THE WEEPING AND THE LAUGHTER

Russian 1919. As the country plunges into revolution, the family of Prince Dmitri Korolev prepare
to flee, leaving home and fortune behind. In the
port of Kronstadt, they are overtaken by the chaos
and turmoil of a nation tearing itself apart. The
Princess is murdered, the twin boys Nicki and
Rudi become separated.

Nicki grows to manhood in the swirling bustle of
Paris, amongst the high-society and demi-monde
of the day. In time he falls passionately and fate-
fully in love.

The Second World War looms, bringing more
upheavals for the family, and news of the long-lost
Rudi. As the tide of war in Europe ebbs and flows
around them all, Noel Barber's magnificent novel
draws towards a powerful climax.

About the author

Noel Barber has enchanted millions of readers with his novels TANAMERA, A FAREWELL TO FRANCE, A WOMAN OF CAIRO and THE OTHER SIDE OF PARADISE. Now once again, he has drawn upon his own experience – the author lived for many of his years in Paris as a leading foreign correspondent – to produce a superbly compelling and authentic story.

NOEL BARBER

THE WEEPING AND THE LAUGHTER

CORONET BOOKS
Hodder and Stoughton

First published in Great Britain in 1988 by Hodder and Stoughton Limited

Coronet edition 1988

Printed and bound in Great Britain for Hodder and Stoughton Paperbacks, a division of Hodder and Stoughton Ltd., Mill Road, Dunton Green, Sevenoaks, Kent TN13 2YA. (Editorial Office: 47 Bedford Square, London WC1B 3DP) by Cox & Wyman Ltd., Reading, Berks. Photoset by Rowland Phototypesetting Limited, Bury St Edmunds, Suffolk.

British Library C.I.P.

Barber, Noel, *1909–*
    The weeping and the laughter
    I. Title
    823'.914[F]

ISBN 0 7736 8040 3

for Tanamera and Patrick,
my grandchildren

Author's acknowledgements

As always my most grateful thanks to my colleague Alan Wykes who has given me such valuable assistance with the research for this book. I may know my Paris – I lived there for more than a dozen years and yet, always in the search for accuracy, more questions have to be asked and answered. Alan's ability to find those answers has enabled me to finish this book six months earlier than I would otherwise have done.

My thanks, too, to John Bright-Holmes, my editor, whose painstaking suggestions have been equally valuable.

Lastly my thanks to Pippa Esdaile for her work in typing the four versions of this volume – or rather, half of it; because circumstances beyond my control made it necessary to use a second typist; by chance, her name was also Pippa – Pippa Mallett. To both Pippas I am most grateful.

I am grateful too to Messrs Faber & Faber for permission to quote from *Poems from the Russian*, chosen and translated by Frances Cornford and Esther Polianowsky Salaman, published by them in 1943.

N.B.
Chelsea, 1987

Contents

PART ONE

1919

1

Rudi, my twin brother, and I were twelve years old when, one day early in 1919, Rudi overheard Papa talking to Mama and Aunt Olga in the next room. As Rudi strained to overhear, Father mentioned one magic word: 'Escape!'

'Come and listen, Nicki,' Rudi beckoned me urgently to crouch behind the door. Eavesdropping was one of our favourite pastimes, especially in this drab, cold winter of murder and looting when it was hardly safe to venture outside.

'Escape?' I echoed in a whisper. 'But where to?'

'Paris!' That was another magic word.

The door leading from our combined playroom and schoolroom into Mama's large sitting-room was old, and sometimes we could peep through a crack and listen or, if the angle was right, we could even see through the large keyhole.

'Paris!' I whispered again. 'But how can we escape?'

'Father was a general,' said Rudi, as though that settled everything. 'Isn't that good enough for you?'

We had known for months that something would happen; and ever since the Tsar Nicholas and the Tsarina Alexandra and her children had vanished, we had been hearing bloodcurdling stories of the Russian revolution, of men being butchered and tortured.

'If we don't,' I could hear my father say to Mama and Aunt Olga, 'we'll all be slaughtered. I've almost fixed up the final details. I've found the right boat to take us from Kronstadt across the Baltic, and then we'll make for our house in Paris. There's no future for a nobleman in Russia. The Bolsheviks drink blood as we drink vodka.'

Rudi turned white as chalk, and I also felt queasy as I pictured Rudi's throat being cut and someone filling an old beer mug with his blood and passing it round. Still, it did not stop me peeping through the keyhole.

My father, Prince Dmitri Korolev, who had just celebrated his fiftieth birthday, was standing with his back to the big open fireplace in which massive logs were sizzling and blazing, with the occasional crack of sparks from a branch of chestnut. He was over six feet tall, beginning to put on a little weight, with thick white hair, a neatly trimmed white beard and huge moustaches. When he attended a ball, he used to say, 'I've got the best moustaches that ever decorated the Winter Palace.'

He was a military-trained autocrat through and through, a commanding figure who had made many a soldier quail if he was slow obeying an order; but he was a general no longer, for a simple reason. The generals had all disappeared – massacred, escaped, or trying to form a White Russian army in the Crimea and to the East. Father's life had been spared for the moment because, though strict, he was known to be just and fair and one of his 'just' deeds was already a legend among the working classes in St Petersburg.

Apparently (as he often recounted to us) Father had stopped the guards on the broad, sweeping two-mile boulevard of the Nevsky Prospekt as they dragged a tired old man to jail, forcing him to stumble, tied to the tail of a horse. My father hated the soldiers, and discovered that there had been no actual charge against the man other than 'degrading the sight of the most beautiful street in Russia'.

The man was not drunk, just half-starved and penniless. My father ordered the man freed, and the officer in charge of the squad to be jailed for a month. It was an act which saved him from murder when the revolution broke out, for many an ardent Bolshevik secretly admired my father. One of them tipped him off that he was on a death list, so we escaped from the bloodstained streets of St Petersburg to our country house in Tsarskoe Selo, a grace and favour house given to my father by Tsar Nicholas. It was in the grounds of the Royal summer palace in Tsarskoe Selo, which is Russian for 'The Tsar's Village'. The house, with several others in the palace grounds, was a reward for valour and friendship. The private park of several hundred acres included the Tsarina's private chapel, where Rudi and I were christened, and where the Tsar himself became my godfather, because I was half an hour older than Rudi. But, having left our house in St Petersburg, on the Moika Embankment near the Winter Palace, we were now in virtual seclusion at Tsarskoe Selo.

The view of my father through the keyhole was suddenly blotted out and we barely had time to scuttle away and look as though we were reading before Father stalked in – yes, that is the word I have in my memory, he *stalked* with the hallmark of power and riches, rather than walked like a mere mortal.

'Hullo boys,' he said. 'Where's Galina?'

This was our seventeen-year-old step-sister, for my father had been married twice.

'I think she's gone for a walk in the park.'

'Damn stupid. Can't trust anyone outside these days.' Father twirled his moustaches, purely an instinctive movement. 'When she comes back tell her I'd like to see her.'

As he returned to the sitting-room we could hardly restrain our excitement.

'Paris!' I exclaimed. 'Are we really going to Paris?'

'I hope so,' said Rudi. 'That's where all the beautiful women live, so Uncle Igor told me.' Igor, who was all of nineteen, had left St Petersburg with us and planned to escape when we did.

'But,' I had sudden doubts, 'I'm not sure I'd like to live in Paris, a horrible big city.'

17

'Not even with lots of girls?' Rudi teased me.

'I'd rather have Russian girls when I grow up – and our own home.'

In fact Father had four houses, including a villa in Switzerland; we were never quite sure exactly where it was because some people said it was on a lake called Léman, while others said it was on Lake Geneva. Even so, that was the house where Rudi and I were born – 'between two trains', my father used to chortle. But there was no mystery about it. Although she was Russian, Mama wanted us to be born in Switzerland because she had more faith in Swiss doctors than in Russian ones. Besides, on Lake Geneva everyone spoke French, and even in Russia all the Russian aristocracy normally spoke French except to the servants.

Still, although we lived in frightening times, we had no wish to leave Russia, our real home. I still remember the lump that came to my throat at the prospect of leaving this beautiful park – beautiful even when, as now, it was threatened by brigands. And would I be able to take Kodi, my beloved teddy bear, with me?

'Russia is the most beautiful country in the world, and the rest of the world is horrible,' I said savagely to Rudi.

'Could we stay behind?' asked Rudi.

'How?'

'Run away when Father escapes. Hide in the woods!'

I shook my head. 'We'd be shot by the Bolsheviks.' And that settled that.

Only twice during that long winter had visitors come to see us. We heard them arrive in the middle of the night, and apparently they went straight to bed for we did not see them until the following day. They were flaxen-haired men who spoke to each other in a strange language and we had to be dressed the following morning in our best long-sleeved sailor suits, the wide V-shaped open-necked collars showing our striped shirts at our throats. They were diplomats, Father explained, and so he, too, was dressed up to receive them, in his full-dress uniform with white kid breeches, gold-embroidered coat sparkling with medals and orders.

After a day at Tsarskoe Selo, with the best lunch that Lilla, our housekeeper, could cook (usually chicken again) the strangers departed once more after night had fallen.

They were high officials from the Danish Embassy in St Petersburg, Father later explained. 'They are very brave men who are trying to help us by sending a Danish vessel to Kronstadt to pick us up and sail away.'

Though we did not realise it at the time, the Danes' friendship with Father was due to the Tsar's father having married a Danish princess, the daughter of King Christian IX. Tsar Nicholas was half-Danish, therefore, and he had visited Copenhagen regularly, accompanied by my father as aide-de-camp. Father had formed a close friendship with the Danish ambassador, who spent several week-ends with us in Tsarskoe Selo before the Revolution, and it was he who contacted Father during the fighting when the Winter Palace was sacked, and begged him to wait in Tsarskoe Selo until he could send a Danish vessel to rescue us. This could not be done until the weather improved for the mouth of the Gulf of Finland, where it meets the fresh water pouring out of the River Neva, was invariably frozen during the winter months.

Now we were in Tsarskoe Selo, isolated and slightly afraid, the vast park empty, blanketed in white, most of the houses shuttered, the branches of trees bending under heavy snow. Although the Tsar and his family had gone our two faithful old servants – Yuri and his wife Lilla – had waited for us to return to Tsarskoe Selo. They would light huge fires for us, even creeping into our bedroom at night to keep a warming glow going. We stayed indoors most of the time with only brief visits to the park because looters had ransacked the Imperial Palace and had only left our house alone because it was an inconspicuous villa and there were greater riches to be found and more people to kill in St Petersburg.

Yuri and Lilla were the only people we saw outside the family. Even the Lycée had been closed – the Royal school situated in a wing of the palace to provide a proper education for future holders of high office, and which the Tsar had permitted us to attend, dressed in a uniform of blue coats with red collars, silver lapels and jackboots.

How sad, I thought, as I peered through the window at the snowy ground looking out for Galina, that the Lycée was closed. What had happened to the twenty or so boys who made up our first class? Gone, all of them. Fled or killed.

It was impossible to dispel these moments of fear, but just as hard to forget the happy months we had spent in Tsarskoe Selo. The blankets of snow and the bending birch trees seemed to add a fairy-tale beauty to the Imperial Palace we knew so well – the marble statues of the Garden Façade leading to the Lycée, the ornamental Chinese village, and the White Birch glade from where you could catch glimpses of gold and green palaces lining the walks which radiated like the spokes of a wheel from the glade itself.

From one point we could see the pagoda with its miniature cupola set in a remote corner of the gardens behind hedges that had been cut into outlines which sometimes pleased and sometimes frightened me; for in winter they would assume ghostly shapes with the weight of the snow, and become monsters against which the wind from Siberia blew howling gusts which shredded their frames.

Sometimes in the summer we had been invited by the Tsar's children, and the royal footmen would organise games for us all after the picnic was spread out near the Milkmaid Fountain, at the far end of the large ornamental lake. At other times the Tsarina would ask us into her beautiful mauve salon in the Alexandra Palace, and on these occasions we were allowed to sit with her daughters, Tatiana, Olga, Marie and Anastasia, the older ones dancing with some of the young guardsmen who were stationed in Tsarskoe Selo, or to listen to the orchestra play while Galina, our half-sister, danced excerpts from a ballet on the polished floor.

Galina had already been attending ballet classes in St Petersburg. She was thin and tall, with long legs, and could stay on her points forever, it seemed, and everyone said she showed great promise, though whether or not Father would allow her to become a professional dancer was a different matter.

Seven years previously Galina had been accepted by the Imperial Ballet School which taught all the usual subjects, including literature, painting and music. Like all the boys and girls of ten and eleven Galina had to pass one of the toughest entrance examinations in the world – indeed only a quarter of those who applied were accepted. There, before dancing a single step, she spent weary months learning to walk gracefully and to 'turn the feet'. Like all the other pupils, she wore a uniform of brown cashmere for academic classes and a special frock of grey holland for dancing.

Girl and boy pupils never met except on formal occasions, and black marks were given for even the most trivial misbehaviour. Every girl entering the classroom had to curtsey to the ballet master and the pianist (this was called 'the reverence'). The ballet master beat time with a long pole which he struck on the floor. Even the commissionaire at the entrance to the school wore a uniform embroidered with the Imperial coat-of-arms on his chest. Galina at least had passed the first difficult tests – she was deemed good enough to be taken to masked balls in the Salle de la Noblesse in St Petersburg.

So in those days before the Revolution, Galina would sometimes have to stay behind in St Petersburg when Rudi and I made our way to Tsarskoe Selo where the atmosphere was less strict, even though we *were* living in close proximity to the Tsar. Of course, we had all been brought up as good Russians to regard the Tsar Nicholas as greater than God himself. Every time the Tsar, as often happened, took a stroll in the afternoon, with the serfs lining up in adjoining fields to pay their respects, we immediately stood to attention and doffed our Lycée hats. Father himself would always stand stiff as a ramrod, eyes unwavering, until the Tsar casually murmured, 'Please, Prince Dmitri', and then turned to smile at us, perhaps pat a shoulder and ask, with a questioning smile, 'Which one of you two is my godson today?' We knew then that we had permission to relax – though not too much, for any bad behaviour would mean no supper that night.

How never-ending those happy memories were – even the rather grim church services, for every Sunday morning we attended service in the private chapel of the Federovski Sobor, in the Imperial Park, built by the Tsarina after she was told that her son Alexis had haemophilia, and where I had been baptised in the presence of the Tsar himself.

It was very 'Russian' – dozens of ikons, candles burning in every corner, an unaccompanied choir singing the Creed. There was a powerful smell of incense, a nun reading the prayer for the day. The bishop's raiment glittered with magnificence in candlelight that cast a mist of light around the altar, a halo that seemed filled with particles of dancing dust reminiscent of the winter snow being blown from the hedges in the garden.

Father came back into the schoolroom again and told Rudi, 'Go outside the front porch and shout. See if you can make Galina hear.'

He must have shouted with all his strength for in a few moments I saw him wave. As I looked out of the frosty window into the park and watched Rudi walking briskly back towards me – a sturdy, well-built boy with brown eyes, like mine, fair hair ('the colour of sawdust', Father once called it), strong legs and broad shoulders – I thought, how is it possible, this business of twins? Each time I looked at Rudi, it was like looking at a portrait of myself. Each time I heard his voice, it was just as though I myself was talking.

'She's coming,' he announced, stamping the snow off his boots.

When Galina came in, she took off her fur hat, shook out her mop of thick, tawny hair, and said, 'It's been snowing, and I'm hungry and cold. I am going to ask Lilla for some tea and blinis.'

'Father wants to see you,' said Rudi.

'I'm going to have some tea first.'

Lilla's husband Yuri had served as a soldier with Father, and though we were never normally allowed in the kitchen without permission, discipline was relaxed because they were the only two servants who had stayed with us. The rest had gone with the wind, some to their villages where they felt safer, some had been killed, others had just – vanished.

'It's a secret, but we're going to Paris,' I announced to Galina.

She clapped her hands. 'Paris! You boys will love it. I went there once with Father.'

'I bet the French don't know how to make real blinis,' I said.

'Father says he wants you to go and see him immediately,' Rudi insisted.

'That means no blinis,' she sighed. Like all of us, Galina loved those caviar-topped thick pancakes. 'Let's hope there's at least a samovar of tea in the sitting-room.'

Rudi and I were playing chess when Aunt Olga came in and beckoned to us.

'Your father wishes to speak to you both and also to Yuri and Lilla. Will you go and bring them in.'

'The servants?' I looked astonished.

'Go on now! Your father has an important announcement to make to the entire family and the staff,' adding with a touch of sarcasm, 'or what's left of it.'

Aunt Olga, who, when referred to formally, was the Countess Olga Arensky, had just celebrated her thirtieth birthday, and with her high cheekbones, enormous pools of black eyes and the longest and thinnest fingers I had ever seen we both adored her. Rudi once said, 'Aunt Olga, you must be wonderful with the piano.' And she replied, 'I'm even more wonderful with the needle.' And Mama said she was too. She loved making cushions, bedspreads, and even at times, and for fun, designing and making dresses. Mama said that the secret of Aunt Olga's prettiness was because everything she did was 'just for fun'. Her eyes were always sparkling, the corners of her lips turned up, not down, as though she was about to start a laugh. And Mama told me that, when she attended the great dances at the Winter Palace, young guardsmen would flock around her, begging to sign her little *carnet de bal* and reserve dances for them. And though at times, in those early days, I wondered why she lived with us when, after all, she was no blood relation, we accepted her presence gratefully. It was only many years later that I learned exactly what the reason was.

'I bet she's always been hot stuff,' Galina once remarked with all the wisdom of seventeen years. Though I did not quite understand – then – how Aunt Olga could be hot all the time, especially in the cold of the winter, I assumed there must be a good reason for it, for Galina always spoke with authority.

We now entered Mama's sitting-room, followed by Yuri and Lilla. Somehow we always felt more in awe of my father in the big sitting-room than when he came to see us in our schoolroom.

He was standing with his back to the fire, a fine upstanding figure, rubbing his hands behind him. Without any preamble, he said, 'Sit down, boys.' He did not offer a seat to Yuri or Lilla. They would never have accepted such an offer and Father knew it would embarrass them. Mama, beautiful but looking tired and worried, sat at one end of a large grey-blue sofa, so long that the back needed ten cushions, most of them made by Aunt Olga. We had been told that Mama was expecting a baby within a few weeks which was why she looked so very large.

'The moment has come for us to leave Russia and make a new home for ourselves in Paris, the capital of France, and the greatest city in the world after St Petersburg,' announced Father, his voice booming, smoke from his cigar wreathing his face.

As this news was received in glum silence – for we already knew – Father added, 'I know we would all rather live in our beloved Russia, but as good soldiers' – with a glance at us – 'precautions against the enemy must always outweigh considerations of comfort.' Father, as I remember him from my first memories, always found a military reason for making a civilian decision, but there was truth in his next words: 'For the moment Russia is engulfed in a civil war against wicked men. Their leader is a man called Lenin, and he plotted his plans from the comfort of a safe country. We must now do the same. We cannot overthrow his revolutionaries from Tsarskoe Selo. But even though our beloved Tsar and his family are no longer with us, we will one day make Russia great again. In the meantime I am not going to allow my family to live in fear.'

As I started to ask a question, he almost roared, 'Silence!' Only then did we realise that he was discussing being involved in a *real* war and, as I wondered about the problems that lay ahead, Father explained more details of our plans to escape.

'The danger we face will be on the trip to Kronstadt. It's only a dozen miles and once we board a neutral Danish vessel, we will be safe. Until then it will be an unpleasant cold trip over the muddy roads, but Igor has been trained

as a soldier and you two boys' – with another look at us –
'you are soldiers in spirit, aren't you?'

'Yes sir,' we chorused.

'But Mama?' I asked. 'She is expecting the baby?'

'I know, Nicki,' he said quite gently for such a fierce-
looking man, 'but we shall do everything we can to make
her comfortable. Cushions, blankets and so on. And once
on the boat, which is called the *Lysberg*, even if she is only
a tramp steamer, she has what is called a director's cabin,
used by shipping line officials from time to time, and your
mother will be given that cabin.'

'And Yuri and Lilla?' The thought of leaving without
them horrified us. Lilla had been far more important to us
than our succession of French nannies. It was Lilla to
whom we could sneak into the kitchen for forbidden cakes.
And it was Yuri who had taught us the tricks of shooting,
fishing, all the mysteries of the great outdoors. We would
be lost without them.

Yuri was turning heavy logs in the fireplace to make new
flames. At the sound of his name he put down the poker
and did his best to straighten up his tired old frame but
before he could utter a word Father said, 'I hope you will
both join us. Apart from the fact that we would like you
to come, you might find life very difficult in Russia if you
have no means of support. You, Yuri, you are an old
soldier and' – with a return to military jargon – 'in the
armed forces, the life of a soldier is as important as the
life of a general.'

Yuri bowed as he thanked Father, who then announced
that we would have to travel without any luggage for, if
the rabble stopped us and discovered expensive trunks or
other trappings of wealth, it would arouse instant suspicion. 'We will leave everything behind except Mama's
best necklace. Mama will look after that. We have some
money in a bank in Switzerland, but we must fit ourselves
out in the dirtiest clothes we can find and leave Russia
looking like beggars.'

'No luggage?' I asked.

'None! Can't you understand French, boy?'

'But Kodi, my teddy bear?' I felt a pang of unease.

'Baby, always sleeping with a teddy bear,' jeered Rudi.

'I'm not a baby.'

'Be quiet, both of you,' ordered Father. 'You can keep your teddy bear. The Tsar gave it to me at your christening to keep for his godson, and a gift from the Tsar should be cherished forever.'

'And is Aunt Olga Arensky coming with us?' Rudi wanted to change the subject.

'She says she would like to come,' answered Father, 'and she will be a wonderful companion for Mama.'

I turned to Uncle Igor and asked, 'Will Igor Treporovitch be coming too?'

Igor was a distant cousin of Father's. He nodded.

'Good!' cried Rudi. 'Uncle Igor Treporovitch is such fun.'

'Not Igor Treporovitch,' roared Father in a voice that made us tremble. 'Plain Count Igor Trepov.'

'But –' began a baffled Rudi. 'You can't just use the same name. Russians always change their surnames when they marry or else –' I didn't understand the name changing myself.

'You can – and we will,' said Father. 'Listen carefully, not only the boys, but all of you. Stop this nonsense about changing names. It might be all right in Russia where everyone understands and expects it. But they don't where we are going. They don't exist there. I will be called simply Prince Dmitri Korolev and your mother will be Princess Korolev. You boys will be plain Master Korolev, and Galina, your half-sister, won't be saddled with ridiculous names no-one can pronounce. She'll just be Mademoiselle Galina Korolev, not Galina Korolevska.'

'It sounds very complicated,' I ventured.

'It's very *simple*,' explained Father, with exaggerated patience. 'Much simpler. Though of course,' he added, 'you, Nicki, being born half an hour before Rudi, will inherit my title of *prince* – if by then it's worth having.'

Our final preparations consisted of collecting what Father called 'the disguise' – making us all look as filthy and as smelly as possible, because, though the fiercest street-fighting and the mass slaughter had been mostly confined to the big cities, bands of revolutionaries sometimes roamed isolated villages plundering for food or horses, and usually ending in an orgy of spilled blood. No-one was safe, except the ragged, the starving, the sick. They had a chance. 'The only hope of saving your life is to look as though you are on the point of death,' said Father.

Yuri had collected all the tattered clothes he could find in the neighbouring palaces, now empty. Sometimes he even had to strip the corpses of serfs who had been killed. Igor also helped us, and we were joined by a labourer named Alexei who had escaped from a nearby farm.

On our last day Father and Igor took off their normal clothes. Father must have been excited by the scent of 'battle' – though of a different kind – for I heard him say almost with a laugh, 'By God, Igor, you *look* and you *smell* like a tramp. We've really managed to turn the old saying upside down – we've turned a silk purse back into a sow's ear.'

It was almost uncanny, the way fear was disguised by laughter. I heard Father laugh – even if only briefly – when he looked in a mirror. Perhaps it was his way of hiding the knowledge that we were still in the gravest danger, especially as Mama was so weak that she should have been in the care of a doctor in hospital. But even she smiled when she stood up in an old, tattered cook's dress, stained and frayed from years in the kitchen. At least the volumin-ous thick calico skirt helped to hide her large tummy.

'Mama isn't an invalid,' explained Aunt Olga as she tore cuts in the ragged trousers and jackets that had been found for us. 'But having a baby makes you *weak*, my dears, and we don't want her shaken about more than is necessary.'

Our house, modest, of course, compared with the villas near the Tsar's palace, had hardly been touched before we left St Petersburg; and once Tsarskoe Selo had been sacked and the Tsar gone, the hooligans lost interest. After all, though we had large stocks of logs for burning nobody was going to steal them when people could cut down the trees on the edge of St Petersburg. And though we had a couple of creaking old farm carts in the farm buildings on the edge of the fields where we produced our few crops, the horses had long since been stolen. The looters, however, had left some hay and oats in the barn, and when we arrived at Tsarskoe Selo on the two old nags that had brought us out of the city at night, we hid them, and because we knew we had no future in Tsarskoe Selo we fed the horses well on the oats we would normally have rationed carefully through the spring and early summer before they could graze in the fields. These two horses had never had such a good winter feed! And now, when the time had come to leave, we could sense their eagerness for action as they were harnessed and backed into the shafts.

The wagons had tarpaulin covers draped over a central pole. Mother could be carried in one wagon by Yuri who knew best how to handle horses. Igor would sit beside him in front. Under the cover one side had been arranged with cushions and mattresses hidden behind the flapping back of the improvised tent, which was tied loosely, like a covered wagon.

Mama struggled as she climbed up then lay back gratefully on the thick down pillows. Aunt Olga climbed in beside her and beckoned Rudi to jump in. He was clasping Kodi. I really wanted Kodi myself but Father persuaded us that it would be a good idea for Rudi to take him, as a bit of extra disguise if Mama's wagon was attacked. I heard Mama almost laugh, 'My protector!' At the last moment Father, as I stood by, peered into the gloomy interior and promised, 'I'll be just behind you, my dear, so that I can see what's happening ahead. You've got them?' Mother said, 'They're quite safe – here.' She patted her breasts.

Then Yuri gave a crack of the whip and, with squeals and creaks as the iron rims of the wheels of the old cart slowly turned on the frosted ruts of the road, we set off.

'Jump in the back,' Father ordered Galina, me and Lilla, while Father and Alexei, who also 'understood' horses, climbed on to the front seat.

Lilla was crying noisily, and Father explained, 'I had to separate them. If we run into any trouble in either cart Yuri or Lilla can do all the talking. If *we* start talking, our speech will betray us immediately.'

'Poor Mama,' I ventured as we started to follow. 'Will she be unhappy without you?'.

'She is a soldier's wife!' Father said sternly over his shoulder. Then he added, more to Galina than to me, 'I deliberately decided to *follow* the other cart rather than go first. It's pointless being ahead, because if any trouble does come suddenly, and our wagon is in front, we'd be involved and could do nothing about it. If we are behind we can see any emergency arriving and maybe cause a diversion. That's why I want to get your mama on board first. If *we* get into trouble, we can run for it, but your mother can't.'

Father seemed quite cheerful as we set off and, leaning back into the covered wagon, he patted me on the shoulder. 'At least we won't starve,' said Father. 'Lilla has cooked the last four chickens, some hard-boiled eggs, some beets and some bread and a jar of caviar. *And* we've got a couple of bottles of vodka, frozen by mother nature.' The bottles were swinging by a string beside the front seats.

'Was that what Father meant when he asked Mama, "Have you got them"?' I asked Galina.

'No, silly,' she replied. 'That was the emerald necklace – the inheritance. Father thought it would be wiser if Mama carried it in case he gets involved in a fight. I don't think they'd touch a woman who's expecting a baby.'

It was a long, tiring, bumpy ride sitting on the bare boards of the old cart and at eleven o'clock we stopped in a side track to eat and to stretch our legs. We were in a quiet, muddy country lane that sliced through a thick forest of birch trees, and Father, without stopping the cart at first, jumped off and ran ahead to order a halt. I clambered out and trotted after him, reaching the leading cart before Galina, and in time to hear Father ask, 'How are you, my dear?' Mother was sitting up on the cushions and answered cheerfully, 'I'm afraid Olga and I have made quite a hole in the vodka. Olga says it's the cheapest form of heating.'

'It won't do you any harm – if you don't overdo it.' Father gave a querying look at Olga, who shook her head and started preparing the food. Then she added, 'I gave Rudi a sip, he was so cold.'

'May I have some?' I asked.

'Of course.'

It was very fiery but it was not the first time either of us had tasted vodka and it certainly warmed us up. And of course Galina then wanted some too. Igor poured a little out and, as she sipped it, teased her, 'You've got to drink the first glass in one gulp. You're old enough to know that!'

'I suppose you drink yours by the bottle,' she laughed, managing to look very pretty despite the old rags she wore. 'I know your sort, Igor. Someone said that all the girls fall for you, and that you go and meet the ballet dancers after the theatre. I bet you wish you could do that again!'

'Ah, happy times. Yes, I loved them. But those days are over.'

'Perhaps in Paris? Old habits die hard. One of the dancers called you a stage-door Johnny.'

Igor laughed delightedly – until Father, subduing his bass voice, whispered, 'Sssh! Listen! Horses!'

The fear was so immediate that our words and laughter

31

froze on our lips. Quite clearly we could hear horses galloping, and the shouts and laughs of a small group of men.

It had begun to snow, the snow falling like feathers over the frozen earth. We crouched behind a rusty tractor, our hearts in our mouths as the dishevelled troops skirted the far edge of the field. We could hear their murderous cries, cries of triumph.

Warning us all to stay behind the tractor, Father slid forward the few yards through the curtain of trees until he could see three men approach a house where smoke was rising from the chimney.

'Brutes,' he gasped to us when they returned. 'Just a bloody *Skopets Gorbusha*! They've got no officers, they're obviously part of a small group that is killing everyone in sight.'

I gasped. To hear a general calling someone 'the son of a stinking castrated camel'! I had heard the oath before.

Rudi was snivelling a bit, and Aunt Olga was trying to comfort us both. Then, as Papa hissed to us to be quiet, I saw a couple of men with bayonets scouting the barn; but they were uncertain who or what might be inside and would not risk a lone attack. 'They'll come back with reinforcements,' Papa said contemptuously. 'They daren't risk their miserable lives in case the inhabitants have got machine-guns concealed there.'

As suddenly as they had appeared, the men vanished. I could hear the thud of hooves growing fainter, until finally Father said, 'All right. Let's get going if we want to reach Kronstadt before nightfall. It's safe now, I think,' he said, adding bitterly, 'as safe as Russia will ever be.'

'Father,' I asked timidly once we were on our way. 'What does "castrated" mean?'

2

It was dusk as we reached the end of the mole that linked the mainland to Kotlin Island on which Kronstadt is built. Scudding clouds revealed the pale yellow glare of the moon, and its reflected light gleamed in the dirty slush where some of the snow had melted.

'Is the ship near here?' I asked. 'And what's this terrible stink?'

'Quiet, boy,' snapped Father. 'This is the part of the journey where we have to keep both our eyes wide open.'

The peace of the country lanes had given place to busy streets, trams, some horse-drawn, and now and then we had to stop as trains, running on gleaming lines, passed alongside the streets, carrying cargo to the docks.

Peeping through the slit in the tarpaulin I could see narrow streets of wooden houses and at the corner of one crossroads the stone building of a forge. We bumped along unpaved or cobbled streets over ruts made by the iron tyres of wagons edging almost on to the doorsteps of some houses. Snow was piled at nearly every corner.

Not far from Kronstadt's two filthy hotels ('The Buffet and the Commercial, both fourth-rate,' grunted Father) was a more ostentatious building – the public baths for men and women, and not far away a tallow-melting plant which manufactured candles and soap. There was also a tannery nearby and the two gave off a combined stench from hides steeped in some horrible liquid and the tallow made by melting animal fat.

It was more than I could stand. Without warning – but just in time to reach the rear of the cart – I was sick, narrowly missing Galina.

'Sorry, Father,' I gasped, wiping the corner of my mouth on my filthy sleeve.

'Don't worry, my boy,' he replied, gently for him. 'You won't be the only one in this stinking town. It's the curse of Kronstadt's two Ts – tallow and tanning.'

Luckily (in one way) the traffic was halted while a train took its time approaching and crossing the roadway on the way to the docks. Father jumped out with a mug he had brought along and bought some boiling water from an old man huddled over a squat iron stove. Normally he sold boiling water for the owners of samovars which they would take on a voyage. Nearby half a dozen men were crying, 'Buy my onions. Onions for sale!'

Father handed me some hot water to sip, saying, 'Sorry we have no tea but this'll settle your stomach.'

'But onions!' I cried.

'They sell them at all Russian ports. They're supposed to prevent sea-sickness.'

The train seemed to take an age to cross to the marshalling yards until finally the clanking of the shunting trucks stopped, the road was opened, and we moved ahead.

Our two old horse-drawn wagons did not excite much attention, but ours had drawn closer to Mama's, and from time to time people shouted at us, and droshky drivers swore and brandished their whips. One neighbouring driver lashed out with his whip at our leading horse and, as it reared with fright, Mama's wagon nearly overturned.

There was a sullen atmosphere of fear about the mean streets and more than once I heard Father say to Alexei, 'Watch out!', and when the man whipped Mama's horse, Father shouted, 'I'd like to kill you, you bastard.'

That, I hoped, would be the end of the affair but we had to stop for a tram, and when we drew abreast with the droshky, the driver shouted menacingly, 'What did you say, you cretin?'

Before Father could betray himself, Alexei answered in

his broad uneducated Russian, 'Never mind that old fool. He's a bit weak in the head.'

'He'd be weak in the arse if I gave him the good hiding he deserves!'

Father was furious, but somehow he managed to contain his rage as we moved forward.

Someone else, who narrowly missed being knocked down by Mama's cart shouted, 'Who the hell do you think you are?' I could see Yuri answer back.

It was becoming more and more terrifying. Red flags hung from high windows, draped like splashes of blood. Small bands of rabble rousers, often drunk, sang and cursed. I was frozen with terror when, without warning, one unshaven man with a red scarf tied round his head jumped on our cart from behind and as he saw Galina, leered, 'I'd like half an hour with you, lady, if you don't mind.'

As Galina screamed, Alexei shouted from the driving seat, 'Do me a favour, comrade. I'll only be twenty minutes, then she's all yours.'

The stink of tallow now began to give way to the fresh smell of the sea; but the wind turned the drizzling rain into driving sleet. The horses, tired after a long day's work, kept struggling for a foothold on the slippery streets. Several times the leading horse stumbled and, though it did not fall, Father, with me peering through the canvas tent, realised that we could not keep too close to Mama's wagon in case we bumped into it.

I began to feel sick again, not only with the stink and the lurching of the cart, the sudden starting and stopping, but for a different reason – the scent of fear. As we neared the docks, I caught glimpses of and heard shouting from knots of people waving red flags. Some men jeered and again tried to climb on the wagon to see what was inside. Galina cowered in the back of the tarpaulin behind the heavy bulk of Lilla. One man who jumped up jeered in a

35

hoarse voice, 'It's one for all and all for one now, comrades, but you're too fat, grandma!' And as Lilla began to stutter with anger, he caught sight of a foot peeping out from behind the screen of Lilla's body.

'What's this,' he pulled Lilla aside. 'Hullo, my beauty,' he said, and as Galina screamed, Alexei looked back through the slit in the tarpaulin and cried, 'Hold on, comrade, she's mine!'

The man shouted to another who jumped on the back of the wagon and taking no notice of Alexei, pulled Galina's foot hard and looked her over, crying. 'Oh, ho! A nice little *kodreetsah*. Bit skinny, but –'

'That chicken's mine, comrade,' Alexei repeated, and I could see him put a restraining hand on Father's knee.

'Well, lend her to me, comrade. Ten minutes'll be enough. I'll pay. Remember our motto, All for one –'

'That's my wife and kids back there. You leave my family alone.'

'Well, if it's the family –' the man said grudgingly. 'But you'd better keep this stripling out of sight. She'd be a beauty if you gave her a good wash.'

The men jumped off, but what we in the second wagon had not realised was that, during the altercation, the wagon had stopped as Alexei tried to protect Galina. Even now, the revolutionary with the red scarf round his neck came round to the front and, looking at Father, asked Alexei, 'Who's this old buffer?'

Because the wagon had stopped, there were cries and oaths from behind and then someone in front tried to pull the horse's bridle to start the cart moving as more and more shouted to stop the crush. Alexei tapped his head and, with a look at Father, cried to the other man, 'An uncle. Not all there in the head.' Father again turned puce with rage he could barely restrain.

For some reason our horse – which was following Mama's – refused to move, even when Alexei jumped down and tried to pull it. It stood trembling as, with sudden fear, Alexei tugged and tugged in vain, and even when, finally, he climbed back on the cart and took the whip to the horse. Perhaps it was afraid of the slippery cobbled street, or after months in the country, frightened by the crowds hemming it in. Two droshky drivers behind us took matters into their own hands – by pulling out into the middle of the road and trying to pass us. They almost succeeded – but then a dray coming the other way got in front of them. The horse pulling the dray stumbled and in a second was on its knees. The droshky overturned, as its horse reared, two screaming women were thrown out, and in seconds there was pandemonium.

As Alexei jumped off the driving seat again, Father cried, 'We've lost them!' Mama's wagon had vanished.

'We're almost at the ship's berth,' Father clambered into the back, almost falling on top of Lilla. Then he shouted to Alexei, 'Go and find them. We'll run to the ship. We're nearly there.' He explained to Alexei, 'Round the corner where you can see the cranes there's a big open loading space lined with warehouses. An alley from there leads straight to the *Lysberg*. I'll go straight there, drop the girls and Nicki, then come back and meet you.'

The square, he explained, was on the left of the street ahead. 'You can't miss it, the loading space is so large. The *Lysberg* is on the other side, only twenty yards through the alley,' he shouted.

'We can't drive into the square through this traffic mix up,' said Father, and as Alexei prepared to run, told him, 'You help get the women and Rudi into the narrow alley, and I'll rush up and help you. It's only a few yards and the boat is moored right opposite.' To us he cried, 'Come on out, all of you. Double quick.'

Father must have seen my look of alarm for he reassured me, 'Don't be afraid, Nicki. I'll see you to the gangplank, then you take over and look after the ladies while I go back and fetch Mama and the others. This is a short cut, it'll save time.'

We shuffled forward on foot, a bedraggled bunch of peasants, so scruffy, smelly, dirty that not even the most dedicated (or suspicious) communist would waste a second glance on us. I shouted, 'I've lost Kodi, my teddy bear.'

'Come on,' cried Galina. 'Rudi's got Kodi. Don't you remember?' I had forgotten.

Father now led us along the short street, which was so curved that we could not see the big open loading square. As we stumbled on the slushy surface, I seemed to imagine hearing shouts and shrieks of pain in the distance, but there was so much noise, so much jostling, that I was too occupied in keeping my balance, and trotting to keep up with the others, to be sure even though Father was holding my hand. He was half-dragging me and helping Galina as she struggled to force the overweight Lilla to keep pace with us; and I could not help admiring Galina for shouting in a real peasant Russian, 'Make way for my mother. She's ill!'

Some people did actually step aside to let what looked like a desolate daughter helping a fat and stumbling old woman seek any kind of shelter in the pelting sleet.

We reached the end of the street and there – suddenly and without warning – was the open water.

'That's the *Lysberg*,' Father pointed out a small steamer which was flying at its stern a red flag with a white cross.

'You're in charge now, Nicki,' Father called out, as he dashed into the narrow alley which we had by-passed as I, my sense of fear much diminished by a sense of importance, led the others at a stumbling run to the gangplank where a large friendly man shouted in bad Russian, 'You must be the Prince's family. Where are the rest?'

As I pushed Galina up the steep plank, with cross struts to prevent slipping, I said, 'Yes, sir. My Father has gone to fetch my Mama and the others. Thank you, sir.'

'Come on all of you,' he turned to help Lilla, who needed most assistance. Then he cried, '*Velkommen!*' A word that even I, as a French speaker, realised must be Danish for 'Welcome'.

It was still pelting with rain and sleet, but once we were aboard, with Father out of sight, the Dane explained in Russian that the Danish ambassador to St Petersburg had sent an assorted pile of clothing for men, women and boys on the *Lysberg*. 'And there's hot water,' he said. 'So ladies' – he was addressing Galina really – 'you all try to get washed first and leave room for the others to wash when they get here.'

'They'll only be a minute, sir,' I said politely. 'Maybe we should wait here until they come.'

Despite my words, I was filled with foreboding. I did not dare go down into the cabin, I wanted to stay on deck until the others arrived. I was almost in tears. My fears were mounting as I leaned impatiently over the side of the gunwale, hearing screams and yells and cries coming from behind the square of sheds, cranes, stacks of cargo, and packing cases.

How long did I have to wait? I will never know, never to this moment so many years later, when I think back to that awful day. I was standing there, fear prickling the hair on my neck. Then I saw two figures approach through the narrow alley, two tramps helping to support each other, stumbling between the walls made by the warehouses.

At first I did not recognise them, one of them limping badly. Then their bodies, their filthy clothes and, finally, their faces streaked with dirt came into focus through my blinding tears.

'Father!' I screamed. 'Where's Mama? Olga? Where's Rudi?'

Father looked badly wounded, gasping with pain but, helped by Danish seamen, he reached the top of the gangplank, where the captain of the *Lysberg* supported him. Following him was Igor, with a soaking patch of blood across one shoulder. As Father collapsed unconscious on the deck, Igor's good looks were distorted with terror so that to me he looked almost nightmarishly grotesque. Then he saw me. He was clutching Kodi, my old teddy bear, the gift of the Tsar, and he told everything in one sentence. Handing it to me, his face still a mask of horror, he cried, 'This is all we managed to save.'

I leaned down in the rain and put my arms around Kodi, sobbing. Poor Lilla had passed out, and was lying on a bench near a coil of tar-smelling rope, for just as Father had returned without Mama, Olga and Rudi, neither had he brought back Yuri or Alexei.

Galina rushed up, also sobbing as she put her arms round to try and comfort me, crying, mumbling words I could not understand, for there was no consolation.

Desperate, I tried to tear myself from her arms as sailors started to look after Igor; and then a hooter sounded, as we prepared to leave. Finally I freed myself, unable to face anyone. I ran round to the far side of the deck where I could not be seen, where only occasional blocks of ice broke the surface of the scene, and I sobbed bitterly, wordlessly, for my lost mother and my lost brother.

Galina followed me across the *Lysberg* and this time I let her embrace me, for in a way it comforted me to realise that we were both torn and unhappy, and her body warmed me and her touch was gentle and kind. Vaguely I heard the throb of engines, guttural cries, and the slap of ropes hitting water as the ship prepared to leave Russia.

As I felt the movement of the vessel, slow at first, but gathering speed, Galina led me back to the port side, near where the gangplank had been, so that both of us could share one last sight of our country.

Father had been carried up the companionway, though with some difficulty, but his leg wound was not as bad as we at first feared. Galina and I were both crying, but Father's face was grim, etched with anguish yet dry-eyed, and I half expected him to reprimand me in his usual stern voice, 'Soldiers don't cry!' But his eyes were wet too, and, instead, he put an arm on my shoulder, another around Galina's and said, 'There, Nicki, go on, cry your heart out, and you too, Galina.'

It is many years since all this happened and it was not until I started to write this history of our family that I found out how Mama was murdered. I discovered the details – well, you shall see how I discovered the details. For now, let me give you the story as it was set down in a journal by Igor in 1921 – only two years afterwards – though I did not find it until the 1940s.

The tragedy need never have occurred. We were all, of course, disguised as peasants, and as Alexei arrived to tell Igor that Father was taking us to the boat and would then return to help Mama, nobody would have noticed them in the jostling crowds – sinister with their red neckerchiefs round their heads, filthy language and an obvious hatred for anyone rich – had it not been for a stroke of bad luck.

As Father's wagon was nowhere to be seen, Yuri had drawn the other one, with Mama inside, to a standstill. He jumped down and was holding the horse's head in case it reared with fright in the awful mêlée. Then another vehicle came up next to ours – this time a carriage, not too ornate, but smart enough to excite the zealous revolutionaries to investigate. The carriage, pulled by two horses, had curtains and one of the two men on the driver's seat jumped off and made to open the door. Even Igor could tell immediately they were the servants of some rich man or woman. Their attempt at disguise was pitifully inadequate.

Igor watched, warning Mama, Olga and Rudi to remain under the tarpaulin, for he could smell trouble, if only in the overbearing attitude of the footman. It was an invitation to mob violence and, sure enough, one great hulk of a man forced the other footman off the driving platform by pulling his leg until the man fell to the ground with a crash that looked as though it had killed him outright and

41

then – how stupid! – the other footman pulled out a concealed knife, jumped on the big man and stabbed him in the throat.

The spurt of blood was the signal for uproar. A great cry of anger erupted and, as the footman tried to stab the man again, the crowd surged towards him, kicked and beat and knifed him until he was a messy, bloody corpse.

All this happened beside Mama's cart. The infuriated revolutionaries were not concerned with an old peasant, however; instead they ripped aside the curtains hiding the interior of the carriage.

'A terrible sight met my eyes,' Igor wrote later. 'Inside was a woman, obviously from her clothes a woman of rank. Her dress and underclothes had been lifted up until the thighs and all the lower part of her body were bare, and they were covered with blood. I didn't at first understand, but then I realised. She was accompanied by two nurses and she was screaming because the shock of the journey had produced the premature birth of a child. She was cradling it as she moaned, as the nurses tried to clean her up. One nurse screamed to the mob to let the patient down. Those nearest to the carriage *did* let her down, and the woman slumped to the ground. One nurse brought out a blanket and cushion and covered the baby and laid it on the ground near the mother and the three corpses – the two footmen and the big man who had been stabbed. All lay dead on the cobbled ground. For a moment I thought the mob would spare her, even though she was obviously a member of the hated aristocracy. But the revolutionaries took a sadistic pleasure in killing for the sake of killing and the mob behind, pushing to the front, had no idea what was happening.'

Igor's sole thought (as he wrote) was to protect Mama, Olga and Rudi, but as he clambered through the slit in the back of the tarpaulin he saw another frightful sight. Two men came up from behind, held up the stabbed comrade by his hair, and one of them shouted, 'This woman is responsible for this murder. They were servants acting on her orders. Death to the aristocrats!'

One man, who did not even see the new-born baby, knelt over the moaning mother and, as Igor watched, stabbed her in the face, and as she died, spat on her. There was a huge roar of approval from the ground. The two nurses were also killed, hacked to death as the raging mob increased its blood lust.

Alexei shouted to Yuri, 'Get out of here.' Old Yuri was so frightened he automatically tugged at the reins and the horse reared with sudden fright, and as it did so Rudi literally fell off the back of the cart. Nobody took any notice of him, his clothes were so poor, but then another man tore open the back and cried, 'Hey, look comrades. What have we here?'

'A pregnant woman,' gasped Aunt Olga, who had heard all the noise and screams around her, but had not the faintest idea what had been happening to the other woman, now dead. Igor heard a man shout to our mother, 'Not *her*! She's pregnant!' But looking at Olga, he added, 'I'll give *you* a good Bolshevik child too if you're clean enough and don't give me a dose.'

Olga and Mama looked so dirty that Igor felt the man had said it more as a joke than a threat but at that moment Mama started moaning and Olga said to the man, 'Help me to get her down, comrade.' Igor remembered hearing then that Yuri cried out without thinking, 'I'm coming, Princess'.

'*Princess!*' Without a word the man, who wore a red sash round his waist, pulled off Mama's skirt, then Olga's, as they screamed and tried to hide their silk underwear. Then one man grabbed two of the pillows that had supported Mama during the long drive, and hurled them high above the crowd.

'Look what we have here, comrades!' he cried, waving a tattered red flag, 'A live bloody princess and her friend.'

They dragged Mother out and, as Igor struggled, old

43

Yuri was felled with a club and never even knew what had killed him. Alexei had disappeared. Mother, large and wearing a silken petticoat, was thrown to the ground near the dead woman and the bawling baby. When Rudi tried to fight with his fists to protect Mama, he was hit across the head. Igor hurled one man away, but was cut badly on the shoulder with a sabre which someone in the crowd had acquired.

Olga got down, fists flying as she cried, 'The lady has started her labour. Let her go.' But Igor heard that same man cry, 'Not so fast my beauty. I promised I'd give you a revolutionary bastard.' Then he grabbed Olga and carried her towards one of the warehouses, crying, 'It won't take long.' Olga was kicking and scratching but the man picked her up by the waist and laughed to the crowd, 'It'll only take ten minutes. Then you can kill her if you like.'

Igor, badly hurt and bleeding copiously, was still struggling to help my mother but he could see the man take Aunt Olga into the warehouse and close the door behind him. Then – all this happening in seconds – Igor saw the ultimate horrifying scene. Half a dozen men and women had set about Igor and Mama. Yuri was dead. Rudi had vanished. Igor, it seemed, almost passed out after one vicious kick to the head, but not until he saw a woman with a red handkerchief plunge a carving knife into Mama's breast. The last thing Igor witnessed was a screaming Rudi trying to reach his mother's body, thrusting the teddy bear into Igor's hands as he kissed the dead face, and below it the huge open gash where the blade had gone straight into Mama's heart.

Igor fainted away, slumped across her body. Perhaps the revolutionaries thought that, as he was covered with blood, he was dead too. Some new sensation must have attracted their attention for, as Igor regained consciousness, he vaguely heard cries as they tore across to the opposite corner of the square. Rudi had vanished again.

44

Neither was there a sign of Olga – or of the Prince. Worse, the bodies of the two women had been dragged away, though a dozen or so dead men littered the square, together with some wounded – and the baby. The expensive coach had been overturned. All the horses had been taken away – extra loot, stolen, no doubt.

But where was my father? He should have come back, even though all this killing had taken place in a matter of minutes. There was nothing Igor could do but try to find him, and at the beginning of the narrow street leading to the *Lysberg* he suddenly saw him slumped on the ground. As my father told Igor later, he had seen the carnage and, when some desperado asked what the hell he was doing, Father knocked him over. He started to run towards the end of the passage when another man arrived who had a cutlass. Seeing the comrade lying on the floor, with Father the apparent assailant, the second man made one lurch at Father, almost missed, but gave him a nasty gash on the thigh. Then he ran on – and was lost in the crowd.

'The Prince was struggling to his feet, trying to reach the square when I found him,' Igor ended his terrible recital. 'But he found it difficult to walk, and so did I, so we hobbled together until we reached the *Lysberg*.'

That was Igor's account of what happened, though other events would later add their particular twists to his account, for he only actually saw the death of Mama, while all witnessed the last pitiful scene – Igor and Father struggling painfully up the gangplank, their first tentative steps towards the start of a new life.

But behind them they left their old lives, with its memories of their own country – a vast, sprawling empire that stretched from China to the Baltic, peopled by over a hundred nationalities from Finns to Mongolians; and their memories in particular of beloved Mama, embodying everything they had lost in the Revolution; for she would be lying not in a royal tomb in the cemetery at Tsarskoe Selo, but in an unmarked grave somewhere in Kronstadt.

3

For three days we wallowed and churned across the Baltic, in waves so angry that at times I was too seasick even to remember the misery into which we had all been plunged. I shared a small cabin with Igor Trepov, and on the second day he forced me to climb up on deck where I hung over the gunwale in torment. But at least I could gulp in fresh air. From time to time I caught sight of my father striding purposefully backwards and forwards across the small deck. Once when he saw me he came over, patted my shoulder and said, 'Chin up, Nicki! Remember, you and Galina and I have to face a new life together.'

The way he said it, as he stalked away, made my grief burst out, and I was racked with sobs. I had no-one to help! Even Galina seemed to have vanished – I found out later that her skinny frame was also nauseated with seasickness, but I never discovered exactly where her cabin was.

It was like that all the second day, but on the third morning the sea calmed and finally a sailor pointed to land ahead and cried, 'Ronne'.

At first I thought this meant Denmark and that we would take a train straight to Switzerland where Father had told us he and I would spend a few days at his house near a town called Nyon. But no! Ronne was the chief town on a tiny Danish island called Bornholm and, as we reached the harbour, we saw towering above us a large vessel.

'We take that this evening,' Igor told me.

'Oh no!' cried Galina, who had braved the fresh air. 'I couldn't bear another night at sea.'

'Don't worry,' laughed Igor. 'This is a proper ship. She'll be so steady, you won't even know you're at sea.'

Father explained that Bornholm – an island famous for

its flat sandy beaches – was visited by droves of visitors each summer, and so was connected with mainland Copenhagen by two large passenger ships – of which this was one – and the trip took twelve hours. Each ship left either Copenhagen or Ronne at ten o'clock each evening, arriving at seven the following morning, thus providing a daily service.

'We're on tonight's boat,' said Father. 'The captain signalled and booked us four berths.' And with a laugh he added, 'So you'll have a good night's rest.'

We had a few hours to wait so we took some rooms at a hotel called Dams, and someone – the captain? – must have told them that Father was a prince. Everyone fussed around us, provided coffee and marzipan cakes and then finally a sumptuous cold lunch which seemed to consist mostly of herrings and other delicacies spread on thin pieces of hard brown bread.

We boarded the ship for Copenhagen before seven and I have only a vague memory of putting on my pyjamas, and then nothing, till a knock on the door woke me and in came Galina.

'We're there, Nicki. Time to get up.'

I was so hungry that after splashing my face quickly, I went straight into the dining-room and wolfed down four sugar-coated pieces of a cake-like bread called *winebrod* and three cups of strong coffee (at home, only tea was allowed).

No sooner had the gangplank been secured than a smart young Danish officer clambered aboard, asked to see Father, and, on being introduced as Captain Sven Jensen, clicked his heels and announced, 'From His Majesty's private office, Prince Korolev. Entirely at your service, sir.'

'Very kind of you,' replied Father gruffly, but obviously pleased, especially as a small crowd had gathered nearby, wondering who this distinguished man with his white beard and magnificent moustache could be.

I stood by, preening myself, as the young officer sat down with my father and explained, 'Everything has been arranged, Prince. Their Majesties are regrettably away, sir, visiting Jutland, but their office has booked rooms for you at the Hôtel d'Angleterre with' – a discreet cough – 'their compliments.'

'That's very kind of you, Captain.'

Listening avidly – together with Galina – I heard the officer say, 'I was told by our ambassador in St Petersburg that you and your son wished to travel to Geneva, and the others –' another discreet cough as he looked at Galina – 'together with Count Trepov and your maid to Paris.'

'That is right,' Father nodded.

'Actually, sir, you all leave on the same train but you change at Brussels. The train goes on to Paris, and you and your son will travel south through France to Geneva on a Swiss train. It's a little longer, but the main German railway lines are still in a mess. Half of them aren't working.'

The young officer led us to a comfortable car and drove into the heart of the beautiful city with its green roofs.

'Why are so many roofs green, sir?' I asked.

'They're made of copper,' he answered, 'and the action of the rain turns them green over the years.'

'What a pity,' I said politely.

'We rather like them green,' he answered with a smile. 'Ah, here's the hotel – and there,' he pointed to a statue in the middle, 'opposite one of our old Royal statues is the Royal Danish National Opera House. More famous really for its ballet.'

Galina craned her neck out of the car window. 'Denmark has a wonderful reputation for ballet.'

'You like ballet?'

'I was studying at the Imperial in St Petersburg. I wonder what they're playing tonight.'

'It's *Swan Lake*.'

48

'Oh! I'd love to see it again.'

'You can, Ma'am, if you wish,' the captain seemed a little uncertain of Galina's place in the hierarchy so was playing safe with 'Ma'am', and as he waved away the hotel porters, for we had little luggage, he said to Father, 'His Majesty thought that perhaps you might be bored spending all the time in the hotel, so –'

'Damned bored!' agreed Father, who had not heard the details of the ballet, and asked, 'Bored and unhappy. When does the train go?'

'Not until tomorrow evening, sir.'

'Hell! Oh well, can't be helped.'

'His Majesty has arranged for his royal box to be reserved for you. If you'd wish it, sir.'

'Daddy! Wouldn't it help us to forget – a bit. Can we go?'

Father looked a little blank.

'Please, Daddy!'

I certainly didn't want to go. I just wanted to go to bed and pray and cry for Mama and Rudi. Father muttered something about, 'Let's see. I don't really feel like it.'

Igor hated ballet but, as he had confided to me, he did like pretty girls and the capital of Denmark seemed graced by an astonishing number of young, laughing blondes with inviting twinkles in their eyes.

I watched the young Captain Jensen gulp, on the edge of a decision, then he said diffidently to Father, 'Perhaps, Prince, as I am at your service until you leave, I might have the honour of escorting your daughter to the ballet. I can appreciate, sir, that you might be very tired.'

'Good idea,' cried Father eagerly. 'Love the ballet myself but – well, I'm sure you understand my feelings at the moment. However, if you don't mind –'

'Of course I understand, sir,' said the young captain almost too eagerly.

'Very kind of you, Captain.' And then with a stern look, he asked keenly, 'Are you married, Captain?'

49

The poor captain actually blushed and stammered, 'No, sir.'

'Well, watch your step. This young lady is going to be a *prima ballerina* one day. You give me your word, young man –'

'Daddy!' It was Galina's turn to blush. 'You can't say things like that.'

'You have my word, Prince,' said the young Dane stiffly, clicking his heels.

'Of course. All a joke, young man. And anyway,' pursuing the joke, 'Count Trepov loves the ballet, so he'll be sure to join you.'

'Honoured sir,' said Captain Jensen, obviously put out – until he saw Igor give him a huge wink, telling him clearly, 'That's what *you* think.'

After breakfast the following day Galina and I went out for a walk, while Captain Jensen was attending Father. Most of the snow had gone and it was a cold crisp day with a sharp wind. We turned right at the d'Angleterre, up a conglomeration of narrow streets, bisected with the occasional square, which we had been told led to the centre of the city.

Galina looked a little happier and smiled. I asked her, 'What's all the excitement about?'

'Nothing really,' she answered, and as we passed the windows of the Royal Danish Porcelain company on the right-hand side, she pointed in the window at a typical piece of pale blue on blue and cried, 'Isn't that beautiful?'

'I don't like it,' I said for I was a little cross. She was holding something back from me.

Finally, she couldn't keep the secret any longer. 'Do you know what I saw? Just about midnight?'

'What? Go on!'

'I saw,' she whispered conspiratorially, 'Igor going into the lift and taking a girl upstairs.'

'Do you think –?' I asked with all the worldly wisdom of a twelve-year-old.

'He'd be a fool if he didn't,' she retorted.

'Galina! How can you say a thing like that.'

'These Scandinavians are red hot,' she said. 'Sven told me.'

'Sven? What sort of a silly name's that? And who is Sven anyway?'

She went a pretty pink. 'He's the young captain,' she admitted. 'Captain Jensen.'

'Oh, I see. And did Sven also see Igor and his girl friend go upstairs?'

Without thinking she nodded.

'So what were *you* two doing together at midnight?'

She went even pinker.

'I know!' I teased her, 'You were waiting to take your friend Sven into the lift when it was safe.'

'Nicki! How dare you! After all that just happened.' But she hugged me. 'He's – was – very sweet, but don't be so silly. He knows how unhappy I am. But there *was* a small dance floor in the back of the hotel and we had a couple of Danish red liqueurs called, I think, Heering. And the ballet – I couldn't take it in. I was so miserable. So as soon as I could, I went to bed.' She looked at me, 'Alone!'

'Promise?' I asked.

She stopped suddenly and looked at me full in the face. 'Why, yes,' she must have seen the look of concern in my face. 'Of course. Promise. But why?'

It was my turn to blush, standing there in the street overlooking the canal while she repeated, 'But why?'

Hesitating, searching for the right word, I finally blurted out, 'We're alone now, and well – you're too nice. I know about these things, and –'

Without a moment's hesitation Galina leaned forward and kissed me. 'That was the sweetest thing anybody has ever said to me,' she said softly.

*

51

After a clanking, tiring journey with many stops we reached Brussels and Father and I got off the train, leaving Igor, Galina and Lilla to go on to Paris where they would open up the house in the *place* de Furstemberg. I saw Father give Igor some money and heard him say, 'That should be enough until I reach Paris.'

'How long will that be?' asked Igor.

'About a week, perhaps,' Father shrugged his shoulders. 'They're so damned slow, the Swiss.'

I knew, even at that age, that Father never liked to make any firm commitments. He had a horror of being tied down, so I had the sense that the 'perhaps' might mean a little longer. But by the time he and I had settled down to dinner and a glass of wine on the Swiss night train, I ventured, 'Father, why are we going to Switzerland? I don't mean just you, but me too. Couldn't I have gone on to Paris with Igor and Galina?'

Father had been given some cigars in Copenhagen as a gift from the absent king, and now he cut one carefully, held it in his hand while he applied a match half an inch from the blunt end and then, as I watched fascinated, put the cigar in his mouth, pulled hard on it and the other end burst into an even brighter glow. Father examined it carefully then asked, 'Sorry, Nicki, what did you say?'

I knew that he had heard my question. Why did Father play games with me? I wanted to shout, 'You heard me,' but I didn't dare. Instead I watched the lights flash by as the train sped through the night.

'Why are we going to Switzerland?' I repeated the question.

He hesitated for a moment, stroking his neat white beard and then said, 'Well, it *is* one of our houses, Nicki. Where your mother stayed when you were born.'

'Then why didn't Galina come with us? After all, she is my sister.'

'Half-sister,' corrected Father almost absently, then

added more briskly, 'I will explain. I am going to collect some money. We need it.'

'And me?' I asked, for obviously there was some other reason I knew nothing about.

For a long time he sat there studying the end of his cigar until finally he said, 'Nicki – this may come as a shock – but when later in life you work out what I'm doing for you, you'll thank your old father for making one of the wisest moves in the world.'

What was it? I wondered, almost sick with apprehension. I did not have to wait long.

'Nicki,' Father puffed on his cigar and watched me carefully, 'I'm going to see if we can give you a Swiss passport.'

'What! A Swiss! Father –!' I jumped up almost screaming. 'I'm a *Russian*. The heir of a Russian prince.'

In my dismay, excitement, together with all my pent-up grief for Mama, Rudi, Olga and Yuri, I upset half of my soup as the plates on the small wagon-lit tables danced and rattled.

'Sit down!' roared Father, furious and oblivious to the way the other diners looked up, startled. Some even put down their knives or forks in astonishment at the thundering noise of command Rudi and I had known only too well.

'I'm sorry, sir,' I sat down, almost in tears, 'But –'

'Enough!' cried Father, and looking at me with a little more commiseration, patted my shoulder as he muttered, 'I know what you've been through.'

'But Mama was a Russian princess,' I could hardly keep the tears back. 'And *you*, sir –'

'I know how you feel,' he agreed, suddenly sympathetic. 'But you know, Nicki, you will still succeed to my title when I die. You'll always be a Russian at heart. All of us are proud to be Russians.'

'But I wanted to grow up and return to fight the Bolsheviks,' I insisted.

53

'You're a true Russian, but I promise you, nothing will change except your passport. Don't you want a passport?'

I suppose I must have nodded miserably, for Father said, again more gently, 'Remember, Nicki, a passport is the most important document in a man's life. The most important. Igor doesn't have a passport. Neither does poor Galina – let alone Lilla.'

'But why?' I asked. 'Igor and Galina don't have passports, but they're travelling around. Haven't they got some – papers, I suppose. Aren't they going to live in Paris?'

'I think they will probably get French passports – of a sort. But I don't want you to be a Frenchman. If there is ever another war, you'd probably find yourself fighting for the French against your fellow countrymen in Russia.'

'I'd refuse!'

'And find yourself in prison,' he said drily. 'Besides, you'll love Paris when we settle down. The only thing is, I don't trust them where passports are concerned. I think you *could* become a French citizen, but then you'd be conscripted and might be sent to Africa or Indo-China. Besides, sometimes your status can change. Here's an example: There are thousands of French Communists who admire the Bolsheviks. Suppose you are a Frenchman and the Communists seize power. It's possible. I know it's difficult to explain, and I'm sorry I told you so abruptly. But believe me, once you hold a Swiss passport, it's forever.'

'But not to be Russian!' The thought appalled me, I was so proud of my period as a cadet at the Lycée at Tsarskoe Selo. Being robbed of my nationality was like watching a disgraced hero being stripped of his medals.

'I should also tell you,' we had both calmed down now. 'You mustn't think that this terrible war in Russia is going to stop suddenly. There are thousands of us already spreading out all over Europe.'

'But who's going to look after me?'

'I don't understand.'

'But if I have to live alone in Switzerland –'

Father laughed, further easing the tension. 'No, no,' he promised, 'you'll live in Paris and go to school there. No, we won't throw you out.'

As he laughed, Father leaned across the table and ruffled my hair, and I could sense how the other people around us almost breathed sighs of relief that the incident had been resolved peacefully. The sudden moment of horror as Father roared angrily was replaced by sounds of normality, the clattering of plates and cutlery, the sound of wine being poured into glasses, the appearance of waiters removing dirty plates in readiness for the next course and, of course, the rhythmical sound of the wheels on the railway track.

We had not been to Switzerland since the summer of 1914 when I was seven, so I had only the barest memories of a villa facing the lake set in grounds so neat and carefully tended that I almost felt guilty if I trod on the grass. But it was a very vague memory, and I recalled nothing of the journey from Geneva until we reached Nyon. Nyon looked like a small lake-side village, consisting of a tiny harbour with a few pleasure yachts, one small pretty street with a few shops, some houses on the left-hand side, lined with clipped plane trees, their barks peeling.

A few hundred yards further on the main road from Geneva to Lausanne, where the road was hidden from the lake by trees, the driver slowed down at a corner. There I saw a plain white wooden sign which I did remember. It read: VILLA MONIQUE. I remembered it because, though the name meant nothing to me, Father had explained years ago that it had been called 'Monique' when he bought the property and he had never troubled to change it, partly because the Swiss did not really like change.

'They'll call a road the *Rue de la Gare* even if the station's been demolished,' he had told us then. 'Can't say I blame 'em. Imagine changing the name of St Petersburg!'

I still remember the moment of shocked silence that had greeted such an outrageous impossibility. It was much later when I discovered that the new régime had already changed the name to Petrograd, but Father always refused to recognise such desecration.

I remembered something else very vividly when we reached the square grey building facing the lake. It was the flowers.

For Father had an extraordinary idiosyncrasy. He enjoyed seeing a wide variety of flowers so much that each July, when we used to come to Switzerland for a month, he always hired a dozen or so gardeners for the season and changed the contents of every single flower bed each Monday and Thursday. It was mad! Especially as there were four large rectangular beds, each one certainly thirty or forty feet long. On Monday there would be geraniums or petunias, on Thursday snapdragons or chrysanthemums or asters, but twice a week different.

Mama used to laugh and whisper, 'It's your father's little folly. It amuses him, so why not? It gives work to the people and helps money to circulate,' adding in her usual placid voice, 'Money's no use to anyone if you keep it in the bank.'

As one who had been encouraged to put any extra money into a money box the remark puzzled me. What could possibly be safer than to put your money into the St Petersburg bank?

Quite by chance on that last pre-1914 visit to the Villa Monique I had discovered the secret of the flower changes. At the far end of our grounds was a forbidding-looking wooden fence, with one door, always secured by a padlock. I was puzzled why our neighbour's door had a lock on our side, but perhaps there was one on each side.

One day the door was half open. Looking around quickly, I slid through – and there, spread out like Joseph's many-coloured coat was a dazzling display of flowers. I realised that this was *our* garden, little more than a field.

56

In one corner was a huge greenhouse, some potting sheds and so on, but for the rest, the field was a blazing mass of colour from, literally, thousands of plants. And every single one was standing in a pot. It had never occurred to me. The secret was out. In the last few hours before dawn, workmen descended on the beds, taking out one pot, putting another in the same hole, racing against time, maybe with the aid of flashlights. What a wonderful idea!

There was an aftermath to this. Just before we were due to leave in 1914, the Press discovered Father's incredible garden. Perhaps a gardener gossiped. A local journalist photographed the beds on Mondays and Thursdays, and printed all the photographs, filling an entire page. We never discovered how. The next day the headline read:

THE PRINCE WHO LIVES FOR FLOWERS.

I had expected Father to be furious, but not at all! Though my memories are a little dim, I remember him being quite pleased. The moment he read the article, he sent out for a dozen extra copies and, almost with a laugh said to Mama, 'Quite a triumph, eh?'

And that night, drinking champagne before dinner, he chuckled to her, 'I like to show a little originality, y'know. You like it, my dear?'

'Lovely,' said Mama cheerfully, then repeated Father's words to me. 'A triumph.'

Indeed it was – until an erudite correspondent called Alexander Lepoint wrote a large article in the *Tribune de Genève*, the first paragraph of which pleased Father, but not the rest, for it read in part:

'The Prince Korolev is to be congratulated on his ingenuity in gardening but readers may like to know that this is by no means a new idea.'

I heard Father splutter with rage as he read on:

'The idea originated with another scion of the Russian nobility who used to visit the French Riviera during the last half of the nineteenth century. Prince Korolev may

57

have changed his plants twice a week, but Prince Cherkassky of Russia went much further – he employed forty-eight gardeners at his winter villa above Cannes *and changed the flowers every night.*'

The memory came flashing back from those annual visits so long ago, and as the car drew to a halt and the two old Swiss who had looked after the house during the war years came to greet us, I ran round to the front of the villa, separated from the waters of the lake by the lawns and the four huge beds. I had forgotten the impact of time, the years of war, for a moment almost everything, I just wanted to see what kind of flowers had been planted there. But the beds were empty. It was still winter – there was even snow on the hills in France on the other side of the lake.

All this was a long time ago, fragments recalled sometimes with difficulty, but I still smiled as I walked into the house – which looked completely unchanged – and Madame Verbier, the housekeeper, folded me into her ample bosom – she was a little like Lilla – and almost in tears whispered, 'Mon pauvre.' And then, holding me out in front of her said, 'You are too thin, Nicki. I shall start to fatten you up. I will start right away – here's a piece of chocolate.'

I never said 'No' to chocolate or sweets or cream buns of any kind – and with a polite 'Merci bien' broke off a large piece of good Swiss chocolate.

We went to bed early that first night, after Father and I had sat in front of the large log fire in the warm sitting-room and Madame Verbier had brought me a large mug of steaming hot chocolate while Father was finishing a bottle of champagne.

Despite the loneliness and the feeling of utter misery – for I still could not assimilate all that had happened to our family – I did receive from Father that first evening a kind of warmth I had never received before.

I had never really been close to him. He was not stern in the sense that I was always in fear of him. No, I was not – but perhaps awe is the better word to choose. He really did have a majestic presence – upright, handsome, always, it seemed, surrounded by beautiful women when he gave a ball.

Tonight, though, it was different. It was as though we were sharing our silent sorrow, and when it was time for me to go to bed, he said, at first in an almost casual way, 'Bed, Nicki! You must be tired after that journey,' and ruffled my hair again adding, 'Tomorrow we're going to see the lawyers in Lausanne. The city where you were born, remember? And don't worry about this citizenship business. We'll go early, down the Rue St François, and buy you some chocolates before we go to see the *maître*.'

And then he added with a heavy sigh, setting down his glass, 'I feel for you, Nicki. This is a sad, sad way for a boy of twelve to grow into a man. But you are a man, now, Nicki – you and I, alone together in the world.'

'I'll go to bed,' I mumbled, for I could hardly restrain the tears – not only for the wretched way I was feeling, but because I could see the tears in the corners of Father's eyes. As I reached my bedroom and burst into secret weeping, which would at least help me to sleep, I wondered whether Father, too, would cry when he was alone.

The name of the lawyer was Monsieur Dubois, and to reach him we had to climb four flights of stairs: narrow, eccentric stairs covered in highly polished linoleum in each of which I could see my face reflected, the reflection distorted as in a teaspoon. I held on to the equally highly polished bannister rail on one side, feeling a little scared of meeting a lawyer – not so much the lawyer himself, perhaps, as of the *concept* of Law (it should surely be spelt with a capital L) and its association in my mind with the immense power of the Tsar, which in turn was associated with the power of God and retribution. Not that I had any misdeeds to atone for: it was just a vague feeling of unease.

M. Dubois was as impressive, in one way, as Father was in another; and by no means forbidding. A solidly built man, he wore a frock coat with silk facings to the lapels and a linking button holding the two edges together. He wore buttoned boots with soft kid uppers and grey sponge-bag trousers. His stiffly starched cuffs protruded to show heavy gold cufflinks, and a pearl pin gleamed in his immaculately folded stock. His beard was trimmed to a point and a gold-rimmed pince-nez hung from a silk ribbon. His hand, extended in greeting to Father, was soft and plump and white.

'I'm honoured to welcome you, Prince.' He turned to me. 'And you, young sir.'

I recognised that the degree of informality was correct: a man of substance and distinction acknowledging the blood royal but avoiding the obsequious.

'And may I offer you a fortifying brandy after your climb to my eyrie? And perhaps some hot chocolate for Master Nicholas?'

'Acceptable,' Father said, spreading his coat-tails before seating himself in the leather chair facing M. Dubois' huge desk. Brandy in a balloon engraved with a crest, and steaming chocolate in a fine porcelain cup were proffered on a silver tray brought in by an elderly lady secretary whose grey hair was styled like a cottage loaf.

'We need not elaborate the preliminaries,' Father said, gently swirling the brandy.

'Exactly.' M. Dubois sat behind his desk now, his fingers steepled together. 'The requirement is for Master Nicholas – Swiss by birth but otherwise resident in Russia and established heir to your Highness's hereditaments in Nyon and Paris – to be issued with a Swiss passport.'

Father inclined his head.

'The procedure,' M. Dubois continued, 'if I may put it as succinctly as our somewhat burdensome legal phraseology allows, is for me to make, on your behalf, initial application for Master Nicholas's Swiss citizenship.'

Father nodded. 'That would seem obvious. To whom is the application made?'

'In this case to the Mayor of Nyon, who considers all requests to become integrated with his commune. He is the figurehead of a specially appointed commission that sits to examine all such requests as receive mayoral approval.'

'No doubt at infrequent intervals,' Father remarked. He touched his moustaches with the hand on which his signet ring gleamed.

M. Dubois gave a small bleak smile. 'The processes of law, Prince –'

'Quite. How long?'

'We must be patient, Prince. The commission is but an arbiter that decides which applications shall go forward to another, more authoritative, senate – this time of the Canton of Vaud, of which canton Nyon is a sub-district.'

'I am aware of that. And no doubt the sacred time of these many grave gentlemen, and the professional services, filing, sealing, travelling – all this is going to cost money.'

M. Dubois gave the smallest inclination of his head, as if the matter were of minor consequence but still had to be considered.

'It is an officially designated fee, Prince. Recorded in the schedules as twenty thousand francs.'

I could not but feel a start at the mention of such a vast amount; but Father, of course, merely flicked a speck of dust from his coat.

'And you, M. Dubois, would that sum include your fees?'

M. Dubois sighed as if with regret. 'Alas, no. The burden of preparation of the numerous documents involved, the fees to the attestors of signatures, all fall upon me – an expensive process.'

'No doubt,' Father said testily. 'How expensive?'

'Five thousand francs.'

'Daylight robbery,' snorted Father.

But there was no more to be said, so as we rose to leave, M. Dubois tactfully helped my father with his astrakhan-trimmed coat. 'There should be no problem. I will let you know when it is resolved.'

We stayed three more days in Switzerland. For most of the time I was on my own. Father had what he always called 'Money business' with his old-fashioned bank. On the third day a taxi drove us to the station in Geneva, just across the border from the Canton de Vaud of which I hoped to become a citizen.

The next morning we were in the noisy glass-topped steamy arcade of the Gare de Lyon and on the way to our first steps of a new life in Paris.

PART TWO

1919–1939

4

Even at my tender age, when I had never really been excited by the physical beauty of objects – always excepting the remembered beauty of Tsarskoe Selo – I found such a responsive chord of excitement in the place de Furstemberg that I immediately fell in love with the house. The small 'place' was square and neat. On its four sides forsythia trees alternated with tall lamp-posts surmounted by clusters of globes like white balloons; and every evening at dusk the lamplighter came with his long stick to set them glowing.

I had not realised that our house was a *hôtel particulier* – which meant complete house – and when the taxi drew up in the square all I saw at first was an unimposing yellow front door, one of the group of equally unimpressive doors along one side of the square.

As I looked, Father pointed to the opposite corner and said, 'That's the atelier where Delacroix used to work.'

I must have looked blank, for Father said, 'You don't know the name of such a famous painter? My goodness, we'll have to send you to a French crammer. Always remember, the average Frenchman won't have the faintest idea where Chagall or Goncharova live but they expect all young people to know every detail of every French painter's life.'

Father opened the rather dirty yellow door – to my surprise it was not locked – but we did not go into the house, instead along a very short passage with a semi-circular brick roof and at the end I could see in the daylight a small splashing fountain. Its music tinkled above the sound of our footsteps. A few steps later we were in the tiniest little courtyard, with a concierge's hut in one corner and steps ahead, and a door with glass panels through which I could see broad wooden stairs.

'Is this our house?' I asked, breathless.

'All of it,' Father seemed amused. 'Like it?'

'It looks lovely,' I breathed and at that moment I saw a flurry of skirts almost tumbling down the stairs, the door flew open, and there was Galina calling, 'Welcome home, wanderers!' She hugged me, kissed Father, and then turned back to me and said, 'This house is a little corner of heaven.'

The reason was not hard to discover. Our house, which Galina and I explored together, had been bought many years ago by Father and furnished slowly. It was as Russian in its atmosphere as our house outside St Petersburg, yet overlaid as though with a thin veneer of French polish so that we had the best of both worlds – a French house of tomorrow filled with the mementoes of yesterday – everything from a samovar to dozens of precious ikons on the walls, and in the living-room an old round table on which stood dozens of framed sepia photographs, prominent among them signed ones of the Tsar and Tsarina. All these stood in one corner of a comfortable living-room, which had a fat, comfortable sofa, its cushions embroidered with the Imperial Russian Eagle. In front of it, with memory tugging at my last mental pictures of Mama, was a replica of the footstool she loved so much. It contained a tiny musical box which played (in the words of one advertiser) 'a restful lullaby for tired feet'. They were enormously expensive, but very popular with the aristocracy.

In Father's study were more photographs – but, in this case, of onion-shaped cupolas, snow, soldiers of the Imperial Russian Guard in their heavy uniform, cannon outside the Winter Palace, army officers resplendent with medals. There was also a silver cigarette box, the lid open, filled with those special Russian cigarettes – half with empty cardboard tubes, the other half with tobacco in saffron impregnated paper.

'I thought I'd fill up the box for Daddy,' explained Galina. 'There's a Russian expatriate here who's set up business as a snuff and tobacco dealer.'

Mama's old room included three boxes decorated with the Imperial colours of blue and gold – which had once been filled with hand-made chocolates, but were now used as glove boxes – dozens of photographs, more ikons and candles, and on a table in the corner a collection of twenty or thirty priceless Fabergé *trouvailles*.

My room had nothing of my own from the past except Kodi, my teddy bear which I had brought with me, while Galina's, next door, contained one photograph.

'Who's that?' I asked.

'It's Marius Petipa,' she answered. 'He was the greatest ballet master of the Imperial Ballet in the early years of this century. A Frenchman who found it impossible ever to speak Russian.'

I never ceased to love our house in the place de Furstemberg. It quickly became a new home to which we all had to adapt as best we could – made easier because, as the years passed, I not only felt that I was beginning to assume the mantle of a man, but I fell in love with Paris itself, especially the Left Bank. I had to go to school, of course, and Father had chosen the American School near Passy, where I enrolled as a weekly boarder; but I lived for the week-ends at home. The Left Bank was a private world of its own – and it was filled with Russians who had escaped the Revolution. Some lived in offices, some were taxi drivers or waiters.

Often I was up before anyone else in the morning, and then I would go and collect the morning baguettes – fresh, still hot, smelling wonderful, and I would – like the French

– nibble a bit of crust off the bread on the way home.

Just behind our house was a large open-air market at the top end of the Rue de Seine. With its wares displayed, it looked like a coloured flag – red tomatoes, green peppers, mauve plums, white asparagus from Cavaillon, green salads and, near the open-air stalls, the *boucherie*, the *boulangerie*, all of it so spotlessly *clean*. It took me weeks to become accustomed to seeing carrots that looked as if they had been polished! It was a beautiful market and at one end were a couple of large flower stalls ablaze with the brightness of freshly-cut blooms. I could happily go to the *marché* in the Rue de Seine for an hour without buying anything.

Sometimes I would stop to watch an artist at work, perched on a tiny triangular stool, or browse among the folding bookstands near the river before strolling back up the Rue des Sts Pères to the famous Deux Magots restaurant on the boulevard St Germain.

Sometimes, peering through the windows, I would see Father talking to friends in a corner and pop in and say 'hullo'. He seemed to know everybody.

'Ah, this is my son,' he would say. 'He is the Tsar's godchild.' He was very proud of that. 'Nicki, this is Mr Ernest Hemingway who has decided to be a famous writer.' The Mr Hemingway was a beefy man with a jovial sense of humour and cried, 'H'ya, young man. I'll give you one of my books and sign it for you.'

'Thank you, sir,' I said politely. 'I will treasure it.'

'It isn't written yet,' Hemingway laughed. 'But I'll write it, I promise you.' As we talked, a very odd woman came in and was introduced to me as Gertrude Stein.

'Miss Stein is a writer like Mr Hemingway,' explained Father.

She almost ignored me, and afterwards I said to Father, 'She looks more like a man than a woman.'

'How observant you are,' said Father drily, but did not explain any more.

Once or twice when I hoped to cadge a coffee from Father at the Deux Magots – and improve my general knowledge by meeting his friends – he brushed me off. One afternoon in particular, I pushed open the glass door – I must have been about fifteen by then, three years after we first arrived – but then froze at what I saw, and hastily left the café.

Father was sitting in a corner with a very pretty but obviously slightly ordinary girl and even I realised how abundantly clear it was that they were more than casual strangers.

'Oh, that'll be Evelyn,' said Galina when I told her. 'I've seen them together several times.'

'He's not going to marry her?' I was horrified.

'Good God, no,' Galina had become very grown up. 'She's just a demi-mondaine. Pretty though, I'll give her that. And poor Father,' she sighed. 'He can't keep his hands off a pretty girl.'

'Galina!' I must have sounded appalled. 'Do you mean –?'

'Of course I do. *And* Igor. He's even worse.' She tapped her snow-white teeth with a pencil and laughed, 'Because he's younger, I suppose. Come on, Nicki, don't look so disgusted. All men do it, you know.'

'Even when they're married?'

'All the more. You must have learned the facts of life at school. Don't they teach you anything?'

I nodded, sagely aware that at the age of fifteen I must at least give the impression that I knew about everything.

Suddenly serious, she said, 'Father has two weaknesses – gambling and women. I'm not sure which comes first. But he seems to have enough money to enjoy the gambling, because he's always popping off to Monte Carlo to make his fortune. It's Igor that I'm really sorry for.'

'He seems all right.'

'Poor Igor. The only money he really gets is what Father gives him.'

'But if he eats at home, and Father – he's got money –'

'It's the *girls*, don't you understand,' explained Galina almost impatiently. 'These wretched females cluster round him like flies – especially the married ones – and actually he can hardly afford to take them out for a drink. So he has to try to wait until they ask him to dinner, then it costs him nothing.'

'And otherwise?'

'He feeds himself on bortsch and boeuf Stroganoff or whatever Lilla cooks him and then, to save money, walks all the way across the Tuileries to the Ritz bar. And then, when it's all over, he usually has to walk home.'

'After – er –'

'Yes, darling brother,' she mimicked me, 'as you so aptly describe it, "after".' Then looking at her watch, she cried, 'My God, I must rush. I'll be late for ballet school.'

For Galina now seemed to spend almost half her time working on the *barre*, and her conversation was studded with words like '*pliés*' and '*glissés*' and '*jetés*' and phrases I could not even comprehend, like '*battements tendus*'. When she was not talking, she was spending hours at home on her toes, wearing her blocked shoes. She had even persuaded Father to buy her a full length mirror like the ones they have in the *salle* of the ballet – the kind of Victorian mirror pivoted in the middle to its standing frame.

What is more, she was doing very well. After her work in St Petersburg, she had had no difficulty in entering the French equivalent of the Imperial Ballet, the École de Ballet at the Paris Opéra, especially as Father had met one of the driving forces of the ballet in France. This was Serge Diaghilev, who had arrived in Monte Carlo before the war and met a coterie of exciting Russians – Chagall, Goncharova, Stravinsky and, later, Nijinsky.

By the end of the war Diaghilev was in serious financial trouble. He had kept together a small troupe of dancers, thanks largely to Princess Edmond de Polignac, more American than her name sounded, for she was an heiress of the Singer sewing machines who loved the ballet. In the early 1920s Diaghilev made an arrangement to join his troupe with that of his own summer ballet season, which started each April, in Paris.

Father's first meeting with Diaghilev was in Monte Carlo and started with a colossal row, as Father was fond of telling us later in life. It seems that Father had done well at the casino and fallen for a pretty twenty-year-old ballet dancer called Lisette. She was only in the *corps de ballet* but Father described her with relish as being as thin as a pencil, with the longest legs in the world. For the moment Father established Lisette in a suite at a small hotel and they seemed to enjoy themselves – until the day when, in the large central hall of the Hôtel de Paris, Father heard someone hail him in a loud voice, 'Prince Korolev'.

Father presumed it was an old friend. Instead he was faced with a heavily-jowled rather plain man who announced loftily, 'I am Diaghilev.'

The name meant nothing to Father. 'Who?' he enquired.

'Serge Diaghilev. I control the Ballet Russe.'

'Oh sorry – of course,' said Father. 'I know your name now. The dancing chap. Congratulations on a fine show. I go to see it most evenings.'

'So I gather,' said Diaghilev, seemingly unimpressed by Father's title. He sniffed the rose in his coat lapel. 'And then spend the rest of the night in bed with one of my dancers.'

'Oh! Lisette!'

'Exactly. And I would be grateful if you could desist.'

'And why, may I ask?' Father began to bristle.

'Because,' answered Diaghilev coldly, 'of necessity ballet dancers are thin, yet they work very hard, so they have only limited strength. If you, sir, spend all your time making love to one of my girls, she won't be fit for work the next day.'

'That's fine!' sneered Father. 'You lecturing me on sex – you a self-confessed tapette.' He used the French word for a homosexual. 'You probably don't know what it's like – the normal way.'

'How dare you!' Diaghilev almost made to slap Father's face, but he did not have a glove. Nor, I suppose, could Diaghilev openly insult a prince who was widely known to have been a close friend of the late Tsar.

'I've lost too many dancers to lecherous old men,' Diaghilev added, 'and anyway, loving women is a morbid business.'

'I don't see how you can know much about that,' jeered Father. 'However, let me assure you of one thing. I enjoy Lisette just as much as you enjoy your tapettes, but I have turned fifty so once a night is my limit.'

Father always chuckled when he told this story. Diaghilev burst out laughing, and after that, they became good friends – indeed intimate in a conversational way, with Diaghilev amongst other things confessing to Father that he had a horror of journeys by water because he had once had his palm read and been told that death would come by drowning.

'Rubbish, of course,' Father snorted. 'But he's a sincere artist and I put some money into the ballet on one condition – that he gave Galina a chance if she was good enough. Diaghilev took one look at Galina demonstrating her skill and gave her a job on the spot.'

Looking back, it must have been in April 1922 when Diaghilev first engaged Galina and she started her dancing career. Because I adored and was proud of my sister, I became more intrigued by ballet – helped too, I admit, by the fact that I was able to get a regular supply of house tickets from Galina which meant that I could ask my schoolfriends and the occasional girl I met at parties.

At school I was a dismal failure. The headmaster had put me into too high a class, so I was always struggling to catch up – and never succeeding. I was told to study subjects I had never studied before. French history was a closed book to me. I could not even understand the rudiments of subjects like algebra. I was good in literature and led the class in French grammar, with its complicated use of the subjunctive, because I had been thoroughly taught it in Russia. So I managed to scramble enough marks to avoid expulsion, and perhaps too because I had by now received my Swiss passport.

I thought we all seemed to be embarked on a happy and normal kind of life in our lovely house – an entire slice of old Russia in a French square – though now and again Igor, always short of money, suffered attacks of melancholia. This, however, was before Galina dropped the first of a series of bombshells into our seemingly happy lives.

I must have been seventeen – yes, I remember for another reason that I was approaching my eighteenth birthday in 1925 – when Galina came into the house with a glum face, lit a cigarette, and announced in a flat, unemotional voice, 'I'm getting married.'

She must have seen the look of utter shock on my face and she looked so unhappy that my first thought was, 'You're not going to have a baby?'

She roared with laughter. 'No, thank you.'

'Then what – and to whom? You don't exactly look as though you relish the prospect.'

'I don't. Not really. Yes, you've met him – a ballet dancer, Jean-Pierre Blondel.'

'Blondel!' We *had* met several times when Galina had brought home a few ballet friends from the Opera. Blondel was in the Corps de Ballet, and a picture of him flashed through my brain – a wasp waist, as small as a woman's, strong leg muscles showing through his tight trousers, longish fair hair, a 'pretty' boy.

'But Galina,' I cried. 'Jean-Pierre. I always thought he was a –'

'A tapette? He is,' she agreed bitterly. 'At present he's madly in love with Serge –'

73

'Diaghilev?'

She nodded.

'But if that's true, Galina – why? You can't marry a tapette – you of all people, darling sister. You've rushed into this –'

'I haven't. It's the result of careful thought.'

'Then can't you – well, explain?'

She sighed, sipped at a glass of tea with lemon, holding the glass in her zarf, the thin silver receptacle with a handle into which you place the hot glass.

'It's a long story. And it's not a love story, though I am very fond of Jean-Pierre. But, Nicki, you don't know how tired I am of going round to the Prefecture and the local police stations to show them my papers. If I were just a poor Russian who didn't work officially, it would be easy, but now that I'm twenty-three, I have to get my work permit renewed all the time. I've no real passport. I'm just a lost soul. I should be more polite to the police officials than I am, but if I *am* polite, they proposition me.'

'But a *queer*!' I burst out.

'I know. And Jean-Pierre's father was livid when he discovered that his son had turned out this way. He's a respectable lawyer, and finally he warned Jean-Pierre that he'd kick him out of the house unless he got married. What's more, the old man told Jean-Pierre that if any girl *would* marry him, he'd give her a hundred thousand francs as a dowry. Jean-Pierre told me, and I said I would. It's a fortune,' she said defensively. 'He's a nice boy and really it's solved all my problems legally.'

I was shattered by the news. I lit a Gauloise to steady my nerves.

'I know, I know,' continued Galina, 'but at least it's got both of us out of a mess. I'll finally have a bit of spare cash and become a bona-fide citizen of the French Republic, and Jean-Pierre'll become a bona-fide man and,' she hesitated, 'I haven't told you this yet, Nicki darling, but we're going to have a quick civil marriage next week and then,

as you know, the ballet season's ended in Paris and Serge
has asked me to go to Monte Carlo the week after, in
September, to work there through the winter.'

'Oh Galina, what'll I do without you?'

'You'll live,' she laughed, even ruefully.

'And Diaghilev will have his little boy on tap,' I added
almost savagely.

And that is how it turned out. Galina was married
quietly. She kept her professional name, but was now
officially Madame Blondel. Father was not angry, really.
He loved Galina, of that I am sure, but he knew he would
see her in Monte Carlo from time to time, and as he said
to me with a Russian shrug of his shoulders, 'At least her
career won't be messed up with lots of kids all around.
And she can always get a divorce.'

A week after Galina had left for Monte Carlo, Father sent
a message through Lilla that he wanted to see me. It was
a quarter past nine and for as long as I can remember,
Father's day had started by being awakened at nine o'clock
and served in bed with half a bottle of cold champagne.

'But only Laurent-Perrier,' he stipulated. 'I don't mind
serving cheaper brands to those –' with a sniff – '*people*
who use swizzle sticks to take out the bubbles, but for
people who appreciate good champagne, it's Laurent-
Perrier or nothing.' Taking the bubbles out after struggling
so hard to put them in the bottles was to him an unforgivable sin.

When Galina first heard that Father drank champagne
in bed every morning, she protested, 'but it can't be good
for you!'

'Nonsense, girl,' he cried. 'Think of all the junk we eat!'
And pointing to some caviar, he said, 'Look at that!
Disgusting! The result of copulation between a couple of
fish. But it tastes good. Pass it along my dear. I'm hungry.'

I was recalling Galina's remark as I knocked and entered
his bedroom.

'You wanted to see me, sir,' I began. I always thought it a good idea to pop in a 'sir' early in the day.

'Did I? Ah yes, of course. Come and have lunch with me today at the Brasserie Lipp. You do like beer don't you – I mean, you drink it at school?'

'When I have any money,' I smiled ruefully. 'Yes, why?'

'Well, I'm very fond of Lipp's, but it's not really done to drink wine there. The food's wonderful, though.'

When we had sipped from the first standard large Lipp glass of beer, Father said, 'Well, Nicki, tomorrow's your birthday – eighteen, and a man. Sorry about your not passing the *bachot*.' I had never expected to pass the baccalauréat, France's toughest school exam. 'It seems a long, long time since we first came to Paris,' he sighed. 'But we've managed to live through it and I'm proud of you.'

I knew Father was very fond of Lipp's for lunch but I had never eaten there because usually I was at school. But even I, knowing of his impressive moustaches and overpowering bearing, was impressed with the way the waiters greeted him and (presumably) the proprietor, who shook hands with him in the traditional French manner. Everyone at Lipp's knew my father but even so, he seemed different today, more mellow.

'I've got three ways to help you to enjoy your birthday,' he announced. 'Let's put the first one to you, shall I?'

I nodded, flushed with excitement.

'I hope you'll be glad, Nicki. I've told the school that you're not coming back. You're wasting your time there.'

I could scarcely believe his words! I was astounded – and almost whooped with excitement. I had never liked school; I had my good subjects, but in general I never felt able to cope with the lessons. And suddenly this joy! Never to return to that wretched place! Yet instinct warned me to wonder why Father had taken this step. He was not the kind of man to let me leave school just because I did not enjoy it. There was a deeper motive involved. But I did not discover what it was until later that day.

'What are the other surprises?' I asked as we finished a thick steak au poivre, followed by a beautiful creamy Brie and we were sipping black coffee, while Father indulged in a large *fine*.

After giving the matter a few moments' thought, Father carefully stirred his coffee and asked me carefully, 'You're eighteen tomorrow, Nicki. Tell me – are you still a virgin?'

Blushing scarlet I cried, 'Father, really! Please!' I was sure everyone near us on the banquette that lined the length of the room could see my blushes. Father had even spoken in a loud voice. Was that a snigger I heard behind my back?

'Come on, don't be so silly,' he said almost testily. 'It's quite a well known practice in France – and especially in Paris – to – er – initiate a young man into the arts of love-making,' adding sharply, 'Don't look as though you're so damned embarrassed.'

'I am embarrassed,' I blurted out. 'I can't help it.'

'I suppose, when you're young' – was there a hint of envy in his sigh? – 'but in the old days in Russia when a boy was eighteen, we'd just look round the workers on the estate and find a healthy young wench and exercise *droit du seigneur*. Not very satisfactory, really,' he added hastily. 'Things have changed. But just regard tonight as though you're going to take a much more exciting exam than your stuffy old *bachot*. You may – er – enjoy yourself, but you'll also gain an elementary lesson in the art of love-making. Trust the French to get it right.'

'I don't want to go.'

'You're not becoming like Galina's husband?'

'No, sir,' I said hurriedly, because I saw that his good humour was turning harsh, 'but you make it sound so – well, businesslike, commercial.'

'It is!' My father suddenly laughed out loud. 'You don't get anything for nothing in this world.' And, whispering confidentially, 'let me tell you something. The most expensive girls in the world are those who don't expect to be paid – especially if you marry one.'

As he settled the bill, Father added, 'You go home now. I've got an appointment in town. I'll pick you up at eight this evening and we'll have a drink at the Ritz first.' He strode off along St Germain towards the Quai d'Orsay, a fine figure of a man in his late fifties, as stiff and straight as his silver-knobbed cane. As I walked off the other way, past the Deux Magots and into the place de Furstemberg, I did feel a tingle of excitement at the prospect of our evening ahead, not because of what Father had rather derisively labelled 'the lesson' which I was supposed to learn, but because, like every healthy boy I was, in truth, aching to try the real thing instead of the substitute which was the lot of most of us still at school, and after which I always felt sordid and depressed.

Sharp at eight Father picked me up. 'Put on that grey flannel suit of yours,' he had suggested. He was also dressed in a grey suit and looked very smart as we took a taxi to the Rue Cambon where the Ritz had a smaller, second, more friendly bar, presided over by Frank, an old stager of the racecourse, who invariably thought he knew the latest hot tip.

As we walked in, he greeted us, 'Bon soir, monsieur le Prince.' I saw a few heads turn and felt a thrill of pride in my father.

'The usual Laurent-Perrier, Monsieur?' Father nodded, said 'Evening, Frank,' and sat down in a corner seat. Someone brought along glasses, an ice-bucket and opened the champagne skilfully without making a pop.

After the bottle was empty – Father drank three-quarters of it for I was afraid of drinking too much – we took a taxi to an address which I failed to catch but which I recognised was past the Madeleine and up the boulevard Malesherbes. After paying it off, Father fumbled in his pocket, took out a note and handed it to me.

knows whether – one day – staring out of a picture – there might be someone you know. You should go.'

I couldn't help asking, 'Do you go, Father?'

Going through the paraphernalia of lighting a cigar, he said, 'Once a week. Every Monday. Just pop in, pay my respects, see if by chance – yes, Nicki, I know how you feel, there is no hope of tracing the past – and yet –'

'I'll go, Father,' I promised. 'Regularly. I will.'

He hesitated, picked up one of the foie gras sandwiches which Lilla had prepared for us, then said shortly, 'Any idea of who runs the Russian Centre?'

'The Russians, I suppose.'

He shook his head. 'No. The Russians haven't got a bean between them, you must know that. You may be surprised to know that it's run by the Red Cross in Geneva – apart from the unpaid helpers, who work so many days a week.'

'The Red Cross?' I was surprised.

His cigar was glowing now.

'It started because so many Russians who can't get out of Russia don't know where to write to – so they write to the Red Cross in Geneva, who organise the whole thing in an attempt to try and bring people together. They've got lots of centres, of course, and if someone writes, they probably duplicate his letter or photograph and the details of a missing man will be stuck up for all to see in places as far apart as – well, Paris, London, Rome, New York. It's wonderful work.'

Unthinkingly, I stifled a yawn, not so much from boredom, but I had had quite a night. 'Excuse me.' We had always been taught to apologise for yawning.

'Go to bed, Nicki,' said Father. 'I think I'll stay up and finish this cigar.'

'And this job – can't I know?'

'Not too tired?'

I shook my head.

As Father puffed his cigar after, as usual, examining the

bright red end, he said, 'I've got you a chance in a lifetime. As a trainee with the Red Cross on the understanding that, if you behave yourself, you take over the Russian section in Paris.'

'The Red Cross!' I burst out. 'But there's no war!'

'There might be before long. Give the Germans a few years to gather strength and they'll be dying to have a crack at the French again. And the Russians, I don't doubt. That's why I want you to leave school – it's the chance of a big job.'

'But what'll I do? Please, Father, don't force me into a dreary job! With a twin brother we don't even know is dead or alive. I'm sorry, I didn't mean that' – I saw his look of anguish – 'you know how we all hope –'

'And yet' – bitterly – 'since you *have* to work, you can't be bothered to work where you *might* be able to help – and why should that be dreary? Your situation is very simple. I discussed the whole thing the last time I was in Switzerland. The boss has to be a Swiss. The man who's in charge at the moment – a Swiss, obviously – is due to retire. After a bit of training, you'll be ideal. *You* try and find a Swiss who has lived most of his life in Russia.'

'But I don't know what to do – even the way around.'

'You'll learn and you'll be paid to learn – that can't be bad can it? Anyway' – as though the matter was settled – 'it's all been fixed. Your main job will be to arrange for others to classify the names that *do* come from Russian sources. And, Nicki, who knows? You will be in charge of the destiny of hundreds of thousands of lost souls.'

And so, knowing that Father would never forgive me if I did not have a shot at it, I agreed. And at the back of my mind, I knew that if I *was* fed up, I could always look around later for another job. But, despite my fears, the job *did* turn out to be fascinating work. And there was something that I did not immediately realise. It took me back to my roots – my Russian roots. Six very formative years is a long time, and during all that time my friends had tried to tear me away from Russia and make me a Frenchman in all but name. Even Father was now such an international that the most Russian thing about him was his title of Prince. Could there be anything more French than the way he had taken me for my 'lesson' with the charming Hélène?

Now, when I started going to the office in the Rue du Bac, I was becoming quickly submerged by Russia. Russia was a living entity in the four rooms we rented almost at the corner where the Rue du Bac reaches the Pont Royal, so that I could even look out of my window at the river Seine.

Our headquarters consisted of four rooms and a kitchen, in an old corner building of great charm but few modern amenities. In a way this made the poor Russian refugees who came regularly to us in search of help feel more at home. They would have been put off the place if it had been surrounded by bright chrome and glass furniture.

Instead, the largest room was warmed with sofas and armchairs and a selection of Russian newspapers and magazines. On a small table was a samovar, filled by volunteers with hot water for impoverished guests. One room had every wall filled with small photos or requests, 'Can anyone trace . . .' and other pitiful pleas for information, often with passport-style photos attached. The most astonishing thing was our remarkable rate of success. It seemed that, for many people, all you had to do was let them know your name and someone contacted them. Sometimes a Russian who was wanted on the OGPU list would defect and throw himself on the mercy of the French, and my job then, after my initial training, would be to extract every inch of information out of the newcomer; particularly names of old friends, what they were doing, where they were living. The only sadness was that we never heard a word, not a trace of Rudi, nor, for that matter, of Olga.

When the head of the bureau retired, a Swiss came in

for a year. He was an agreeable young man from Geneva, a few years older than I was, called François Savin, and he could not speak Russian, did not like work and confided to me almost on the first day we had lunch together that he had grabbed the chance to come to Paris because he wanted to live in the French capital. Somehow the age-gap between us shrank, no doubt because by the time François arrived I had grasped all the elementary rules of the game of tracing unknown and missing persons, and so did most of the work.

François turned out to be a wonderful character, who had a great desire to experience the seamier delights of Paris. After our first meeting he said cheerfully, 'You don't mind if I call you Nicki, do you? And I hope you don't mind acting as a guide and showing me the hot spots. And I don't mean art galleries, thank you.'

Yet he mixed his pleasures with tuition very skilfully, asking adroit questions so that I hardly realised how much he was teaching me. Was I good at figures? Fair. Could I type? No, but willing to learn. Did I top six feet? Just on. Did my twin brother have the same sandy hair? Yes. And 'You've got a tough body, and you don't look as though you eat too much. Let's hope that your twin's the same as you – a smiling, good-looking fair-haired broad-chested man who ought to be able to do your job on your head.'

'Thanks for the compliments. I hope so too,' I laughed.

He was a perfect companion. He had plenty of good Swiss francs to spare, was a generous, cheerful spender and his carefree attitude infected all of what I called the 'Left Bank crowd' with his determination to enjoy himself. He smoked so much that I found myself smoking a pack of Gauloises a day almost out of sympathy.

He was prepared to do anything. He was a big man, but no match in size for the man Father had introduced me to, Ernest Hemingway. One day, when we met at the Rotonde, Hemingway looked at his watch and said, 'Hell, I'm late for boxing.' Hemingway loved to box a few rounds.

'If you ever want a partner for sparring . . .' François Savin offered eagerly.

'Sure you're tough enough for me?' Hemingway smiled tolerantly.

François persisted, and finally Hemingway did have a few rounds with him. Then it turned out that François had been university champion in Berne and, though he did not have Hemingway's height and reach, he gave such a good account of himself that Hemingway asked him to box again.

The exciting common denominator of the Left Bank in those lovely, gentle days of the free 1920s was that everyone was struggling. Even Goncharova, the exiled Russian painter, could not always pay for canvases and paints, but we often saw her leaving her two rooms in the Rue de Seine for a coffee in the Deux Magots. She could make a coffee last twice as long as anyone else. She had to. She did not have the price for two. But whenever François caught sight of her, he would grab her gently – she always seemed so thin and frail – and take her out for something to eat.

He seemed to know everyone. One day he arrived late at the office, his hands, even the cuffs of his sleeves, covered with grime.

'What on earth –' I began.

'I promised Fernand Leger' – who had a studio on the Left Bank at the top of some circular iron stairs – 'that I would help him to light his fire with some *boulets*.' Then he said, 'That is only his studio, of course. Do you know where he lives?'

I shook my head, though I had met this tough exponent of what someone labelled, 'The engineer school of painting'.

'He comes from Normandy,' said François, 'but when I asked exactly *where*, he just grunted, "Half way between Camembert and Pont l'Évêque".'

They were happy days, those Left Bank times where

everyone seemed equal, where there was always tea or coffee for any one of them in our lovely house, and where, when I could spare the time, I used to go round the corner from home to the English bookshop, called Shakespeare and Company, and browse in the latest books. And each spring the pink and white candles of the horse chestnuts signalled the end of winter, and when they were blown away, sometimes like pink snow, it was the birth of a new summer and coffee on the terraces again.

At the end of my second year in 1927 – I was almost twenty now and complete boss – I qualified for a month's holiday and Father was so pleased with my progress and enthusiasm that he took Igor and me off on a trip to Monte Carlo early in September.

'It'll give Igor a chance to make some money,' said Father when I thanked him, 'and of course you'll be able to go to the ballet and see your sister every night.'

5

Monte Carlo turned out to be bliss. It is the only word I can think of to describe its particular brand of old-world charm. It was like travelling overnight from today into yesterday. We arrived there in the early morning on the *train bleu* and Galina was at the funny little brown and gold toy-town railway station to greet us.

She was twenty-five now, a girl turned into a woman and she looked ravishing, with a new sparkle to her eyes, as though specially to welcome us. We had always been very close friends, filled with teasing behind the warmth, and it was this that made me, after the kissing had stopped, ask her with a touch of irony, 'How's your husband?'

'Marvellous. We're playing opposite each other in the *soliste secondo* in *Romeo and Juliet*. It's a terrific step up for both of us. Next week. I've got house tickets for you. The last two!' She squeezed my hand.

'And – er – *love*?' with a wink.

'Non-existent.' With a giggle, she added, 'It *is* Jean-Pierre's job to look after me, so we've solved the problem perfectly. Jean-Pierre stays with Diag – yes, they've got a house together – and Jean-Pierre or Serge provides me with a tiny apartment on the avenue de Belgique, a stone's throw from the theatre.'

'But you can't go on like this,' I protested. We were in a taxi now, on the way to the Hôtel de Paris.

'Can't I? You'd be surprised. He's playing opposite me. Jean-Pierre's wonderful. As a dancer, he's a genius. The sort who gives everything.'

Galina had suggested on the phone to Paris, when making all our arrangements, that I should stay in her apartment, which had two small bedrooms, so after Father and Igor had signed the book, and their luggage had been taken to their room, Galina and I, with my one modest suitcase, walked the slightly downhill road past the gardens with their ornamental palms, to her flat, which was on the third floor, overlooking the blue sea and the casino like a sugar loaf.

'It's strange,' she left a question-mark in the air as she made some coffee. 'And I don't expect you to understand it really, Nicki – ballet is such a special thing – but when Jean-Pierre is dancing a *pas de deux* with me, he puts so much of his heart – no Nicki, not his heart – the other vital part of his anatomy – into it that it's almost as though he's had an orgasm. You may not believe it, but his entire body is so driven by sex that he can't consummate in any other way.'

'Except with Diaghilev?'

'Oh him! I doubt it. I don't think they do it together. I may be wrong, Jean-Pierre and I have never discussed it. But when my husband dances with me in the way he does, I think – it's terribly sad really, but I believe they just (you're grown up now and will understand) I think they just, well, stroke each other, and play around.'

'What a waste!'

'Oh that! Diaghilev has other things. He may be rather selfish and repulsive at times, but instead of doing *that* all night long, Jean-Pierre pours out his artistic soul into the dance. And next week we get star billing. And if our *soliste secondo* is successful we're going to star in Paris next summer. You wait! I'll be a *prima ballerina* before you know what's hit you.'

'What is that Italian term you use?'

'*Soliste secondo*? Literally, it means a soloist of the second degree.'

I put down my coffee cup. 'I'm so glad for you, darling. But do *you* feel drained like he seems to?'

She nodded.

'In a way, especially if it's a difficult part. But I get over it quicker. The most important thing is that, although we don't love each other, we're the closest of friends, we dance divinely together and we respect each other's talent.'

I was unpacking in the tiny spare bedroom, and Galina was standing by the door while this conversation was taking place.

'But he's got a boyfriend – while you –' I said.

'Oh *that*.' It was a phrase of which she was fond, 'Don't you worry your head about me. You'd be surprised how popular ballet girls are with the boys,' adding, with a twinkle in her eye, 'No problems on that score. I'm careful. I do take the occasional lover but I'm very very choosy and I take good care never to fall in love. And what about you?'

'I'm doing fine,' I lied, thinking of the few girls I had slept with occasionally, including one dreary volunteer of eighteen at the Russian Centre who insisted that she was in love with me. That dark-haired married woman, Hélène, had rather spoiled me.

'Well, I've got the girl for you,' Galina suddenly turned

practical. 'She's a friend I met here – an American called Brig – a bit older than you, about my age, but you don't look the shy type. And she's enormously wealthy. Her father comes from Chicago and he's so rich that when she fell in love with a man her father didn't like, he packed her off to Europe to live and forget. Treat her with care, though. We don't want a nice boy like you marrying for money.'

'I promise.'

Galina's tiny flat bore few traces of old Russia, as she was only in Monte Carlo for the winter ballet season. There was one beautiful ikon over her bed, and a few Russian prints, but it was more French than Russian. The French influence had over the years partly transformed her too. She was a coffee drinker now, and she loved croissants and preferred onion soup to borscht. She had only one other picture in her room. It was not very large but it was striking, consisting of large blobs of red and blue, like flowers on the ends of thick but not joined green lines, the stalks. From the distance, you could see immediately what it was – a bunch of flowers, blazing with colour, joined with lots of empty white spaces.

'That's stunning,' I cried. 'Where did you find it?'

'It was a gift,' she said, adding a trifle demurely, 'from the artist. For services rendered.'

'Galina. *Never* talk like that,' I cried angrily. 'It's disgusting.'

'I didn't mean it that way. This daub isn't worth a kopek to him. But though we only met one night, I obviously meant a little to him, however unimportant.'

'Do tell me all about it.'

'It doesn't matter if I do,' she shrugged her shoulders. 'We met at a party. Goncharova and Larionov, her lover. They're one thousand per cent Russian, and she's been doing some fabulous dress designs for the new ballet. Diaghilev was there. So was Jean-Pierre, one or two others, but only one man who was obviously a foreigner.

He seemed to know the others. He was a big man with huge, tough shoulders, and I heard someone say that he lived in Paris but had rented a studio here for a few months to paint in the sun.'

'And what happened next in this fascinating saga?' I asked.

'I went to bed with him,' said Galina simply, instead of being cross. 'He came up to me, we talked, and I was fascinated. And finally he said to me "You're beautiful" or words to that effect, "This is boring, isn't it? Would you like to come and see my studio?"'

Galina looked at me, still smiling, perhaps at the memory. 'Well, you know what that sort of thing means with the French.'

'But you *did*?' I asked almost incredulously.

'I don't know why,' she nodded, 'except that he had such a strong personality. The whole studio smelt of paint, there were canvases everywhere, he hardly said a word as we took off our clothes. I never felt embarrassed or anything. And then! Nicki, I've never known anything like this in my entire life – with his bull-like shoulders he – well, he simply *pounced* on me. Always in silence. It was an unbelievable experience. I've never known anything like it.'

'All this sounds very exciting,' I said sarcastically, for I was angry in a jealous sort of way. 'Who is this silent monster?'

'I haven't finished the story yet. When it was over, we dressed. He poured out a glass of brandy for me. I needed it, I can tell you. I was trembling all over, and then he said, "It's exciting like this – just the two of us, no yesterdays, no tomorrows. Don't let's spoil it by doing it again. It's never so good the second time. Let me take you back to the party".'

'As we opened the door of his atelier, he took this lovely painting,' she indicated the flowers, 'off the wall and said, "Here – a little keepsake". And here it is. Like it? And

you don't recognise the painter? Honestly Nicki, you'll
have to brush up your artistic knowledge.'

I walked to the other side of the tiny room, and there
in small letters below the jumble of reds blues and greens
all arranged with superb skill to make it look haphazard,
was a powerful signature with a strong line underneath it.
Just 'Picasso.'

Two days later, in the lovely autumn warmth that seeped
on to our tiny balcony, and with flowers in the gardens
below and around us, I met Galina's friend Brig.

'I guess it's short for Brigitte,' she said with her mid-
western drawl. 'Somehow it just became Brig.'

She was hardly the world's most beautiful girl, but she
was such good fun and always laughing that we all laughed
too, though once or twice I thought that she might be
tougher than she looked, because there was a line that
became very firm if she was annoyed, and showed. At the
Russian Centre I had learned to judge the character of
strangers from quick summings-up, and I wondered if she
might have inherited any of the less laughable qualities
that had made her father a millionaire.

It was a passing thought, dismissed easily, for she had
one delightfully amusing habit: except at the Casino, she
never carried any money with her. She frequented the
places she knew, and whenever she had to pay, she just
cried to baffled barmen and waiters, 'Just chalk it up, Joe!'
At first the mysterious 'Joe' was a secret that baffled
everyone, until Galina explained with a laugh. 'We're
trying to educate all Monte Carlo that everyone here is
called Joe.'

'And you may ask, who the hell is Joe,' said Brig, and
I saw that she was glowering. 'Joe,' she explained, 'is
the sonofabitch who refused to marry me after another
sonofabitch, my father, said I couldn't.' But she said even
that with a laugh.

That second night we met by appointment in the Hôtel

de Paris bar because Galina was working, and in the most charming way, with an openness which I found touching, she leaned a jewelled hand on my arm and said, 'Galina told me that you boys at the Red Cross don't earn much dough. So don't get angry with me when I ask you, let me stake you.' And as I stiffened, she called for champagne and said, 'Come on now, Nicki. Don't spoil my evening. And don't be so stuffy. What the hell's money anyway?'

'I shouldn't, and I can't – but I will,' I smiled. 'But only for one reason. It's my twentieth birthday tomorrow. I was born in September – the ninth day of the ninth month.'

'Gee, what an omen. Nine. That's my lucky number. You put the lot on number nine. Come on now.'

'I can't take all this,' I was aghast. It was a bill for 1000 francs.

'I told you not to spoil my fun!'

We crossed over to the Casino, walked into the Salles Privées, where a uniformed flunkey in velvet breeches looked at me doubtfully, until Brig handed him a note and told him cheerfully, 'This is my friend Joe.' He bowed and I was in. She cashed my note for me into chips, and said, 'Now! No messing around, Nicki. Remember you're the son of a prince, not a pork butcher like my sonofabitch old man.'

'Not all this!' I begged her, but I put the thousand francs on number nine, and since it was not really my money, I didn't even feel much of a quiver as the tiny silvery ball spun round and then clacked and bounced and slithered to rest – on the number nine.

'You've made it, Nicki!' cried Brig and gave me a kiss in front of the croupiers and players. I received enormous plaques for nearly 40,000 francs. As I walked off to the bar, I heard from behind an agitated voice call, 'Monsieur, monsieur. C'est à vous encore. Vous avez gagné encore.'

I could not believe it. I had never played this game before, I had no idea that when you were paid your winnings the original stake remained on the table unless you took it off. Mine had been left there, and number nine had turned up again. I had doubled my winnings.

'Okay,' agreed Brig when I tried to insist that at least I repay the original stake money. 'Forget it, I'll let you stand me one glass of champagne. Only one. After that, the night's on me.'

'But that's not fair.'

'Silly boy. I like you – enough to bet ten times what you did on number nine. See you in a few minutes. I'm just going to the powder room.'

I was so excited that I went straight out of the main salon to the cashier near the exit and immediately cashed my chips in. I wasn't going to waste one sou of that money on gambling at some stupid game! I had never had so much money in my life, and I was determined to keep it.

Later, after we had met up in the tiny bar in the corner, and I had ordered her glass of champagne, she said, with that easy smile, 'I'm just plain bored with this casino, and I don't want to watch you lose all that dough. We'll celebrate with a bottle of Dom Perignon – I'm told that's a good marque – in my suite. Let's order supper there. It'll be more comfortable.'

And what else, I wondered. Not that I minded.

'Okay,' I said cheerfully.

'Did you know there's an underground tunnel back to the hotel? Kinda convenient if you carry your hotel key, 'cos then you don't have to check in at the lobby. Get the drift?'

'I think I do.'

I had known nothing of the underground lift but was fascinated to take one – 'we call 'em elevators back home,' she explained – down to the cellars, then we walked underneath the roadway, filled with people walking on top of us, until we reached the next lift.

'Fourth floor, Joe,' she said firmly and I knew what was expected of me.

Not until we entered her luxurious suite did I realise that Brig had no real sense of decorum.

'Let's have a bath,' she cried cheerfully. 'You ever do it in a bath?'

I shook my head.

'You will now! This suite has a double-size bath. Come on – don't be so goddam slow.' She had turned on the bath, steaming at double speed, and while the water gushed in she slipped out of her clothes and stood there naked, legs apart, wearing nothing but a few blonde curls in the middle.

But after a while, we reached for the towels, for the bath did not work.

'Kinda hard on the knees,' she agreed. 'But I've always wanted to try it. Okay – bed it is, with champers in bed.'

All in all, the evening was quite an experience. I had never shared the luxury of a huge double bed, silk sheets, soft lights, down pillows – it was beautiful, even to the touch, and though I had no deep feeling for Brig, she seemed to enjoy herself and even said:

'That's what I like about you European guys. You know how to wait for a gal. With Americans it's bang, bang, thank you Ma'am, and then when they've put on their goddam pants you're left frustrated and you've got to finish it off yourself and alone. But Nicki! For one so young, you're quite a performer. Staying power. You're great. How come you learned up on all this so young?'

'I took lessons!' I pretended solemnity.

'In sex?'

'Exactly. Quite fun, the lessons.'

She was baffled and obviously thought I was pulling her leg. If an idea is preposterous enough, it is quite easy to tell the truth and let the others think you are joking. Anyway, she said, in quite passable French, 'Merci, monsieur, pour votre patience. It's been great. We must do this again, after supper.'

We dressed informally when the waiter brought in cold

lobsters, and then it was back to bed until I made the first tentative move to get up.

'Hey! Watcha doing, Joe? Sorry, Nicki. You stay. Half the pleasure of making love is to sleep afterwards. Pure goddam bliss. Think I'm such a bastard I'd turn you out in the cold after behaving with such old-fashioned gallantry? I sleep on my right side, so I'll tuck my ass into your crotch and then we'll fall asleep. If you get a horn in the middle of the night, carry on, have it on me, but try not to wake me up.'

'But later?'

'Forget it. We're paying a fortune for this suite. I told the clerk at the desk to serve two cooked breakfasts – the works, everything from orange juice to bacon and eggs sunny side up.'

'But they'll be horrified.' I sat up in bed almost with a jerk.

'I ordered for nine-thirty. Okay? The other side of the bathroom you'll find an extra bedroom. If it makes you happier, you can sneak in there. But not until daylight. No walking out on me in the middle of the night. You're one of my creature comforts.'

'Anything you say, Ma'am,' I tried to enter into the joke because it *was* fun; the luxury trappings appealed to me, awakening some sense of a nearly forgotten past. The silk sheets stirred vague memories of being frightened when I was very young and running into Mama's bed and cuddling up to her for protection. These sheets felt just like those.

The next day Brig presented herself for lunch, which she insisted on paying for, and then presented me with a square package wrapped in fancy paper and, as we drank champagne in the Hôtel de Paris bar, she smiled and said, 'This is a small present for a dashing young man,' adding, 'one who has done all his homework.'

'But I can't –' I began.

'Go on. Open it. It'll last you all your life.'

'But you shouldn't,' I said. 'Brig, darling –'

97

I fumbled with the silken cord and finally the tissue paper, then the box – a square of velveteen and, inside, the most beautiful watch I had ever seen. One look as I took it out and I realised what it was – a solid gold Cartier, with its distinctive Roman numerals, black on white, and its black leather strap that closed with a clasp shaped like the letter 'D'.

'Brig, darling – I can't –'

'You can and you will. And anyway, I put it on Pa's account so forget it.'

'Thank you – again and again. But I'll thank you properly I hope after dinner tonight.'

'You bet your life, lover. Here's to the next time.'

But there was no next time. Never. For the most astonishing thing happened. Though I flattered myself I had pleased the lady, she met another friend that afternoon and did not keep her appointment with me that night. Worse, just before the end of our holiday, Brig took a man with her to the American consulate at Nice and, after the briefest of ceremonies, she changed her name and became Madame la Contesse Trepov.

We were all staggered. At first Galina said, 'Nicki! It can't be true. And if it is, I'm going to stop it.'

But there was nothing to be done, and soon Brig had another idea. As Galina said, 'All she wants is to be – what do the Americans call it? – a dollar princess.'

And Igor said, equally simply, 'I've got no money. She's agreed to make me a handsome allowance. We had the document of settlement drawn up by a solicitor – and Brig is a good sort, easy to live with.'

There was one other thing that Brig was also determined to have – a formal Russian wedding. It might be a bit unfair of me to think so, but as Galina put it, 'It's her one chance of fame and she's going to make the most of it.' So, as Father told me later, Brig paid for everything, leaving Father to arrange it. He was very good at organising when others paid! And this was a very, very expensive occasion. Brig wanted the world to take notice, so Father started by inviting half a dozen reporters from Paris to visit Nice on an all-expenses-paid week-end.

And news of the impending wedding, to quote the *Nice-Matin*, 'of a Russian nobleman and an American millionairess' so excited the locals that they flocked to the Russian Church in Nice.

When the bride, dressed in white satin, arrived, the gate crashers – mostly girls anxious for a glimpse of the 'handsome and dashing young Count Trepov' (to quote the *Continental Daily Mail*) – jostled forward to try and enter the church. A red carpet had been laid along the path leading to the front entrance and from somewhere Father found dozens of artificial rowan tree fronds whose red berries are supposed to be a Russian guarantee of eternal life, and which we so often saw on the walls of the Tsarina's chapel.

The interior of the church was beautiful, the white walls lined not only with dozens of ikons and hundreds of candles, but, in keeping with the sunshine outside, with huge branches of palm trees, a startling green to contrast against the white.

There were no bridesmaids – there never are at a Russian wedding – and the service was conducted entirely in Russian. The bearded high priest in his cloth of gold raiment circled round the altar twice, followed by six Russian ushers, assembled hastily from the ballet line. Taking it in turn, they held crowns above the heads of the bride and the groom.

All this was very tiring, for by tradition there were no pews and we had to stand for the entire ceremony which lasted more than an hour, ending with a moment of beautiful poetry when the couple knelt in front of the altar and exchanged their marriage vows.

When it was all over I stepped forward with all the others to kiss the bride and wish her well. Why not? I did not mind, of course. I was in no way jealous. And I had made some money. But I *did* realise that Brig was the sort of woman who would always be determined to get what she wanted out of life. She had entered into a contract. I saw again that sudden flash of straight lips when she was annoyed. Dangerous to cross! I wondered how long she and Igor would be happy. One thing was certain. She would not easily give up the status of her title for a mere trifle like an American divorce. Cynically, for one so young (but I knew Igor!) I also caught myself thinking, I wonder how long Igor will be able to keep his hands off another woman when this one starts to bore him.

The only thing that did irritate me, however, was that Brig never said one word to me. It was as though I had never met her, let alone spent a night with her. She took the greatest care never to be alone with me. It did not matter, not really, for after all, I was the real winner – eight thousand francs and my independence preserved!

When the time came for me to return home to work, Igor and his wife decided to stay in Monte Carlo a little longer. So did Father, and in the end I returned to Paris on the *train bleu* in solitary splendour, but at least able to afford a good dinner on the train.

What a time it had been! My mind was dazed as I tried to sum it up. For I had also met the rather unpleasant but nonetheless gifted Diaghilev, who seemed almost to smirk as we first met Galina's husband Jean-Pierre. But Galina did not mind, and gave me a wink as though to say, 'Take no notice. It's all one monstrous joke!' Then there was her night with Picasso. And *my* night with Brig, how she staked me, the enormous amount of money I won; and everything culminating in the extraordinary marriage of Igor and Brig and the very moving ceremony.

All this, as I devoutly hoped, was enough excitement for one whole year. But there was more to come, even more surprising.

The *train bleu* arrived in Paris in the morning, so I

dumped my bag in the place de Furstemberg, went and said 'hullo' to Lilla, then walked round to the office in the Rue du Bac to see what, if anything, had happened while I was away. Very little had so after a sandwich, I went to a cinema, had a few drinks, and arrived back home just before dark.

I passed through the tunnel and there, by the fountain near the front door, which was always locked at night, stood a woman and child. The little girl was clutching the hand of the woman, and my first memory is that the girl had a mass of golden curls but, in the dim light, I could see few details.

And then, suddenly, stabbing into my subconscious, a voice asked lightly, 'You don't recognise me, do you, Nicki?'

And I didn't – not for the first few seconds – not even the happy trill of a voice from the past that had always filled us with laughter.

Bewildered, unable to believe what I could barely see, baffled by the presence of a little girl of seven or eight, I almost screamed, 'Aunt Olga! Oh, darling Aunt Olga. Where have you been?' I fell into her arms, and burst into tears. 'We never thought we would see you again.'

'Nor me,' she kissed my face all over. 'And how is your father? Aren't you going to let us in?'

As I brushed past her to open the door to the stairs, she said gently to the little girl,

'And aren't you going to say "hullo" to your Uncle Nicki?'

'Uncle?'

'What's so odd about that?' Aunt Olga trilled with laughter as I ushered her in through the front door.

'This is my daughter Tasha.'

101

6

It was strange but, in the girl's eyes, there was an echo of Olga's instinct for merriment. She had beautiful lashes shadowing her high cheekbones, and, so far from being fearful or dejected at her new surroundings, she was filled with fun – her face enhanced by her colourful dress with its row of tiny scarlet buttons down the front of the bodice, and the green beret slanting on her golden curls. Any sign of melancholy came only in flashes yet, for some reason, from the very first time we met, she seemed to look to me for protection and friendship. There lurked in her eyes what I came to recognise as an appeal for affection which was surprising, considering her devoted mother. She was certainly an exquisitely beautiful child.

'I'd quite forgotten this damned staircase,' Aunt Olga was breathing heavily as she followed us up the two flights. 'I haven't been up these stairs since before the war. It's time Dmitri installed a lift. Absurd, all this walking at his age.'

I paused, still holding the girl's hand as we climbed up and said, 'He has thought of a lift, Aunt Olga. Sometimes he *does* get a little breathless, but it won't work. We'd have to take out all the stairs.'

'Then why on earth live on the second floor if Dmitri owns the entire building?' The years – and what else? – seemed to have made Aunt Olga a little more grumpy! Surely she remembered that the ground floor was always a glorified warehouse for storing the enormous amount of luggage with which we always travelled in the past, combined with a sitting-room and bedroom for Lilla and her husband before he was murdered? They had always travelled with us. Above the ground floor were the bedrooms, though I had not the faintest idea why the bedrooms should be below the living-room until Father explained that, when he relaxed, he always liked to look out of the windows at the surrounding scene of the roofs of Paris.

'I know,' sighed Aunt Olga, 'but the work gets harder every year.'

'We don't mind do we, Tasha?' I was trying to inject a little good cheer.

'No. You're a very strong man,' she replied almost gravely.

She refused absolutely to let me withdraw her hand from mine, so I couldn't get to my key and asked Aunt Olga to ring the bell for Lilla.

I almost wish I hadn't.

Lilla opened the door and saw Aunt Olga. She gave a shriek, swayed, turned white, and shouted in Russian, 'The resurrection of the Dead!' Then she fell to the floor in a faint, with a terrific thud.

Tasha immediately started crying, almost howling with fear. I knelt down and tried to calm her.

'Try and make Lilla comfortable,' I said to Olga as I wiped Tasha's tears away. 'I'll go to Father's bathroom and see if I can find some smelling salts.' I found them quickly in the small medicine cupboard in the bathroom and put the dark blue bottle to Lilla's nose. She stirred, spluttered, opened her eyes, saw Aunt Olga again and started to whimper with the ignorance of the peasant.

'Pull yourself together,' I cried sharply. 'Stop making a panic.'

'Sorry, sir,' she managed to stagger up, 'it's like seeing a ghost.'

'That's no ghost, Lilla. This is the Countess Arensky,' I had almost forgotten her surname after all these years. 'And this is Tasha, her daughter.'

'Oh Countess,' she sobbed, and kissed her hand. 'I can't

believe it. The wonder of having you back. Can I get you some broth or tea or something –?'

'No, no,' Aunt Olga smiled as I watched her take Lilla into her arms and let the woman sob on her shoulder. I was thinking, now I could see her better, that dear Aunt Olga was certainly eight years older since I had last seen her, and that by 1927 the lines of pain were showing on her face. She must have suffered, and I wondered what had happened in the intervening years – especially in the first months.

'You're back, Madam,' breathed Lilla, trying to recover her composure. 'It's so wonderful, so exciting – and this beautiful little baby –'

'I'm not a baby, I'm a little girl!' Tasha had recovered her child's dignity.

'Yes of course,' Lilla soothed her. Then, almost absent-mindedly, she began to croon the age-old Russian lullaby –

> 'Now fall asleep, my lovely babe,
>   *Baioushki, baiou;*
> The moon into your cradle looks
>   The clear night through.
>
> A story I will tell you now,
>   A song I'll sing for you;
> So shut your eyes and fall asleep,
>   *Baioushki, baiou.*
>
> Father is a warrior bold.
>   A fighter hard and true;
> So sleep, my baby, calmly sleep,
>   *Baioushki, baiou.*'

For a little time – it could hardly have been more than half a minute – the haunting little cradle song held us spellbound. Then suddenly the spell was broken and Lilla was once again the practical domestic. 'And your husband, Madam?'

'He's dead,' said Aunt Olga so abruptly that I was shocked, until I realised that perhaps he had died only recently.

We walked into the lovely big sitting-room. Aunt Olga, quite self-possessed and with no sign of grief, looked round, gave a nod of approval, a kind of sigh of satisfaction, and said to me, 'Nothing's changed, Nicki. It makes coming home doubly welcome. When you return to a room that's exactly the same it's as though the terrible eight years in between never happened. As though I had been here yesterday.'

Then she brightened up and cried, 'But where is everybody? Where is your father – and Galina, and Igor?'

I explained that Galina was married to a ballet dancer and was playing big roles in Monte Carlo – though I did not bother to explain his proclivities. Father was down there too. Igor, having just married an American heiress, was on an extended honeymoon.

'And you, Nicki. You're so big! Filled with brawn.'

'I've grown, Aunt Olga. It's as simple as that.'

'I know. But so much. Of course,' she too sighed, 'it is eight years. An age. How old are you now?'

'Twenty.'

'Oh dear. No, I'm delighted for *you*, but it does make *me* feel so old.'

'And Tasha? How old is she?'

'Eight.' And after a pause she saw the old samovar and cried, 'That takes me back to Russia. Maybe we *could* have a cup?'

'Of course, I'll go and see that Lilla has some blinis or something for Tasha.' And at the same time I asked Aunt Olga, 'Give me a few minutes without thinking me rude. I've an urgent job I simply must attend to.'

It *was* urgent – and it couldn't be hurried. I *had* to tell Father. It took me nearly half an hour to get through to Monte Carlo but finally I heard his voice, his almost testy, 'Is anything the matter?'

'No, Father. But I've got an astonishing piece of news for you.'

'Don't tell me *you're* going to get married too,' was his immediate reaction.

'Not that. But Father – hold tight,' and choosing my words very carefully so as not to give him any false hopes, I said, with an accent on the right word, 'a *female* friend of ours has arrived in Paris from Russia. An old friend of our house.'

He knew immediately.

'Olga Arensky. It can't be!'

'It is. She arrived a few moments ago and she's having a cup of tea with her eight-year-old daughter.'

'Daughter!'

'Yes. She's married, but she told me that her husband was dead.'

This time I thought I heard a sigh of relief on the phone, but perhaps I was mistaken. Father was becoming a little set in his ways nowadays, and he might not have relished having a male stranger foisted on him in place of Igor who would now, presumably, be moving to a house chosen by Brig. Aunt Olga, I was thinking, would take the place of Igor, and it would be no problem absorbing Tasha into the household.

It was then that Father made a quick decision.

'I've got an hour before the *train bleu* leaves. I'll catch it – the concierge'll get me a ticket – yes, tonight – and I'll see you all tomorrow morning.'

Never had there been such a reunion! Nor so many tears – of happiness or sorrow, it was hard to tell. Father kept on hugging Aunt Olga, then holding her away as though to examine a new possession. Then he called to Lilla, 'Champagne!'

'So early in the morning?' asked Olga.

'Absolutely', and out came a bottle of the Laurent-Perrier.

'Let Tasha have a sip to celebrate,' suggested Aunt Olga.

'Bit young, eh?'

'I'll bet you started before you were eight, you old reprobate!'

'I'll give Tasha a sip of mine.' I beckoned to her and she came and sipped gently. 'I like it, but the bubbles go up my nose,' she laughed.

'Beautiful little child,' I heard Father say to Olga. 'Wonderful gold, her hair.' He sighed and muttered, 'Reminds me of the hair of –'

'Don't, Dmitri. Don't torture yourself, thinking of the past. Nicki told me last night what happened when you left for the boat. She's – well, it's eight years ago, now, and we're making our way in a new, live world.'

'Of course, I'm an old fool. It was just catching a glimpse of her hair, with the light shining through it – just the same.' He sighed again and then as Tasha cried, 'Mama, I'm hungry!' Father laughed and cried, 'They always are!' and suggested, 'Take Tasha to the kitchen, Nicki. Lilla can give her something to eat and drink. Then you come back and Aunt Olga can tell us something of what has happened to her.'

Perhaps it was drinking champagne so early in the morning, but when I returned, I tried to recall those few terrible moments when we last saw Russia, but of course they were all mixed up, mingling reality with imagination, truth with the terrible stories I had so often heard and read about, the nightmares which had haunted my sleep for so many years; twisted faces shrieking out in my sleep as knives sank deep and blood spurted. Everything was mixed up in those dreams – jackboots and whips, rearing horses and the stench of ordure, the vats of stinking tallow. Sometimes, for the first few years of our new life, I would wake, stifled, screaming; but it had all gone by now, the weeping of the past overtaken by the laughter of the present.

Those thoughts and memories returned briefly now – though this time I was awake – at the hint of anguish in Olga's big dark eyes, the tiny lines that had become etched at the corners of her mouth, changing her once laughing smile to one that was touched with caution, as though she was no longer sure of life. I shuddered – visibly, I suppose, because Olga looked at me and asked, 'Nicki – you're cold?'

'Not really. Footsteps on my grave. I just shivered, remembering –'

'Remembering! Ah! That is something we all do from time to time.' She looked directly at Father, almost attaching a significance to the glance that at the time meant nothing to me, though I was puzzled at its apparent reproach, as though something that lay in the past was best forgotten.

Father stood dominantly beneath our daguerreotype of the Tsar, his hands behind him, rocking slightly on his heels. 'Account for yourself, Olga,' he said with a note of joviality that I sensed as false, as if Olga's look of hostility had aroused in him a feeling of guilt he wanted to allay. 'Tell us the whole story. For a start, you've certainly lost a terrible lot of weight.'

'I lost twenty kilos at one time, but I've managed to put a bit back.' She hesitated as though preparing a long set-piece which would take time, as though she wanted to set the facts in proper order.

'Well,' she said at last, as though forcing herself to speak. 'I escaped for one reason. Just after the Princess had been dragged from the cart and lay on the ground dying, a carriage near to us overturned and a woman was killed. I tried to help but at that moment a man grabbed me, shouting something like "You're for me!" and – I was fairly slim in those days – held me by the waist and carried me off to one of the warehouses, leering "This won't take long, dearie" or something like that. Fortunately, another man had the same idea, and as I was dragged into the warehouse I shouted to Rudi, but he had vanished. I never saw him again.'

She stopped for a moment, thinking. Father poured her another glass of champagne and she sipped it gratefully.

'This other Bolshevik had evidently got designs on me too, and my captor was forced to let me go while they fought over the delicate matter of which of them should rape me first. There was no light except the little that crept in from the moonlit street, and I edged away from the fiercely battling men in terror behind what I took to be some packing cases. One of them, though, was the raised trap-door leading to a cellar below – as I found to my cost when I fell through it. Mercifully I had enough wits about me – the wits that come with desperation, no doubt – to grab at the edge of the opening as I fell and found that my feet tangled with the iron rungs of a ladder that led down to the cellar. I was so shaken that I felt that every bone in my body had been put on the rack, but I managed to pull the trap-door down, knowing that my violation was only being postponed but seizing with gratitude on the respite that had been granted me to hide.'

I held my breath. Aunt Olga had always been a good raconteur, entertaining us children amusingly in the nursery whenever we got bored with games; and I suppose I had enough of fairy-tale romance left in me (though at twenty I would never have admitted it) to think of some knight in shining armour rescuing the captive princess.

It seemed, though, that a more gruesome explanation afforded her her chance of escape. The two men had gone on fighting until evidently one of them had received a blow so hard that he fell back and struck his head on the ironbound corner of one of the chests stored in the warehouse. The force of the blow penetrated his temple and killed him; and his assailant, horrified, ran from the place to escape the consequences of the revenge of the dead man's comrades.

'So,' said Father, 'evil overcame evil and you were left to pursue your way unsullied.'

Olga laughed; and this time her mouth turned up at the corners in her merriment. 'My dear Dmitri, you are too impulsive in your conclusions! It seemed hours before I realised that the claimants for my body had ceased their battle; and ages before I ventured, trembling with fear, up the ladder and raised the trap an inch or two. I nearly screamed when I felt globules of coagulating blood fall on me over the edge of the trap. The dead man lay but a few inches away, and as I saw the ghastly wound that had opened half his head I really did scream. But when my heart stilled its frantic beating I realised that the activity in that part of the town had died down. Evidently the revolutionaries had moved on. When I at last emerged the streets were relatively quiet, and in my torn and stained clothing I aroused very little interest . . .'

'And what then?' I said eagerly.

'Patience, young man,' she said with mock severity as I sat listening to the unfolding drama.

'There was no sign of anyone?'

She shook her head. 'I felt like a mad woman, I went roving round. No sign anywhere. Suddenly I realised that while I had been hiding, perhaps you and Igor had come and rescued the others.'

Aunt Olga turned to Father, 'You remember you told me, if we got separated, to run through the passage. Maybe you had all reached the vessel and everyone was safe on board. I ran down the narrow alley and reached the quay-side and there I saw a sight I shall never forget, so terrible it will haunt me until I die. The boat was sailing out. I screamed. I yelled. I waved. But the noise of the engines, the screaming and whirling of the gulls, made it impossible. I could see your boat, you could not see me. I just fell to the floor in a faint.'

What happened later was quickly told. When Aunt Olga came away from the quay, feeling utterly desolate and alone, she retraced our path past the two hotels in the place, the Buffet and the Commercial. She had no money, but she walked to the Buffet to apply for a job washing dishes, sweeping floors – anything for a bed and a square meal. She found a hag at the desk who was half drunk but she gave Olga shelter and a meal of beans. And to cut a long story short, 'Then I realised that she wasn't just the concierge,' said Olga, 'as I'd thought, but the proprietress – "Madam" would be more to the point – and she let me stay on as a sort of maid-of-all-work.'

The 'Madam' soon found that Olga had some ability with her needle and could patch and repair sheets and could relieve her at the desk and cope with rough customers, so for a year she became a sort of second-in-command.

'A whole year!' Father smoothed his moustaches. 'And then?'

'And then, my dear Dmitri, I fell on golden feet, as they say. I saved all my roubles, then advertised that I could make and repair uniforms. The Bolsheviks love dressing up; but so many tailors had vanished that I had more or less a clear field. Meeting the commissars meant that I also often met their wives and mistresses; and though those ladies don't like the rich dresses of the parasites (as they call them) they enjoy serges and heavy wool. In Petrograd I found one particular firm that could supply me with good quality materials – and fell head over heels in love with its boss, a widower, and his daughter. I didn't want to complicate the story at the outset, but Tasha is actually my adopted daughter. She was born in 1918, and I adored her from the word go. And the father was so handsome – and then he died, suddenly, of a diseased heart, and I was left alone with a little girl I loved, but with no money. I – well,' she coloured slightly and gave father a wink, 'I found a protector – a good man, someone to look after us,' she lowered her voice and nodded towards Tasha who was reading a picture book.

111

'Ah!' Father nodded disapprovingly. 'I know what you mean only too well –'

'You certainly *should* know,' whispered Aunt Olga angrily, solving in one astonishing whisper a puzzle I had never been able to understand: why did Aunt Olga always live with us? Now I knew. She had been Father's mistress! Of course. That explained everything. The only thing I did not know was whether darling Mama knew. My guess is that she did, that it all happened before I was born, and that Mama accepted the situation gracefully because the two women had been bosom friends before Mama married Father.

As to the rest of the story, it did not take much telling. Olga succeeded in developing a thriving connection among many high-ranking communists and saved up all her profits. And by then she had enough influential friends to arrange for her to travel to Paris.

It did not really surprise me, the way in which we all settled into the large family house. Igor returned for a few days and was greeted effusively by Aunt Olga, while Brig was suitably impressed by meeting yet another title in the 'family'; Galina was still dancing in Monte Carlo, and could not return until the winter season was past.

And a miserable September and October it was, as though the warmth of autumn had been stolen by a cold and lifeless winter. The leaves blew off the trees, turning them into black skeletons and it was cold after Monte Carlo. When the Paris rain pelted down, the tops of the tall buildings in the Rue Jacob vanished in the wet dark.

You should never be sad in autumn, I thought, it is the world's richest season, and at least in one way the presence of Aunt Olga blew the sadness and the cold away and on a Sunday, when it was not raining, she and Tasha and I would walk down the Rue de Seine to watch the river traffic from the banks with their huge elms and plane trees with peeling barks.

There we could see the plodding barges, each one a home for a family in which to live and sleep and die, sometimes half a dozen barges being pulled by one fussy little tug. We had a great game with the tugs, Tasha and I. When one reached a bridge like the Pont Neuf, its funnel had to be folded back mechanically, otherwise it could not get through. Tasha could not grasp the reasoning behind all this, but whenever the tugs and their string of barges approached, she would grip my hand tightly, almost trembling with excitement.

'Uncle, will the funnel fall down?' she asked, and when the funnel *was* folded down, she shrieked with excitement, 'Uncle! We knocked it down!'

I had not been in Monte Carlo since September, of course, but after the winter and as the time for Easter the following year approached – that would be the beginning of April 1928 – it was Father who said:

'Olga hasn't seen Galina since she returned. Yet surely the ballet season will soon be over in Monte. I'll phone her and see if she can get here for Easter. Without that damned husband of hers.'

We were in luck. There was a month's wait between the end of the Monte Carlo season and the start of the Paris rehearsals, and Jean-Pierre was happy to remain in Monte with Diaghilev while Galina came to see us. It suited everyone because Easter was Russia's most exciting annual festival – greater in many ways than Christmas.

Galina seemed to be in good luck too. She told Father that Diaghilev had given her into the charge of his choreographer, George Balanchine, to study *prima ballerina* rôles. 'Quite ecstatic, she was. Well, I suppose she would be. She's getting near the top of the ladder.'

Galina arrived four days later, in the midst of the pre-Easter Great Fast which, as so often happens, was always observed much more by the poor and the peasants than by the rich and powerful.

In our house, during the period leading up to Easter, Wednesdays and Fridays were meatless days and for most of Lent there was, in theory, nothing to eat but vegetables, kasha (or buckwheat as the Americans called it) bread and fruit. All this was supposed to prepare us for the mystery of the Resurrection.

Lilla was devoutly religious and ate nothing except vegetables and a slice or two of bread, though in the final days of fasting she always seemed to be cooking dozens of Easter eggs for us to paint later. The rest of her time was spent praying – and looking disapprovingly at us for smuggling in hams, cold chickens and caviar. As Lilla would not even prepare them, the task fell to Aunt Olga – not very difficult, since all Olga really had to do was put the food on plates.

Sometimes when I was not busy, I used to take Tasha to the Deux Magots for a soda pop and an extra croissant. And there we often met Hemingway busy scribbling away in a corner, but always, it seemed, pleased if he caught our eyes, for then he would close his exercise book almost with a slap or a bang and say, 'Enough for the moment!'

He took Tasha on his knee and said to her, 'If I was younger and you were older, we'd get married.'

'Thank you, sir,' she looked worried. 'But I've promised to get married to Uncle Nicki.'

'Okay. Can't win 'em all. Here's something for you, Nicki. He handed me a book in a bag bearing the inscription *Shakespeare and Company*. The book was called *This Side of Paradise*. I had seen it in Shakespeare's where I was a constant browser, for after my years at the American School I spoke English almost as easily as I did French.

As I took it, he said, 'It's by a friend of mine. Wait a minute. I'll sign it.' Taking a stub of pencil from his pocket, he wrote in the book before giving it to me.

'That's yours, Prince. From me to you.'

Thanking him, but not quite understanding, I read the

flyleaf. He had written *To Prince Nicki, another of the Lost Generation, from E.H.*

'It's most kind of you. I saw Mr Fitzgerald's book in Shakespeare's.'

'He's doing great these days. Fine writer – and American too,' he added aggressively, as if he expected a challenge on Scott Fitzgerald's status.

He must have noticed my puzzled look as I stared at the inscription.

'Read the book and you'll get the message.'

I was more puzzled than ever. 'Get it?'

He laughed jovially. 'Understand what I'm getting at?' He paused, then struck his forehead with the ball of his fist. 'No, maybe you won't. I ain't sure I understand myself right now. But Stein . . . you remember her?'

'Certainly,' I said almost indignantly, as if offended at the challenge to my memory. How could anyone forget that strange woman with her hair cut straight like a mop-head and her insistence on wearing a man's fedora hat?

'Sure. Well, she was telling me about Scottie's book' – he pointed at *This Side of Paradise* – 'and said, "They're all a lost generation, Ernest, the people in that book." What she meant was, the people out of it too, I guess, the post-war people . . . the displaced . . . so you're of them. Get my meaning, Prince?'

'I think so,' I hesitated, not really pleased with his nickname for me. Nor did I quite grasp his tone of significance.

'Sure. Well, you will one day, I guess.'

'Are there any pictures in it?' asked Tasha, the croissant and drink long since gone.

'Gee, sorry, no. But we'll go right now young lady and buy you the latest *Tintin*.'

'I love *Tintin*, though I don't read very much. Will you read to me?'

'We're going home to paint eggs,' I said firmly. We had to paint as many eggs as we could to celebrate Easter, for in Russia – and to a lesser degree in France – the egg was the symbol of new life. 'Say thank you to Mr Hemingway and then we've got to go, or your mother will be cross.'

'Thank you, Mr Hemingway. Can I kiss you?'

'Sure.' The big man squatted on his heels until he was roughly level with her height. 'Tasha, you and your Uncle Nicki will be very lucky if you get married.' Adding cryptically, 'All you have to do is wait a bit and the years will disappear.'

'Thanks for the book,' I laughed. 'And now,' to Tasha, 'your mother and the eggs!'

All eggs had to be painted before Easter with natural dyes, sometimes depicting holy symbols or scenes, the ones painted by Tasha – who loved 'the game' – usually in red, the traditional colour of Easter. Special eggs were painted by friends who had a talent – a number with the insignia of father's regiment, while someone at the Russian Centre even painted one with the badge of my cadet school at Tsarskoe Selo. And Olga herself, now running our home, decorated eggs with beautiful 'lace' patterns.

'All very dull,' she said cheerfully, 'they're based on the stitches and patterns I used to employ when making dresses.'

Though it was true that none of the wealthier Russians – except those who were deeply religious – bothered too much with the fasting, Father was very strict about observing Easter Sunday. I believe this was because for years he had walked up the church steps behind the Tsar and his family, and the habit had, so to speak, stuck.

Around eleven on the Saturday evening, we all trooped to the Russian Church and the priest arrived together with his acolytes.

'Is he God?' whispered Tasha, half lost in the swirling congregation. I grasped her hand firmly as I whispered, 'Nearly!' He certainly looked impressive in his voluminous gold and red robes. Slowly he led the procession of worshippers all the way round the outside of the church,

followed by the Church dignitaries. Most of us grasped
ikons. As the clock struck midnight, there was a great cry
from every throat, '*Christos voskresa!*' the Russian for
'Christ is risen'. The priest led the way into the church,
now ablaze with light, candles everywhere, ikons on every
patch of wall as the priest intoned again, '*Christos voskresa*'
and we responded '*Voistino voskresa!*' – 'He is risen indeed!'

Poor Tasha started to fidget during the long and dreary
sermon that followed the waving of incense burners, and
then in a twinkling, without a second's warning, she fell
fast asleep against me. When the service was over I carried
her home. She never woke, not even as we started ceremoniously to break the fast.

The table truly *did* 'groan' with food every Easter – for a
very good reason. Even in the greatest Russian palaces, the
peasants were always given Sunday and Monday off, and no
servant was even allowed in the kitchen. So all the cold food
had to last until Tuesday. Nothing could be cooked, all the
food and much of the drink (*we* could go to the kitchen for
iced vodka!) was laid out on our large dining-room table.
There were deep bowls of grey caviar, large dishes of
smoked sturgeon with onion rings, a gravy boat of smitane
sauce, a tureen of bortsch, a cold koulibayaka consisting of
sturgeon, kasha, and hard-boiled eggs baked into a long
round pastry that looked like a large French baguette; and
of course the painted eggs, champagne, vodka kept cold in
a block of ice, with tiny silver cups for drinking.

'I eat more than at Christmas,' cried Galina who still
looked as slim as a pole.

'Can I have some more sturgeon?' asked Tasha.

'You shall,' I helped her to some. 'This is one of the
finest Russian dishes in the world.'

'Mummy,' she asked. 'Why didn't we have sturgeon
when we lived in Russia?'

'Ah!' Aunt Olga sighed in reply. There was a world of
sadness in the sound.

'We'll have some more and make up for lost time,' I laughed and stooped to kiss her.

Quite sharply (for her) Aunt Olga, watching me kiss Tasha, snapped, 'Don't mollycoddle the girl, Nicki.'

'Me?' I was astonished.

'I want to kiss Uncle Nicki,' Tasha's mouth turned down at the corners, a sure sign of her proficiency in bringing tears into operation.

'There's too much kissing,' Aunt Olga said, and added crossly, 'and don't stand there pretending to cry.'

All this passed in a flash and was forgotten when Aunt Olga told her, 'Time to go to bed, darling.'

I was slightly baffled, but didn't give the matter much thought. Aunt Olga was not normally cross. Far from it. I put her bad temper down to tiredness, after the rigours of Easter, and she did in fact apologise.

'Sorry, Nicki,' she smiled, after tucking Tasha into bed. 'I'm exhausted and there have been so many revolting people in my life during the last few years that too much kissing makes me feel sick.'

'Having you here is the most important thing,' I smiled back. Yet I remembered.

Poor Tasha! She always seemed to be in trouble. She was never exactly 'naughty' in the accepted sense of the word. More, she was 'wild'. She did no-one any harm – her jokes and misbehaviour were never based on cruelty, though several times she did dodge classes at the Lycée. One day, by sheer bad luck on her part, she was spotted taking coffee with Hemingway in the Deux Magots. Aunt Olga saw her daughter through the window and stormed in furiously.

'Young lady, what the devil are you doing here?' she asked. 'You are supposed to be at school. Come at once.'

Tasha did not panic – I never in my life saw her frightened, her eyes always danced with laughter – and she just said, as though it were a perfectly valid excuse, 'I'm sorry,

Mama, I thought I'd learn more from Mr Hemingway than from the nuns.' She spoke with such an air of innocence that one felt she really believed she was telling the truth.

It is strange, the way in which an unexpected turn of events can change a person's life. All our lives had been switched around, goodness knows, but now, at last, Aunt Olga's seemed to be settled – and despite our shattering loss of Mama and Rudi, she had suffered physically worse than we had ever done, though she had the solace of Tasha. She had come to terms with life bravely.

Yet now her life was on the verge of changing again – and quite by chance. During the year that followed, we saw a fair amount of Igor and Brig, for the simple reason that, though Brig had bought a lovely house in the Rue St Dominique, it was in such a hopeless state that it would take a year or more to repair.

'One day it will be beautiful,' said Brig. 'In the meantime Igor and I get so fed up with our suite at the Ritz that we just love to come here and chat.'

This time she was dressed in a stunning gown, for she and Igor had popped in for a drink before going to a big ball.

'It was made by Chanel,' said Brig, and though I find it hard to explain about clothes, it was in the mode of those days, short, yet long, a subtle combination! The actual dress was pale blue georgette, and barely reached the knees but from the waist hung a string of beautiful long darker blue flounces almost like petals. The effect of the dress was like a flower. And with its glimpses of knees, just suited the age of 'le jazz'.

Then it happened. Father was pouring out champagne, when he turned and tripped, almost fell over. He just managed to grasp a corner of the table to save himself and then there was the most awful ripping sound as I rushed to hold him up.

It was Brig's skirt. She was sitting down. Father had

stepped on a corner and ripped away two 'petals'. Brig gave a scream – more of dismay than anger.

'Oh my God!' she cried. 'The whole bloody dress is ruined.'

Father was so embarrassed that he almost dropped the bottle.

'Accidents like this never happen to me,' he spluttered. 'I can't begin to tell you –'

'We'll have to cancel the dance,' wailed Brig.

'But can't we dash back in the car and change dresses?' asked Igor who had bought a Delahaye by now because it was so safe and easy to park in the place Vendôme at night.

'You men never understand,' she was almost in tears. 'This is Chanel's very latest creation – and absolutely exclusive. It's *meant* to cause a sensation – and it would've done. Now, I'll have to send it to be repaired – and this is the end of the dancing season. No, Father,' she always called him that, 'it wasn't your fault. I shouldn't have spread out those long strips of dark blue. But they looked so pretty like that, and –'

It was Aunt Olga who now surprised us – though we should not have been.

'Don't worry,' she smiled.

'Don't worry!'

'I'll fix it.'

Brig's mouth set in her straight, disapproving line. 'This just happens to be a model dress,' she almost snorted. 'I don't see how –'

'My dear Brig,' said Olga with a kind of wry tolerance, 'I've spent years making dresses for the Bolsheviks. Why not let me try to move one rung up the social ladder? And I do have a needle and thread.'

'She stitched away for hours making me a practice dress,' said Galina, who was not performing that night. 'I'm sure she could.'

'But even if you could –' Brig still did not believe it

120

possible – 'where can we find the matching blue cotton at this time of night?'

'Upstairs,' said Aunt Olga, adding with a firm finality, 'I have every coloured cotton you can buy in my sewing box.'

'You have?' Hope began to bring back the colour to Brig's cheeks.

'Let's try.' Olga cast a professional eye over the dress. 'These two petals might be an eighth of an inch shorter than the others, because we'll have to make the tiniest seam, but nobody'll notice.'

Nobody did notice. I was not in Olga's bedroom so I never saw what she did, but when Brig came down and twirled round, it was as though the accident had never happened, and in fact two newspapers the next day carried photos of Brig at the ball, one of them with the caption, 'The most feminine dress of the year'.

It heralded the beginning of a success story that would last for years, though it started in a small way. Brig was so impressed that she begged Olga to help her with dresses that needed alterations if she put on weight, or then take them in when she had gone on one of the new diets that were all the craze. She introduced Olga to friends. They begged for help too.

All this went on until one day about a year later Olga asked Brig, 'I'd like to design and make a dress for you. An evening gown. Short, elegant, and if you didn't like it it would cost you nothing except the material. I could probably sell it to someone else. Would you like to take a chance?'

Brig was doubtful. It was one thing to have a tame seamstress. It was something else again to design an evening gown.

'I have designed them for the mistresses of the Communists!' There was an edge of scorn in Olga's voice.

'Ghastly! What did they know about dresses?'

'They knew what they wanted, and I made what they

121

asked me to. I know what you want – yes, I do Brig, even before *you* do, and I promise you, I'll make you look sensational. It's worth a try isn't it?'

'All right,' agreed Brig. 'You've got my measurements. Let's see what we can do.'

While all this was going on, a devastating event took place in the world of the ballet. On 19 August 1929 Diaghilev died in a hotel in Venice – that city of water of which he was so afraid. Father accompanied Galina to the funeral. As he put it, 'A prince of the blood attending the funeral of a prince of art' – and they told me afterwards how Diaghilev's body had been conveyed in a gondola draped in black and gold to the island of San Michele for burial. Even Father, who was well used to grand ceremonies, was impressed.

'Imagine, Nicki! A cortège of gondolas.'

But there was another, less pleasant, side to Diaghilev's death – as Galina told me later.

Apparently Boris Kochno, his secretary and *aide* – for want of a better word – and Serge Lifar, his protégé *balletore*, were at daggers drawn in the feline way of many tapettes. And at his bedside they kept vigil silently and tearfully until he died; but the moment the last breath was out of his body they fell on each other across the bed, clawing and scratching like cats after a *bonne bouche* of fish.

'It was disgusting,' Galina said. 'Even Jean-Pierre thought so.' She shrugged. '*Mais c'est bien ça.* They are all the same.'

I shuddered. And still worried for her, despite her growing success.

7

The most prestigious social event of the Paris season – in fact the first ball of the winter of 1930 – was undoubtedly the Columbus Day Ball at the American Embassy on 13 October. For weeks the gossip columnists had been feeding the public with promises of famous guests who would be present, the bands chosen for the jazz age, the marquees that would be erected on the lawns behind the imposing white embassy at the corner of the avenue Gabriel and the Rue Boissy-d'Anglais near the Hôtel Crillon.

Father had been invited, not only as head of the Russian colony in Paris, but because he was a good friend of the ambassador's, and somehow I too had been invited – which meant acquiring my first full white tie and evening tails – for which Father gallantly paid. But I feel sure he had arranged my invitation with the ambassador.

The main guests, however – as far as we were concerned – were the Countess Trepov and the Countess Arensky, or, to us, Brig and Olga, locked in nearly six months of secretive planning, cutting, needlework, re-shaping – all done in what had once been Mama's bedroom, and now, with its dummies and hangers and bolts of cloth and pins, was more like a junk shop.

Both women were convinced that Olga would produce the 'dress of the year' but no-one was allowed to see it. Galina *did* see some of the early developments but, by the time of the ball, she had started her season in Monte Carlo.

The 1920s had not only been symbolised by the Charleston and the new short dresses and new hair styles for women, but by 'le jazz'. Although named by a Frenchman, it was, of course, the product of the black race, and so it was rumoured that the singer 'Hutch' would entertain.

'I wonder if he'll insist on bringing his girlfriend along with him,' Father wondered.

'And who's she?' asked Olga.

'Edwina Mountbatten,' said Father. 'Married to Lord Louis Mountbatten, Queen Victoria's grandson. Fine way to carry on,' he snorted, 'but they say she's fond of dark-skinned men.' He added with a loud laugh. 'They're particularly well endowed, y'know.'

The invitation cards had said, in embossed script,

'22.00 – Carriages at 4am.'

When the great night arrived, Father, Igor and I made our way by taxi so that if there was a crush we could alight and, as it was a fine night, walk the last few steps. Igor had joined us because of the 'secret' dress which had been transported to the Ritz, where Brig and Igor were still living in luxury. The two ladies would then make their way in Brig's chauffered car to arrive sharply at 10.30, where Igor and Father would be waiting on the steps to escort the ladies to the ballroom entrance.

The front of the embassy blazed with *flambeaux* – the electric bulbs encased in globes shaped like torches. These had been attached to the tops of all the gilded railings, while floodlights spotlighted the Stars and Stripes and the Tricolour, intertwined above the portico. Marines, the traditional guard of every American embassy, stood stiffly to attention as the guests – including ourselves – poured in.

Everyone had been warned to be in the embassy before the principal guest of the evening arrived at 11pm. This was Raymond Poincaré, and so I hardly had a chance to see Brig's dress when she and Olga arrived late, only five minutes before the French premier, who was precisely on time, his motorcade of Panhard limousines escorted by American police on their huge 'Indian' motorcycles. Gendarmes in capes flicked their batons irritably at pedestrians who edged too near the motorcade.

Preceded by a long drum roll, the band played The Marseillaise and The Star-spangled Banner, and the ambassador and his wife stepped forward to greet Poincaré. Tremendous clapping broke out. Poincaré, having recently rescued the franc from its plunging fall into disastrous devaluation, was a popular figure in France, and by squeezing the Germans to the limit of reparations had scored in the United States too.

'It's like another *entente cordiale*,' whispered Olga, 'but all this business of Liberty, Equality and Fraternity amuses me. The French ladies in their jewels look as if they're being presented at the Tsar's court. Equality my eye!'

Very little notice was taken of other ladies' dresses, for every eye was on the staggering new dress and cape of Brig. Everyone seemed to turn in her direction as though magnetised.

It *was* a sensation. Again I find it difficult to describe clothes, but this one was so exquisitely feminine that even I gasped! Somehow Olga had changed the 'line' of Brig's body, slimmed it, so that she could do the Charleston if she wanted to, made it straighter, perhaps because the evening dress barely covered the knees. It was of gold brocade with coral beads and brilliants, low at the neckline, shoulders bared, the dress kept up by a bra of flesh-coloured tulle and with a diamanté circle around the neck.

Even I could see that it was not only beautiful but daring and, to set it off, Olga had designed and made a cape of green and gold shot lamé with a green lining and a huge black fur collar.

Brig made a 'stage entrance', walking slowly the length of the room. The black fur collar was so large that it almost covered the back of Brig's blonde hair, but she had left the cape open, of course, so that we could see the dress as well.

'They'll be ecstatic,' exclaimed Igor, pride in his eyes. 'It's the most wonderful dress I've ever seen.'

*

Shortly after midnight, when the plates had been cleared from the champagne supper, Brig was given a respite from the adulation of her friends. Guests were invited to watch a cabaret in a large room always known as the 'concert hall' where from time to time up-and-coming American musicians gave performances to encourage American culture. This time, though, it was different. All the gilt chairs and tables had been placed well apart so there was room for champagne and glasses, and the room was more like the setting for a cabaret. And what a cabaret!

The American embassy officials had surpassed themselves to entertain distinguished guests. Names that appeared in lights at the Folies Bergère, the Hot Club de France, the Moulin Rouge, stepped upon the dais with delight at the distinction of their audience. 'Hutch' *was* there, singing. So was Josephine Báker, the black girl from the slums of St Louis who had become famous for her outrageous dances; Mistinguette, whose legs were insured for a million francs, was there; so was Maurice Chevalier, his charm already legendary.

Alas, I did not see all of the cabaret because poor Igor was taken ill with a sudden attack of dizziness, almost causing him to faint. Nobody noticed, apart from those at our own table near an exit door. He looked glazed and drawn and we had to get him out.

Brig helped me to help him.

'Damn!' She was furious. 'Chevalier is just about to go on.'

'Well, he *is* ill,' I retorted.

'He's always getting these dizzy spells,' she said, stamping her foot with impatience. 'And he won't go to a doctor.'

'He's got to go home,' I said. He hardly recognised us. And then I added, because I had always been so close to Igor, 'You go back to the show, Brig – if I borrow your car I'll tuck Igor into bed, get a doctor, and be back in half an hour.'

126

'You will? You're an angel.'

'You thought so once,' I said with a snide smile.

'That remark is in very poor taste,' her mouth turned into that hard straight line I had occasionally noticed. 'But I'll forgive you, as you're helping me. Thank you for that.' She swept back into the concert room, looking like a million dollars.

Igor presented no problem. The dizzy spell had almost passed by the time I got him into bed.

'We'll lunch one day,' his speech was faintly slurred, but not by drink, that I could tell. I made sure that he was asleep, tried my best to take his pulse, called the Ritz resident doctor, then went back to the embassy. The cabaret had ended by that time and the dancing had started in the main ballroom.

'That was kind of you,' Brig thanked me. 'As a reward you can have the next dance with me. Do you like the quick fox?'

I did and we danced, and I could sense the envy of all the other women at the sight of Brig's dress. It gave *me* quite a curious sensation.

'Let's hope Igor's all right,' I clapped for another dance from the Hot Club de France. 'You said he has had them before?'

'Several times. Never serious, just dizziness. And no after-effects . . . I'm going to take him away for the winter.'

It was about now, towards the end of the evening, that a most extraordinary event occurred.

Among the guests was one American who had been introduced to Brig – as the Countess Trepov – and when he begged her to tell him the name of the 'house' which had made her dress, Brig with a smile said, 'She's here. I'll try and bring her along for you.'

She managed to find Olga, who was sipping champagne with Father and me. She explained that a certain Mr Gordon Selfridge wanted to meet her.

'He owns a store in Oxford Street, London,' she added. 'Maybe he wants to sell some copies of your clothes. Don't do anything rash, Olga.'

'Selfridge,' chortled Father. 'I know him. He's a great gambler –'

'He told me he's just come from Biarritz for the ball,' said Brig. 'He's American.'

'Did he bring two girls?'

'I saw two pretty girls, yes.'

'His joint mistresses,' said Father, while I muttered enviously, 'Two!'

Father told the story of how Selfridge had fallen in love with a couple of dancing girls called the Dolly Sisters, and somehow managed to keep the two girls happy in bed, often together, and still find time to gamble and run his big emporium, supposedly the largest in Britain, which sold virtually everything.

When Brig introduced Olga to Mr Selfridge he said very politely, 'I'm sure delighted to meet you, Countess. May I present the Dolly Sisters, friends of mine?' and thus they met the famous twins who were, in fact, Hungarians with the difficult names of Janzieska and Roszieska Deutsch and had been discovered by the famous Ziegfeld.

'Would you excuse the countess and myself for a couple of minutes?' Selfridge asked Brig and the Dolly Sisters.

'I've got an idea that might amuse you, Countess. Let's take a glass of something.'

He escorted Olga to one of the several bars erected on trestle tables for the ball, and offered her champagne.

'Your clothes are supposed to be wonderful,' he began. 'The dress I've seen is staggering and the Dolly Sisters want one each. Could you do it?'

Almost reluctantly, Olga shook her head. 'It's not only the time it takes, but I did promise the Countess Trepov that there would never be a copy of this one made.'

'Appreciate that,' said Gordon Selfridge, thinking – Olga remembered how she could almost *see* him thinking.

128

'Tell you what, though,' he suggested. 'Why don't you set up in business – a salon, or whatever they call 'em in this part of the world?'

'Lack of money.'

'No difficulty. I'll stake you. I'll advance the money so you can engage staff – all you need. I've been investing in property, and I can let you have a nice little shop – sorry, salon – in the avenue Montaigne just off the Champs Elysées. I'll let you have it rent free for as long as it takes you to get the place ready for business. After that you pay. Then you can start up in business and all the profit's yours. On one condition.'

Olga could hardly believe her ears as this white-haired man so casually made a suggestion beyond her wildest dreams. Was he a practical joker? Was he a fraud? He *seemed* all right, but men did not go around offering shops to strangers just because of one dress. There must be a catch somewhere. And, she thought, since he already seemed besotted with a pair of twins and shared their bed, it couldn't be sex! Somewhat nervously, she asked what the one condition was.

'You design the dresses and make them with your assistants. Then you'll send over the *toile*, the calico-type base of the finished gown, so that our store in London will make copies. You'll be exclusive in Paris. We'll have what the French call –' he was searching for the right word, his French wasn't that good.

'*Prêt-à-porter*?'

'That's the one. This way you'll be exclusive here, and we'll have a stunning line of fine clothes for England. That'd work, wouldn't it?'

'I don't see why not.' But she still didn't believe it.

'We won't go for this kind of stuff,' he indicated the highly expensive dress of Brig's. 'But I know all about you. I'm sure you can make enough exciting simple day clothes and simple evening dresses to please our customers. Is it a deal?'

'It is – how do you call it? – a deal, Mr Gordon Selfridge. When do we start?'

'Tomorrow morning? I'm staying at the Lotti in the Rue Castiglione. Meet you there at 11 am. We'll go round, case the joint, then set you up.'

The next day they drove round. The salon exceeded all she could have hoped for.

'The possibilities are fabulous,' she said breathlessly. 'We could put our mannequin area there you see. Then –'

'Yes, yes,' said Selfridge. 'I'm a busy man. I leave all that to you.'

'What shall I call it,' Olga wondered.

'What do I call my store?' retorted Selfridge. 'Not Selfridge and Co, not The Selfridge Emporium. No, just Selfridge. And you do the same. Already you have worked for dozens of clients recommended by Countess Trepov. Just call yourself "Olga".'

8

Brig did take Igor on an extended holiday and I did not see them again until early in 1932. It was partly because of Igor's illness, of course; but also, I think, because Brig could no longer stand living in the Ritz, and decided that a year or so of travelling by sea to parts of the world they had never seen before would be good for them both, if for different reasons.

They took ship first to Singapore, then lingered in Bali, before going to Australia. From there, they travelled the seven seas in great comfort, safe in the knowledge that the restorations in the Rue St Dominique, which she had ordered, were in the safe hands of the most expensive interior decorators in France.

The only worry was that Igor did seem to have contracted

an illness which, if not dangerous, was at least worrying. In a letter to me, he wrote, 'It's a damned bore, but I've got something called fibrillation, a mild heart condition which causes my heart to beat irregularly. Bloody bore. I've had to give up tennis and squash *for life* and I'm on pills to thin my blood. At least I can drink, but very little smoking, just the occasional cigar.'

I mentioned the matter when I met a friendly doctor, and he told me not to worry. 'All will be well so long as your friend doesn't overdo it. Thousands of people suffer from it and hardly realise they're ill.'

During the absence of Brig and Igor, I was working harder than ever because more and more Russians were emigrating to France. And there was something else, very different. It took poor Olga years to put her dream salon into order, for she had, in effect, to design an empty shell of a building, to say nothing of designing clothes. As Gordon Selfridge had said, 'It'll take quite a few years to put this place in order *and* design a collection.'

He was right, and I was able to give Olga a little moral help by visiting her regularly, often with Tasha who, by 1932, had grown into a lanky, beautiful girl entering her teens, with golden hair hanging over her shoulders, and large grey eyes set far apart.

Originally Olga's boutique had been a town house for wealthy owners with servants who had lived in numerous bedrooms which Olga commandeered. 'A *couturière* needs premises as well organised as her sewing-box,' she explained. 'Indeed, a house divided into boxes is really what I aim at.'

She took me past the general litter made by carpenters, glaziers, painters, plumbers, electricians, and general workmen, up a magnificent staircase which led to the finely proportioned drawing-room (as it once was) on the first floor.

'Here' – she gestured sweepingly – 'I shall display my materials – not as bolts crowded on shelves like books, but

131

draped to display their beauty and colour and texture by a clever young window dresser I know who works in Galeries Lafayette. He is sensitive to the differing effects of clinging and transparent fabrics such as chiffon and georgette, tulle and muslin, and where and how to contrast them with taffeta, gaberdine, moiré, crêpe velvet, and wool. He tells me there is much to be done with a new material called rayon.'

'Olga!' I protested, 'you make me giddy!'

'Of course I do. You men with your love of serge and flannel! We need change and gaiety.'

She was right, of course. And those who led the Bright Young Things of the era – the designers and painters and entertainers – reached out for those extravagances that came to be associated with 'le jazz' age. Gleaming chromium, and tiers of fan-shaped lights, and strangely veneered woods in cubist designs, were all incorporated in cinemas and shops. Erté, the son of a Russian admiral, de Tirtoff, influenced Paris from New York, where he had been attracted by fabulous sums of money. The curious combination of clean lines and sensuousness that typified his clothes and theatre designs also typified this Art Deco period.

Olga, however, though certain that change and gaiety might be needed, refused to have any Art Deco in *her* salon.

'That's for others,' she said, with a touch of hauteur. 'I want traditional dignity, with some sense of the palatial magnificence that vanished with the Revolution.'

A short flight of marble steps outside, with wrought-iron balustrades, led up to the entrance, which was flanked by plate-glass windows framed in the same pale pink marble, each with the name OLGA in discreet gold-leafed lettering surmounting it; and, at the extreme ends of the fascia the family crest, also in gold leaf. 'In due course,' she said with a certain wistfulness, 'I hope that the patronage of royalty may be indicated by coats-of-arms. But that is for the future.'

For the moment the progress was in purely practical directions. The spacious drawing-room floor had been panelled in a neutral colour of pale oak and a corner of it had been set aside for a tiny boutique in which she intended to display what she called 'frivolities' – the knee-length strings of beads and long cigarette holders that were the rage, jewellery influenced by Indian and Egyptian designs, and pochette handbags ornamented with antelopes and gazelles, inspired by the décor of Poulenc's ballet *Les Biches* which Diaghilev had staged.

'One must have echoes of the present, Nicki. The past is done with.' She paused. 'Of course I mean the *evil* past.'

That was evident in the glittering chandeliers that hung from the ornate ceilings in both the 'upper floor' (as she called it) where the materials were to be displayed, and the 'grand salon' on the ground floor, where she intended her clientele to sit on gilded chairs while the mannequins came slowly down the dramatic staircase wearing her latest creations.

'But,' I gave a puzzled frown, 'I thought you were going to design dresses exclusively for those who can afford to be unique.'

'Certainly, Nicki. And those ladies will be entertained privately with champagne and a view of my portfolio of sketches while we discuss the materials to suit their personalities. But I have to think of multiple buyers – those to be sold by Mr Selfridge and the dress shops here in Paris which now attend collections shown by such as Worth and Chanel. They are the people who will copy from the *toile* when the gowns no longer have to be exclusive. And whatever Monsieur Worth and Captain Molyneux and Madame Chanel do, I must do better.'

Looking back, I realise that Olga had begun to take an active part in the dress-making business at just the right time. The late 1920s and early 1930s were *alive* with changes, typified by the almost wild abandonment of any-

thing that linked the 'Lost Generation' to the war years.
Freedom and ease were now watchwords – in clothes and
morals as in everything else. Young men students appeared
along the boulevards wearing bright red jumpers, sandals,
and slicked-backed brilliantined hair. Their girl friends
sported knee-high Russian boots (whatever the weather)
copied from those in the Russian ballet. The beret, once
worn mainly by Basque peasants, was adopted by some
middle-aged Parisians and often replaced the formal silk
hat. The artists who sat on their little stools sketching in
the place Vendôme or along the banks of the Seine had
always been a law unto themselves in manners and dress;
but now their floppy bows and trousers of a new canvassy
material made in Nîmes in the south of France, *Serge de
Nîmes* (quickly abbreviated to 'denim') could be seen worn
by quite respectable clerks on their way to offices near
the Bourse. Father was quite outraged, however, by the
'flat-chested look', as he called it, which had been adopted
by girls to go with their boyish bobbed and Eton-cropped
hairstyles. 'Apeing,' he called it and challenged Olga to
tell him what it all meant – 'this determination to crush
the figures the Almighty gave them.'

Olga shrugged. 'Always there have been changes, my
dear Dmitri. This transformation from solemnity to gaiety
is quicker than you care to accept, that's all.'

'I like to see a woman's shape,' Father protested.

'I am aware of that, Dmitri,' Olga retorted.

Soon she was supervising the fitting-out of what she called
'the working heart' of the business. The bedrooms near
the top floor were furnished with long wooden benches
with linoleum tops that would give a perfectly smooth
surface that could not damage the delicate fabrics. Each
room was designated for a different purpose. In the
pattern-making room lengths of stiffened paper were outlined in chalk with the many different component parts
that made up the bodice, the skirt, the ankle-length train

if it were for an evening dress. In the cutting-room the materials were laid out on the benches and the patterns superimposed for heavy, razor-sharp shears to follow the pattern with a precision that must make allowance for hems, turns and darts – and woe betide any cutter who defaulted on measurements by so much as half a millimetre. In the embroidery-room powerful green-shaded electric lamps lit the scarcely visible stitches that made pin-tucks lie flat yet at the same time made their narrow presence visible, and where beads and sequins could be knotted to the thinnest of voiles to give a shimmering effect like mother-of-pearl. Next door was a big room for adjustments and alterations – both inevitable when the fitting came.

'Our bodies are not geometrically perfect,' Olga said, 'as I have discovered to my cost. One shoulder is a little higher than the other, one arm a fraction longer than the other, the curve of one hip a little more pronounced. I see this when I measure the client, but all the same, the finished dress will need to have a dart unpicked and resewn, a collarette given its proper balance.'

The pressing-room was vitally important. Here, a dozen gas rings ensured constant heating for varying sizes of flat iron, each with goose-neck handles. The temperature of the irons had to be judged finely and their heat applied through squares of dampened linen to avoid scorching the fabric or imparting a shine. And from there the completed dresses would go to the packing room to be folded in swathes of tissue paper, packed in flat boxes, and given into the care of trusted midinettes to deliver to the client.

'Today,' she said one morning, 'is a great moment for me. I am starting to choose my staff.'

We were at home having breakfast, and Father, who always rose later than we did, came in angrily in his dressing-gown. We had run out of half-bottles of his Laurent-Perrier.

'We haven't got any, sir,' cried Lilla.

'Well, get some whole bottles,' shouted Father, angry at not being awakened in the proper manner with champagne. 'Haven't we got *any* champagne in the house?'

'Yes, Prince.' She scuttled away to find a cold bottle of whatever marque was available.

'All right,' growled Father when it arrived. 'I'll drink this until the new supplies arrive. I'll drink half.'

'Will the rest keep for tomorrow morning?' I asked timidly.

'Don't be so silly,' cried Father. 'You think I'm going to go through life drinking half-bottles of flat champagne? Throw the second half away right after breakfast, or drink it yourself. Understand?'

When he heard Olga talk about picking her staff, he growled.

'Choose well, especially in the upper echelons. Remember, there are no bad soldiers, only bad officers.'

Aunt Olga called back, 'My dear Dmitri, it is skills I seek, not heroism under cannon fire.'

'Can I come, Mama?' Tasha wanted to know.

'You'd be bored.' It was Olga's way of saying No. 'It's a long job, examining seamstresses' stitches and deciding whether they have the flair and the patience for the finest work.' Seeing Tasha's look of disappointment she said, 'But I tell you what – if Uncle Nicki can spare the time, he can bring you along at midday and you can have a croissant and a glass of lemonade.'

Poor Tasha! She was adorable – although Father used to call her one of the 'fauves', the name for the wild post-Impressionist painters. And soon she was in trouble again – well, hardly trouble, but I found Aunt Olga in tears.

'Tasha?' I asked.

She nodded angrily. 'I've locked her in her room. Do you know what she's done? She saw an advertisement for apprentice hairdressers who offer to pay you to act as a model while they practise waving, setting and perms and so on.'

'And what happened?'

'They bobbed her hair. Her beautiful golden hair!'

'Oh no! She can't have done,' I cried.

'This time I'm going to punish her,' said Aunt Olga. As I started to make my way to her room, Olga almost shouted at me, 'Now don't you interfere by molly-coddling her. She always runs to you for help in trouble.'

'No, I won't.' What a savage remark! After the initial shock, I thought, Well, her hair will grow again in a year. But it was yet another instance of Tasha's ability at experimenting for fun – even on life itself.

Once, long before, I had heard a shriek and the sound of Aunt Olga giving Tasha a slap. She had just caught Tasha in Aunt Olga's old bedroom, holding a magnifying mirror in her left hand and beginning to pluck out all her eyebrows with her mother's tweezers.

'*You* do it!' Tasha cried to Aunt Olga. 'I want to be different – the only girl in the world with no eyebrows at all.'

There was never any *malice* in Tasha's antics, and it was hard to be angry with her. I never could be, and Tasha had long since realised this, even before I realised why. She just had an insatiable appetite for trying to live her own way with a total disregard for the normal rules of life.

As Olga had suggested, Tasha and I slipped in to the salon at noon and found all the signs of approaching completion. The grand salon had been fitted with pier-glasses endlessly reflecting each other from opposite walls; and all assembled, waiting to be interviewed, were some twenty or more women whose ages stretched from the teens to the fifties. The younger ones were accompanied by their mothers or guardians, who hoped by paying a premium to set them up as apprentices to the new house of *haute couture*. Their job, whatever talents they had displayed at their school sewing-classes, would be merely to make themselves useful by tidying up the bits of material littering the floor, watching the seamstresses at work and anticipating their needs by picking out the proper sized needles, selecting from the numerous spindles of cottons and silks of every colour, threading the needles, and seeing that they were always to hand in the velvet pincushions that stood on the lino surface of the work tables.

The 'improvers', who also were very young, but could be expected to have proved their skills to some extent, were one step up from the apprentices and would be allowed to do some of the tacking and perhaps, under supervision, to feather-stitch a short hem or sew on a button or hook-and-eye. Top of the hierarchy were of course the seamstresses, whose skills were subdivided into those who specialised in buttonholes, tucks, embroidery, sleeves, collars, and in the early stages of a dress's creation, would assemble its component parts on the jointed lay figures and wicker and sateen-covered tailor's dummies.

Tasha was wide-eyed as I led her up the great staircase, where delivery men from the warehouses were bringing in bolts of material carefully wrapped in stout canvas to protect them, each bearing on its surface a swatch of the material to be found within. Olga was in what she called her *salle privée* ('Where the sordid business of ledgers and accounts is attended to'), interviewing each candidate for a job, so I was able to show Tasha the top floor, where there was a strong smell of fresh paint and wood shavings were still littering the floor.

'It doesn't look like a place to make pretty dresses in,' Tasha pushed fastidiously at the shavings with the toe of her shoe. 'It's – *untidy*.'

'It won't be,' I assured her, 'when the time comes. Or rather,' I added, 'it won't be *this* sort of untidiness.'

We were suddenly joined by an unexpected friend after a voice had yelled, 'Anyone at home?'

It was Igor.

'My God! It's over a year since we saw you!'

'I know. The wanderer returned!' he hugged me.

'And fatter too. How's your health?'

'Okay thanks, so long as I don't exert myself too much.'

'How long have you been back?'

'A month. Sorry I haven't seen you. But it's been hell getting installed. It's all been *done* at last – the house is fine. But you know what Brig is –' he shrugged his shoulders. 'She's a glutton for perfection. When do you open, Olga?'

'After Easter. I'll send you a card.'

'You'd better. It was your dress that started all this excitement, and it was Brig who introduced you to a backer.'

'That man Selfridge!' Olga held her hands in the attitude of prayer. 'Bless him – and the Dolly Sisters – and all the others!'

I walked round to see Igor the following afternoon, and after that, I went fairly regularly for dinner at their house.

'An extra man with a black tie is always welcome when a girl drops out at the last moment,' said Igor honestly.

'I know my place,' I grinned, for of course I did not mind. As I said, 'So long as the caviar's good, I'll help you to eat it in surroundings like this!'

For the house, now finished, really was magnificent. It was the only word for it.

Conscious of the fact that she was no run-of-the-mill phoney *French* countess – an illegal title anyway – but a real, genuine *Russian* noblewoman (if only by marriage) Brig had filled her house with treasures of Russia. She (or her interior decorator) had scoured Paris, searching out Russian relics which the less fortunate refugees, struggling to make both ends meet in a strange city, had been forced to sell. She, in effect, even 'bought' many actual Russians; well, not quite, though she did employ a virtually all-Russian staff of waiters, butlers, chauffeurs, and ladies' maids. It was quite amusing sometimes, when Igor presided at our formal dinners there, for me to see Igor wink at Kornilov, who was also a count, reduced to doing the butler's job wonderfully well, with Igor on the other side of the plates.

Well, not *always*. On the first Easter Monday after their return in 1932, Igor invited me to have a Russian lunch at The Cossacks, the finest Russian restaurant in Paris. On the first occasion, when I had thought we were lunching alone, I was surprised to find a dozen or so other male guests, some of whose faces were vaguely familiar.

'This is my secret get-together,' Igor raised a glass of ice-cold vodka in a toast as we sat around a large table, and whispered to me, 'This is Brig's staff! They're not allowed, by tradition, to work on Easter Monday, but the Russian restaurants – which serve lots of non-Russian clients – are open while the house is virtually closed, so I decided to have a binge here. You recognise Count Kornilov, the butler, of course. Next to him is Brig's chauffeur.'

At The Cossacks there was always a small orchestra of balalaikas, the players in traditional Cossack uniform with crossed bandoliers and tall hats of astrakhan. They played gopak and czardas music, alternately melancholy and exciting, and sang songs of battle and yearning:

'That day the foemen learned aright
The way we Russian soldiers fight –
    Fierce hand to hand,
Horses and men together laid,
And still the thundering cannonade;
Our breasts were trembling, as it made
    Tremble the land.'

Then a fine bass singer stepped forward and sang Tchaikovsky's *None But The Lonely Heart* and a setting of Pushkin's sad love song:

'Dear, I have loved you, and my heart maybe
    Has not quite lost the love that once it had.
Grieve not: I would not that one thought of me
    Or any thought on earth should make you sad . . .'

We expatriates shed our tears and thumped our feet
when the music drew to its frenzied climaxes, and for a
short while were back in our far-off country . . .

It was a wonderful meal which never seemed to end and,
as we drank vodka and champagne, all titles and positions
vanished. At one stage, after some discussion, Kornilov
roared with laughter, 'I've got a better job than you, Igor!
I get three days or nights a week off – and all the perks.'

'My perks aren't *that* bad,' Igor protested.

'Ah! But you have to pay for them – to perform your
duties.'

'So do you! Different sort, but just as hard!' Igor
smirked.

What I found so wonderful over that lunch, as it lasted
well on into the afternoon, was that, as though by magic,
we had all flown away from Paris and were now part of
the mosaic of life in a Russia that we had almost forgotten.
I remembered Vron, as he was nicknamed, the chauffeur,
for he had given me a lift one evening. He had been quite
well off in Russia. But he did not manage to get much
money out, and one by one over the years he had sold his
jewels, everything except his signet ring, and yet with that
wonderful temperament of the Russians, there was not a
hint of discontent in his laughing voice.

'I even sold a beautiful Fabergé egg,' he sighed. 'It was
my pride and joy. You can see it any time you like.'

'How, if you've sold it?'

'In Igor's sitting-room. His wife bought it,' he replied
with another laugh.

Like all the many others, Vron's fortunes had dwindled
miserably, and there was one other man whom I had not
seen since I was a boy. He had worked at Tsarskoe Selo

and was now a gardener in the Rue St Dominique. The men – some titled, others not – were all old friends or acquaintances of Igor's and in many cases, he had been able to recommend them when they were really hard up.

'This will, I hope, be the first of our annual Easter Monday lunches,' he cried in another toast. 'To all of you my blessings. We are all equals in the sight of God.' I remember thinking, 'Maybe, though there, but for the grace of God, go any of us.'

The Cossacks was a long restaurant behind the avenue Gabriel, parallel to the Champs Elysées, and when Igor had signed the bill, and the others were dispersing, he said to me, 'Let's walk up the avenue Matignon to the Travellers and have a beer. All this vodka is fun *during*, but it gives you a hell of a dry mouth *after*.'

It was a sunny day. We strolled past Markos, the art dealer, who was exhibiting a mixed collection of paintings from the unsold left-overs of the Salon d'Hiver in the Musée des Beaux Arts behind the Rond-Point. On the other side, the windows of Jacqueline, the furriers, provided no temptation.

'That's for the girls to buy,' said Igor, and I thought, even after we were sipping cold beers in the Travellers, that suddenly he seemed melancholy.

'Something worrying you?' I asked.

'Not really,' he confessed. 'But if you could do me a small favour –?'

'So long as it's not money.'

'No, it's not that.' He extracted an envelope from his inside jacket pocket. 'It's this. I wondered – could you look after it for me?'

'Of course I will.' I took it from him. 'Dare I ask what's in it?'

He shook his head and laughed, with a quite noticeable sense of real relief that I found puzzling.

'No, I don't mind telling you. I've fallen in love –

hopelessly. I can't see the girl very often because of Brig, so I have these photos of her. We're both in love.'

'But Igor,' I said in a voice almost bordering on desperation. 'You can't *afford* to be in love!'

'I can – as long as I'm not discovered. Nicki, this is the first time in my whole life that I'm really serious. I adore this girl – young woman, if you prefer. She's kind and gentle – everything that Brig isn't, though I shouldn't say that, but you know what I mean. And if Brig ever finds out, she'll kill me.'

'You've had a row perhaps? But a few photos!' I must have looked puzzled.

'I took the photos myself,' he confessed, 'and they're all – well – all nudes.'

'Oh no! You are an ass.' I sighed and because his revelation suddenly conjured up a picture of the beautiful black-haired Hélène without a stitch of clothing on, in Father's lesson, I said, 'Can't you *remember* what she looks like?'

'I suppose I can,' he admitted.

'But haven't you got a desk or something in which you can lock them?'

'It's not that. If I'm carrying them – like now – and something happens to me –'

'Why should it?'

'Quite seriously,' he said, 'something *has* happened. Not really dangerous, but frightening.'

'What do you mean?'

'I went to the cinema not long ago – and suddenly, without warning, I couldn't see properly. I blinked my eyes, but the left half of the film – I couldn't see it. It was as though half of my left eye wouldn't function. I was terrified. I got out of the cinema, I still couldn't see properly through my left eye. I got home, phoned my doctor at the American Hospital, and he said not to worry. He called it an ischaemia. I wanted to rush round to see him, but he told me – and this sounded silly – to take a couple of aspirins. My blood was already thick; aspirin, he said, would thin it down quickly. It did, but obviously I had a small clot in the bloodstream.'

'A blood clot!' I cried. 'That sounds like a minor stroke.'

Igor reassured me that it was not as bad as that. In his words it was 'the fifth cousin to a stroke', and he said it would probably never occur again.

'All the same, I can tell you, it scared the hell out of me. And that's why I'm asking you to keep the photos. Just in case. And if I need them, I'll walk round and pick them up. You're sure you don't mind?'

I shook my head.

'Of course not. But remember – look after yourself. You've got yourself a full-time job.'

I had not been surprised to discover that, except for financial arrangements, Igor and Brig were ill-suited. It always intrigues me how age diminishes differences between people. When I was twelve, Igor at nineteen had been an unapproachable member of 'the older set', bridged only by Galina. Now, over the years, we had grown into contemporaries.

With those passing years his good looks had matured into a kind of sophisticated charm, enhanced by blonde hair which now curled a little at the back of the neck. He was quite dashing – as many girls discovered. He bore his title well and was used to the splendour of the life imposed by his wife who relished the acquired title which he took as his birthright, but which was always a thrill to her.

Just over six feet, he had played excellent tennis and squash at the Passy club on the edge of the city. He had the money to dress well – Brig insisted on that, even though she was paying the bills – and he was a popular member of the Travellers' Club. He always stood his rounds of drinks and everybody liked him.

It sounded like an idyllic life for a young man who had started without a penny; and so it would have continued to be, had not Igor reverted to type and included a large number of pretty girls, most of whom discreetly ended up in bed with him, if only for a couple of hours. Women never could resist Igor! I once asked him to tell me the secret of his 'fatal attraction', and he answered simply, 'I just ask them. Most of them say Yes. Try it sometimes, Nicki. You'll be surprised how many women are so bored with the dull routine of married life that they'll do anything for a night in bed with someone else.' And on another occasion he said, 'Of course you've got to be clean and well mannered. You've got to be respectable – and preferably married, because then if a girl wants a flirt, she knows it won't go too far.' He laughed challengingly.

It all seemed slightly cynical to me – I was always romantically waiting for love and lust to mingle; the second without the first seemed just like taking exercise, but Igor seemed to enjoy the thrill of the chase if the girl was attractive.

'Only don't get caught,' I warned him. 'If Brig ever finds out, she'll flay you alive.'

'She would,' he admitted. We were having a quiet drink. 'I've had one or two narrow squeaks, but thanks to the ikons of mother Russia, I've managed to play safe.'

I was glad for, as one would expect of the daughter of a self-made Chicago meat packer who had become a countess, it was Brig who was the real boss in the ménage, who organised life completely – and very efficiently too. When Igor's attendance was requested at a dinner, lunch, cocktails, or even at one of the great balls that studded Parisian social life, Igor could be relied upon completely. And Brig's social events were regarded as so important that, if you did not receive an invitation to her annual Pré-Catalan ball for four hundred or so guests, 'Well,' as Father said, 'you might as well go and live in Timbuctoo.'

9

The moment of Olga's opening ceremony was growing nearer, but one day in 1935, a few weeks before the actual date, she asked me if I would take her to an address near Clichy, on the outskirts of Paris. She badly needed, it seemed, to woo an expert dressmaker as an assistant, and Father had given permission for me to use his ultra-modern Renault with its unusual front-opening coal-scuttle bonnet. In a way I would rather have gone by bus. I loved the French buses where you could stand on the platform, swinging as the bus turned a sharp corner, and happily puffing an acrid Gauloise. But the car it was to be, and I reached the address without any problem. After I had dropped her, I had to drive back along the boulevard Malesherbes. Halfway along the all-grey façade of uniform flats, I recognised the house where Father had taken me so long ago on my eighteenth birthday. I do not know why I recognised it – perhaps because that girl Hélène had certainly left a memory, and I often wondered what had happened to her.

Almost without thinking I parked the car, then ran up the stairs to the second floor and, heart pounding, palms damp, and pulses quickening – quite out of character for me – I pressed the doorbell.

A girl answered the bell and without any stretch of memory I asked, 'Madame Lefarge please?'

How had I remembered that name after all these years? I believe that after you have lived through a momentous event – and for an eighteen-year-old, mine had certainly been that – all the tiny, incidental items that make up the whole – names, colours and shapes of furniture, carpets, wallpaper, atmosphere – are indelibly imprinted and can be instantly recalled.

Madame Lefarge entered, examined me almost suspiciously, and asked, 'Can I help you, monsieur? I don't think –'

'You don't remember me?' I laughed. 'The son of Prince Dmitri.'

'Oh, dear me! An old woman's fading memory. But you have changed so much, monsieur. How agreeable to see you again. And can I help you?'

I hesitated, almost getting cold feet. Then I plunged in, 'I was wondering if –' I searched for words – 'if the young girl called – Hélène, her name –?'

Incredibly, the almost ingratiating smile vanished as though wiped off a slate, and her mouth hardened into a straight line.

'She no longer comes here,' she said brusquely.

'Oh, I'm sorry.'

'But if monsieur would like –?' The smile of money reappeared.

'No, no,' I said hastily. 'I just wondered.'

'I'm sorry, monsieur,' Back came the frosty tone. 'But she left.'

'I thought – well, she seemed happy and –'

'Elle est une *putain*,' Madame Lefarge's voice was suddenly furious. 'She did the unforgivable thing.'

Now that the prospect of seeing Hélène had gone, so had any sudden feelings of desire. I found Madame Lefarge repulsive and I would have left immediately, only I was intrigued at her sudden outburst of anger.

'I'm so sorry,' I mumbled. 'I must be going.'

'Do you know, Monsieur, she walked out with hardly a word. You are a gentleman, Monsieur, the heir to a Prince, you will scarcely understand this *putain*.'

'I'm still not quite sure?'

'She did say one thing. Why should I give her only half of her earnings? Think of it! The impertinence. I provide all the creature comforts. What about the overheads, the lighting, the heating? Monsieur, she is an evil woman. Now she is on the streets – it serves her right.'

I almost started to laugh. The inside quarrels of a bordello – whatever you called it, that was the basic name for this establishment – could almost be fun. Squabbling over nothing.

'Well, I'm sorry, Madame.' I picked up my hat. 'If you'll excuse me – er – this time.'

'A bientôt, j'espère,' she smirked and took me to the door.

This kind of adventure often seems to run in pairs, and within a month of visiting the *maison de rendezvous* I bumped into Hélène – literally.

I had promised to meet Olga and Tasha in the Jardin du Luxembourg and take them for tea, and I was in danger of being late. Aunt Olga rarely took an afternoon off, and shared with Father a hatred of unpunctuality, so, darting across the square in front of the Odeon Theatre, I saw Olga almost by the Palais itself. I shouted, Tasha spotted me and waved back.

What I did not see was a figure in front of me, and I all but knocked the poor girl down. Luckily I grabbed her, held her from falling, but some books, a parcel and the contents of her handbag splashed all over the pavement. I started to mumble apologies, and bent down to retrieve everything. She also bent down, anger at first in her voice, but then her eyes met mine and she said, almost laughingly, 'I forgive you. I'm sure you didn't do it on purpose.'

I saw a black-haired girl, the hair all over her face so that I could hardly see it, but I knew that hair!

'You're Hélène?'

She looked up, brushed the hair away from her eyes, and asked 'How on earth did you know? Who are you?'

'Nicki Korolev.'

'Of course. I remember you now.' She smiled, then,

148

with a touch of mischief, added, 'I remember the occasion too. How's your homework?'

'Homework?' I was genuinely puzzled.

'The lessons I gave you. I hope they weren't wasted.'

'The lessons were the best part.'

With an easy laugh, but making her meaning quite clear, she said, 'Any time you want a refresher course? But I'm a very expensive professor.'

'Really expensive?' I was tingling but still not thinking very seriously of what we were saying.

'Twenty-five thousand.' The tone was businesslike.

With the franc having been so devalued, that was not, in fact, too bad. But –

'I must go,' I pointed out Aunt Olga who was waving for me to join her and Tasha across the square. 'But I'd love to see you again.'

'So would I.'

'Where?'

'Here,' she indicated the theatre. 'Or better, *there*,' she pointed to the bar and café across the street. 'The Relais St Jacques opposite. I'll be there tomorrow at four.'

'Can you make it five?'

'Fine. What a beautiful little girl,' she added. 'She's not yours is she?'

'Good Lord, no,' I laughed. 'She's my niece, Tasha.'

'Bon. Á demain.'

I ran across the road. Aunt Olga had seen how I had helped to pick up the girl's parcels, but, I thought, it was just as well she had not heard what we talked about.

Sharp at five I sat down in the St Jacques and ordered a glass of red wine. At home we always had champagne and/ or vodka, but not at five in the afternoon. Vin rouge was cheaper and safer. And since I never really enjoyed wine by the glass without food, it lasted longer too. I was not being mean, it was just an instinct that had grown over the years, not to drink strong liquor too early in the day.

Almost at the same moment Hélène arrived, waved, sat down and almost begged me, 'Coffee please – and would you think I'm awful if I asked for a sandwich?' She smiled. 'I'm starving. Haven't eaten all day.'

'Of course.' I ordered a typically French long sandwich, lots of butter on a crisp, freshly baked roll, the ham dripping over the edges. She wolfed it down and I had the sudden uncomfortable thought that perhaps she did not have enough money to buy food, and I also caught myself thinking, What the hell am I doing, here in a café making a date with a tart I'll probably never see again? And I don't even really want to go to bed with her. Especially not at 25000 Fr a time! But if I take up too much of her time, talking in a café, she'll probably charge me something anyway. No, she wouldn't do that, I thought. She was good-looking, a pale face framed by a black halo, and she wore a black dress edged with white, and a white belt, silk stockings and neat shoes.

'So, what's happening in the world?' I thought it might be difficult to make conversation, but not at all, she was quite frank and smiling.

'Could be better,' she admitted. 'But that's my fault. I'm too choosy. I never go with anyone who doesn't attract me – I mean reasonably. I can't stand what the girls call the rough trade. I have a clientele, very select, I like men like –' she smiled again, quite unaffected – 'like you.' Then she laughed again, like a muted peal, and said, 'Don't worry. I'm not trying to seduce you. It's just so nice to see old friends.'

'Me too, and,' slyly, 'you *were* very hungry.'

'Much better now. But never mind me – what about you? Are you married yet? I don't see a ring.'

Shaking my head I said, 'No. Too busy.'

'In love?'

I shook my head again.

'That's bad!' There was something very attractive about her outbursts of unexpected frankness. 'It's men in love

150

who are good for business. It's the married men who are the best for –'

'Don't worry about me,' I ordered a round of drinks and she asked the barman, almost absently, if she could have an egg, and the barman returned with a basket of the hard-boiled eggs that decorate almost every Paris bar.

As she started to peel one, she laughed, 'I just wanted to see if you thought I was greedy.'

'Of course not. Why should you be? If you want a dozen eggs, take them!'

Then a curious thing happened, and to this day I do not know why. I found Hélène fun, pretty, but as for sex – nothing doing. I can only think that I could picture her in someone else's arms, or hear the noise of crinkling notes passing, or perhaps it was just one thing she said, 'Your father, the Prince! What a man!'

For a moment I wanted to ask if she still saw my father, but had second thoughts. Even the thought that she *might* be seeing him – and if not him, who?

Being a woman, she instinctively read my thoughts.

'If you don't feel like bed,' she touched my arm gently, 'Don't worry. One day perhaps, but for the moment –' she shrugged her shoulders, 'you can take me to the cinema one day instead.'

And so we drifted into a friendly, almost happy-go-lucky type of companionship in which she phoned me sometimes at the office, we went occasionally to the theatre, sometimes for a bistro lunch, and one time, when I borrowed Father's Renault again, we drove out for a picnic on a beautiful summer day to the forest of Fontainebleau, and that time we *did* make love, on a grassy bank deep in the forest, and it was exquisite. But that time it was Hélène, a girlfriend, not Hélène a high-class tart. And that made all the difference.

We were relaxed and as intimate conversationally as we were physically. She told me what a harridan Madame

151

Lefarge had turned out to be. Then she laughed delight-fully. 'But I am having a little revenge. Not a cruel one, you understand, but satisfying.'

She went on to say that she had enough money to buy the lease of the house in the boulevard Malesherbes, which was for sale as Madame Lefarge was failing in health. 'So I shall be running my own little house of pleasure – and Madame will be so cross when she finds out it is her old employee who is taking over. Is that not *ironique*?'

I joined in her laughter, and we parted that afternoon with great affection, Hélène giving me the Malesherbes telephone number – 'In case of sudden need,' she added with her own brand of mischief.

And there were other girlfriends too, many of whom I met simply after people insisted on addressing me as 'Prince Nicki'. In a silly sort of way, I never minded. Certainly the higher their 'ranking' in the phoney world of café society, the easier they were. When I met really pretty girls – or rather young women – at big dances, the ending was almost predictable.

The American girls led the field, many behaving with the same abandoned vigour that Brig displayed before she 'settled down'.

Of course Paris itself was the perfect backdrop for excit-ing adventures. Every city has its character, and the charac-ter of Paris was to the Americans one of enchantment, arising from its carefree gaiety seen most clearly in the village atmosphere of Montmartre and St Germain; its sophistication in the luxury shops of the arcaded Rue de Rivoli and the Rue St Honoré; and its mercenary concerns reflected in the narrow faces of the Normans who had established themselves in the Bourse quarter. It was the mingling of these characteristics that to tourists seemed typified in the lingering smell of Gauloises and Gitanes in the Métro; the half-smiles of the *grisettes* hurrying home from work to eat a supper of baguettes and Brie in attic rooms, with their gas rings heating saucepans of bitter coffee; and solemn children being herded unwillingly to Mass in the chestnut-shaded churches to be found in narrow streets where the bus drivers shout curses as they pass within inches of each other.

It was all part of the multi-coloured life of the capital and, once the tourists had absorbed that picture (and it did not take long), it made them feel that they had been given a free passport into a liberated world. They were 'fun girls' anxious for a good time, convinced by legendary stories that the French were the world's greatest lovers. One evening a girl actually told me that her friend who had visited Paris the previous year had told her, 'You *can't* go to Paris without trying a Parisian.'

'Well, I'm willing,' I said cheerfully, and we ended up in bed. Of course, there was a certain element of truth in what these 'foreigners' from America and Britain said – although the French were not particularly *good* lovers in themselves, many *had* done their homework with the Hélènes of this world, and so they did not find it difficult to astound girls whose sole experiences had been with their own countrymen, who had often left them flat and unsatisfied.

Sometimes I brought the girls home for a drink and occasionally, if they were really pleasant, for dinner, as I knew they would be impressed by our Russian house in its charming French square, the best of both worlds.

Father, too, was a 'draw'. If he was present, the girl would be even more impressed, for although he was by now well into his sixties, he was still upright and could ooze charm if the girl was attractive. But as he grew older he was becoming more and more obsessed by what he called 'continuing the line'.

'Time you got married and produced an heir,' he said to me bluntly as we drank champagne before dinner. I had a girl with me that night, a Melanie Duprez from New Orleans, and to my embarrassment, Father turned to her

153

and said, 'Why don't *you* marry my son, young lady? He's a good chap.' Adding with a chuckle, 'Takes after his father. And you'd be a real live Russian princess, m'dear.'

'Father – stop it!' But I had long since resigned myself to his embarrassing outbursts about heirs.

'I won't stop it!' he boomed. 'You see what's happened in Germany? That man Hitler has finally won the peace – he's managed to become Chancellor of Germany. A madman. If we don't put him in his place soon, he'll lead them into another war.'

'Gee, that's kinda real sweet, Prince,' said Melanie who spoke with a lilting sort of Southern accent, and had probably never heard of Hitler. 'I'd just love it, only Mr Duprez might have something to say.'

'Nonsense! I'll take care of your father.'

'Not my *father*,' Melanie said sweetly. 'My *husband*.'

'Husband!' For once Father was nonplussed. 'But I thought that you two –'

'We are, or we do,' she was almost laughing, 'but we Americans have a saying that once you cross the big pond anything you do doesn't count. Rather like the American doughboys in France during the last war. Goodness knows what they were up to, but I sure can guess. Now the husbands are busy making money, but for the girls it's a tit-for-tat season. Otherwise,' with a bow to Father, 'I'd be only too happy to oblige, Prince.' She twirled her glass.

'Thank you, Melanie,' I said, for all this conversation had been conducted in a slight air of banter, though with an undercurrent of seriousness. I am sure Melanie cursed the day she had married, and would have loved to be a princess. In fact, I was thinking, 'There but for the Grace of God – and the state of marriage – goes another Brig.'

Aunt Olga was having dinner with us that evening. She had moved from our house as the work of preparing her building and designing a collection mounted up, so she had converted three of the old bedrooms at the very top of the house in the avenue Montaigne into a tiny flat, very small, very pretty.

'I live over the shop,' she smiled. 'I don't drive and I can't face the bus journey twice a day.'

'But you have a daughter?' asked Melanie.

'Tasha is sixteen now,' Olga nodded, 'and she's living here. She goes to the Lycée round the corner, and I can't look after her at the salon. She's gone with a friend to the cinema this evening.' And then, changing the subject, she asked, 'You know we're opening next week. Would you like to come?'

'Gee, I'd love to.'

'I'll take you,' I offered, 'I'm taking Tasha, and we can all go together.'

Olga had previously shown me her invitation list. 'Everybody who is *anybody*,' she had said proudly. I looked with surprise at some of the names. 'Surely,' I said, 'Chanel's another *couturière*?'

'Of course. So are Captain Molyneux, Monsieur Patou, Monsieur Worth, and Signor Schiaparelli. There are also a couple of young Englishmen, Norman Hartnell and Digby Morton, who are planning to open London houses. You invite your competitors because if you didn't they would simply assume I had nothing worth showing and would gossip accordingly. As it is, they'll come and drink my champagne and eat my caviar and admire my salon and wish me luck with exaggerated politeness and go away thinking that they must keep on their toes – which is the very essence of the *couturière* game.'

'And who,' I asked, puzzled, scanning the list, 'are Mrs Tom Lewis and Mrs Edward Titus? Actresses?'

'Not in the sense you mean. They are ladies who have invented a new word, a new profession: cosmetology. They manufacture, at minute expense – and sell at considerably greater expense – preparations to keep the skin young. They're both rumoured to be contemplating divorce so

155

they can marry Russian princes exiled like us to Paris. Their professional names are Elizabeth Arden and Helena Rubinstein,' she added mischievously. 'I have invited both, knowing that they never accept joint invitations. Indeed they never meet. But I can't leave their names off the list. The wrong sort of gossip can be very damaging.'

She had asked me to help with preparations and circulate among the guests, and I arrived before ten in the morning (the reception was at eleven) to find Boris, a Russian émigré who, like so many, had fallen upon hard times, and whom Olga had engaged as a major domo, guarding the portal in his splendid uniform of dove grey frock coat and cockaded silk hat, the trimmings of pink silk braid to match the marble and an embroidered O in gold thread on his lapels. He bowed with exactly the right degree of formality.

'The countess is within and begs you to help yourself to the champagne you will find in the salon. The *sommeliers* are not yet here.'

If the wine waiters had not arrived, everyone else seemed to be there except for the guests. I could scarcely move amid the rushing about that was going on. *Grisettes* and apprentices were helping to put gilt chairs into groups, *commis* chefs were putting the finishing touches to an elaborate buffet table that clearly had been set out by a master hand. A glazed boar's head was centrally placed and shiny white jars of caviar and *foie gras* were flanking gilt dishes of salmon, Parma ham, pheasant breasts, and quails' eggs. 'I can see you took note of the Embassy ball,' I said to Olga as she swept by me to speak to a group of worried-looking women who stood aloof at the far corner of the salon.

'My outworkers,' she explained.

'Outworkers?'

'As distinct from those who work inside,' she replied, as if to a rather dull child. 'They are the very experienced ones who collect the finest work and take it home to work on it there. They're freelance and in theory will work for anyone for a set fee agreed in advance; but in practice they prefer to attach themselves to one house. That half dozen have come to wish me well – which is tantamount to wishing themselves well, for if I do well, so will they.'

The bustle seemed to settle down and I had a chance to tell Olga how amused I was by the two tanks of tropical fish that flanked the foot of the grand staircase.

'My *décorateuse* Syrie Maugham – she's the wife of the novelist who's become so popular lately – assured me that fish in a tank have a tranquillising effect, they *hypnotise*. When I replied that I wasn't sure I wanted my clientele tranquillised she said – with some wit, I thought – that I probably would when they learned my prices. I matched her by telling her that I was not really interested in clients who worried about prices. Now – I see the *sommeliers* have arrived; I think we are ready.'

One of the earliest to come was the actress Gertrude Lawrence, accompanied by Captain Molyneux, who designed her clothes. Thereafter, I could see through the open door the succession of Citroëns, Renaults, Panhards, Signor Schiaparelli and his *couturière* wife Elsa in his Isotta-Fraschini, and humble taxis and fiacres bearing press reporters and photographers and some of the buyers and senior assistants from the Bon Marché, Galeries Lafayette, Liberty, and other stores and the more exclusive boutiques. Then, in a limousine with coachwork resembling wicker, an elegant woman with the fashionable cupid's bow lips and feather-trimmed cloche hat.

'The Marquise de la Falaise de la Coudray,' Boris announced.

'Honoured,' I said, thinking she looked familiar.

She smiled enchantingly. 'You needn't be, honey. You can see me in ciné any time for a few francs. Only there I'm called Gloria Swanson.'

Thus it went on, and well into the afternoon. If Mesdames Arden and Rubinstein were not there in person the scent of their perfumes and cosmetics hung heavily in the air, as if we were enclosed in a bower of flowers.

Handsome young men in faultlessly cut single-breasted suits with double-breasted waistcoats spanned by fine-link watchchains, their feet shod in patent-leather boots, moved languidly about, talking in cultured voices of the seasonal rise and fall in dress sales. The ladies – some of them dowagers with faces masked stiffly beneath cosmetics – toured the premises, their sharp eyes taking in any detail of the displayed designs and completed dresses that they could use to their own advantage, at the same time sycophantically congratulating Olga on her originality.

'I am not deceived, Nicki,' she said to me later. She was telling me how Gordon Selfridge, delighted with his investment, had whizzed in and out again with customary American hustle, warning her that smiles on the faces of tigers did not diminish the danger from their teeth and claws. 'And it's true, Nicki. It's a cut-throat profession.'

Melanie was so enchanted that she almost immediately ordered two dresses.

'They're dee-vine,' she breathed happily. 'I'll be the sensation of New Orleans.'

She was not only delighted with the choice of designed clothes, but fascinated by the famous people with whom she was rubbing shoulders.

Tasha was loving the occasion as much as Melanie, especially when I invited the two of them to lunch at Fouquet's which was within walking distance, just around the corner. We had a table outside on the sidewalk of the Champs Elysées.

'I chose this place,' I explained to Melanie, 'because I feel that I must spend most of the day at the salon. It's a bore, and I hope you'll come back – if you want to, that is. You're coming, aren't you, Tasha?'

She nodded. 'Of course – if you are.'

'She's not only a beautiful girl, but a *good* girl with a sense of duty,' laughed Melanie, 'or perhaps it's just because she likes being with you, Nicki?'

'Do you really think I'm beautiful?' Tasha had over the

years developed an almost unnoticed kind of breathless excitement that gave her a vitality and zest for living that was wonderful. And she *was* beautiful. No doubt about it. On the verge of becoming a woman, she had grown into a tall, lissom girl with legs as long and as shapely as Galina's, steady grey eyes that looked into mine almost with a secret smile in the eyes as much as on the lips. She had high cheekbones, accentuating the best of Russian stock in the past, perhaps from a father who had a faint touch of the east in *his* past. And above all this was the golden curtain of her hair, so much like Mama's that at times the memory hurt. The ill-fated bob had grown again. She wore it long once more over her back, well below the line of her shoulders.

'You like the dress?' she asked Melanie. It was blue and yellow in vertical stripes that made her look even thinner than she was.

'Olga made it for me,' she explained before Melanie had a chance to comment. 'She said she didn't want her daughter to look dowdy before all these people. A little present, she called it.'

'Lucky you.' Melanie crumbled a croissant.

'So perhaps I'd better go back to the salon in case Mama needs me,' she said. 'Will you excuse me?' and as Melanie nodded, she turned to me, 'You will come back, won't you?'

I nodded as she got up.

'I must go, but don't be long,' she laughed to me. 'I'm not used to being alone in large crowds.' She leaned forward to kiss me on the mouth and then after shaking hands with Melanie, dashed back to the salon.

'You're right,' I agreed with Melanie. 'She is a stunning looking girl.' I put down my coffee cup.

'She sure is,' and looking at me without malice said, 'I can see why, as far as you're concerned, I'm just a surrogate.'

'A what?'

159

'A surrogate.'

'I can't even spell the word,' I laughed. 'What's it mean?'

'A substitute.'

I felt myself colouring slightly. 'You girls do talk a lot of nonsense.'

'Nonsense? My dear boy,' Melanie said, 'that girl's madly in love with you – okay, don't shout, maybe it *is* only calf love – but she's crazy about you. Stands out a mile.'

'Puppy love,' I laughed. 'I'm the only man to look after her. Good old Uncle Nicki. She'll grow out of it.'

'I doubt it, but that's not really the point. I'm the surrogate.'

'That word again!'

'Which means that *you* are in love with this under-aged girl.'

'Me! Don't be silly.'

'I'm not silly. You probably don't even realise it yet, but you're mad about her. No, you don't realise it, but all the signs are there, believe you me.'

'Come on, let's go.' I paid the bill and linking my arm through Melanie's, asked her, 'What on earth gave you that idea? And if I *did* love her, how on earth could I love her and go to bed with you?'

'Oh, *that*! It's just exercise. I'll tell you Nicki, and I'm not trying to compliment you, but you're the best I've ever had. And I love it – and I'd like it again before I go home. You're so goddam mature.'

I couldn't help laughing.

'One moment I'm mature, the next I'm a baby snatcher.'

'I'll tell you one thing, Nicki,' she confessed, and this time her arm was in mine, 'I adore my husband. He's the greatest. Works like a demon, absolutely terrific. But as for love-making – that's different. He's a morning man, I'm not a morning girl. I do it because I love him and it makes me happy, but that's about all *I* get out of it. Whereas here – I'm hurting no-one, I'll be delighted to see him again, but as for what we're doing – what the hell, you only live once, might as well enjoy it. For me, I'm in love with a good guy, but he just can't provide the creature comforts at the right time. Afternoons, let's say. Guess he's too busy making money for me. Can't have everything in this world.'

'Quite a philosopher.'

'Sure am. Learned the hard way. But as for you and Tasha – that's something else. I'll be back, expecting to see you – no, *hoping* to – unless you're married to your beautiful Tasha by then.'

'Not a hope.'

Of course it was absurd really, she was little more than a schoolgirl, but the serene beauty that I saw developing day after day before my eyes hid a passion laced with laughter and mutual happiness that I could see only too plainly. It was as though we both shared a secret – not for having *done* anything, but of knowing that we both wanted to. I remember thinking once, 'What awful thoughts to have about a girl of sixteen!'

The trouble was that I could not *say* anything. There was nothing in her character against which I could cry 'Stop!' She just looked at me – through me – tall and beautiful, her breasts growing into beautiful, firm shapes, mouth wide and inviting. At sixteen she looked eighteen – and old enough to be married.

And of course my half-formed, half-roused desires were increased by that good old-fashioned word: propinquity. If you live with a desirable girl/woman in the same house, what can you expect but desire? And I was only human! Sometimes propinquity leads to unexpected encounters. One day I heard a sound in the bathroom between our two rooms and quietly opened the door, as though by accident. Tasha was standing up naked in the bathwater which was draining away. She was drying herself, standing legs apart, facing me, pulling the towel with both hands across her back.

She started a shriek, stifled at birth. Then, with a curious

161

little smile, she carried on drying her back, not moving her legs, making no attempt to hide anything, not saying a word as I watched those long, slim legs, taking in every golden detail.

'Sorry,' I muttered as I closed the door, my sexual urge so immense that I ran to the privacy of my bedroom and locked the door.

She never referred to the incident but she had the instinct of true love – she knew that no accident had led me to the bathroom door. I had done it deliberately.

Why? I wasn't a peeping tom! I never went to the Paris *spectacles* where every taste was catered for. I no longer even bothered to meet Hélène for a drink. Yet I had secretly *wanted* to see Tasha – something to remember, an image firmly imprinted that would last until she was a few years older.

That evening, I remember lingering over a last nightcap after Tasha had gone to bed, and thinking, Are you being a bloody fool, Nicki?, and then I said aloud but alone, 'Yes, I'm in love. Dammit! I'm in love with my own niece.'

Well, not quite; but, I thought . . . what a preposterous idea! In love with someone little more than a schoolgirl! And when I returned to the salon after seeing Melanie off to lend Olga a hand, I gave Tasha a long, hard look. Yes, she *was* beautiful. Melanie was right. And Tasha was not just a beautiful doll. I must take care not to encourage her.

But any thought of Tasha and Melanie became submerged and forgotten in sudden, momentous news.

I had returned to the Red Cross at about half-past four, more out of duty than because my presence was needed late in the afternoon. Our office was really a sub-office of the Headquarters in Geneva, and now that the USSR was firmly established, and people were beginning to forget our old war, we existed mainly to deal with the thousands of displaced Russians. Even they were slowly dwindling. We still received letters from Russians hoping to trace friends and relatives, but in many ways our office was only a card index, with offices for me and a couple of young English girls (at the moment). They were called Millie and Daisy, and the girls would change regularly, for they usually consisted of youngsters studying languages in France. Since they had only small allowances from their parents, they looked for jobs like the ones I could offer to supplement their income.

This they could do providing we did not force them to work fixed hours. So I never worried them as long as one was present to deal with the filing, the telephone calls, and act as receptionist.

We had a row of japanned steel filing cabinets, and on the wall opposite the window, overlooking the Seine, we pinned photographs, drawings, cuttings – anything visual to help with identification. On the carpet – beginning to be worn – were three ancient desks. Mine was distinguished by a blotting pad and an old-fashioned Olivetti typewriter with a three-bank keyboard and double shift keys.

I had hardly turned the lock in the front door when Daisy came tumbling to the top of the stairs shouting, her voice trembling with suppressed excitement, 'Come quickly, Nicki! Quickly!'

'What's the trouble?' At first I thought that something terrible must have happened to the other girl. 'What on earth –?'

'There's a picture of your twin brother!' she cried. She knew all about Rudi. 'It's just arrived in the package from Geneva.'

10

For a moment I thought my heart had stopped. Perhaps it had, as it is supposed to stop every time you sneeze. I almost lost my footing, swaying, unable to take in what this English girl was shouting, 'It's him all right, I promise you.'

Bounding up the stairs to our first floor offices, I felt a physical tug of pain in my chest, a sudden shortage of breath. 'It can't be,' was my first thought.

But it was.

'There!' she cried, pointing to the cutting. My hands began to shake. The picture showed two men in tattered working clothes, pausing in their task as they leaned on pickaxes and faced the camera in some surprise. One was a square-faced man with cropped hair. The other was – Rudi. There was no doubt about it. A haggard Rudi, but Rudi nonetheless, an aged vision of myself.

Infuriatingly, the photograph had been cut from a newspaper without leaving any of the surrounding columns, so there was no indication of date, and the reverse showed no more than a section of an advertisement. Still, at least Rudi was alive! But when had the picture been taken? The inquiry did not concern Rudi, but the other man, called Georg Krauss, who was looking for his mother, last heard of in a transit camp 'several years ago' – hardly helpful.

Rudi! I sat down, my legs like jelly, studying the photo again and again. Then, my hands still shaking so that I could hardly control them, I tried to phone our house.

'My father, please!' I asked Lilla, who answered the phone.

'He's out, Prince.' She never could overcome her habitual use of Russian titles. I nearly blurted out to her the news about Rudi, but remembering her hysterical reaction when she first saw Olga again, I decided to leave it till later. I knew how fondly she felt about Rudi.

Next I phoned Olga. No reply. There was no real ring in the phone. She had obviously taken it off the hook until the party was over and the salon closed. How bloody infuriating! The most wonderful news in the world and I had no-one to tell it to!

164

Equally infuriating, of course, was the fact that I could do nothing myself. I asked Daisy, 'Any message with this newspaper clipping?'

She shook her head, then added, 'except this.' She handed me a small card on which were the words 'Georg Krauss pictured with a friend sends his love to his mother wherever she escaped to and says that all is well!'

So poor Rudi was just 'a friend'. I wondered if he even knew whether Krauss had sent the newspaper clipping to the Red Cross in Geneva. Perhaps it was just chance – that the clipping should have been smuggled out, that Rudi should be on it, that I should be put in a position, with assistants to help me, to sort out and recognise the face of my twin brother. But what could I do about it? The answer – for the time being – was nothing.

The picture gave me one clue, however, for as I studied it again, the ill-kempt clothes and the thick coat brought to mind the dreaded word 'Siberia'. But, no. Who on earth would bother to take a photograph in Siberia? No, it was probably just a cold spell in Moscow or on some country farm. The other man looked decent enough, and I could not help wondering if he would ever make contact with his mother – poor devils, both of them, separated by oceans or hostile land masses. At least if the mother learned that her beloved son was safe it would be wonderful news. But Rudi? What of him?

I felt ashamed now of how little I knew about the inner workings of the head office of the Red Cross, but surely they must have agents – friendly ones even – in Russia? Perhaps they could help – though goodness knows how. I studied the picture again. Rudi looked tired, almost re-signed, bored. I wondered why these two men had been photographed and the picture printed. Odd. I felt a sudden dull fear that maybe they had been photographed when arrested, but that could not have been possible, for if they had been jailed, how could they have smuggled the picture out? So at least these two men were free, it seemed – or had been when the undated photo had been taken. And it could not have been all that long ago because Rudi looked very much as I looked myself, even though worn and older.

I had to tell *someone*. It was now six o'clock and so I phoned Galina in Monte Carlo. Even if she were dancing that night, she would not yet have left for the theatre.

I could sense the feeling of excitement in her voice when I told her.

'Oh Nicki, darling, I am so glad – not only for him, but for you. And don't worry. Now we've had this first contact, you mark my words – you'll hear from him. I'm so glad for you. It's the most wonderful news.'

We talked about Rudi, we wondered how he might have changed during the interval, what kind of life he had been leading since, as kids together, we had been jostled in that creaky old cart that took us to the waterfront – and me to freedom.

Changing the subject Galina asked, 'How's Olga's show?'

'Wonderful. A sell-out.'

'I sent her a telegram but I couldn't get a reply on the telephone. I wanted to congratulate her.'

'She's taken the phone off the hook.'

'Ah! That explains it. Now, hold your breath, darling brother – *I've* got some news too. Not exactly as exciting as yours – but still –'

'Tell all,' I laughed, breaking the tension.

'I think it's now virtually certain,' she said, 'that they're going to give me the chance to dance a leading role.'

'You're joking!'

'I'm not.'

'In what?'

'*Casse*.'

'Casse? The ballet name from the *Nutcracker*!'

'Yes. It's a wonderful role. I'll dance opposite Jean-Pierre.'

'A husband and wife team!' I laughed again.

'Sort of. Oh Nicki, my dear, it's a dream come true. I will actually be a *prima ballerina*.'

'I'm so proud of you, Galina. *So* excited. Tell me, when?'

'It'll be in the repertoire next year at Monte Carlo. We'll probably have to dance it ten times through the season. And then of course in Paris the following summer. I can't wait for it. But I'll see you before – this coming summer. It's wonderful. Everything seems to be conspiring to make us happy.'

Soon after I had finished telephoning, I walked home up the Rue de Seine and on the way, opposite the Beaux Arts, I climbed the three flights of narrow stairs to tell the good news to Natalie Goncharova, who lived with her artist friend Michel Larionov. She was delighted at Galina's triumph.

'I'll tell Balanchine that he must advertise more extensively – and I want to have a chance, if I can, to do some of the costumes,' she said. Goncharova had already carved out a name for herself as a designer for the ballet, and she had designed most of the costumes for *Les Noces*.

And when I told her about Rudi she said, 'When Balanchine comes back to Paris I'll tell him. He's got a lot of influence with the present Russian rulers. He might be able to trace Rudi.'

I stayed a short while, talking, then walked round the corner of the Rue Jacob until I reached the front of Michel's restaurant – an unpretentious but good eating house, with its newspapers rolled on racks. There, in the window, leaning over a checked cloth, stroking the hand of a pretty girl who could not have been more than twenty, was Father, obviously working hard at what he once described as 'the charm game'.

I *had* to tell him about Rudi, so I opened the door and walked straight in. It was still early for dinner, but the two were drinking champagne and Father, spruce, moustache neatly clipped, white hair beautifully combed, was murmuring sweet nothings into this young girl's ear.

As I opened the door, he looked up as I waited. You never knew with Father whether he would be angry or polite at an interruption. But I had noticed an increasing tendency for him to show off when taking out girls younger than his daughter. It was his way of shedding a few years.

'Ah!' he cried jovially. 'A rival attraction enters! And what do you want, young man?' Before I could answer he turned to the girl and said, all in good humour, 'You know this young feller? It's Nicki, my son, who seems,' with another chuckle, 'unable to find pretty girls of his own, so he haunts me, trying to pick up girls that I'm finding for him. Nicki, this is Katerina.'

She smiled shyly.

'Pretty eh?' asked Father, with the proprietorial air of someone saying, 'You can stay for a few minutes but, then, bugger off!'

'I congratulate you on your good taste, Father,' I said politely. 'She's absolutely adorable.'

Katerina turned a little pink.

'Now now my boy, don't overdo it. No poaching!' And to Katerina with a shake of his head, 'Too young, m'dear. Far too young. Now, why this intrusion? You must want something! Money?'

'No,' I didn't quite know how to break the exciting news. 'Father, don't get too excited, but –'

'With this little piece? You expect me not to get excited?'

'Father, *please*!' I cried and gripped his arm so hard that he suddenly stopped the banter, realising that I was not joking. 'Have a drink.' He signalled for a glass, slanted it and poured out the Laurent-Perrier. 'What is it? Anything wrong?'

'Nothing *wrong*,' I replied, 'but don't get excited, Father, because there's no clue, no way of finding him – nothing; but I've seen a photograph, a newspaper clipping of' – I paused instinctively for dramatic effect – 'of – Rudi!'

Father's face went as white as his beard, and as he held the checked tablecloth, I could see the knuckles showing white with the power of his grip.

'Rudi!' he breathed. 'Our Rudi.' Then, turning to the girl he said, 'My long lost son, Nicki's twin brother.' He started to bombard me with questions, 'Where? How? When?'

My throat was dry from talking to Galina. I felt a kind of lump at the back of my throat, slight but it gave me a tendency to croak a little when I was tired, but I took a gulp of champagne and that helped. Then I told him, as simply as I could, what little I knew. He had gathered his wits by then. 'This calls for a celebration,' he ordered another bottle, a little unsteadily, not from drink, more from emotion. 'I can't get over it. I just can't absorb it. It's a miracle.'

Katerina said very politely, 'You'd like me to go, Dmitri? I understand.'

'No, no, not yet. I'm overwhelmed, I can't take it in. But you must share in our joy.' The waiter brought the bottle. We drank a toast, 'To Rudi – God bless you, wherever you are'. Father drank the champagne as though it was vodka, sat there looking at his empty glass for a full minute or more – one of those moments which are endless – and then, finally, as the truth came to him, he laid his head on the table, couched on his crossed arms, and started weeping, racking sounds, studded with almost indecipherable phrases, 'Thank God! I'm so happy.'

He did not notice the girl or me, and finally I whispered to her, 'I think you might as well go home,' adding with a smile, 'He'll probably drink so much champagne that he won't even remember where you are!' She nodded and quietly left the restaurant. Father raised up his eyes, waved but said nothing, then wiped his face with a silk handkerchief and gave his nose an almighty blow.

*

There was one more person I could talk to, and that was Igor, though he had changed a lot since his return from abroad. Once he had become installed in Brig's grand new house – and after his confession to me about the girl whose photographs he had asked me to look after so carefully – he had become more and more introspective. It was almost as though he now lived a double life – one as the perfect host, doing what he called a job, the other his secret life.

This news, however, was something that none of us could ignore, and as soon as I had finished looking after Father, I went home and phoned Igor.

'It's not possible!' he cried. 'God is looking after us! Don't say a word – I'll jump into the car and come right round to drink a toast to Rudi. Where are you? At the Red Cross or at home?'

I told him I was at home, that Father had said he wanted to digest the news alone. 'Father's probably getting drunk in some bistro.'

As soon as Igor arrived, I told him all I knew. 'Which isn't very much,' I confessed. 'But it's a start.' It was wonderful to see the enthusiasm that lit his eyes. There was nothing lack-lustre about him now. I had almost forgotten the 'real' Igor, the man who had been such fun in Tsarskoe Selo, now the master of such a grand house, for Brig still gave superb parties – to which I was occasionally asked as a spare man. Father often came along too, because of his rank, and if Galina was not dancing she would be invited as well, not only because she was a Russian, but because of her growing success with the ballet. She wasn't yet 'the best' but she was on the way, and even Balanchine commented on what he called her 'luscious and tantalising quality'. She had developed an exotic beauty, and she danced with a gentle lyricism subtly mixed with sexual allure.

Brig's dinners, always served by the immaculate Kornilov and his staff, were more Russian than at the court of the Tsars. She certainly provided the finest Russian food in Paris – and with no nonsense like beetroot soup and sour cream masquerading as bortsch. Her hot koulibayaka, with its base of kasha, sturgeon or salmon and hard-boiled eggs encased in a long tube of shining pastry, melted in the mouth.

'You are the greatest hostess in Paris,' I heard one guest gush as he helped himself to a large second portion. 'Your food –'

'Ah! The Russians!' She toasted Igor with an ice-cold vodka. 'For the Russian head of the table, only the best is good enough.'

It was said very sweetly, but it was all part of an act, I could tell that, a phoney war of manners.

There were indulgent murmurs of 'To Igor!' as the guests raised their glasses to the host who had not the faintest idea what he was going to eat before he sat down and was served.

Now, with Father out and Tasha at the cinema, Igor and I were alone and relaxed in our old house in the place de Furstemberg. Igor sighed, 'This is my real home. If only I'd never got married!'

'And your girl?' I asked.

'She loves me, but I hardly ever see her. She lives at Avallon, two hundred kilometres away and we meet only twice a month. That's all.' He sighed. 'If Brig has to go away, then I can go to her place and see her when her husband is working. The same thing if her husband goes away. I can put her up in Paris.'

'It sounds very complicated,' I hesitated over the word, 'and depressing. And not really like you,' trying to lighten his emotion. 'You never *used* to allow any woman to get under your skin.'

'It was different then. I might have loved women, but until this happened, I was never in love. Never. But now I am, and I miss her terribly. I feel utterly wretched. That is why I would like to ask if you would give me back my photographs.'

'Of course you can have them if you wish,' I replied. I went over to my desk, unlocked the drawer where I had kept the wallet, brought it over and gave it to him.

'But supposing you are caught,' I added. 'Or you faint. What then? For God's sake, promise me you will put them away in a safe place.'

Not long after Igor left, Tasha returned. She had been to see Elizabeth Bergner in *Catherine the Great*.

'You know what's happened?' I cried. 'Rudi is alive! I've seen his photo in a paper. He looks tired and much older, but he's alive.'

She kissed me and said, 'That's wonderful, Nicki.' She dropped the 'uncle' these days. 'When is he coming?'

I explained that perhaps we would never see him, that this was only an untraceable newspaper clipping which I had come across by chance.

'Poor Nicki. I know you love him so much,' and then, as though to comfort me, she added, 'He'll come. I'm sure he'll come.'

'I doubt it,' I replied. 'Of course I'm terribly excited, but we know nothing at all of his whereabouts.'

'Poor you,' she said once more, and it passed through my mind that there was a hint almost of a sigh of relief in her changed voice, accentuated when she sat down on a footstool at the foot of my armchair, and asked, almost wistfully, 'You'll never love Rudi more than you love me, will you, if he comes back?'

'It's a different kind of love,' I stroked her hair, 'but you'll always be first.' The trouble was that I meant it.

'Good,' she said and seemed to dismiss the subject, though none of us could forget it entirely. Indeed, for the next few days the house seemed wrapped in silence, almost as though we were waiting for the doorbell to tinkle and for Rudi to be ushered in. My work at the Red Cross, of course, made me realise how unlikely it was that we would

172

ever hear from him again. Still, hope and reason always travel hand in hand.

Work in the Red Cross had also given me a certain edge of hardness in dealing with this sort of problem. Though we did rejoice in some triumphs, the sad, sometimes tragic, failures largely outweighed them, and gradually we all realised that the coincidence of seeing the double photo could never lead us anywhere except by a miracle, despite the fact that my boss in Geneva, Philippe Peter, had promised to try to trace the clipping.

All I could do was to have the clipping photographed, then framed and hung over my bed. If I had still had my floppy teddy, Kodi, I would have put them together as my sole mementoes of Rudi. But I had no idea where Kodi was now, presumably lost or given away.

Galina returned from Monte Carlo in the spring, ready not only to dance in Paris but to start preliminary rehearsals for the following winter performances of the *Nutcracker*.

Perhaps the frenetic quality of life made it easier to put Rudi out of mind. There was so much happening all around us, life taking a new hold on all of us. Already it seemed years since Lindbergh had flown solo across the Atlantic to Paris, or D. H. Lawrence's *Lady Chatterley's Lover* had been a sell-out at Shakespeare and Company, or, for that matter, our old friend Hemingway had produced a magnificent bestseller in *A Farewell to Arms*. And the 'talkies' were now a commonplace. On a more sombre note, there was even discussion of the new Soviet Russia – our mortal enemies – being admitted to the League of Nations. And in Germany, Hitler had banned all political parties other than the Nazis, while Spain was teetering on the verge of civil war.

'It's no time for good business,' said Olga, 'yet somehow we're doing better than I ever thought we would.' In fact Aunt Olga was thriving because internal tensions tend to make people spend more, to adopt a 'live for today' motto.

Of course to one person – and through her, all of us, really – at that time – life centred round the future of Galina, who had never looked more beautiful. She was in the full bloom of her life as a dancer, filled with years of experience yet still young enough to be blessed (as she had to be) with a perfect figure, as thin as a wraith, as supple as though she had no bones, and radiating intensity.

I did not see any of her rehearsals in Paris because they were not going through the entire ballet, but concentrating on sections of the dancing which were particularly difficult.

The date for the opening performance in the fairy-tale Opera House in Monte Carlo had been fixed for December 16.

'My birthday!' cried Tasha. 'I'll be eighteen.'

'A grown-up lady,' said Father.

'We've been promised star billing,' Galina announced. 'Oh, Father, you must all come to the first night. Can we arrange it?'

'Of course we will come! And to one or two of the rehearsals – the others, I mean,' he added hastily. 'I might have business to attend to.'

'Darling Father!' Galina kissed him. 'You're a fairy godfather. It'll be so wonderful.'

'Will you take me to the rehearsals?' Tasha whispered to me.

'Anywhere you want to go –'

'I don't see why Father should be the only one who gets a kiss. Here's one for you.'

She planted a firm but lingering kiss on my lips, slightly opening hers. 'You're adorable, Nicki,' she squeezed me.

Father had mellowed a great deal with advancing age, though he would still roar with anger if he could not get his Laurent-Perrier before breakfast. Indeed, he could still be really angry if something displeased him, but such occasions were becoming rarer, and if things were going well, he needed no prodding to arrange a celebration. As *I* grew older, I sometimes wondered where all *his* money was coming from. But it was none of my business really, and he just seemed to have unlimited funds in Switzerland.

'Yes,' Father cried, 'we must do this in style – a double celebration.'

'Double?' Igor had suddenly arrived, catching the last phrase. He had popped in for a drink, though I thought he looked far from well, with a grey, pasty complexion.

'Galina's première and Tasha's birthday – both on December 16. Surely you haven't forgotten Tasha's birthday? You must come too, Igor,' cried Father. 'And Brig.'

'Come where?'

'To Monte Carlo. For the première of Galina's *Nutcracker*. We're all going to Monte Carlo for a couple of weeks,' adding with an expansive wave of his hand, 'Don't worry. It's all on me. I'll invite you.'

'I'm afraid –' Igor hesitated. 'I'm not sure I'll be able –'

'Nonsense,' cried Father. 'Why on earth not?'

'The doctor. He says I shouldn't travel.'

'Fiddlesticks! How can you tell what you'll be feeling like by next December?'

We made no final decision that evening about Igor, but later Igor told me that his dizzy spells were becoming increasingly frequent and that the doctor had advised him, in his words, 'For a few months it would be better to stay close to me where I can keep an eye on you.'

'And,' I added warningly, 'better to leave those photos in a safe place. Never in your pocket.' He nodded, although somewhat distractedly.

Olga also could not come to Monte Carlo – at least not for the first ten days of the holiday.

'I can't ignore the Christmas rush,' she said, 'but I'll arrive on the fourteenth – so I'll be in time for the opening and Tasha's birthday.'

Father set about booking our train seats, and hotel rooms. In the end, the Hôtel de Paris was virtually full – the Christmas rush, of course – but Father did manage to secure a small suite for himself, while Tasha and I had two single rooms at the Metropole, the haunt of the British, in front of the far end of the Casino gardens. It would suit us perfectly, I thought, for Galina would be busy rehearsing, and Father would be equally busy losing or winning money.

Tasha and I could explore the small bistros and even walk down the hill to that toytown station and take the train to have lunch in Nice with its splendid Promenade des Anglais and, always that extra blessing, sunshine in winter.

Perhaps it was the romantic promise of the forthcoming celebration that brought some verses to my mind – verses I had read long ago at my boyhood school in St Petersburg:

> I come again with greetings new,
>   To tell you day is well begun;
> To say the leaves are fresh with dew
>   And dappled in the early sun;
> To tell how over everything
>   Delight is blowing in the air –
> I know not yet what I shall sing;
>   I only know the song is there.

11

Galina, of course, was already hard at work with the Corps de Ballet in Monte Carlo – rehearsing in the mornings and playing in the Opera House in the evenings. I had not intended to watch her early rehearsals, though I did want to see one of the three dress rehearsals before the opening night. Galina, though, persuaded me otherwise.

'Do come along, Nicki,' she begged me. 'Rehearsals aren't going well and I need moral support.'

'But you've got darling Jean-Pierre,' I said flippantly.

176

'Jean-Pierre certainly helps with the steps,' she agreed with a small smile. 'But your presence in the theatre would help my frayed nerves.'

I shrugged. 'If you say so. But is Balanchine such a slave-driver?'

'He's not a slave-driver at all. He's endlessly patient. But that's because by now all the choreographic work's been done, and the *régisseur* takes over.'

'The what?'

'The *régisseur*. Well, stage director if you like. He does far more than watch the props, make sure the scenery flats don't fall over, check on the costumes, and act as a general factotum. Once Balanchine's choreographed the first part of the ballet – act, scene, whatever it may be – he hands over to the *régisseur* and leaves him to develop things and take most of the rehearsals.'

'Sounds an important job.'

'It is; it's also scarifying with Adolphe.'

'Adolphe?'

'Our *régisseur*. Real name Horley-Bentinck, very classy English. But we call him Adolphe because he's got one of those thin moustaches and brilliantined hair like the film actor Adolphe Menjou. He's terribly affected and bitingly sarcastic at times. He wears a sort of kaftan under which he's rumoured to be naked, and beats time with a shepherd's crook. He's also rumoured to have been Balanchine's lover.'

'Sounds like an immoral eccentric to me.'

'He encourages everybody to think that. But he is marvellous at his job; it's just that he's such a mixture of hot and cold that you never know where you are with him. But if you're just sitting somewhere in the theatre, our –' she gave my hand a warm clasp – 'our *rapport* will help.'

'He'll probably be furious,' I pointed out.

'Not him. He loves showing off.'

'I'll be there,' I assured her.

*

177

Galina met me at the stage door half an hour before the rehearsal was due to begin and conducted me through a maze of back-stage corridors, illuminated by popping gas jets. We went through the scene dock where great scenic flats stood against the wall and dozens of thick cords hung from the flies. There were plaster 'props' everywhere. The chaos seemed to defy solution.

'How on earth do they ever find anything?' I asked.

'Believe me, the stage hands know exactly where to put their hands on anything. Chaos is the medium they work in.'

There was a great deal of hammering going on and, in the workshop adjoining the dock, men were busy constructing wooden frames for the canvas flats. The acrid smoke from their Gauloises drifted against the boldly written notices – 'No Smoking' – understandably, with open pots of paint everywhere. I raised my eyebrows; Galina shrugged. 'There's no stopping them.'

We slid through the pass-door in the proscenium and found ourselves in the theatre. Acres of plush stalls draped in white dust sheets stretched away to the back. A single bulb hanging from the end of a wire was the only illumination on the stage. The backdrop, I recognised. It was for the 'Kingdom of Snow' scene in *Casse-Noisette*, but its scintillating beauty was diminished by the feeble light.

Diagonally across one of the upstage corners was a piano. A bored young man with long fair hair and an unending supply of Gauloises sat before it. A saucer filled with cigarette ends stood on top. Trios of dancers lounged about in groups. They wore a curious mixture of loose jumpers, thick woollen legwarmers, and skirts or shorts that looked like leftovers from a jumble sale.

'I must join them and limber up a bit,' Galina said. 'Find yourself a seat in the stalls and introduce yourself to Adolphe when he comes. You'll find him quite agreeable.'

I did. The monkish robe he wore was bound round his waist with a thick cord and he wore elegant red leather slippers. He was, he said, delighted to meet me. The tinny sound of a three-four strumming came from the piano and the dancers rearranged themselves in anticipation of his commands. But he passed one hand across his face in an extravagant gesture – an extravagance that matched the frequent emphases in his speech.

'My *darlings*, I have the most monu*me*ntal hangover this morning. I simply cannot think of a *single* step. Do, I *implore* you, dance your little hearts away.'

Whereupon he sat down a couple of seats removed from me with a hand over his eyes. It must have been a translucent hand, for it did not stop him observing and crying out at the frequent faults of the Corps de Ballet.

'Julie, dear child, what is the matter with you in that *glissé*? The foot is to be *slid*, not dragged. Are your knickers coming down? Or are you just weary after cavorting like a cat on heat with some dreadful *garçon* last night? Whatever it is, do try to pull yourself together, dear child. I am weary unto *death* of your woodenness.'

A few minutes later he cried, 'Esmée, you are supposed to be a *snowflake*, dear child, not a clodhopping peasant.'

The ever-smoking pianist tinkled away on his badly-tuned piano until stopped by the irritated Adolphe, who suddenly abandoned his languid pose and leapt up the short flight of steps on to the stage and seized his crook from the wings.

'Etienne, how can *any*one possibly keep time when you yourself are so far adrift from the regular beat?'

'Rubato,' Etienne said without taking the cigarette out of his mouth.

Adolphe thumped his crook furiously. 'I want none of your Chopinesque rubato here. Keep the beat, the beat, the *beat* – one, two, three; one, two, three – thus. Now again, my darlings, group for the *adage*. Let's start with Clara – Galina – and Nutcracker Prince – Jean-Pierre. Get ready for your *pas de deux* . . . and remember, Nutcracker, that the knee thrown out in front during the *grand pas de*

179

chat is *bent* during the jump. I shouldn't have to tell you, but I do . . . Clara, I am constantly having to remind you that this whole ballet is a fairy tale of a little girl who falls in love with a monstrous toy and *dreams*; it is the elements of fantasy and reality that we are mingling. Do try, dear child, to *mingle* . . .'

I watched for a good hour, after which the dancers began to show signs of weariness – understandably after Adolphe's remorseless and sarcastic demands, such as '*Please* – throw the right leg higher when you spring forward off the left in the *jeté fouetté*'; or 'make a level diagonal with the arms to match the rearward level of the leg in the *épaule*'; or 'Remember to reverse the feet in the *entrechat dix*.' He was ruthless, but he seemed to get results – as Galina confirmed when I saw her in her dressing-room afterwards.

'He *is* a monster, as you say; but at least we have confidence in him.'

When I was introduced to Balanchine I found him charming. 'Come to as many rehearsals as you like,' he smiled, 'and now, while Galina and the Corps de Ballet are having a break, let me show you some of the props.'

The ballet was always such a glittering affair that I had expected nothing less than cloth of gold for the dancers. Astonishingly, sackcloth seemed to be used for most of the stage costuming.

'Brilliant illumination of the stage makes silks and taffetas look dowdy and coarse,' explained Balanchine. 'Velvet never looks like velvet on a lit stage. But old flannelette sheets suitably dyed could come straight from the silk looms of Lyon, and hessian and canvas, suitably painted, enhance the effect of luxury.'

What an artificial world I had plunged into! I saw the rows of tutus, every one of them sixteen layers of starched net, the leg holes looking like scissor handles, and next to every tutu, a freshly-laundered jock-strap.

'*A jock-strap!*' I laughed aloud.

'And why not?' asked Balanchine. 'Men aren't the only people whose pelvic muscles need support during strenuous activities.'

In another room were at least fifty pairs of block-toed shoes for the Corps de Ballet. I thought it must be very uncomfortable, balancing on your toes.

'Not as bad as you think,' said Balanchine. 'The toes are blocked with horsehair which gives a resilience to the toes as you balance.'

In another room, a gang of back-stage workers was finishing the final costumes for the men, making sheets of armour from cardboard painted silver, while someone else had made a suit of chain armour out of knitted string and was dipping it in aluminium paint.

'You've seen the other side of ballet now,' said Balanchine. 'I hope you enjoyed it. Next comes the dress rehearsal.'

I awaited it with impatience but, though I was fascinated, I was anxious to shake off the uninviting atmosphere of the unlit theatre, the dust rising from the chalk lines on the stage, showing the positions to be taken up by soloists and groups, and the grubby practice clothing of the dancers. And the transformation to the proper glamour of the theatre was delightful.

The costumes for the scene set in the Kingdom of Snow were exquisite, with multi-coloured spangles decorating the diaphanous skirts of the Corps de Ballet, and the Snow Queen's headdress a masterpiece of imaginative fantasy. And those for the Kingdom of Sweets were not only pretty but witty too – the chocolate-bar sweetmeat looking like a gold-and-red Toblerone packet, the barleysugar swathed in orange spirally encircled with black diamanté, the nougat and Turkish delight looking almost edible in beige and pink with bite marks on them. As for the Sugarplum Fairy, as queen of the Kingdom of Sweets, she was dressed simply in a tutu and fondant headdress.

181

The costumes reflected all the stages of the disillusioning fantasy through which the little girl Clara went in her dream – and, very daringly, in the scene in which she creeps up to the Christmas tree to find the freakish doll on which she dotes, she wore a nightdress that was to all intents and purposes transparent.

'Won't you have the City Fathers complaining?' I asked Galina afterwards.

'Not them. They'll love it. I can see them licking their lips,' Galina said with a sideways glance at me. 'I've no doubt your lascivious eye detected that I've had to shave my pubic hair off, since I'm supposed to be a little girl of ten. It's awful. It itches.'

'Well,' I said hesitantly, 'I –'

'Of course you did. So will others. But as I'm an innocent little girl of ten, any reproach would only reveal the under-cover thoughts of dirty old men.'

'Ah. They'd be hoist with their own petard.'

'*Some*thing would be,' Father added with one of his outrageous laughs.

As things turned out, one or two newsmen – stringers for the Paris papers – had smuggled themselves into the rehearsals, and their brief paragraphs implying eroticism had created such a rush for seats that the house could have been filled twice over.

I had taken Tasha to the first dress rehearsal, because the theatre would be half empty. It would be filled much more for the second and then the final rehearsals with guests of the cast; but now, as we sat down in the middle of the stalls, Balanchine, Kochno and 'Adolphe Menjou' were a few rows ahead of us.

When the house lights were dimmed, and after the first beautiful music heralded the rise of the curtain, Tasha's hand searched for mine, squeezed it tightly and then, in the most natural way, she turned her face to mine and kissed me – but this time she gently opened her lips.

The moment was totally unrehearsed, perfectly natural, and I was quite sure that never before had she touched any man's tongue with the tip – only the tip – of her own against mine.

'Be a good girl,' I whispered. 'You mustn't do that here.'

'Didn't you like it?' she whispered back.

'That's nothing to do with it. Behave yourself!'

There was a loud 'Sssssssh!' from an angry Kochno looking back, as the rehearsal got into its stride.

'See?' I whispered.

For a short time we watched, with me more entranced than Tasha in the ballet, and I thought that the kissing had been stopped by Kochno's warning. But then something else happened. She had been clutching my hand, and suddenly, without warning, she gently undid two buttons and pulled my hand inside her blouse. I felt a surge of excitement at the feel of her cool bare skin. It was not erotic, but it was exciting. Nothing happened for a few minutes. Then, very gently, almost imperceptibly, she pressed my right hand hard on her breasts. She was wearing no bra. I tried to take my hand away. She held it in position with a firm grip, clasped over mine, and she kept the hand there for a few minutes longer. Then, without warning, still gripping me tightly, she slid her whole body forward.

'You mustn't!' I whispered. '*Please*.'

'Don't you like it?'

'Of course I do, that's the trouble.'

'Do you love me?'

'Yes I do, darling Tasha.' The music was very loud at this moment. 'I'm almost afraid to say so, but I do. But stop this.' I kissed *her* this time and lovingly stroked her cheek.

The occasional whisper between us passed unnoticed because from time to time Balanchine would interrupt and then there would be long discussions with the cast.

'Anyway,' I said, 'we'll see the entire ballet again in four days – the full version.'

'Don't worry,' she answered. 'I'll tell Galina how beautiful everything was now – even if I haven't seen a thing.'

'You're a naughty girl.'

'In four days' time I'll be a naughty woman.'

Aunt Olga arrived on the *train bleu* two days later, and we all set out to greet her and hear her latest news, with Tasha, exquisitely polite and on her best behaviour, saying 'Yes, Mama,' and 'No, Mama.' Then, the following evening, on Tasha's birthday, we all dressed up to the nines, and set off to witness Galina's first appearance as a *prima ballerina*.

The stage-door keeper was old but alert, up to all the tricks of unwelcome Lotharios who tried to bribe their way into a star's dressing-room. But Galina had warned him I was expected.

'Ah, M'sieu, for the moment Mam'selle asks to be excused. The wardrobe mistress is with her . . . advising, helping . . . the costumes, you know. She will call on the telephone –' He pointed to a speaking-tube projecting from the wall. 'Be seated, M'sieu. The flowers you bring are very beautiful. Her dressing-room is already a garden.' He closed one eye with a conspiratorial air. 'I *know*. The bouquets have all passed this way.' He paused, realising that I, too, was nervous on Galina's behalf and, his hands clasped across his ample belly, set out to relax me with conversation.

His favourite subject – indeed I suspected it was his only subject – was the theatre. It had been built on to the casino in 1878 and Charles Garnier – the architect – had also built the Paris Opera House. Sarah Bernhardt performed the opening ceremony ('Think of it, M'sieu! The great Bernhardt!') and Garnier had been summoned to the royal box and presented with a decoration.

'Ah! The gala nights I have seen, M'sieu! Pavlova, Paderewski, Chaliapin, Karsavina, Kreisler – all have performed here. Still do, those who are with us. And tonight is another gala – for Mam'selle and for you too, her brother, and for His Excellency the Prince, your father. He will of course sit with *our* Prince in his box, as you will yourself, M'sieu.'

He chattered on, reminiscences pouring from him until at last there was a whistle from the speaking tube as the little cork popped out and Galina was ready.

Her dressing-room was indeed a bower of glowing colour. My own yellow roses were lost amongst the profusion. 'Sweet of you, Nicki. Everyone has been so kind and encouraging. I'm overwhelmed.'

The costume for the first scene had met with approval, and the dresser actually had to stitch the back in when she wore it, it was so tight. Galina had only the first terrifying moment of her entrance to overcome. I gave her an affectionate kiss and wished her luck before making my way back to the stage-door and then to the front of the theatre, where the audience was already arriving, since the entire house had to be seated by the time Prince Louis of Monaco entered five minutes before the curtain rose.

Father and I, being his princely equals, were the Monegasque ruler's chief guests in his box, and because of protocol we had to await his arrival at the door of the box so that His Serene Highness could enter first. He arrived exactly on time with a fanfare of trumpets from the orchestra pit below. He was accompanied by Prince Rainier, his grandson, a handsome young man. Father looked very impressive in his formal evening dress with the glittering orders bestowed on him by the Tsar ornamenting his white shirtfront and, after the formalities of bows and handshakes, we entered the box as the entire audience stood.

How different the theatre looked in the full beauty of its lighting, its red plush stalls, gilt frescoes, candelabra, and sky-blue ceiling painted with cherubs and goddesses! The audience glittered with jewels and orders. Visitors staying at the Hôtel de Paris had turned out in force and included Sir Basil Zaharoff, the armaments king (who owned the hotel anyway); the Grand Duke of Liechtenstein; and Gordon Selfridge (Olga had persuaded him to come with his Dolly Sisters). Somerset Maugham was there, and so was the 'Scarlet Pimpernel' novelist Baroness Orczy. It certainly was a star-studded audience.

When the curtain rose after the overture there was a gasp of astonishment, following by spontaneous applause. Balanchine had rejuvenated the ballet. The party scene with the toys and the Christmas tree was a wonderland of glitter, with Clara's godfather, the magician Drosselmeyer, creating his toys in his workshop that glittered behind the scrim, the translucent curtain through which a second scene is visible to the audience. The party went on, and Harlequin, Columbine, and the Moor began to jerk from dolls into life.

Galina's entrance in her *pas de seule* got a ringing round of applause; and indeed she looked the embodiment of fairy-like childhood. As the ballet unfolded its story of enchantment, adult perfidy and childhood disillusionment, the audience applauded time and again, and especially the Chinese dance and the gobbling noises made by the bassoons and double-basses. The Arab dance, with the Corps de Ballet in the dreamlike sequence of fluttering veils, brought a gasp of appreciation. The spectators loved the Waltz of the Snowflakes, during which Clara and the Prince dance their way to the Kingdom of Sweets; and as the Russian trepak exploded in its final burst of speed and sound they cheered. But despite my obvious bias, I could see that it was Galina they loved. She *did* dance most beautifully – not faultlessly ('Nothing in this life is faultless,' as Olga might well have said), but with a depth of feeling I had never seen before.

At the end of the first act the principals had to come before the curtain, and in the interval the hum of conversation drifted up to our box, as Father, with a proprietary air, pointed out to Prince Louis, 'They seem to like my daughter.' I noticed the Prince hide an indulgent smile.

The final curtain, as it fell on the brilliant scene of the dance of the flying bees as they danced in ecstasy around the hive of their queen was received with rapturous applause and cheers and many people rose in their seats as Galina, smiling radiantly, took her call. She curtsied to our box and then, in an expressive gesture, opened her arms wide in tribute to the audience.

Attendants trooped into the theatre with the baskets and bouquets of flowers I had seen in her dressing-room and soon she was enclosed in a floral bower. Eight times the curtain rose and fell, each time with undiminished applause.

Of course there had to be speeches, with René Blum, the theatre manager, paying tribute to His Serene Highness for gracing the occasion with his presence; George Balanchine recalling the work done by Diaghilev in restoring the ballet to its original beauty 'after so much hacking about by choreographers'; and Boris Kochno, who spoke reverently of Diaghilev 'during the time I acted as his secretary and adviser'.

'And no doubt other things too,' Father whispered (rather too loudly, I thought) in my ear.

And of course there had to be privileged visitors to the star dressing-rooms, and long lines of autograph hunters waited patiently at the stage door. Galina was exhausted, drained of emotion, but she knew that artists can only fulfil themselves with audiences, that they are the ones who make or break a show.

There was no doubt about one thing, I said as I hugged her, 'You've certainly got a huge success on your hands.'

'Isn't it wonderful!'

I was still talking in the crowded dressing-room when the old stage-door keeper came in, and tugging my sleeve, said, 'M'sieu, a telephone call for you – from Paris.'

'Can't be,' I smiled. 'Are you sure it's not for Mam'selle Galina?'

'No sir, she specified you especially, Nicki Korolev.'

She? Irritated I went out into the hall near the stage door, and barked, 'I'm terribly busy. Who is it?'

'This is Brig,' I recognised the shrill, sometimes aggress-ive tone of her American accent.

'Thank God you're there, Nicki.' She sounded panic-stricken.

Assuming that she wanted to congratulate Galina, I asked, 'Can I help – give her a message?'

'Can you help! For Christ's sake!' Then she almost screamed into the phone. 'It's Igor! He's had a stroke!' Her voice was choking. 'He's paralysed and can't even talk!'

12

What a disastrous and tragic finale to such an exquisite evening! I was so stunned that when I returned to the noisy dressing-room – the babble of talk mingling with the clink of glasses – I did not dare to tell anyone.

I *could not* spoil Galina's wonderful triumph. She had now *arrived*. No doubt about it. Every instinct told me that she had reached a tremendous climax in her life, one that would lead her on to permanent stardom until the time came for her to hang up her ballet shoes. And even then she would become a legend. But it was this very moment that was so triumphant. The frenzy of clapping, the encores had been rapturous. Never before had I seen or heard such enthusiasm in an audience. Why, even the Prince of Monaco was standing up in our box clapping!

Yet the news about Igor was so sudden and shattering that I could hardly absorb it. The fact that only a few moments ago I had been hailing Galina's success, wonder-ing what the *Nice-Matin* would say the following morning, preparing for the grand supper at the Hôtel de Paris – Father's special offering for Galina, and for Tasha's eighteenth birthday. Now as Tasha and Galina celebrated their great and glorious day, disaster lay concealed. What is more, I knew perfectly well that Tasha hoped it would lead to a more intimate relationship with me. It was not going to – I was determined that I would fight her passions, and my own. Still, I could no more spoil her birthday than I could douse the high spirits and the achievement of Galina.

What to do? For a few moments I stood just inside the tiny dressing-room, hot with the background of costumes on pegs, the smell of greasepaint, the frame of small bulbs round the rectangular looking-glass before which Galina made up each evening. Everything about the room tended to make me panicky.

And not only that – any decision that I would *have* to make in the next few moments had to be set against an imaginative picture that stared at me from the recesses of my mind – Igor lying on a bed as lifeless as a corpse, or nearly. I could *see* him – that was the trouble. The picture was etched in my mind. So, loving Igor as I always had, how could I conceal from our family and close friends in this room the magnitude of what had happened?

I felt sick, beckoned to the waiter and took a gulp of champagne, then, even before the waiter could move away, I drained the glass and held it out for more. I drank that too. Everyone was so busy – and I was so tormented – that I hardly noticed as Tasha, looking much older than her age in an elegant model Olga dress – her birthday present – sidled up to me and said, 'You look awful Nicki. Are you all right?'

'No, I'm not,' I replied savagely. 'I feel bloody awful.'

'What's the matter, darling?'

'Don't darling me in public – or in private either.' Instantly, as her face filled with an expression near to tears, I added, 'Sorry, Tasha dear. I've just had a terrible shock.'

'Can I help?'

I shook my head miserably. 'Only by leaving me alone,' I muttered. 'Please leave me. Go and talk to the others.'

As she walked away – and there were plenty of young men eager to meet this ravishing young lady – I saw Father staring at me. I nodded, almost like a signal. He recognised it and edged across the crowded room.

'Never seen you drink champagne like that,' he started. 'I need some myself. I'm having a terrible run at the tables. Terrible. Something the matter?'

I nodded. I had forgotten his tale of woe at the tables, it was always very good or very bad. Of course! Father was the one to confide in, to make the decision.

'Can you come outside for a moment, please?' I asked him.

Without a word he made for the stage door and when Galina saw us, she cried, 'You're not going?' I said to her, 'I need a breath of fresh air. I'll be back in a moment.'

'What's the trouble?' asked Father abruptly as we stood outside, gulping in the late evening air.

'It's Igor,' I was equally abrupt. 'He's had a serious stroke. Brig's just telephoned me.' I didn't need to elaborate immediately.

'My God!' Father echoed my words of reaction. 'Is it – bad?'

'Paralysed.'

'Poor devil.'

'I was wondering – should I ask Galina to cancel the party and then tell the family?' I jerked my head in the direction of the dressing-room.

'No! Absolutely not.' Father never hesitated. 'It's the girls' party. Both of them. Don't let's spoil it for them. But I'm glad you told me.'

With that he walked heavily back into the room and clapped his hands and cried, 'Come along, the Korolevs! Time to eat!' I was astounded – and proud of him – at the way in which he seemed to have switched off a clock, though I could imagine his thoughts.

But he was an old soldier, used to putting on a good front when the enemy attacked – and what an insidious enemy we faced! At least his cheerfulness, assumed though it was, made me feel a little better. How true is the old saying that a tragedy shared is a tragedy halved.

'Come on all of you!' And as the uninvited hangers-on left, we trooped over the road to the Hôtel de Paris. Father led the way into the large ground floor dining-room overlooking the Casino and the gardens, and then there was a moment of wonderful and unexpected delight. The guests already sitting at table, many of whom must have been to the ballet, stood up and clapped as Galina led the way into the room on Father's arm. It was a spontaneous gesture and both Father and Galina gave slight bows to show their appreciation, Galina in the seventh heaven of delight, especially when Somerset Maugham walked from his nearby table, kissed her hand, and in that peculiar reedy voice of his, said, 'Let everyone here drink to Galina. I have never seen beauty more exquisitely danced!'

Somehow we managed to keep our spirits from flagging, helped no doubt by the fact that Galina began to look exhausted soon after midnight, and was surreptitiously glancing at her small Cartier wrist watch, as though thinking, 'Won't bed be wonderful!' We broke up at one in the morning, and although the shadow of a threat had fallen across it, it had been a glorious evening.

Father broke the news to the family the next morning, and I telephoned Brig to find out more details. It seemed that the previous day Brig and Igor had been walking near the Champs Elysées when, without warning, Igor collapsed in the Rue Marbeuf.

'I screamed,' Brig told me. 'I didn't know what had happened. He was talking and fell to the ground in the middle of a sentence. A couple of policemen came along quickly, and called for an ambulance. Thank God I was there, we *never* go shopping as a rule. If he had been alone he would have been sent to any old hospital. But I was able to order them to rush him to the American Hospital at Auteuil. I wasn't going to have him looked after by the French.'

'And then?'

'Nicki, it was terrible. He lay there on the pavement looking up at me, while we waited for the shriek of the ambulance. His eyes were wide open, but he couldn't move, he couldn't speak. I cradled him in my arms till the police came. I tried to coax him into talking. It was hopeless.'

I could hear on the phone how overwrought she was, facing a battle that she would have to fight alone. Her speech was disjointed, 'Do you think he'll get better soon?' Even the question made no sense.

'I'll catch the *train bleu* tonight and go round to the hospital first thing,' I promised her. 'And in case you need me, I'll stay near the hotel all today so that they'll know where to find me.'

I wanted to reach Paris as soon as possible, not only because I naturally wanted to see Igor, but for another reason. During the night I had dreamed about poor Igor and woke up in a cold sweat as (in the dream) I saw Brig showing me what I always laughingly described to myself as Igor's 'gloating photos'.

My God! Igor had taken them back before we all came to Monte Carlo. Had he got them hidden away? Or had Brig? And if not now, would she get them soon? Short of burglary there was no way I could find out – yet I must try to find them and destroy them if I could.

Next day I went straight from the train to the hospital. It was an agonising experience. One look into Igor's cold impersonal room gave me the immediate impression that he would never recover. Oh God! I hoped I was wrong, for Igor and I had grown up together, indeed he was only seven years older than I was. With every passing year, we had grown closer, but close in a different way from the happy days of Tsarskoe Selo. And now all I could see was a pitiful, helpless hulk, his mouth half drooping, his body still as death. He lay on his back, his face an unnatural pink colour as though the blood had rushed to his head and stayed there. His hands had been placed by his side and when I touched one hand to squeeze a welcome, there was no response.

His eyes had been closed when I arrived, but without warning he opened them – and then there *was* a response. He could not see me at first, of course, not even when I squeezed his hand, but though he could not move his eyes, it was quite extraordinary the way they lit up the second I leaned over them and he saw who I was.

They *shone* with pleasure.

'He can recognise me, Nurse,' I cried. 'Fetch the doctor.' The doctor was a tall grey-haired man whose short white coat crackled with starch.

'I know he can't speak,' I told the doctor. 'But he *did* know who I was. It looks as though he can understand me.'

'I'm sure he can,' said the doctor. 'He can hear. These are early days, but we've already given him some elementary tests. He can move his eyelids, so we asked him to blink once if he wants to say "Yes" and twice for "No". He can do that.'

'So what are the prospects, Doctor?' I took him aside.

'Not good, I'm afraid – but miracles do happen. At least he's kept his senses. When we found that he can use his eyelids, we asked him, "Bed pan?!" and then "Bottle?" and he responded immediately. No to the first, yes to the second. The Countess insisted, rightly as she can afford it, on day and night special nursing, and if the *patient* wants anything – a bed pan, say – he can change the look of urgency in his eyes, just as he did when he saw you, and then one of the nurses can ask him. This is the most important hope – not only for the chance of a breakthrough, but as it's obvious that you're close friends –'

'I am Prince Korolev's eldest son and heir –'

'I understand you might be able to find a way of talking to him, by asking leading questions,' suggested the doctor.

'I'll try as hard as I can,' I promised, 'but, Doctor, there's rather a delicate matter I'd like to discuss with you.'

'Yes?'

'What happened to the Count's clothes – or rather, the contents of his pockets?'

'They've been put away in a locker. Not in this room.'

'There was a wallet containing letters' – I thought that easier to explain – 'to the Count which I had been keeping. I've never seen them of course, only the wallet, but I'd – er – hate for them to fall into the wrong hands. And if I could take them and keep them for the Count –'

'So that his wife doesn't?' the doctor said drily. He thrust his hands into his crackling pockets.

'Well – exactly.'

'I understand,' he said. 'It's not the first case of this sort. But my own concern is with the patient, and I don't want him to suffer. It might make an enormous difference to his peace of mind if we can find the letters and show them to him. Let's go and see.'

'That's very considerate of you, Doctor. Very.'

The locker room was only a few steps down the corridor and I recognised Igor's camel-hair overcoat immediately, and the dark grey-striped jacket.

Every pocket was filled with the sort of things most men carry – keys, coins and, in the hip pocket, a bundle of currency notes. It was as though they had never been touched. But the inside breast pocket was empty. Nothing, not even a cheque book.

Whatever else he might forget, Igor always carried a cheque book. But not this time.

'Thank you, Doctor,' I said. 'I'm baffled about the inside pocket –'

'It's not my business.' It was not; but his voice was conspiratorial. 'But I'll make a few discreet enquiries. He may not have been carrying the letters, of course.'

'That's true. But it gives me the shivers.' In the meantime there was nothing *I* could do – except wait and see.

As soon as I had tried to cheer up Igor, I went out to buy copies of all the Paris morning papers to see if there had been any reviews of the ballet. Even if Galina was not well known, a new ballet choreographed by Balanchine would be of interest in serious newspapers. I was delighted. The reviews were ecstatic – and more about Galina than Balanchine. The *Figaro* said, 'A new star has been born in Galina.' And *Le Monde*, more conservative and loftily employing the royal 'we' said, 'She has the greatest possibility of any *prima ballerina* we have seen for many years.' Another headlined, 'Triumph for husband and wife team.'

I telephoned the good news to Galina and then promised to send the papers off to Monte Carlo in a large bundle.

'I'll post them from the office,' I promised her. 'They should reach you in a couple of days. They're really terrific.'

'And how's poor Igor?'

I explained all that I knew. 'It's terrible, Galina. Frankly, I'm glad the family can't see him. It's like a page from the Inferno, like the living dead. Just lying there, staring, with me wondering what the poor devil's thinking about.'

'Poor Igor, poor devil,' softly she echoed my words. 'And here's someone who wants to talk to you.' She must have handed over the telephone for the next words came from Tasha. 'Darling Nicki, ' she started.

'Now stop that!' I laughed. 'Just because you're a couple of days older.'

'I'm eighteen now,' she cried. 'I want to see you.'

'Me too, of course,' I was determined to keep the

conversation light, 'but when we do, no nonsense, understand?'

The trouble was – I said it, but I didn't really mean it. I yearned for the 'nonsense'. I wanted her to kiss me, yet behind everything else was the niggling question of her age. I was still a young man, of course, I could still be a healthy and willing lover or husband to a young girl but, I was thinking, I am nearly twice as old as Tasha. Of course it does not matter if one of you is two and the other four, or if one is seventy and the other sixty. But at this particular moment a girl of eighteen was virtually begging to go to bed with me, and whatever my own feelings, I knew Aunt Olga would not take kindly to hearing that I was having an affair with her step-daughter. And if we kept meeting, it certainly would end in bed. It was impossible to hold Tasha back, she was too wild, reckless and exuberant to be kept in check. There was no way *she* would ever take 'No' for an answer!

And I would be the first to cry if she *did* say No – if, that is, we ever did get to the point of Yes or No. There was only one real solution: wait and see if we both felt the same in a couple of years – if, that is, we were given two years of peace. There was so much talk of war, so much was changing in our lives! The threat of war was always close – from the posturing Il Duce in Italy or from the insane ravings of Hitler in Germany; to say nothing of the psychopathic Stalin in Russia. Making plans for the future seemed impossible.

When I hung up the phone after listening to Tasha's goodbye kiss, I was thinking, it is getting on for twenty years since we had clattered along those rutted, dirty, smelly streets, resounding to shouts and curses and oaths, with the gleam of knives in the half light, most of us escaping to our various alternative lives – life, death, the unknown. I was now thirty. How much had happened! We were all growing older! Aunt Olga must be nearing fifty – though she did not look it; and Father, well on the way to seventy, still looked as straight-backed as ever. He had even boasted secretly to me, in a stage whisper, 'But I can still do it, m'boy! Not so often I grant you, but still –'.

But to what end, all this living and dying and suffering? My senior officials in the Red Cross, who always entertained me when they were in Paris, gloomily prophesied that war was inevitable.

'The French and the British have no heart for war,' one warned me. 'The Italians and the Germans are bent on conquering Europe – and Communism. It's a difficult world we live in, Nicki, and my God, when war *does* break out, you are going to be kept damned busy.'

Father returned early from Monte Carlo a week after me, the day after the doctors had decided that, having made all their tests, Igor was what they could call 'stable'.

'It might be just as safe for him to be moved to his own bedroom. We even think that being in surroundings he knows might help to make him better,' said the doctor.

And so, he was taken by ambulance from the hospital back to the Rue St Dominique, and three trained nurses – devoted nuns, all of them – were engaged to keep an eye on him twenty-four hours a day.

The night Father left on the *train bleu*, Olga telephoned me with a warning.

'Treat him carefully,' she said. 'He's not ill you understand, but very upset.'

'About Igor?'

'Partly of course, but it's himself really, though the trouble is more – what's the word? – more psychological.'

'What on earth do you mean?' I asked her.

'He's taken an awful beating at the tables.'

'Oh *that*! I understand. I'll treat him gently.' I promised all this with a half-laugh, for I knew how depressed Father always got when he did not win. Over the phone I could hear a shout in the distance and Olga added, 'He'll live. That was Tasha sending you her love,' adding drily, 'What

197

little a girl of eighteen thinks she knows about love.'

'More than you realise!' I did not *say* the words, only thought them, remembering that inviting look in her eyes when I had opened the bathroom door.

By the time Father arrived I had left for the office, for his train was late reaching Paris. But when I returned home for lunch he was there, looking pretty awful for a man who always prided himself on keeping up a neat appearance. His white beard and hair looked more like cotton wool.

'You look terrible, Father.' The years had given me leave to be more forthright than I would have dared to be when younger.

'It's Igor,' he seemed close to tears. 'It's far worse than I expected.'

'He's been a member of the family as long as I have,' I agreed.

'And poor Brig – I wonder how she must be suffering.'

I wondered. The extent of her grief might depend on whether or not she knew about Igor's secret lover. Then I added, with last night's phone call from Olga in mind, 'No other problems?'

'Should I have?' Out came the old bark and (or was it my imagination?) his handsome moustaches twitched.

'Nothing,' I replied airily. 'But we covered a lot of ground at Monte Carlo. And you,' with a moment's hesitation, 'you played at the tables a lot. Specially at baccarat. I didn't see you win a lot.'

'That's because you don't watch all the time,' growled Father, and called for Lilla to bring in the iced vodka. 'Well, Nicki, I don't see that it's any of your business, but – yes, I will admit that my luck was out.'

'Badly?'

He hesitated. 'Badly is an underestimation,' he muttered bitterly. 'Never saw such bloody cards. Catastrophic. I got into a very big game,' his face reddened as he decided to confess. 'In fact – well, no good beating about the bush, I got *right* out of my depth.'

'That bad?' And half-bantering, 'we're not broke?'

'Not quite,' he replied gloomily. 'You're not going to like this, Nicki, but I needed cash badly –'

'And so what did you do?'

'I – well, I hate to admit this, but I needed the cash so badly – I had to sell the Monique.'

'Father!' I gasped. 'You're joking! You *must* be. The Villa Monique in Switzerland. Oh Father, how mad can you get? Oh no, Father.' My face drained of colour, half anger, half sympathy. 'And all those beautiful flowers,' I added inconsequentially.

'Oh yes, son,' he retorted. 'It's hardly been used since your mother died and that's twenty years ago – and I needed the cash. Otherwise I'd have been drummed out of the casino.'

'I know we didn't use it. But as a capital investment –' I started. 'With all this talk of war, if Switzerland remains neutral, it would be a fantastic haven.'

'Let's hope then that there isn't going to be a war,' he retorted. 'But don't go on blaming me.'

I was appalled. That beautiful if unused villa, which we had visited perhaps three times since we fled from Russia. Gone! Sold to some bastard we had never seen. Thrown away at the turn of a wheel or on the cut of a pack of cards.

'But couldn't you have borrowed money from the Swiss bank?' I asked.

He shook his head. 'I couldn't cash the bonds that give me my income. And the overdraft rates are so exorbitant in Switzerland the interest would have cost me more than our income. It was best to cut my losses. And' – the past flashing into his mind he cried, 'Oh! If only I hadn't entrusted our emerald necklace – the heritage – to Mother. If I'd had the sense to hide it myself. It's worth enough money to buy a dozen Swiss villas.'

'But it's gone,' I said bitterly. 'And we don't have the emeralds. My God, Father. How could you?'

'Stop badgering me!' He was suddenly furious. 'What I do with my money is my affair.'

'It won't be for long, the rate you waste it,' I shouted.

'Meaning what?'

'Come on, Father. We haven't got limitless pockets. How much did you lose? For God's sake tell me the truth – and don't try to minimise anything.'

Suddenly he looked older, more dejected, and I put an arm on his shoulder. 'Cheer up, Father,' I said more gently. 'And I'm sorry I shouted. It's not the end of the world. Let's have another vodka.'

We gulped down a glass each, the fiery ice-cold liquor burning my throat. 'How much?' I asked.

'Ten million francs,' he muttered in a voice so low that I had to repeat the words.

'Ten million francs,' I groaned. 'How *could* you?'

It took a little time to hear the full story, but I got it out of him in the end. Father had fallen into the company of the famous Greek Syndicate – five professional gamblers who had pooled their financial resources in 1919 and had since dominated the highest gambling echelons of Deauville, Cannes, and Monte Carlo. Their combined wealth ran into astronomical figures, which gave them the edge on any opponents in a game of chance, because they could weather a bad run of luck that only the wealthiest could match – men like André Citroën, the Aga Khan, Farouk of Egypt, Baron Henri de Rothschild.

It was into this company that Father's social status naturally admitted him – for, as I heard him say many times after the débâcle, 'They were all *gentlemen*,' as if he were puzzling like a child over the pain that could be inflicted by such attractive things as flames.

Simplified, baccarat is a game of chance. Between three and eleven players can pit their chances against the bank. The cards bear their face value, though all court cards count as ten, and the player who scores nearest to nine wins. Six complete shuffled packs are used – 312 cards – and are dealt from what is called the 'shoe' – a wooden contraption from which the banker slides the cards out one at a time.

Each man is dealt one or two cards, and the Greek Syndicate runs the bank with limitless credit. The player on the left – acting for all the other players – tries to get eight or nine, and thus beat the bank. Each player can bet what he likes against the bank – but any player can bet against the whole of the banker's stake by calling 'Banco'.

On this night, Nicolas Zographos of the Greek Syndicate was running the bank. It had been a tumultuous week of fantastically high playing, so that in the end it was a question of keeping your nerve if you wanted to win. Zographos, small, dark, sunburned, apparently incapable of fatigue, had won more than he lost – because he had one small but distinct advantage. He was able to remember the run of every single card that was played from the shoe – all 312 cards – and so was the only one who knew, towards the end of the shoe, how many eights and nines were left. It was not an advantage in itself, but the fact that he was the only man who *did* know there were only one or two nines left as the shoe began to dwindle, made him bet big.

Earlier in the week, Zographos had won eight million francs against Hilmy Pasha, King Farouk's uncle. Then he won nearly as much from the Aga Khan. But the next night he lost fourteen million francs.

On this night, too, Zographos was losing heavily. According to Father's story, Father had seen the run of bad luck that threatened to cripple the Greek Syndicate. It was astonishing. Four times in a row the bank lost. Then another four times the bank lost, and the punters made big money. Three times more – a run of eleven losing banks. Zographos sent for ten million francs to keep the bank afloat. Father had only been watching the baccarat table, where of course he was well-known. The bank *must* lose now, he thought. It was beyond all the laws of average for it not to. Zographos cried 'Tout va!' meaning 'You can bet the lot if you want to!'

Father cried Banco! – to ten million francs.

Zographos, who was almost cleaned out of money, knew one thing – there were only a few cards left in the shoe – all the eights had gone, and only one nine remained. Father turned up a five and a two.

Zographos pulled his card out of the shoe. It was the nine of diamonds.

13

During the spring and early summer of 1938 I hardly realised the shattering events that were building up under my nose, nor the deepening shadows which fell over the Paris of that fateful year. I had Igor to think of. I had a gloomy Father to think of. I even began to wonder how long our money might last.

Yet, ironically, everyone seemed tranquillised by the splendour of the spring and summer. The Tuileries and the Luxembourg Gardens had never seemed more beautiful, or the chestnuts more brilliant with their candelabra of blossom. Wealth and luxury had driven anxiety away, and gloom was also banished by the presence of Tasha, now more beautiful than ever and – I knew, I knew that it was only a question of time now.

Added to this, the Seine had the mysterious quality of a painting by Monet. Even Father, giving a twirl to his moustaches and eyeing the girls in their summer dresses from his table outside the Deux Magots, said, 'Love is in the air.' The papers announced a state visit in July of King George VI of Britain (a cousin of my murdered godfather the Tsar) and his queen. Versailles and all the showpieces of the capital would be displayed *en fête* and there would be banquets befitting an *entente cordiale*. Nothing seemed more remote than war.

But as the weeks passed from spring to early summer the headlines in *Le Temps*, *Le Populaire*, *Le Petit Journal* and the rest became more urgent. Until then I had scarcely known the names of Daladier, the Premier, or the President, Lebrun, let alone Bonnet, the Foreign Minister. Now these, and others even less familiar – Chamberlain, Beneš, Gamelin – seemed to crowd into my consciousness like shadowy figures. But there was reassurance in the gaiety of the city, in the familiars of my life – Galina, Tasha, Olga, Igor, Father – and in events close to me. Games of political chess were easy to shrug off, though out of curiosity I did ask Father what his opinion of it all was.

'It's that madman Hitler, Nicki; he wants to trample over Europe in jackboots. He's trying to grab the Sudetenland, which is part of Czechoslovakia. Says that the Czechs are ill-treating the Germans in the Sudetenland. All balls! But he says he can only stop the grabbing by force.'

'You mean he'll send an army in to fight Czechoslovakia?'

'That's it.'

I had only a hazy idea where Czechoslovakia was – somewhere miles away on the eastern side of Germany, I thought. I suppose I showed my indifference by shrugging.

'Ah, but Nicki, it's not as simple as that. France, Britain and Russia have treaty obligations. They've promised to fight if Czechoslovakia is attacked.'

As I looked down from the window on to the place de Furstemberg with its pretty lamp-posts alternating with the forsythias, I could hardly imagine armies mustering, the ring of marching boots. But then, as the summer advanced to mid-July and the state visit of the British king and queen took the headlines the threat of war seemed to recede again.

I was brought back to reality with a bump – in the shape of a particularly nasty person I had never met before.

I had gone to the office on a Saturday, not really to work, more to try and overcome the shock of seeing Igor who, far from recovering seemed, as each month passed, more and more unhappy and frustrated. We never worked on a Saturday, and I could not face another morning doing nothing except entertain Father, who was bored to tears without any gambling. I decided to go for a walk and my footsteps led me to the banks of the Seine and when it started to drizzle I automatically sought shelter in the office, empty of course for the weekend.

I was riffling over the mail at my desk on the first floor, which was over an antique shop. In order to climb the stairs you had to press the front door bell and await a response before we in turn pressed a bell upstairs to open the door.

The buzzer sounded. A voice asked, 'Monsieur Korolev.'

I said, 'Yes, what can I do for you?'

'If I could have a word –'

Assuming some poor Russian refugee needed help or advice, I pressed the bell near my desk and waited as I heard light footsteps climb the stairs.

'Monsieur Korolev?' the man asked in a soft voice, and I nodded and waited for him to speak again.

I did not like him. He was thin, short, his dark hair cropped close, he wore an ill-fitting suit, and the straight line of his mouth had the cruel, hard twist of a man who could easily become a sadist. But what I disliked most of all was the limp hand which he held out for the obligatory handshake in the French fashion. Unprepossessing was the first thought that leapt to my mind.

He offered me his card, and I raised my eyebrows. It informed me that he was Inspector André Verron of the Paris police.

'Oh yes?' I was not really interested until he added softly, 'I am in charge of a new specially created force at the Sûreté concerned with tracking down undesirable Russian émigrés in France.'

'Are you?' I was surprised. 'Then we are allies, M'sieu. If we find any Russian spies who've been planted in Paris by the Kremlin, I shall be the first to let you know.'

'Very kind,' he said – was he being ironic? – 'but we know the names of all the spies.'

'Good for you,' I said, uneasily aware of something I could not understand.

'Yes, we arranged their cover stories and so on,' he added smoothly. 'I don't think we'll be looking for the same people.'

'I'm not quite sure what you're getting at.'

Inspector Verron gave me a hard look. 'I have just returned from Soviet Russia.' He announced in a flat sort of voice, 'where as a member of the French Communist party I was the guest of the NKVD.'

'Oh!' I was really surprised. 'I'm sorry.'

'Nothing to be sorry about, M'sieu – or should I say Prince – Korolev?'

'Monsieur. We don't have titles in Switzerland. Nor, for that matter, did I realise that you have Communists in powerful posts within the Paris police force.'

He gave a thin smile. 'You seem surprised. Since the Communists in France will come to power before long, I was ordered to visit Moscow to pick up a few hints on how a police force should be run.'

'And how will you start?'

'By routing out all the Russians whose papers are not in order. There must be hundreds of them in Paris alone. And when we catch one he or she will be shipped back to be greeted by Mr Stalin.'

'Well, we don't have any here and I can't help you, Inspector. And I don't like people who are friends of *Smersh*' – I used the catch phrase derived from two Russian words, *smert shionam* meaning 'Death to the Spies'. 'Good afternoon.'

Apparently impervious to my studied insult, he asked, 'I appreciate that you may be annoyed, but may I have a look at your photographs – your rogues' gallery.'

'Why?'

'In case,' with a Gallic shrug of his shoulders, 'I recognise anyone?'

'Have you got a search warrant?'

'Well, no. But I hoped –'

'No, you may not,' I said shortly. 'The Red Cross is an independent organisation.'

'I can easily get a warrant,' he persisted.

'Then get one. Good day, Inspector.'

'Just a moment, Korolev.'

'*Monsieur* Korolev,' I cried even more angrily.

'My apologies. It will be Korolev without the Monsieur if we lay hands on you.'

'Don't be such an idiot,' I shouted. 'How are you going to dare to touch a Swiss citizen. Now, get out of here.'

'*You* may have a Swiss passport,' he sneered. 'But a lot of your friends don't. And when the war comes – and it won't be long now – I wouldn't give much chance to men like' – he consulted a list – 'the so-called Count Kornilov and so-called Count Trepov, or Count Sergei Mensky.'

'Like most Communists, you're a man of filthy bad taste,' I cried furiously. 'Your Count Trepov is a cripple, Count Mensky works in the Hotel Meurice, and your Count Kornilov works a damned sight harder than you do – as a butler.'

'And their papers? And your father?' He sneered again. 'A very close friend of the late Tsar's. He must be about the only friend of the Tsar's who hasn't been shot – yet.'

'Get out of my sight before I kick you down the stairs.'

I made a threatening gesture, and he backed toward the stairs.

'*Á bientôt*, M'sieu,' he said sarcastically. 'And don't worry, we'll be meeting again.'

'I hope not,' I shouted. 'Get out!'

Without another word he walked out of the room, leaving with me a vague sense of fear, of menace.

How curious that this horrible little man should have picked on Igor, because that very day I had come to a decision. Over the weeks we had learned to communicate so well – and Brig did not *seem* to have seen the tell-tale nude photographs – that after a lot of thought I decided to try and communicate with Igor's girlfriend, to tell her what had happened to him. It was bad enough for poor Igor, but if these two really did love each other, it must be terrible for her too. All I knew was that she lived in Avallon. I determined to discover her name and then write to her.

I cannot detail the months of agony I had undergone in learning how to communicate effectively with Igor. Fortunately Brig had hired as day and night nurses the nuns who were his devoted attendants. But otherwise Igor seemed as though he was doomed to live the rest of his life as a cabbage. He could not move, speak, open or close his lips. He lay there, growing strangely pinker, fed intravenously, a man whose life had been ripped apart on a sunny afternoon in the middle of Paris.

How cruel fate can be! He was an inoffensive friend – or was he, as a philanderer, being paid back for sexual deceits? Yet his hours of dalliance, coupling in strange beds, had never hurt any of his female partners. He had never attempted to break up anyone's marriage – on the contrary, his only fear lay in becoming too involved. So why was he being punished in this wicked way? Or, I wondered as I squeezed his hand, was it just sheer bad luck, the way some people sheltering under a tree during a cloudburst are killed by lightning, while everyone around escapes with nothing worse than a drenching.

At least Igor and I established a firm rapport. We had learned to 'talk'.

The art of 'blink talking' depended on my asking only leading questions that could be answered by one or two blinks. There was no point in my asking 'Whereabouts do you feel any pain?' For there was no 'yes' or 'no' answer to that.

But when I had learned how to steer a conversation through leading questions, I decided that the time had come to find out how to contact his girlfriend, for I realised that his girl must be uppermost in his mind. Several times his eyes seemed to glaze over as though hiding a secret pain. Once or twice I thought something might be hurting him physically, but after I asked him he blinked a firm 'no'.

'Mental?'

He blinked once.

'It's the girl isn't it?'

'Yes,' he blinked.

'Is there any way I can let her know what's happened to you?'

Two blinks.

Thinking quickly, I asked, 'Does she write to you?'

'Yes,' he replied in blinks, and even more quickly I guessed, 'Poste Restante?'

A blink – and his eyes started to shine, because I felt that the nearest Poste Restante to his house was in the post office in the Rue des Sts Pères, opposite the plot of land earmarked for the building of a new medical college – one day, no-one knew when.

'Rue des Sts Pères?' I asked.

He blinked once. Eyes shining.

'Now we have to discover the name,' I told him, not for the moment asking questions but trying to formulate a method by which I could discover it. At first everything proved abortive, until finally I told Igor, 'We'll find it out the tough way. First of all we'll concentrate on the surname, letter by letter. It'll take a bit of time, but all you have to do is blink an affirmative, but don't bother to blink if I've got the wrong letter. I'll go through the alphabet slowly and when you blink I'll stop, and check. This way we'll build up her name. Is that clear? It'll be tiring – for both of us,' I almost gave him a grin, 'but with repetition we can do it.'

So we started and soon reached the letter 'D' and then we had a bit of real luck, the second letter was an 'A'.

Painfully we built up the name. It was D'Arcy.

'That right?' – a single blink that I can only describe as a sign of joy showed that we *were* right. That was the first stage. Knowing the passion for red tape in the Post Office, I next asked the doctor to write a letter to say that Count Trepov had suffered a stroke and could not move or speak.

Armed with this and my official Red Cross card, bearing my photograph, and showing that I was head of the local bureau, I confidently went to the Poste Restante guichet.

The man examined my card, then read the letter. He returned my card, saying, 'That's in order, Monsieur. But this' – he waved the doctor's letter – 'one moment, Monsieur. I'm not sure, I will have to consult with my superiors.'

'But this is from the American hospital!' I cried.

'One moment, sir,' he walked away, only to return with a regretful shake of his head and say, 'I'm sorry, Monsieur, but we cannot accept this. Anybody could have written this – we have no proof of its validity.'

'But what the hell can I do?' I felt so exasperated that I was raising my voice.

'It's not very difficult,' he tried to soothe me. 'All you must do is to get the doctor's letter legally certified by a *notaire*.'

'But that's preposterous! Anyone could sign this with his hand on the Bible and still he wouldn't know if it was true.'

'That is not a matter that concerns us,' said the Post

Office official almost primly. 'The law must be obeyed. Get it stamped and the correspondence will be given to you!'

And, incredible though it sounds, that was just what I did. I sent one of the Red Cross girls – our office was almost at the bottom of the Rue des Sts Pères – and our solicitor, in the Rue Quatre-Septembre, near the Opéra, who had no idea if the document was genuine, signed it and stamped it with his notary's seal.

The Red Cross girl paid the fee, I collected the letter and the same assistant – with the smug, self-satisfied face of an underpaid clerk who has illustrated his superiority – handed me a letter in a blue envelope.

I knew that Brig was going out for dinner that evening. Indeed she had thanked me when I promised to pop in for a few minutes to see if I could cheer Igor up.

'You're an angel,' she had said. And I wondered how her opinion would change if she knew of the letter I carried. I flattered myself that I had pulled off quite a coup in finding the girl's name.

Now I faced the problem of tearing it open in front of Igor and reading out its contents, without having the faintest idea what they would be. I rushed round and, entering the door, smiled at him and waved the letter.

'Do you want me to read it to you?' I asked.

He blinked once – a blink that I can only describe as an ecstatic 'Yes'. I tore open the thick blue envelope. Then, asking the nurse to leave us alone, I read a short note – poignant – amidst tears. It read:

How can you not write, beloved? You leave me in anguish. After promises of eternal love, you cannot even write to say 'goodbye' if that is your intention. As a good Catholic I have sinned. I have given all my love to you in the hope of an eternal bliss. Or have you – God forbid! – been taken ill and I cannot find out in any way? Please write. Silence is a cruel way of breaking a woman's heart.

Underneath, she drew a heart and nothing else.

I was horrified at the look of pain etched in Igor's face, almost as though the shape of his mouth had changed. His eyes glistened with tears which he obviously had no muscular power to shed.

'Now Igor,' I said, brusque on purpose. 'Obviously she hasn't got a clue what's happened. I'll write a good letter on your behalf. You agree?'

He blinked, once.

'So if I write to Madame D'Arcy, Poste Restante, Avallon – is that the address you use?' With a signal of pathetic eagerness, as though to ask me, 'You will?' he blinked once.

'I'll do it now and then send it on Red Cross notepaper and sign it, then she can phone me if she wants to.' I sat down, took out my fountain pen and wrote:

Dear Madame,
Igor has been taken very ill and is unable to communicate with you. I am a great friend of his and am writing this letter to let you know. If you wish to contact me, please do so and I will help all I can. Igor asked me to send all his love.

Then I read it through to Igor and asked him if that would do,

'Wonderful!' He did not say it, of course, but I knew that this was what his blink conveyed.

14

We Russians have a reputation for sudden outbursts of temper, even for an occasional bout of the sulks, but I have never been involved in such a row as the one I had with Aunt Olga – when she found me passionately kissing Tasha.

It was high summer. I had heard no word from the unseen Madame D'Arcy, and poor Igor was becoming gloomier and more miserable by the day, especially as the threat of war seemed to be approaching more inexorably by the hour.

This was in the month of August 1938, in the city of an empty Paris when everyone who could had left for the sea, and you could hardly buy a litre of milk or get a suit pressed, so many of the shops were closed. It was like a ghost city. Before long Tasha – still at the Lycée – would be nineteen – almost the same age as when Mama had married Father – and by then, who knows, France and Germany would once more be at each other's throats.

All that high summer the tension had been mounting, and it was confined to the prospect of war; there was Father's moodiness, with so much of his money gone; Igor with his tragic life; and somehow, within a week after the King and Queen had returned to England, the mood of depression which they had helped to lift from the country started to engulf Paris once again.

Added to that of course we now had to watch the pennies more carefully. We were not poor as such, but (though I did not know this at first) the house in Switzerland had for several years been profitably rented, and Father had quietly pocketed the cash to use on gambling or girls. It was his secret income. Thus, when he *did* sell the property, not only did his extra capital vanish, but his income as well, all handed over to the Greek Syndicate. Father still had an income from shares in Switzerland but even this, with the threat of war looming, had been sharply reduced.

So we all lived on the edge of our nerves, and on this particular evening I arrived back from the office about five to discover a message from Lilla, who had been unwell for several days but had managed to carry on as best she could. The doctor had ordered her to spend a couple of days in hospital while she had some tests. Father, I knew, was out meeting Kornilov, the Trepov butler who was having a day off. Tasha was evidently out shopping.

I let myself into the third-floor living-room, adorned with its ikons, a battery of silver-framed photographs and everything that made this a little corner of Russia. I went to the kitchen fridge for some cold Perrier as I intended to have a Scotch but could not be bothered to decant the ice. On the way back I heard the key turn in the lock and in walked Tasha.

'Just in time for me to offer to take you out for dinner,' I said. 'We're all alone until Father comes home.'

'Don't waste your money now we're broke,' she laughed. It was a standing joke. 'I'll cook something.'

'You'll do nothing of the sort. You're far too attractive to be slaving away in the kitchen.'

'You always say the most beautiful things,' she said softly.

She *did* look beautiful – beautiful but, even more, *desirable*. And with every passing month she became more and more a woman. She did not look in the least like a girl from the Lycée, bored by preparations for her *bachot* exam ('which,' she once announced, 'I have no intention of passing'). She was old for her age, but it was not powder and paint that added to her years; it was the more subtle mixture of beautiful facial bones, a slightly Slavic look, golden hair, long legs, a bewitching smile from her generous mouth, and eyes that sparkled with a devil-may-care

look, always with the unwritten question taunting me,
'Come on – come to bed with me. I dare you to!'

'I'll cook something simple,' she said. 'Blinis. I know
we've got some sour cream, and some red caviar. Okay?'

She had picked up the word 'okay' from American films.

'Nokay,' I retorted. 'We'll go to our little restaurant in
the Rue Jacob. I know it's open in August, and we can
have steak au poivre.' I knew she loved the peppery meat,
covered with its thick creamy sauce, because we had tried
it before.

'I agree!' She laughed and threw her arms around my
neck. 'I'm won over. You're an angel!'

'So are you,' I replied, but huskily. And somehow – no
process of thinking, planning, analysing, even wanting
– our lips met, mouths opened, hearts quickened, and,
breathless with the joy of it all, we locked into an embrace
which I prayed would never end – joining each other in
the first real unthought-of kiss of our lives.

There had been kisses before, one or two passionate
enough to arouse stirrings of physical desire, hastily suppressed – but this kiss was different. It was *pure* – a natural
love kiss, not sex as such, more as though we had both
been touched by the beauty of genuine love. Looking back
over our turbulent lives, I knew that this was the first
moment of real loving. I told her, 'God! I love you. I
always will – you and nobody else, ever.'

Wild and impulsive, she wrapped her arms even more
tightly round me, squeezing me as she whispered, 'We're
alone in the house. Let's go to bed.'

I must have hesitated before taking the final step. Yes,
thinking back, I *know* that I would have finally agreed.
But at that moment, unheard in our excitement, the door
of the sitting-room opened as we stood, locked in love,
mouths joined and transported with love in a way that
made it clear this was no ordinary kiss.

In the open door, her face contorted with sudden fury,
stood Aunt Olga, who had always had a key to the house.

'You bloody bitch!' she screamed, advancing, hand up-raised.

We separated, faces suddenly ashen. Olga's face lost none of its anger. Turning to me, she screamed, 'What the hell do you think you're doing, trying to seduce my daughter.'

Tasha started to talk, Olga cried, 'Shut up, you slut. I'll deal with you later.' Turning to me, she shouted, 'She's only a girl – but you – you dirty bastard. By God, if I were a man I'd kill you.'

'Well, you're not a man, so you shut up,' I cried. '*Shut up*! All right, I was kissing Tasha. Lots of people kiss pretty girls.'

'Not *that* way!' Still angry she made another threatening gesture.

'Touch one of us and I'll –'

'Please, Mama,' Tasha pleaded, 'we were –'

'I know what you were doing, but you keep out of this,' she cried. 'You're a bloody whore.'

'You're a dirty liar,' I shouted. 'How dare you say a thing like that about Tasha? You of all people!'

'You're a sex-mad beast. You're just like your father.'

'You would bring *him* into it,' I jeered, and blurted out, 'after all, you used to be screwed by my father before he married my mother. And I've no doubt you paid for your precious salon in the same way.'

'What do you mean?' her voice had suddenly become dangerously quiet.

'You know perfectly well. They tell me that Mr Selfridge never gives anything away, but he *will* accept payment in kind.' For a split second her mouth opened in shock.

My voice was reduced to short sharp breaths. 'And don't ever call me a dirty bastard again. Understand?'

'I've had enough of this,' said Olga defiantly. 'I've seen what I saw. God knows what you've been up to before in this house.' And to Tasha, she shouted, 'You're not pregnant, are you?'

Still breathing hard, I said, 'Olga, I give you my word nothing has ever happened between us. I give you my word on Mama's head.'

'Nothing happened,' echoed Tasha.

'Be quiet,' cried Olga. 'Go and pack your things.'

'Pack?'

'Of course. You're leaving. Do you think I'm going to leave you here in his – this *brothel* with –' contemptuously, '*him.*'

'But I can't leave, Mama,' Tasha begged, 'after all these years – and close to the Lycée.'

'You can – and you will,' cried Olga.

'But school?' I could see that Tasha was on the edge of panic.

'To hell with school. You're not going back to school. You're starting work tomorrow, young lady, in my salon. And you'll sleep there – so I can keep an eye on you.'

'I won't go, I won't, I won't,' Tasha started to shriek.

'You will.' There was a new, grim, quality to Olga's voice.

Poor Tasha. She burst into a flood of tears, wailing pitifully, 'Don't take me away from here, Mama, please, *please*. I've been so happy –'

'I'm sure you have,' Olga darted a savage look at me.

'Don't be such a damn fool,' I looked at her. 'Can't you see you're breaking her heart?'

'And what about my broken heart? And Rudi's, and all the Russians who are dead – don't you talk about broken hearts to me.'

'You make me sick.' Walking out to the kitchen to get some more Perrier, I heard Tasha cry to me, 'Don't let her take me away, Nicki.'

'Don't be such a baby,' snapped Olga. 'It's time you had a bit of discipline drummed into you.'

As I returned, Tasha, sitting defiantly on a chair shouted, 'I won't go, I *won't*.'

'You will!' As she spoke, Olga walked across and slapped Tasha hard across the face.

'There!' she panted, 'I didn't want to do it – but that'll help you to remember that you're the daughter and I'm in charge. I've looked after you since you were a baby, I lavished all my love on you, and this is all the thanks I get.'

And that was that. With the sweep of a Russian *grande dame*, to whom authority came naturally in the salon, she gathered up all of Tasha's few possessions in the small room she occupied, bundled them into an ancient suitcase, took Tasha by the hand, carrying the case, and led the way out without another word. I heard her clump angrily down the stairs and the door banged as she reached the place de Furstemberg.

My first instincts were of furious resentment that Olga would not believe me, a member of the 'family', after I had given my word that nothing had happened. But then I began to calm down. Alone in the house, lacking the presence of Tasha, I felt lonely. Already I missed her sparkle and sense of fun as much as her passion. The sunshine in the house was missing. But the main reason for my calm was because I was aware that Olga knew instinctively that, in the end, I would not have trusted myself.

When Father arrived later in the evening, I told him.

'Tasha's gone – left home,' I said flatly.

'What on earth do you mean – left home – where's she gone?'

'Olga took her.' I thought I had better explain what had happened.

'And did you go to bed with her?' asked Father.

I shook my head. 'Absolutely not. Just gave her a kiss.'

'She's a damned high-spirited girl,' Father admitted. 'A beauty, too. You're sure?'

'I'm sure.'

'Well, can't be helped. We'll miss the girl, but Olga'll

217

regret it. She won't want to be saddled with a girl around the house all day long – or rather, all night long. She's no spring chicken, but she still can't say no to a man. She'd better enjoy them while she can – before the war comes.'

'You and the war! You've got the war on the brain,' I laughed.

'Well, don't laugh. It's on the way. Don't you read the papers?'

'Yes, I do. But can you believe them?'

Certainly the newspapers were doing their best to scare all of us. WILL THERE BE WAR? *Le Matin* asked in huge type; less dramatically *Le Temps* told its readers that the British envoy in Prague hoped to settle the dispute between the Czechs and Hitler by negotiation. But the negotiations always seemed to break down.

'With German troops massing on the borders of Czechoslovakia and Mussolini ready to fight France, the threat grows every day,' Father said solemnly. 'And as for the statesmen – they're damned cowards, before that lunatic Hitler –'

Yet, deceptively, the heat of summer continued to lull us all. When the papers were not headlining words like 'Mobilisation!' or reporting Hitler's ranting speech to the Nuremberg rally, they printed pictures of people frolicking in 'the longest, driest summer on record'. One of them appeared alongside a declaration by Bonnet that 'France rejected any solution by recourse to arms.' There was a continuous airborne traffic of statesmen to Hitler's hideout in Berchtesgarten. They talked in Paris, in Prague, in Munich, in London; and as the first leaves fell from the chestnuts toward the end of September there still appeared to be no solution. Suddenly the beautiful summer had gone; on Wednesday 28 September thick clouds rolled in from the west and a great storm killed people and cattle in the Loire valley, while in Paris, though there was no storm, the day quickly became dubbed 'Black Wednesday' because war seemed inevitable. There were photographs

218

in English papers of guns in Hyde Park and men digging trenches. The clearest thing of all was that Czechoslovakia was being urged by France and Britain to surrender to Hitler's demands and to allow him to occupy the Sudetenland. And that is just what happened.

Premier Daladier made a nationwide broadcast that evening. All France listened. He had been going to announce that France would honour her commitment to Czechoslovakia and that general mobilisation would begin immediately.

'I have postponed that decision,' Daladier said, 'because Signor Mussolini has interceded and persuaded Herr Hitler to hold back his attack on Czechoslovakia for twenty-four hours. There will be a conference of the heads of the Four Powers at noon in Munich tomorrow, and the only item on the agenda is to settle the Czechoslovak problem. I shall do all in my power to contribute to that settlement.'

When he returned from Munich on 30 September, the world knew that his 'contribution', and that of the British Prime Minister, Chamberlain, had been to give in to every one of Hitler's demands; but on landing at Le Bourget Daladier was greeted by cheering crowds.

The following day the French papers carried pictures of Chamberlain at Heston aerodrome, where he had landed on his return from Munich. He was waving a document which he read to the assembled newsmen, and at the window of No. 10 Downing Street: 'I believe it is peace for our time.'

A few days later Churchill growled to the House of Commons, 'We have sustained a total and unmitigated defeat,' and he was subjected to a storm of abuse. The Czechs had been abandoned. But a respite from war had been achieved.

I was in the office, thinking idly of Rudi, wondering, as I so often did these days, where he was, what he would be doing, whether he would be drawn into war, and trying to

219

fill in pictures of the life he must be living. Almost always these thoughts ended with a sigh of despair. There was *nothing* we could do. That tattered old clipping with its offer of hope of a new life, had quickly proved to be a dead end.

The phone rang.

A gentle voice asked, 'Mr Korolev?'

'That's me.'

'My name is Madame D'Arcy.'

I tingled with excitement, sitting in my old office chair. It was two months since I had sent off the letter, and I had assumed that it was lying in some pigeon-hole behind a grille awaiting collection.

'I'm so glad to talk to you, Madame,' I said. 'Are you – er – in Avallon?'

'No, no,' she gave a small laugh. 'I'm here in Paris. At the Meurice. Tell me please, your letter about Igor was so mysterious?'

Starting with a sigh, I told her everything. 'And that really, is all I *can* tell you,' I finished somewhat lamely. 'But I would like to meet you, Madame D'Arcy.'

'With pleasure. Why don't you come and have a drink at the Meurice?'

'Now?'

'If you can.'

'Half an hour then?' That would give me enough time to walk through the Tuileries and along the Rue de Rivoli. I felt I needed the fresh air.

'Do you think,' she hesitated, 'that I'll be able to see Igor?'

'I don't know,' I confessed frankly. 'We'll talk about it. I realise it would give him enormous pleasure.'

'Me too.'

'But I wouldn't bank on it,' I warned her. 'He's not a very pretty sight.'

'Please come right away. I'll be in the small sitting-room next to the ground floor bar.'

*

She turned out to be charming. I put her age as being late twenties, and she was more warm and appealing than classically beautiful. Her auburn hair was a mass of obviously natural close curls. As I studied her dark blue coat and skirt with its white piping, I revised my opinion. In fact, she was beautiful in her way. Perfect hands, good legs, but it was as though she used the warmth and charm of her character to disguise the beauty that lay behind the first impression.

She was drinking coffee and offered me a cup. 'Or would you rather have something a little stronger?' she asked.

'I wouldn't say no to a whisky and Perrier,' I admitted. 'It's not every day I meet a mystery lady.'

I beckoned to the waiter, who was Sergei Mensky – Count Mensky – and she ordered one, and then, in a low voice said, 'I feel I know you already, Mr Korolev. Igor spoke about you so often and your eccentric father. Is he still a great gambler?'

I laughed. 'Yes, at heart, but he's got little left to gamble with. Perhaps it's all for the best.'

'And poor darling Igor,' she used the 'darling' quite naturally. 'Tell me again what happened.'

I hesitated. It was a struggle to find the words to make a flat statement. And she was the sort of woman who instinctively one wanted to help.

'It's strange,' she said quietly, 'I wondered immediately why he hadn't written to me – and the most ghoulish thoughts passed through my head – and I did even think he might have had some sort of stroke.'

There was nothing I could do at first but nod miserably and mutter, 'Yes, that's exactly what it is, I'm afraid. He's in no pain – or doesn't seem to be. Just, well, immobile.'

'But he must be talking. Otherwise how did you find my name and address?'

I drank some Scotch, and then explained in detail the laborious way in which we had learned to communicate after the doctors had found that his brain was functioning, and that he could wink. 'But it was hard work,' I said.

'How wonderful of you,' she said. 'You must have been very, very patient to help him – and me – so much.' And then she asked the all-important question. 'Tell me – his wife?' It was the only reference she made to the marriage. Then she dismissed the subject. 'I asked you before, is there any chance of seeing Igor?'

I hesitated. I did not really know what to say – the fact was, I did not want to get *too* involved. I *should* try to arrange a meeting – in my mind, not so much because they 'deserved' to meet secretly in the house of a lover's wife, and I would abet it, but because such a meeting could have a therapeutic value. Who knows, the shock might even jerk Igor into some power of speech.

To gain time, fencing with words, thinking over how, if or when, I said politely, 'I feel I know so much about you I can't keep on calling you Madame D'Arcy. It sounds so formal.'

'My name is Anna,' she replied. 'And you are Nicki. Are you a relation of Igor's? I never quite understood why Igor always spoke so warmly about you and your sister Galina.'

I shook my head. 'He's a distant cousin, but we all lived together when we were young and we escaped together from Russia in 1919, disguised as peasants. Then we lived in my parents' house here in Paris until Igor got married.'

'And his wife lives at home?' she sighed.

'Yes. But perhaps I can arrange something. Brig' – Igor must have mentioned her name, I didn't have to explain – 'does go out for some dinner parties, and the butler, a Russian count who's fallen on bad times – he's a very old friend. I'll try to find out when, and then maybe we can slip you in for a few minutes. It would do poor Igor a world of good.'

'I just want to see him. And if I can't be all alone with him, never mind.'

'But you'll have to be careful,' I warned her. 'The nurses

– three nuns – are chatterboxes and they're bound to tell Brig that a beautiful strange woman visited him. I'll have to think hard.'

We did arrange it, finally. Kornilov tipped me off, telling me the first night when Brig was definitely committed to attend a large dinner. I went to fetch Anna in my Renault and we waited until we actually saw Brig leave in her chauffeured car.

Once inside the house, luck was on our side. I was about to explain that I was bringing an old friend when we reached the landing. The nurse on duty was at Igor's door. By now, I knew each of the nurses by sight and one said, 'Would you mind looking after our friend for a few minutes, Prince? He's been sweating and I've got to change his pillows.'

'Of course, Sister, with pleasure,' and as the nurse walked to the other end of the landing, I whispered, 'You've got three or four minutes clear. When I hear the nurse returning, I'll come in before she arrives. That way, it'll look normal, just a casual friend.'

She nodded and I led the way in. Igor of course was expecting Anna, but even so, nothing could hide the almost unbelievable light of joy that burned from his eyes. I left then, closing the door behind me, and so I shall never know what happened; for as soon as I heard the nurse's footsteps I knocked, and walked into Igor's room.

Anna was crying gently, stroking his forehead and Igor's eyes glistened with unshed tears. I had to wait there while the nurse carefully lifted Igor's head and put new pillows underneath.

We 'talked' a few moments by blinking, while the nurse sat in a corner knitting, then ten minutes later we left.

'Poor darling.' Once in the car she started crying bitterly. 'It's the curse of God for the way we've been behaving!'

'No, don't ever think that,' I tried to comfort her, trying to put a few thoughts into words. 'Perhaps these few moments with you have been worth all the suffering, all his life.'

Anna and I had a quiet lunch together two days later before she returned to Avallon.

'You've been so kind and understanding,' she said, 'and I want to thank you. And I want to tell you that I won't be coming again. I think it better. Seeing Igor lying there – it *is* like a punishment from God for what we've done.'

I could say nothing, for the thought had already been implanted in my mind.

'It's heartbreaking,' she said, 'and my heart is already broken. But I'll phone you from time to time at the Red Cross.'

She thought for a moment and then scribbled a few numbers on a piece of paper.

'This is my telephone number at home,' she said. 'Yes, take it. Just in case you need to contact me urgently.'

'But is it wise?'

'I think so. If it's – well – inconvenient for me to talk, I'll just say it's a wrong number and then I'll telephone you when I can. Only as a last resort. But you never know. I might be able to help.'

I took the piece of paper, not really thinking about it, certainly never dreaming that one day I would have to phone her urgently not about Igor, but to help me in an act of life-saving deception.

15

It was three weeks before Tasha telephoned me. Before that not a word. Then suddenly, her voice, husky and pleading with love and misery, she said, 'It's been like prison. But today I've managed to get a couple of hours off. Mama's going out for lunch.'

224

Breathlessly, she added, 'I miss you terribly, but I'm going to sneak out to the Red Cross. Stay in for me, will you? I'll be round in an hour.'

She arrived at half past one, and I was appalled at her appearance. The desirable young woman had been demoted to an overgrown school-girl, simply by wearing a standard French-type school smock, rather like a grey apron. She looked terrible.

'And you look exhausted,' I said, wrapping my arms around her and kissing her. 'You're even out of breath,' and then suspicion dawning, I asked, 'How did you get here?'

'I walked – or trotted.'

'You *walked*? You've no money? How can your own mother do this to you?'

'It was the only way I could get to see you. I never have any money – not a sou. Mama says it's a punishment. I work like a slave, but not for money, only for food.'

'Darling, I'm going round to see that you get a square deal,' I said savagely. 'You're right, it's like being in prison. And at your age – dressed like you are. It makes you look like –' I hesitated for words.

'A freak?' Tasha laughed. Nothing could daunt her sense of fun.

'I didn't say that,' I laughed too. Despite everything, she was shining with happiness, and her laughter made me smile too. 'But you *walked* – all the way from the Champs Elysées – past the Concorde – along the Left Bank.'

'It's a nice day,' she smiled tenderly, 'and it was worth it.'

'What a bitch Olga is. How *could* she do this to you.'

'It's a mother protecting her young,' Tasha answered sardonically.

'Well, I won't tolerate it,' I said angrily. 'First of all it's disgraceful, so we'll start at the beginning.' I unlocked the drawer in my desk, 'Now, here's a supply of French francs. No, darling, don't argue. It's not a fortune, but keep it

225

and the next time you can sneak away, you'll be able to grab a taxi.'

'Or a bus.'

'*No buses*! Taxis.'

'But Nicki –'

'Don't you understand? If you take taxis both ways, we'll have more time together.'

'That's *worth* it,' she almost giggled. 'If only we had a place to make love! But it took so long walking here, I'll have to rush back soon.'

'Don't worry, I'll think of something, if you can come again.'

We discussed ways and means – as yet without doing anything, simply because there was no time or opportunity.

'What's the best time for you to get out – if you've got the money to come quickly?'

She never hesitated. 'Lunch. Mama regards business lunches with top clients, often at their own homes, as what she calls her "selling priority".'

'That's wonderful. How often?'

'Two or three times a week.'

'Marvellous. Leave it to me. I'll fix something.'

And I did. I kissed her goodbye, we fondled each other, and then she had to rush back.

The following day I went to the Salle Drouot, the auctioneers behind the Rue Lafayette. They specialised in job lots of second-hand furniture and I found a splendid long leather button sofa. The next day I picked up a bargain – a second-hand refrigerator, then a mahogany-style cupboard with two doors and above it a three-tier bookshelf. I also bought a couple of armchairs – grey loose covers dotted with blue birds. On the Left Bank I bought some cheap prints and had them framed at the 'instant frame' shop, the last shop before the Rue des Sts Pères meets the river.

In a few days I had transformed a drab office into a reasonably pleasant sitting-room-cum-office with its bathroom next door (into which I put the fridge) where I kept a bottle or two of champagne, some white wine and Beaujolais and of course a bottle of vodka and some safe-to-store items like jars of pâté, butter or *céleri remoulade*.

I arranged with Tasha to phone me whenever she had advance warning. If she did not phone by half past twelve I went out for lunch. If she *did* phone, I nipped out to the *marché* at the top of the Rue de Seine and bought cold meats or chicken and a baguette.

Only one problem remained – the girl assistants. The earlier couples had long since left and had been replaced by two American students. Both had boyfriends and they both knew the 'facts of life'. That was obvious and so, since they did not expect me to be a virgin at my age I decided to tell them everything.

'I've got an – well, a friend,' I explained to Betty, the elder girl, with the other listening, 'and we can only meet at lunch time, and I have no place of my own and neither has the girl. So we meet here for lunch when we can. That's why I've decorated this room and had a lock fixed for my private office. I'll probably stay here for lunch twice a week, so I suggest that we change our work schedules. From today you can both take from twelve to three o'clock for an extended lunch, as I would like to be left alone then. That's generous, don't you agree? Who else in Paris gets three hours for lunch? Agreed?'

With little squeals of delight and the slightest giggles of conspiratorial laughter they made it clear they were delighted – and understood exactly.

The new system worked perfectly. And oh! how wonderful was the excitement and after all this waiting, the blind, mad rush of desire. We lay, almost naked on the sofa in each other's arms for the very first time in our 'courtship'. We kissed each other – kissing mouths, chests, breasts and then further below. The feeling was delirious.

'Be careful, remember this is the first time,' she breathed. 'I've waited so long, my love. Remember that

227

day in the bathroom – you peeping Tom! I'll never stop loving you. Never! Never! Do it now – please. I can't wait any longer or I'll come.'

I could not wait either. As gently as I could, afraid to hurt a virgin, I pressed her to me, and somehow, without any help, she was so excited that I needed no guidance, but just slid inside her and we both started to move with love. It was pure exaltation and I never wanted it to end until at last, with final cries of joy, she gasped and it was over.

'Darling, darling Tasha,' I kissed her, her heart banging against my rib cage. 'At last! Isn't it wonderful when you've waited so long?'

'I'd die if you ever left me,' her breath was coming in short excited gasps.

'I won't!' I cuddled her closer, stealing a glance at my watch. Only two o'clock.

'Now, let's have something to eat and drink,' I said and suddenly thought, 'What about – well, babies?'

She laughed. 'Don't worry. One of the girls who doesn't want babies told me what to do. You didn't notice that I left a small package in the bathroom. A douche. I just fill it with warm water and pour in a spoonful of vinegar. That should stop anything – but you have to do it right away.'

Five minutes later she came back from the bathroom, crying, 'Food! I'm famished. What's for lunch?'

'That's what love-making does for you – gives you an appetite.'

We feasted on paper tablecloths spread out on the old desk, a cold vodka in one gulp to start with, then some paté and crisp bread, followed (on the same plate) with some cold chicken which I had brought along after her phone call.

'The best meal I've had in all my life,' she cried. 'Here – you finish my chicken leg and I'll finish yours!' We swapped the last pieces of chicken, each tearing it off the

bone with our fingers, and I said, 'Darling Tasha. I've
got no coffee. Shall we go and have coffee at the Deux
Magots?'

'I daren't,' she shook her head. 'Someone might spot us
and, without thinking, tell Mama. No, let's be happy and
take no chances. I'll walk through to St Germain and pick
up a taxi there. And God bless you, beloved. I'm crazy
about you. And I love the way you make love. All our
lives until we grow old,' she sipped the cold Beaujolais,
'we'll do it.' Gnawing the chicken bone – my chicken bone!
– she looked up with apparent anxiety and asked, 'How
long does this beautiful love-making go on for? When does
this divine fire die out?'

'You'll be fed up with me long before that happens,' I
laughed. 'But now you *must* go,' I ordered her. 'It's twenty
to three. Off you go, don't let's spoil this beautiful arrangement.' I took her to the front door, kissed her before I
opened it, and she ran off, looking a happy schoolgirl, to
find a taxi.

We *did* take care, our secret was undiscovered through
most of 1939. One weekend, when Olga had to go to
London to see Selfridge, I borrowed Father's car, which
he rarely used now, and took her away to a small hotel
called Le Forêt de Fontainebleau, deep in the forest itself,
surrounded by painters and young lovers, and there in a
huge double bed, with coffee and croissants in bed for
breakfast, we lived for two glorious nights as man and
wife.

Naturally, it was not like this every day. Life had to go on.
I paid regular visits to Igor. I had to look after Father,
becoming easily irritated by now, and even Olga finally
started visiting the house again from time to time, bringing
with her a docile Tasha, secretly laughing behind her
mother's back, especially on one or two occasions when,
earlier on that very day, we had secretly made love, and
now were talking politely to each other as though the

family quarrel had made us half strangers. We never mentioned that fight until, on one visit, Olga said to me, when she caught me alone, 'I have forgiven you for that disgraceful episode when I caught you kissing. I believe you were telling the truth.'

'I was, Aunt Olga,' I replied, conveniently forgetting to add the word, 'Then.'

Suddenly, almost without warning, we were in the summer of 1939, and on the brink of war. The first official warning details came in an urgent phone message from the Red Cross in Geneva on 23 August. It was from Philippe Peter, my boss in Switzerland. He pronounced his surname 'Petter' – and he was always known as 'PP'. Without preamble, he said, 'Thank God you were in, Nicki. Yes, I'm fine. I want you to catch the night train to Geneva.'

The prospect of a trip to prettified, orderly Geneva, hopefully with the sun shimmering on the lake, excited me.

'When?'

'Tonight.'

'*Tonight!*'

'That's it.' PP affected a crisp authoritative language which he felt went with his image.

'Of course, PP. How long for?' I was thinking of the next lunch with Tasha. How to let her know I was going.

'Only one day. Two or three if you want to. On expenses. I'm organising informal meetings of our European agents to decide particular problems when war breaks out.'

'*If*, you mean.'

'No, *when*. It's certain now. And we've got more Russian refugees in Paris than anywhere else. In America we've been able to gain full citizenship for thousands. But, as you know, it's not so easy in France.'

I did know. Plans to settle Russians living in Paris had foundered like so many corpses drowned in the wash of sloppy French plans, and even worse, lack of putting them

230

into operation. It was an old story which had started back in 1917. France had lent Russia ten billion francs. After the 1917 Revolution the Bolsheviks refused to repay the loan. As a direct result, Russian exiles in France officially became internees, and that meant regular reporting to the police. This condition prevailed throughout the 1920s, when the Red Cross tried to intercede on the Russian emigrés' behalf by certifying their innocence with a *carnet d'authentiquer*. These *carnets* were issued by our offices and in Paris included co-operation between me and the police. Declarations had to be made by the émigré concerned in the presence of a notary.

In Paris there was a flourishing unofficial trade in 'citizenship deals' and crooked lawyers made fortunes out of bribes – often jewels – though by 1934, when Russia joined the League of Nations, this eased the citizenship situation. Then Russia was expelled from the League for her attack on Finland. Immediately the Russian colony in Paris faced renewed internment laws, though few were treated harshly. The main problem was that some went underground and allied themselves with Communist organisations and were sometimes imprisoned as 'enemies of the Republic'. For the most part, though, Russians were treated with tolerance as members of a fallen aristocracy.

All this, of course, I knew, especially as Inspector Verron had obtained the necessary powers to examine our books and made frequent visits to our office to check on any new information. I found it highly ironic for now, with war on the doorstep, everything had changed, thanks to Hitler's shrewdness and the antics of a German champagne salesman diplomat called Ribbentrop.

It had happened mainly because the dithering French and British politicians had lost the chance to sign a non-aggression pact with the powerful armies of Communist Russia. They had banked on the fact that Hitler was Russia's mortal enemy.

How little they knew! Hitler *did* loathe the Communists,

but as Father had said, 'Even Hitler can't be mad enough to fight a war on two fronts.' So, on 14 August 1939, he sent Ribbentrop to Moscow to talk with Stalin. Twelve hours later these mortal enemies, Russia and Germany, signed a non-aggression pact. It was announced on 21 August – and meant one vital thing: Hitler could now be confident that he would not have to fight a two-front war.

All this flashed through my mind as PP was talking on the phone, telling me, 'Each man who's visiting us will talk to one top man from head office. We don't want any seminar-type lectures in which nobody really learns anything.'

'I agree.' And for the moment, left it at that. 'Tonight,' I promised. 'I'll be on the night train. See you tomorrow,' adding as an afterthought, 'By the way, will I have the chance to see my old chum from Geneva?'

'Who's he?'

'The man who taught me my job – François Savin.'

'I rather think you will,' said PP with a half chuckle. 'It just happens that he's the man deputed to talk to you about our plans for handling the Russians once the French are at war.'

'That's wonderful,' I cried, my mind recalling the young Swiss who hated hard work, who came to Paris when I started learning the job at eighteen, and spent a year there before he handed over the bureau to me. François – the man who had boxed with Ernest Hemingway, who loved Paris night clubs in those happy-go-lucky days and nights in the second half of the twenties – must be getting on for forty, I reckoned.

I was put up at the Richmond, right on the lake, and told to report to the League of Nations in the Parc de l'Aréna, with its adjoining Botanical Gardens facing the lake; and there François was, waiting to greet me.

He had hardly changed, still the same big bluff friend, though now he had the hint of a paunch.

'Wonderful to see you, Nicki,' he threw his arms round me. 'Welcome to Geneva. We'll get through the business first. PP wants you to dine with him tonight.' He was much more serious now; as happens so often, a spell of 'fun life' is often followed by a serious settling-down, and François certainly knew his subject.

'Sorry to drag you away from your beloved Paris,' he said. 'Those were great days. Nothing to do really!'

'It's changing now.'

'It certainly is. Everybody in the Red Cross is really worried. Including me.'

'It hadn't escaped me,' I said drily.

He cleared his throat. 'No. Well, you'll know all about this nonsense that's going on.'

'Half the time I can't make head or tail of it,' I admitted. 'We went through it all last year, and it seemed as if we were on the brink of war, then the threat cleared off. Now –'

'There's no doubt about it, this time, I'm afraid. I'll lay you a hundred to one that there'll be war inside a couple of weeks.'

'And you –?' I left the sentence unfinished.

'Well, Switzerland's neutral as always, and we've got Swiss passports. We'll have other work to do.'

'I'll meet my liabilities, whatever they are,' I said.

'Of course, of course. Your liabilities will go towards helping your true compatriots, the Russian émigrés. It's going to be intensified from now on. You saw the announcement of the non-aggression pact Ribbentrop signed with Stalin? The Germans really beat the French and the British to it.'

'So Russia and France are now enemies!'

François nodded. 'You've said it. But it isn't so much Russia the *nation* you've got to worry about: it's *individuals* – the Russian colony in Paris. They'll all become enemy aliens officially.'

'But –'

His face looked worried. 'I tell you this: when war flies

233

in at the window tolerance goes out through the door. There'll be a round-up.'

'Internment?'

'Could be.'

'But they're all living there quite legally,' I protested. 'As you know Geneva's been issuing *carnets* for years.'

'When it comes to war, Nicki, *carnets*, naturalisation papers, what-have-you – these don't count for much. It's a man's country of origin that counts. The authorities will be going through the records like mad. What they're afraid of is the underground Communist organisations. And if they find any irregularities – papers obtained through crooked lawyers and so on –' He made an expressive gesture with his hands. 'You're going to have your work cut out, Nicki.'

I could see his point. 'Maybe there won't be a war,' I said with a cheerfulness I did not really feel.

But of course there was, on 3 September 1939. That infamously memorable date.

Tasha and Olga and I took a walk in the Luxembourg Gardens. The last trumpet-shaped blooms had fallen from the heaven-trees and lay shrivelled in the sun-dried earth. It seemed like the end of life.

PART THREE

1940–1941

16

Those first months of the *drôle de guerre* had a somnolence that was sinister. Superficially little happened. There were reports of advances and 'resistance to the enemy' and changes in command, as if some leisurely chess game were being played – until, at the end of May 1940, the British Expeditionary Force was cornered after an unbelievably fast 'Blitzkrieg' through Belgium by German troops. The BEF was evacuated at Dunkirk, Belgium surrendered. We were shocked with the horror of it all; Rouen and Dieppe fell and on 11 June Paris was declared an open city. Three days later German troops marched down the Champs Elysées and goose-stepped under the Arc de Triomphe.

Then came the final blow. Marshal Pétain, a doddering old man of eighty-four, the hero of Verdun in the Kaiser's war, asked Germany for an armistice. On that morning even Father, old soldier though he was, saw no hope for a defeated France. 'Not vanquished, my boy, but defeated; yes – defeated.' His voice had lost something of its booming splendour. And so it seemed. There had been a great exodus of refugees, so that barely a fifth of the population was left in the city; but now German troops, carrying cameras instead of rifles, began to wander the streets like tourists gazing at the sights. Officially they were allies of Russia, and they allowed us, as Russians, freedom of movement; but they were not people I could take to. Once the French were beaten, however, my work changed. Before then my task had been twofold – to weed out subversive Communists, and to protect refugees who were fleeing the Communists. But after June 1940, I had no more 'protecting' to do because Germany, now the master of Europe, was 'friends' with Russia even though she nursed a secret hatred of *all* Communists.

This eased my work considerably, for I had spent a lot of time providing legal papers for Russians, finding jobs for them now that so many Frenchmen had first been mobilised, then taken prisoner. Getting jobs for refugees was the simplest way of preventing them falling quickly into the clutches of men like Inspector Verron. In fact I had to go to the Prefecture to arrange for some passes from the Germans who had an office there, and I took the opportunity to pay the inspector a visit in his small cubbyhole of an office opposite the Palais de Justice.

'Good morning, Inspector,' I started cheerfully, thinking 'God! what a loathsome creep this man is.'

'What do you want?' he growled. He glared at me from beneath vulturine eyelids.

'Had to come to the Prefecture, so thought I'd pop in just to thank you for not annoying my Russian friends.' I gave him a smile, knowing he would dearly have loved to throw them all in jail; and after waiting for a split second, thrust the barb of hate deep into a wound where I knew it would hurt most.

'How does it feel to be an inspector of police who has to take his orders from a German?'

He stood up, almost shaking with fury. 'Get out of my office!' he screamed at me, and then shouted to a young policeman standing just outside the inspector's door, 'Kick this man out of here!'

Startled, the young policeman looked at him, then at me, and I smiled to him, 'Don't worry. I'm going anyway,' and, with a final sneer, I added, 'My best regards to Major Konrad Ullmann. He's your boss, isn't he?'

Without turning to see the effect on Verron, I walked across the courtyard and through the main entrance, and breathed long and deep draughts of fresh air. 'That tastes marvellous,' I thought.

I had already been asked to meet Ullmann, a major of the old school. I had arrived at the Crillon where he had an office, and later he came to see me in our Red Cross headquarters. He was in his late fifties perhaps, a quiet, rather handsome man, tall and thin, who seemed more at home with books than guns. He wore his uniform with a certain elegance and only in his thin, straight mouth did I detect a touch of cruelty. He was in charge of Red Cross and all 'foreign' activities. This included rounding up Britons who were interned in Fresnes. If they caused any problems, Ullmann sent for subordinates. He did not want to be party to any physical violence himself.

Always mindful that I was not a beaten Frenchman but strictly a neutral, I said. 'Please sit down, Major.'

'Thank you, Mr Korolev. I hope I'm not interrupting you?'

'Not at all,' I replied. 'I'm just waiting for a relation of mine. She wants a paper signed.' This was Olga who needed some official document. She was coming in an ancient taxi, and had announced, 'I shan't stay. These taxis cost a fortune, but he has promised to wait for a few moments while you sign.'

'I quite understand,' said Major Ullmann. 'War is a bad business,' he lit a small cigar, 'and it seems so crazy for people such as us to be fighting each other. But,' with a shrug of his shoulders, 'what can we do?'

'Stop it!' I cried, and I wasn't being facetious.

'If only we could, my dear fellow. Sometimes I envy you Swiss more than anyone else on earth. A country of eternal peace! Ah well! To business.'

He seemed so pleasant that I offered him a vodka from the refrigerator, and he accepted with alacrity.

'Not *quite* the same as German schnapps perhaps,' he smiled, 'but an excellent drink. Prost!'

'What can I do for you, Major?' I asked him.

'Just a courtesy call. I wanted to reassure you that, providing people behave properly, I have no intention of causing any trouble, particularly among the Russian colony in Paris. I am hoping that our relationship will continue as quietly as it has begun. The – er – next best thing to peace, *hein*?'

'Thank you, Major, I appreciate that.'

'I know that most of the men with whom you are dealing fled from the Bolsheviks,' he continued. 'I appreciate that. We Germans do not like Communists – no-one, not a single one – but alas, we need their raw materials for war – and the certainty of having them as allies so that we won't be threatened with a war on two fronts. But,' he twiddled his glass as though hoping for a refill, 'after we have finished off the British,' his voice suddenly went soft, 'then we may have to deal with the Russians.'

'But the British? Why are you so sure –?'

'My dear friend, yes, thank you, this vodka tastes so good. The British? It is only a question of time. Meanwhile, let's hope that we can meet occasionally! I have had a few words with the office in the Sûreté which deals with the Russian refugees –'

'Verron?'

'That's the man.' He gave a gesture of distaste. 'Not quite what we would call a gentleman.'

'A horror!' I couldn't stop laughing. 'And a double-dyed Communist as well.'

'Is he now? I must keep my eye on him. And if you have any trouble, don't hesitate to let me know. I have a suite at the Hôtel Meurice as well as my office in the Crillon.'

'That's very considerate of you. I may take you up on it.' I was thinking, how easy it was, when discussing business with a civilised enemy, to get on easily with the representative of a country I disliked.

At that moment the entry bell rang on the outside door, and I buzzed Olga so she could climb the stairs.

'This is my relation,' I explained and when Olga arrived at the door and came in, I presented her, 'Countess Arensky, Major Ullmann. The Countess owns a salon called Olga.'

'A famous name!' The Major clicked his heels.

'Sorry if I interrupted anything,' said Olga. 'But I did tell you I was coming. I just wanted –' she spread out a paper requiring my signature.

'Please,' said the Major politely to me, 'ignore me if you wish to help the Countess.'

'Thank you, Major,' Olga smiled, and turned to me. 'It's just this signature please. For my *carte*. The usual – the annual guarantee of my good behaviour for another twelve months.'

'And how is Tasha?' I asked her, explaining to Ullmann that Tasha was Olga's daughter.

'Fine. Being properly looked after in the salon,' replied Olga stiffly. 'Thank you for your help. Good afternoon, Major.'

'Good afternoon.' He bent over her hand. 'But – may I give you a lift home, Countess?'

After the shortest possible hesitation, Olga smiled gracefully and said, 'That's very kind of you. I'd be most grateful.' She gave him a dazzling smile, and added, 'You go down first, Major. I'll follow.'

In the few seconds when Olga, following the Major, was left alone in my room, she hissed, 'I've got my special taxi waiting. Go and send it away after the Major's driven me off. I want to cultivate this man. He might be useful.'

Taxis were hard to get in Paris, unless you paid over the odds as Olga did. I walked down the stairs, just in time to see the back of the Major's Mercedes, and told the driver that he would not be needed.

He had seen Olga drive off in the German car. No doubt about that, for he looked at them speeding towards the Tuileries, and he spat with disgust, saying one word only, for both of them.

241

'*Salauds*!'

Apart from my work at the Red Cross, the first year of German occupation is one that I find difficult to describe in simple narrative form because at times the reasons for certain actions were not always easy to understand. Only in hindsight does the past unravel itself.

One thing *was* quite clear: the increasing friendship between Aunt Olga and Major Ullmann. The lift he gave her at that first meeting had been followed by regular discreet dinners – and the attraction of a good meal was not to be underestimated, for life in those days of 1940–1 was miserable.

Everything from taxis to tobacco, from whisky to coffee was in short supply. The easiest liquor to buy was 'bathtub gin'. Life was regulated by an inventive *marché noir* supplied by farmers who provided butter, bread, cream, joints of beef or lamb, bottles of brandy, all for newfound 'friends' or newly invented 'relatives' ready to pay fortunes for food. Everywhere we were stifled by the atmosphere of lackadaisical acceptance of the facts of existence, with the underlying shame of a cowardly defeat. Even the Ritz could not shake off the lethargy though Maxims managed to provide the best food in town, presented by the wobbly-jowled maître, Albert, who always kept the best cuts of steak for the Germans, reserving the corner table on the right of the main salon for Reichsmarschall Goering on his visits to acquire masterpieces of art for his rapidly growing collection.

The cafés in Montmartre and Montparnasse existed in an equally dismal fashion. There might be stocks of real coffee at Maxims, but the Deux Magots was reduced to acorn coffee and whatever drinks, other than red wine, they could scrounge from friendly but avaricious suppliers.

But for me, though, one real happiness remained that no war could change – the joy of my love for Tasha. It was more difficult to meet frequently, for the fall of France had been followed by acute petrol rationing, which meant fewer taxis, until the ingenious French started running their taxis on liquid gas, stored in silver grey balloons anchored to the roof of the taxi, with a pipe leading directly to an adapted engine. If she was lucky, Tasha, being beautiful, got one of these, but it was becoming more and more difficult.

Then a miracle happened. One afternoon Olga telephoned Father while we were drinking a precious *fine à l'eau*, and when he sat down he said, genuine astonishment on his face, 'Well, I'll be damned! That was Olga, and do you know what she's doing? She's going to live in the Hôtel Meurice.'

'What's going to happen to Tasha?' was my immediate reaction.

'That's the only thing that'll make you happy,' Father almost chuckled. 'First she asked me if I knew that she'd caught you kissing Tasha. Wanted to warn me. Of course I told her that I knew, that it was quite harmless and so on. Finally, she came out with it – the Meurice was too expensive for two, so she's decided, if you please, to send Tasha back here to the place de Furstemberg.'

My brain gave an enormous leap of excitement, my heart began to bang against my ribs.

'To this house? *Here?*' I could hardly control my voice.

'That's what she says, for she made me promise that I'd be responsible for your good behaviour. I ask you! Tasha must be over twenty by now. How can I tell *her* what to do?'

I tried to take in the news: to have my darling Tasha home again! A gift from the Gods! – But I was also thinking, 'Can Olga really afford the Meurice? It sounds absolutely crazy, however many dresses she sells to the Germans.'

'Maybe she won't be paying,' suggested Father drily.

'You don't mean –'

'A gentleman friend? Why not?'

243

'Impossible,' I said firmly. 'Olga is too occupied with her work.'

'Well, we'll see, she's arriving soon.'

Two hours later Olga and Tasha arrived. Our joyous reunion was muted, first by caution, secondly by the fact that Olga was as usual in a rush because she had a precious taxi waiting.

'I hope you take good care of this girl,' she warned Father, and then stared at me, almost accusingly. But I had eyes only for Tasha; and my mind echoed words from the past:

> I come again with greetings new,
> To tell you day is well begun . . .

'What's this nonsense about staying at the Meurice?' asked Father. 'I thought it was filled with Germans.'

'What nonsense you do talk,' she snorted. 'Chanel is staying at the Meurice and what's good enough for her is good enough for me. Staying at an hotel is one easy way of halving my work. Now I won't have to bother with ration cards, housekeeping – it's as simple as that. Now I've got to go. Be a good girl, Tasha, I'll be visiting again soon.' She went. And Father followed her, muttering, 'I've got to go out. Back for dinner.'

I grabbed Tasha under her arms and twirled her around, swinging her like a baby. 'Oh! my darling Tasha.' I led her instinctively into my bedroom. 'Isn't life wonderful! Let's make love now, this minute.' For, although we were already lovers, this occasion was different – a kind of celebration. From now on we would be able to meet every day, and she would sleep in my arms each night. As she slipped off her clothes, I fumbled, rushing, trying to take off my trousers. 'Never mind your shirt,' she gasped. 'Let's do it now.' She had only a small slip on now, she pulled it up to her neck. I stroked her young and beautiful breasts, then her thighs and the join of her legs and she moaned,

'Put it in. *Please*.' And I knew that she – no less than me – would not be able to wait.

Instinct, love, lust – it was as easy, and as natural, as two animals mating; and as I tried to reach as far as I could into her body – just one thrust, then one more – I felt the rush of her inside me, all over me and I poured my love to mix with hers at exactly the same moment. She shuddered gently, then arched her back and gasped, 'Ah! That's the last half-second of pleasure,' and I panted, 'I will love you forever, Tasha. For ever and ever.'

I was still lying on top of her, my trousers dangling over the edge of the bed, as she stroked my face with her own particular brand of gentleness and whispered, 'We're together now. Nothing will ever part us again. You're all my heart, Nicki. All I ever want – except –'

'Except what?'

With that slow, teasing smile, she kissed me gently, and said, 'You're getting hard inside me.'

I was. I could feel myself growing once more.

'Again,' she whispered, and this time it was gentle and controlled, bathed in our internal warmth, and I moved so slowly that I could feel the grip of her nails each time I reached the end of a slow thrust and this time it was she who could not wait and as she came I gave one final gasp of pure joy and it was all over.

I had hardly spoken so far, I was too excited, and with the clarity of thought that follows an orgasm, I was already busy visualising plans, formulating schemes. Where would we sleep? Dare we let Lilla into the secret? Now that we did not need transport Tasha's return to our home opened up an entirely new world. Supposing that? Supposing this? My thoughts were flitting across the exciting prospects of our lives.

'Calling me a girl!' said Tasha. 'I'm a *woman*. And as for staying at the Meurice – a likely story!'

'What do you mean?' asked Father, who had returned.

'It doesn't matter – really,' Tasha hedged.

'What's the likely story – wasn't that what you said?' Father asked.

'All right, I'll tell you, although you've probably guessed already. She's not paying a sou at the Meurice. Not a damned sou.'

'Who is, then?' Father frowned.

'A German. She's become the mistress of a Nazi officer.'

I could scarcely find words, my throat was dry. 'I don't believe it. Yes, I do. I bet I know who it is.' I felt suddenly sick.

'That man she says she met at your office. Major Ullmann,' Tasha continued.

'Him!'

I had never seen Father so red in the face. 'I know the chap.'

'You know Ullmann?' I asked incredulously. 'How did you meet him, Father?'

He hesitated, then muttered, 'Only a casual acquaintance. We met playing cards. I go to the Meurice occasionally.'

'You play cards with Germans!' I couldn't believe it.

'Ullmann isn't a bad sort.'

'Not a bad sort,' I exploded. 'Seducing Aunt Olga then playing cards with you.'

'We don't play cards together,' said Father stiffly. 'It's a few others. I just happen to see Ullmann there from time to time. And anyway, there's a hell of a difference between having a drink with a German and sleeping with one.' He was on the defensive.

I could not help laughing. 'Point taken. One tapette in the family is enough.'

Even so Father, for all his anger over Olga's behaviour, *was* meeting Germans.

'No riff-raff,' he said. 'Only the good type, and senior officers – majors, colonels, generals. Damn it all, you can't be cut off from everybody, and –' he tried to explain but uneasily, adding, 'After all, the Russians and the Germans may be strange bedfellows, but we *are* allies.'

'But you still hate them!'

'The gentlemen are not so bad,' he said cagily.

'Perhaps not to meet at big functions – but to *gamble* with?'

'What do you mean?' he blustered. 'All right, we do have the occasional flutter, but it's quite harmless just to pass an evening with free drinks for me. You know I haven't got the money to play for big stakes. We only play *zehn*' – this was a dice game called *passe-dix* in French – 'and,' he added, 'I always win anyway. They're real suckers, the Germans.'

'They're still Germans,' I retorted.

Defensively, again, he replied, 'These are different. The kind of well-bred officers with whom I get on well. Fellow officers, friends or enemies. They're my kind of men. And after all, *I'm* not at war with them.' Yet there *was* something odd about Father's friendship with them, and his going two or three times a week for an evening of dice.

Zehn is quite simple, a dice game parallel to baccarat, popular in America, called *ten-spot* or *birdie*, and is played with three dice. Each player becomes banker in turn. Every time a player throws a total below ten, he and all the other players lose their stakes to the banker; but when ten or more is thrown the banker must double all the stakes in a pay-off to the players.

The most curious thing about these meetings, though, was that Father always won, yet I knew that he was not a good gambler, especially at a game like *zehn*. I could not help wondering why, until one day Sergei Mensky – Count Mensky – told me what was really happening.

I had gone to the Meurice, ironically enough to meet Ullmann. I was half an hour early, and Sergei was serving the tables in the cocktail bar. As soon as he saw me he hastened to take my order, giving me the proper deferential smile of waiter to customer but somehow conveying anxiety. He carefully placed my beer on a fresh coaster beneath which I could see the edge of a slip of paper.

'Merci, M'sieu.' He withdrew – my glance telling him I had seen the note. The place was full of German officers, but I read the message by holding it against the list of drinks as if I were merely checking prices.

'I have important information. Must produce my *carte* for routine inspection at Gestapo immigrés branch tomorrow. Be in the vicinity.'

Knowing Sergei as well as I did, I realised it must be important. The next day I hung about for over an hour while the queue filed in to have their papers checked by Ullmann's staff. In a bookshop opposite I could browse while keeping an eye on the diminishing queue. At last I saw Mensky come out. We strolled on opposite sides of the road to the nearest Métro, then when we entered the train, sat on adjacent seats.

'It's your father, Nicki. I begin to be a little worried about him.'

'His gambling, you mean?"

'His *successful* gambling, rather.'

So someone else had noticed Father's run of good luck – with the Germans.

'But surely –'

Sergei put a hand on my elbow. 'Please, Nicki. We are friends, off-duty friends now, we do not have to be customer and servant, I can speak honestly.'

'Of course,' I reassured him.

'They have a private room for their little games, and your father is accorded his proper title – Prince – and it pleases him. Because he is an aristocrat, and Major Ullmann and his friends always speak deferentially of aristocrats in the German hierarchy – the Habsburgs with their Archdukes and their Emperors, and so on – they gain his confidence. And tricksters need to gain the confidence of those they are to trick.'

I failed to see how they could be cheating him when he

won so frequently, even though I had no doubt the stakes were small since Father could no longer afford to play for big sums.

'It's what the Americans call "a come-on",' Sergei explained. 'I'm often on duty in that room and I listen. Sometimes when the Prince goes to the washroom, I hear snatches of conversation. Remember my father was at the Russian Embassy in Berlin and I was with him? I understand enough German.'

'And –?'

'Nothing incriminating of course – but the stray remarks I've heard make me believe they're gradually getting your father in their grip.'

'By cheating?'

Sergei shrugged as the train thundered into a station. 'Not loaded dice of course. Too obvious. The routine politeness is always gone through before every game begins.'

I must have looked baffled, for Sergei added, 'When I'm on duty, I'm summoned to bring a glass of water and three dice are dropped into it one by one. Loaded dice turn over when dropped in water, always landing on the weighted side. It's as simple as that. I heard your father protest once, wave his hands and say, "We're all gentlemen here, no need for such a demonstration." But they're equally insistent on the *politesse*, which I'm sure they wouldn't be if they weren't leading up to something.'

'But,' I said, 'if the dice aren't loaded –?'

Sergei smiled at my ignorance. 'There are plenty of other ways of loading dice in your favour. One is to have dice that are not precisely cubic: two surfaces are a fraction longer than the others. Such a die will land most often on its long sides. And of course it's not noticeable. Another is more blatant – the dice have slightly rounded edges on certain sides and will land less often on these. And an expert can conceal crooked dice in the palm of his hand and substitute the straight ones when it's to his advantage.'

'You seem to have learned in a good school,' I said with a hint of sarcasm.

'One is not an attendant in the washrooms of seedy bars for nothing, Nicki; and I was not always a waiter in the Meurice, as you know. More goes on in washrooms than the purposes for which they are provided – and that doesn't exclude our Meurice.'

Sergei got off at the next station, leaving me worried, for I knew that if the plan were to lure Father into a big stakes game and he lost and could not pay his debts, he would be an easy prey for the Gestapo.

But for what reason? What secrets could he possibly give to the Germans?

Barely two weeks later I thought the trap had been sprung. I arrived home at about seven o'clock to find Father sitting alone, slumped in his favourite chair, examining, yet not seeing, an old Fabergé watch. His face was a mask of fear or pain, and I thought as I looked, 'Uh-uh. He's blown it!'

As gently as I could, I asked, 'Bad news, Father?' Though I must admit I was feeling more anger than pity. 'What is it?'

To my astonishment he started crying, then mumbled, spluttering through his tears, so that I could hardly hear, one word that tightened all my nerves until I thought I would explode at the terrible sense of unexpected shock.

'Galina,' he stumbled over the word.

'Galina!' Every thought of Father's gambling debts was wiped away. 'Galina?' It was a question now. 'What –?'

He was almost choking, trying to force the words out. I wanted to shake news out of him; I could control myself only by an effort. It seemed ages – though in real life barely a minute – before he managed to straighten a few words out of a hesitant jumble.

'Murder – killed a man –' Father clenched his hand over the little Fabergé watch. 'Not Galina – that husband of hers – that Jean-Pierre –'

17

The world seemed to collapse around me.

'Try and talk sensibly, Father,' I pleaded, taking his hands and unclenching them. Trembling myself, I poured us both stiff brandies. 'Now – take a sip of that.'

He gulped at it and the colour returned to his face. I sat on a chair directly opposite him and listened when, at last, the words came in a vague sequence.

'Those tapettes, Nicki: they're so unstable emotionally – so *violent* when they quarrel between themselves.'

I remembered the grisly story of Diaghilev's two boy-friends snarling at each other across his dead body, and nodded.

'Well, Jean-Pierre picked up an Italian soldier in Monte Carlo – the place is full of them – and made a – well, the two went off together. Then the trouble began. The Italian already had a boyfriend and a jealous row started. Jean-Pierre apparently threatened the Italian with his own re-volver and it went off accidentally –'

'Well,' I tried to be calm, 'if it was an accident –'

Father gestured impatiently. 'That's what Jean-Pierre says. The fact is that an Italian has been killed – by an enemy. Jean-Pierre was arrested and Galina was picked up later as a probable accomplice; but she managed to give them the slip – I don't know the details, this is all I heard from a 'phone call on a bad line from Vichy.'

'Vichy!' I asked. 'What on earth's she doing in Vichy?'

'I don't know. But you must go at once, Nicki.' His voice was trembling with emotion. 'You're the only one who can travel more or less freely with your Swiss papers and your Red Cross authority. Vichy's swamped with

Germans, as you know, all conniving with that ghastly Pétain government. She's probably already in jail.'

I did one thing before anything else. I telephoned Ullmann, and told him what little I knew.

'Yes, go to Vichy,' he agreed, 'and when you come back, let me know. I'll find out the facts, and maybe I can help you.'

It was a good two hundred miles and the train, with the dozens of long stops for inspection of papers and interrogations by the Gestapo at main line stations, took thirteen hours. But at last I reached Vichy, tired and bedraggled, and went immediately to our sub-office there. It was scarcely more than a cupboard adjoining a warehouse in the modern part of the town, separated from the Allier river and the Pétain headquarters by the ornamental gardens which teams of gardeners still kept in order with fanatical enthusiasm.

My opposite number was quite comical about his cramped office. 'Acres of floor space stacked with crates of *Source des Céléstins* next door, and I can hardly flourish a pen. And over there,' he gestured out of the window, 'those fat slugs of French traitors wallow in the hot springs as if they hadn't a care in the world. But evidently you do have cares, my friend. Tell me.'

I explained and he made enquiries of the local Gauleiter. Yes, there was a French citizen, Galina Blondel, being held for questioning in connection with the death in which her husband had been involved in Monte Carlo. And no, in no circumstances would I be allowed to see her.

I thought I saw a way round that. The fact that Galina had been permitted to phone Father showed there were loopholes in the rules – probably only arbitrary rules laid down by the local Gauleiter. I would go and see him and asked my opposite number how to find him.

'The name is Klaus Köhler. He's a giant of a man, well over six feet and must weigh twenty stone. Something of a – er – deviationist in matters of – er – sex, I believe. Those who've seen him in the baths mutter about lash marks on his back. "Der Elefant" he's called.'

Köhler was staying at the five-star Hôtel Véronique, which he had taken over as his headquarters, and where he occupied what was obviously intended as the suite for royal visitors. He was courteous all right; but it was the courtesy of a man who would wear velvet gloves while measuring you for the rack.

'You see, Herr Korolev, our interrogator has not yet been able to get at the truth.'

I felt a chill down my spine. 'Interrogator' was a hated and feared word since the Nazis had arrived.

'I may be able to help. We are very close, my sister and I.'

For such a giant of a man his lips were oddly cherubic and they were moist as he smiled. 'I wonder what exactly you mean by that, Herr Korolev.'

There was no doubt in my mind as to what he *thought* I meant.

I returned 'der Elefant's' smile with a scornful, 'Just that she has always confided in me. And I am as anxious to know the truth as you are – as is your Paris colleague Oberstleutnant Ullmann.'

Mention of the name shook him, I could see that; and I pressed my advantage. 'Indeed, Konrad's instructions –' I could hint at an implied threat as well as anyone else.

Köhler's demeanour changed when I used Ullmann's first name. Evidently respect if not fear was part of the Köhler–Ullmann relationship.

'Ah! I see. You should have mentioned before that your visit is under his direction. I would have been more immediately co-operative.' He rose, taking from a drawer in his desk a pair of thin black leather gloves and a riding crop. 'Accompany me, please.'

His great bulk occupied most of the back seat of his open Mercedes. He motioned me to sit beside the driver.

'To share a seat with one of my size is a little difficult,' he said.

We did not go to any jail, but to a pleasant house on the outskirts of the town overlooking a square in the centre of which was a statue of Napoleon III. Köhler pointed with his crop. 'But for him Vichy might well have crumbled away. He revived interest.'

My lack of interest was evident, for he brought the subject back to the present. 'With the man Blondel we have had to be more secure. After all, he has shot a soldier of our ally, Italy.' He puckered his cherubic mouth as if he had little esteem for Italian soldiers. 'But your sister is under house arrest only, she was allowed to telephone your father, as you know. She is after all a star of some magnitude. You will find her . . . unimpaired.'

Which indeed I did. I kissed and hugged her, but our reunion was in no way tearful. Galina was always practical when coping with immediate problems.

'What on earth happened?'

'Need I say, Nicki, that it was simply a spitting and clawing affair like two cats fighting over a bit of fish. Jean-Pierre's room was next to mine and I could hear them quarrelling and then rushing out of the house. I thought that was the end of it. But Jean-Pierre came back half an hour later, white-faced and crying. "The gun went off, Galina," he kept saying, "and there was Luigi in a pool of blood . . . but it was an accident. I never meant –" and so on. I was disgusted more than frightened. But now Jean-Pierre faces a murder charge – or manslaughter if he's lucky. The Italians will prosecute as it's a military case. I asked to leave, hoping that if we got to Vichy we might be able to get help, pull some strings. I'm being held as a material witness.'

She had not been able to do a thing because, being under house arrest, it meant very literally that they never let her out of their sight.

'It is really quite embarrassing,' she smiled weakly, 'I

haven't even been able to take a bath without constant
. . . attendance. Though I must say I'm given plenty of
food and I'm allowed to walk in the garden – with an
armed sentry at the gate of course.' She cupped her chin
in her hands in a gesture I had seen so often in the ballet.
'Poor Nicki. God knows you have enough troubles of your
own.'

I poured myself a glass of water from a carafe on a side
table. 'I think I know how to deal with this one,' I said,
firmly. 'I'll go back to Paris. You hang on here until you
get your orders."

Ullmann was courtesy itself; but it was a courtesy that had
none of the underlying threat of Köhler's. 'Am I not here
to help our Russian friends?' he asked.

He was, of course – but only if 'helping' also helped the
German war effort. There was an edge of ruthlessness in
Ullmann; and in his job of looking after Russian emigrés
it sometimes showed.

When I had explained to him Galina's situation he
looked grave. 'Murder can't be treated lightly,' he said,
'and even if your sister isn't directly involved, she could
be held as a material witness.'

'But as you know, she wasn't there.'

'Even so – enemies killing soldiers –' he thought carefully before adding, 'However – there are what the English
call "strings to be pulled". And in certain circumstances –'
He let the sentence die away.

Here it comes, I thought.

'Yes?' I said. 'A quid pro quo?'

He smiled. 'You are very understanding. And of course
it would be an absolute deprivation to the world of art if
the name Galina were to be – shall we say – "locked away"
for the duration. Yes, indeed. But there is a solution, a
quid pro quo, as you so engagingly call it. I could arrange
her release and her return to Paris if –' he hesitated – 'if
in her capacity of *première danseuse* she can arrange a brief

German tour of her ballet company. Dr Goebbels insists that we must keep the spirits of the people up. It is an important facet of propaganda; so every artist of international repute –'

It was an obvious solution, and one that could be accepted without loss of face, and although Galina did not relish the prospect of visiting a victorious Germany, she didn't say no, perhaps because Maurice Chevalier, whom she admired tremendously, had also agreed to sing for French prisoners of war in Germany.

'If he doesn't think it's traitorous, then neither do I,' she smiled when she was once again back in Paris, and the trip was being arranged. 'But first, I must go and see Igor.'

We all sometimes tended to forget poor Igor, now resigned to a dismal, twilight existence in a bedroom. I was glad that Galina was going – because Igor needed cheering up.

'I'm only going to Germany for three weeks,' she instinctively dropped her voice to a whisper when he saw her, 'then I'll be back and when we're not dancing – we are planning a season at the Opéra – I'll come and see you every day.'

I knew she would. She kissed him gently when she left, and I told Igor that I would come and visit him the following day – because the truth is, he *didn't* look well. Something was troubling him, I could tell that. I had to try and find out what it was.

The next day, after I had seen Galina off on the train, I made my way to the Rue St Dominique.

Poor Igor. His once handsome and elegant face was a furrowed wreck of wrinkles and pouches and a turtle neck. His sunken haunted eyes were those of a dying man – but a man who would not, or could not, die. The most pitiable moments of the day always seemed to come if I visited him before lunch. Brig invariably spent an hour a day alone with Igor between noon and one o'clock. The nurse was given a rest during this time and Igor's bedroom door was

locked. It was all vaguely sinister – or was I exaggerating?
– but there was nothing I could do about it. But what *was*
it that disturbed Igor? On one visit I even took a cursory
look around Igor's bedroom, but discovered nothing.

Through our blinking system I had discovered that Brig
knew about the nude photos, but I did not know how.
Even so, what could she do? She could not rage for day
after day. She could not slap his face or physically ill treat
him because he could feel nothing. Doctors had even
pricked him in several parts of the body to test his reaction,
and Igor had not even noticed the pricks. Yet *something*
terrible was happening behind the locked doors in that
hour which husband and wife spent alone.

The most awful thing was that, to everyone but Igor
and me, Brig gave the impression of being the soul of
compassion. She was attentive, solicitous for his welfare.
Yet I knew this was make-believe. I was convinced from
the wordless conversations with Igor, that she hated him.
Why, then, keep up the pretence?

The time had now come when I felt that I could stand
this secret agony no longer. I had a longish 'conversation'
with Igor by asking leading questions. It went something
like this, and though he could not *say* yes or no, I have
substituted, as I always did, those monosyllabic words for
the single or double blinks of his eyes – one for yes, two
blinks for no.

'Now, listen carefully Igor,' I began, 'I'm right in thinking that Brig doesn't worry you in the morning, afternoon
or night because then there's a nurse around? It's in the
lunch hour?'

He blinked once.

'When the nurse is having her meal and Brig comes in
she locks the door of your bedroom?'

'Yes.'

'You see, Igor, I just can't imagine what her hold on
you is. Yes, I do know she's seen your nude photos. But
can they cause you recurring agony?'

One blink – which meant yes.

'So it *is* a recurring agony?'

'Yes.'

'In that case,' and I have to admit my qualms as I put the question to Igor, 'the only chance is for me to break the door down when she's locked it at lunchtime and find out for myself what's happening? Dare I do that?'

His eyes were shining as he blinked once.

'Not scared? For the future I mean?'

'No, no, no' again the rapid succession of blinks.

I was thinking carefully. I didn't want to burn *all* my boats, but I had to try and worm out a few more thoughts.

'If I break in,' I asked Igor, 'will she be able to denounce me – and you?'

'No.'

'Am I right in thinking that if I threaten her to tell everyone – she wouldn't dare to breathe a word?'

'Yes.' Eyes shining.

Something was happening in the room. I couldn't think what it could be. It certainly caused poor Igor intense mental agony. Then I had a thought.

It seemed to me that whatever happened during that time with a helpless invalid involved some sort of apparatus that had to be set up. I asked him if that was so.

One blink.

'Then it must be kept in that wardrobe. That's always locked isn't it?'

'Yes.'

'All right then – if I break open the door with a mighty push at half past twelve – will that be all right?'

As I watched, Igor gave one blink, waited a moment then gave two blinks.

'You're not sure,' I said.

One blink.

'But you still want me to get in?'

'Yes.'

'But another way?'

'Yes.'

Suddenly as though he was talking, I knew what he was trying to tell me.

'Am I right in saying that there's another key to the door, so I won't have to break it down?'

'Yes,' he blinked. Somehow a part of his face seemed – only seemed – a reflection of the eyes, to light up, almost as if he had tried to smile. Had his lips actually moved as he tried to say 'Yes'?

Who had the spare key, I wondered. It must be the butler.

'Kornilov?'

One blink.

'I'll go and see him this evening. Don't worry, Igor, I'll clear this mess up as soon as I can.'

The beginnings of tears glistened in the corners of his eyes – tears of despair or hopeless love. I could not tell.

That evening Kornilov and I met at the Deux Magots and each drank a *fine à l'eau* before approaching the main topic of conversation.

'I'm very worried about Igor,' I felt the time had come to drop his title. 'He's afraid of *something*.'

'I am aware of this – and –'

'You are?' I was astonished. 'You know?'

He nodded. 'I too am deeply concerned about Igor – and I know he's my master, he found me the job, but to me he'll always be Igor. I never miss a night without going to see him – when I'm sure the Countess has gone to bed or is out for dinner. The night nurses understand. They are grateful if they have ten minutes in the middle of the night to get a coffee or something while the butler looks after the boss.'

'That's wonderful of you, Boris,' I used Kornilov's first name. 'Igor has these moments of intense depression – no, not depression, almost a *fear* of Madame, his wife.'

'You noticed it too?'

'Of course I have. That's all we talk about. Haven't you seen it?'

'I *have* noticed signs of alarm when she's entered the room suddenly,' he admitted, 'but I have to say that Madame is most kind to Igor. She and the nurses talk to him, even though he can't reply.'

I asked Kornilov, 'Do you think that Igor and the Countess *really* love each other, or is Igor tired of her?'

He hesitated, studied the refill of his brandy and water, and muttered, 'It's not really for me to say. I *do* work for Madame.'

'Thanks to Igor,' I retorted. 'You owe him *everything*. And don't think I don't know that Igor has a girlfriend. I just wanted to know if you and the servants knew.'

'There has been some – talk,' Kornilov admitted after more hesitation. 'But nothing that we really know about definitely.'

'Well I'll tell *you* something, Boris. She *knows* that Igor has a lover.'

'But my God, how?'

'Because like a fool Igor, when he had his stroke, was carrying some photographs on him of a girl in the nude. And she found them. They're quite – well – revealing. The – er – absence of clothes you understand.'

'My God,' Kornilov signalled for a third refill. 'Poor devil. So that's why he's frightened – of the hold that the Countess has on him.'

'Yes, and I want to find out what that hold is.'

'I don't understand,' he sipped his brandy slowly.

'I don't know what happens. But *something* does, and I mean to find out. I intend – as soon as it's possible – to burst into the room when she's locked it. You have a spare key to his room. If I borrow it, I could open the door with complete surprise and find out what's happening. Will you do it? Have you got the spare key?'

'Yes, I do have it.' He hesitated.

'Then I'll borrow it.'

'I shouldn't – you won't tell? Isn't it a bit risky?'

'Don't be such a coward, Boris. You know the secret of the bedroom lies in the large dressing wardrobe and there's no question of you having a key to that?'

He shook his head and explained to me, 'Exactly. It's a kind of walk-in wardrobe – with only one key. She took it suddenly and it's been locked ever since.'

What *was* in the cupboard – or in the room itself, for she locked that room the moment she had entered it for her hour of 'tenderness'. For a moment I forgot this secret cupboard and wondered if in some way she abused him – for by now poor Igor had increased in size and looked like a bloated caricature of himself. He had also turned a vivid pink from top to toe, only the eyes watchful, fearful, but impotent and helpless.

'It's time I was going to bed,' I said to Kornilov and paid for the drinks, 'I'll be in to see Igor tomorrow morning before the Countess arrives at noon. Slip me the spare door key before she arrives. Then we'll wait for a day when we know she'll be lunching out.'

'I will,' he agreed, 'but be careful, she's a *wilful* woman and isn't to be trifled with.'

'She certainly isn't. But cheer up. It's not the end of the world.'

'It's not far off. I felt safer escaping from Mother Russia,' Kornilov said gloomily, then let a Gauloise droop out of a corner of his mouth and with a final wave of the hand vanished in the direction of the Rue St Dominique.

As it happened, I could not go immediately because I was suddenly overtaken by a catastrophic chain of events. I was thinking what a month of filthy news it had been – first Galina, next Igor. Now, though, I was occupied with Father. He had been acting in what I can only describe as a secretive, almost furtive manner. I went to the Meurice to have a drink at Sergei's bar, and later, when we met outside, he told me that Father had taken a terrible beating at *zehn*. 'I think this is the crunch,' he said gloomily.

I still had no idea what was worrying Father. The one certain thing was that if he *was* in trouble, he could not repay large debts – simply because he did not have the money. His only real assets came from his capital in Switzerland and that had been blocked since the start of the war. So I determined to find out what *was* happening – and from Father himself.

My suspicions had deepened because I noticed that Betty, our American office girl, her country still neutral, was working harder than usual, and when I asked her what she was doing, she replied, 'Only a few notes your father the Prince asked me if I would help with. It's a pleasure, and helps to pass the time.'

'Well, don't let him boss you around,' I laughed, knowing perfectly well that Father must have tried – or succeeded? – in 'entertaining' Betty. No pretty girl was beyond his flirtations.

But at first I thought nothing of it. I was much more worried about Father's appearance. Finally, I confronted him.

'You're in trouble,' I began abruptly. 'For two weeks you've been moping. I know you've lost a lot of money.'

'Where do you get these crazy ideas?' Shiftily he tried to brazen out my questions.

'Father,' I began patiently, 'don't try to fool me. What have you been doing? Apart from losing at *zehn*?'

'Nothing!' he cried. 'Absolutely nothing. All right, I *am* in debt – but only to Germans who are behaving like gentlemen.'

'A German a gentleman!'

'Yes, Nicki. Officers and gentlemen. You know what one of them told me? All debts are waived until after the war.'

'He did?' I found it hard to believe that of *any* German. 'Didn't he ask any favours in return?'

I caught the slightest tremor of hesitation. He was searching for words that would seem innocuous.

'Well, come on, Father,' I said crossly. 'Have you been passing secrets to the enemy?'

It was the sort of joking remark anyone might make when irritated and baffled.

'What do you mean?' Father's face paled, and I could see a pulse throbbing on his left temple.

'Well, what was it?' I asked.

'Nothing,' he grunted in reply. 'The General did suggest that I might be able to help the Russians, make life easier for Russian emigrés if I compiled a list of their names and addresses.'

I was astonished. 'And you did that?'

'Yes, between friends. Betty helped me to copy them out.'

'You got them from my office? My private office?'

'Do you mind?' He tried to bluster. 'Those names are common property. It can only help.'

'How do you know?' I retorted. 'Anyway, that's not the point. Those files are – well, private information. I knew you'd seen them because Betty told me.'

'Well, they can't be that secret if Betty can see them. It's only a list of names, after all.'

'I call it bloody cheek. Yes, I do Father. You've been tampering with Red Cross documents – and it's absolutely forbidden to use them for information to a country at war.'

'Damn it, the Germans are *friends*,' he exploded, 'and you've no right to speak to your father like that!' He flushed with anger.

'I have. It's absolutely disgraceful, poking your nose into my private business.'

'Well, I'm sorry if I offended you,' he said angrily. 'But I don't see –'

'I'll tell you one thing, you *can't* see anything. If I told the Red Cross what had happened, I'd be fired on the spot. You really are bloody stupid.'

I spoke more in sorrow than in anger really, for I could

not see that giving the Germans a list of names could do any harm. But to give the Germans *anything*!

I was still puzzled by these German 'requests' when, three days later, who should turn up at our office, unannounced, but my old chum and mentor François Savin.

'François!' I cried. 'It's great to see you. Come on up.'

He flopped into my comfortable sofa and said admiringly, 'You've tarted up this room of yours quite a bit.'

'Thought I might as well be comfortable,' I said airily.

'It's great to see you again. Just like old times, eh? Except that the food isn't as good.'

'It is in the restaurants patronised by the Germans. Anyway, when did you arrive?'

'This morning, after an agonising night, clanking and banging and Germans shouting all night long, and I had to have my papers examined three times – each time just as I managed to get to sleep.'

'Where are you staying?'

'Don't know yet. I must return tomorrow latest. It's urgent I get back.'

'Stay the night with us. No argument! Remember the beautiful young Tasha. You can have her bed.'

'And what about her?'

'She always sleeps with me anyway.'

'Wow! She does? Shows good taste anyway. Remember, I was the one who taught you the facts of life in Paris.'

I didn't say anything, just smiled, with a sudden fleeting memory of Hélène. Laughing, I said, 'What brings you here anyway?'

At my question, his face suddenly went grim. 'Let me ask you a question. Do you have a complete list of all the Russians living here in Paris?'

My heart not only stopped a beat, it was as though I had been dropped from an aeroplane, or knocked out by a blow from a sledge-hammer. *That* question! That of *all* questions, the only reprehensible thing that my father had done. And here was François Savin asking me about it. I knew what I had to do. Keep quiet.

'Sure I have a list,' I said. 'It's here in my desk.'

'Then, Nicki,' he said urgently. 'Burn it. Destroy it. Tear it up. Quickly. I mean *now*. That is why I came round to see you before even looking for a hotel.'

'But François, what happened?' I was completely mystified. My heart was sinking with fear at the tone of his voice – and the knowledge of what had happened to that list behind my back.

'Well, you don't have to *burn* it – literally. But hide the list. Not in this office, but with some trustworthy friend – like your father.'

Bitterly I thought, 'Father?' Aloud I asked, 'But what's happening? What's all this about?'

He hesitated for a moment, and then in a very sombre voice said, 'You obviously don't know what Operation Barbarossa means?'

'Never heard of it.'

'Operation Barbarossa is due to start in three days' time.' He took a long, deep breath. 'It's the codename for the German invasion of Russia. It's been the best kept secret of the war, and because there are so many Russians here I was told I must come and warn you in person. Because, my God, I pity the fate of the Russians in France. Every man on that list of yours who hasn't got correct papers will be shipped out right away to Dachau. You can bet your life on that.'

18

Barbarossa, of course, was a massive operation – one of the greatest in military history. Hitler did not intend to be defeated by the weather as Napoleon had been, and he did not intend to go for Moscow directly. Ullmann told me that Hitler's attack was three-pronged – on Leningrad in the north, Smolensk in the middle, and Kiev in the south. He had assembled some three million men in 140 divisions and each prong of the attack had the support of a complete *Luftflotte*, nearly 3,000 aircraft.

'The key to success is speed,' Hitler told his generals. 'The campaign must be over before the winter.'

The start was spectacularly successful. Stalin's generals seem to have been obtuse in not realising why Hitler had massed his armies on the borders of the Ukraine, and the Russians were taken completely by surprise. On the very first day the German forces in the north had spearheaded forty miles into Russian territory, and in the centre most of the bridges over the Bug had been captured intact. Within a week, advances of three hundred miles were being publicised by the German propaganda machine.

But for a few moments on that first day, I did not even think of Germans, more of what would happen to Russians here in France. Standing in my room, looking out over the Seine, I was too staggered to speak. I did not even dare to admit to myself that the Germans already had the list. Or that it was my father who had provided them with it. Of course – I was wrapped in thought, silent – Father had not consciously betrayed his country, for he had no idea what was about to happen. But even so, nothing could undo the terrifying consequences, the awful deaths that were bound to follow.

François broke the silence. 'I think you ought to act quickly,' he advised me. 'Warn anyone you know who has any kind of record, and make sure that your family has adequate protection.'

'Yes, I will,' thinking, ironically, I imagine Father will be safe. And of course Aunt Olga, nicely tucked into bed with a German officer. But there was also Tasha. She was truly a stateless person. She had no real papers, only 'casual' ones issued when she first arrived by the Prefecture.

'Your father'll be all right.' Funny how François echoed my thoughts. 'And – what was her name – Auntie someone –'

'Aunt Olga. Yes,' I said drily, 'she'll be all right. She's sleeping with a German officer.'

François gave a low whistle, looked astonished but only for a moment before saying with an affected casual air, 'Ah well! Takes all sorts. At least she'll be able to vouch for Tasha.'

Almost before the first shots had been fired in Operation Barbarossa, I had two expected visitors: Ullmann, followed a day later by Inspector Verron.

'You will have heard the latest High Command bulletin,' Ullmann started. 'I just want to put you in the picture. First the good news. Your sister Galina has been exonerated, partly because her husband gallantly insisted that she had nothing to do with the event.'

'And her husband?'

'Ten years for manslaughter. Very lenient.'

'I see.'

He *was* lucky not to be shot by a military tribunal. He only received a light sentence because the dead man's homosexual record was appalling.

'But now, old friend – if I may still call you that? – the war has suffered a drastic change,' Ullmann went on. 'For the Third Reich it is for the better – successes all the way along the line – but I wanted to come and see you personally to tell you that as far as your family is concerned, please do not worry. You will be safe. You have my word. I can't examine every case that causes trouble, you appreciate that, but I *have* given the most explicit instructions that none of you is to be harassed in any way.'

'To our old friend Verron?'

He nodded.

'He has to do as he's told,' explained Ullmann, then hesitated before adding, 'but be *careful*. Specially with details. Be sure your family's papers are in order. And carry them always. Don't forget or let them run out, because,' he paused then sighed, 'I say be careful because the Gestapo has expanded in Paris, and a new commander with a somewhat – unsavoury – reputation has been appointed. Apparently the old one, whom you never met, was a bit too soft. He's been transferred to the Russian front. So watch out. The Gestapo has a habit of snooping behind the boss's back. Just checking, but I don't want any slip-ups.'

'Don't worry. I'll take care.'

We did not shake hands. He did not offer to, and though I did have to admit that he behaved, in Father's words, like 'an officer and a gentleman', and was very considerate to us, I still found it difficult to grasp his hand when I thought of how the Russians were suffering.

No problems of that sort faced me when Inspector Verron rang the bell and climbed the stairs to my office.

'Well, what do *you* want?' I asked truculently – but *not* angrily as previously because, after all, the Russians were Germany's enemy now. And although Verron – who kept his job simply because the police still had to function, but under German supervision – was also an enemy; and, further, although he was an enemy of Germany, his Communist-inspired hatred of the Russian élite made him a kind of willing collaborator with the Germans.

Verron, I was sure, was the kind of man who, if he worked for the French Resistance, would not be averse to betraying French underground patriots who also despised Communists, for the underground in France was now split into two camps and already many brave Frenchmen were being executed by fellow-Frenchmen who did not approve of their right-wing politics.

'*You* may be safe,' Verron almost sneered, 'but we shall be going through the records of Russians in France with a steel comb so fine it'll bring out the dirt as efficiently as the nits from dirty hair. That's what the steel comb was invented for, isn't it?' His eyes glinted beneath his hooded lids.

I had to warn everyone who might be in danger – and urgently. I had a list, but was it complete? Many Russians had simply crossed a border on a dark night and melted into France, especially as educated people in Russia always spoke French, and the language had rubbed off on to many lesser mortals. Some had married, had babies, but had those children papers that were in order?

Even before the war, we had formed a committee (of sorts) which met every six weeks, more in good fellowship than to discuss business. It was convened in a large, cold hall near a one-time convent in the Rue du Cherche-Midi where nuns had once distributed free bread to the poor each noon.

Russian violinists from night clubs like 'Scheherazade', off the Champs Elysées, would thin out their ranks for the night and, together with dozens of others, produce a typical Russian evening with dances and old Russian songs. Here the yearnings for a distant homeland would flow in poignant songs like Rachmaninov's *K detyam* ('To the Children') and *Vchera mī vstretilis* ('When Yesterday We Met') – which vocalists would sing to the accompaniment of a small Pleyel piano which had been donated through my Red Cross office by the Swiss-French pianist Cortot – and in passionate renderings of Slavonic dances on violins, balalaikas, and cimbalom.

Men contributed to a special club to pay for the vodka (when they could get it) and women provided the food – what little there was since the war broke out, but there always seemed to be plenty of good bortsch, and blinis with herrings instead of caviar. I went occasionally, for the one thing that did impress me was the determination of the old Russians to cling to their own customs and their love for their country.

The committee was headed by Kornilov, the butler of Brig and poor Igor, and I telephoned him at half past twelve in the morning, knowing that Brig would be busy with Igor. I wasted no time, but warned him, 'No, I can't come and see Igor on our arranged business. Something terrible's happened. We're in deep trouble. This German attack on Russia has changed all our lives.' Briefly I warned him of the consequences of Barbarossa, and told him to pass the message on to the committee.

'You see, Boris,' I begged him, 'you've got to call a meeting of the committee *immediately* – tomorrow if you can. And whatever else you do, warn people they must *always* carry their identification papers and so on. There are going to be spot-checks everywhere – and no time for excuses. Can you do this?'

'I'll try.'

I knew how the committee worked. Twenty or so key Russians with steady jobs and impeccable documents each ran a different cell. They were able to spread their contacts very quickly. The band leader at 'Scheherazade', for example, ran one cell, and his orchestra of twenty Russian violinists each alerted their friends. Kornilov's cell included everyone working for Brig – and they warned their friends as soon as Kornilov had had a word with them. Sergei at the Hôtel Meurice was also a cell leader. Once the spark had been touched off, the word galloped round with the speed of a bush fire.

Not always was it quick enough, though. Within two days, disastrous news started to pour in. Two chambermaids in the Ritz had been picked up. The French police – always with a Gestapo man – using the French because they knew their way around Paris, lined up all the Russians in dozens of places, demanded to see their papers, and if they did not have them at that moment – even if they cried despairingly, 'I've got mine at home!' – they were arrested on the spot, rarely to be seen again.

'Sent to God knows where,' I groaned to Betty, who was also in tears because her father felt there was soon going to be trouble with the Japanese and wanted her to return to America.

'I think, as American citizens you'll be safe here. A tiny island like Japan could never attack a giant like America,' I almost laughed, 'but if you feel you should go, I'll understand.'

A dozen men and women were roped in by the Gestapo that first morning, four of them girls, two of them teenagers. Poor girls! Little more than kids. Both had been born in France of Russian emigrés, and had flaunted their Russian connection as safeguards because they believed the Germans were their friends. In fact, the girls were French in everything except blood, yet overnight their lives had been switched back. It was as though they had travelled a road which the Germans told them led to heaven, and suddenly the Germans decided it led to hell.

In the next three days 213 Russians – men, women, children, one a baby – disappeared, literally, from the streets of Paris. One minute they were there, the next they had vanished. Queues of tearful relatives, besieging the Prefecture, begging for help or at least information, were ignored, all questions unanswered. The crying men and women were pushed back brutally, often left falling on the pavements.

I heard reports of another Russian who went berserk. He was at the corner of the Madeleine, walking harmlessly, when he was stopped by a Gestapo man who demanded his papers. He did not have any, but he did have something else.

Pretending to fumble for his *carte* he instead whipped out an old revolver he had brought with him all the way from Russia.

'It's oiled and loaded,' he grinned, and fired instantly at

the Gestapo man, killing him on the spot. He then put the barrel into his mouth and shot himself.

Many others killed themselves. For days bodies were found floating in the Seine. Others took their lives after overdoses of drugs, including a husband and wife and their two small children, all discovered 'sleeping' peacefully in each other's arms.

As the rumours of German successes turned out to be true, they arrested more and more Russians, loading them at the Gare d'Austerlitz into cattle trucks destined for the concentration camps where (according to other rumours) they would be tortured, subjected to genetic experiments, finally to end up in a gas chamber.

In desperation – for in reality I was powerless – I stormed round to see Inspector Verron.

'What the hell are you doing to the Russians?' I yelled. And peering out of the dirty window into the street below the massive entrance to the Prefecture, I said, 'Look at that woman lying in the street.'

He peered down at the scene below. 'Filth,' he shouted back. 'Offal. I know that woman – an upstart Russian countess. She should go home.'

'I know her. Where's her son?'

'Where he belongs. In Germany, doing forced labour, I hope. About time he did an honest day's work.'

'Honest! You're supposed to be an enemy of Germany!'

'I'm proud of the Russian stand against the German forces. But I'm the enemy of all plutocrats.'

'You're a pig,' I shouted. 'I don't care who hears me. You're a pig.'

'You *will* care one day,' he said softly, eyes vicious with hate. 'I'll see to that. It's just a question of time – of waiting, and I've got a very long memory.'

There was nothing I could do. Another hundred were deported the following day. Finally I asked for an appointment to see Major Ullmann in his office at the Crillon.

'Can't you do *something*?' I begged him. 'Can't you at

least issue some sort of instructions so that distraught relatives can be told what's happened – even if the news is terrible. It's the lack of knowledge that's driving people crazy.'

'I wish I could. I do help when I can. The French inspector is a swine. I'd have him shot if I could. But the Gestapo is taking an increasing interest in the Russians, and the new man admires your inspector. And I have to be careful – once I'm seen to be lenient – I'll be sent to the Russian front. No, I mean it. No-one is indispensable, and I feel that, as long as I'm here, I might be able to help a little. If I were to be replaced, who knows what would happen to your family – to anyone?'

'I know. For God's sake don't do anything to land yourself in trouble. You *have* been a great help. I realise that. But if only I could see some of the Russians – speak to them –'

'Don't,' he begged me. 'I *have* seen them. I don't want to upset you, but they're just herded, bemused and bewildered, into cattle trucks. There is no other means of transport. And even that's so overcrowded that sometimes the people squeezed inside have to stand up. If they faint – or die – they do it standing up. They sleep standing up. They vomit standing up. Oh! Nicki, I'm so ashamed – and powerless. Nazism? I'm beginning to wonder. The dream might have sounded perfect. But a dream is only a dream. Reality – making a dream come true – is different,' he shrugged his shoulders. 'Once upon a time war was heroic – about living and dying and behaving like gentlemen. Now – it really affects the innocents, with torture, degradation. It wasn't like that in the history books.'

'History,' I said bitterly, 'is a luxury.'

I had been so busy – the Red Cross offices were crowded every day – that for three or four days I had not been able to visit Igor who, I knew, must be missing me. Besides, I now had the key which Kornilov had given me, and finally

I decided that the time had come for action – at half past twelve. So I reached Igor's house the following morning at a quarter to twelve to talk to him first.

'We'll do it today,' I promised him.

At exactly noon as usual, the door of Igor's room opened gently and there was Brig, using her sweetest voice.

'And how's the patient today?' She stroked his face. 'It's your beloved wife come to cheer you up, darling,' and to me, 'Off you go Nicki, dear, this is our daily hour of bliss together.' With every semblance of a sweet and gentle nature she said, 'Thank you, Nurse, now you go for your break.' Igor looked piteously at me, afraid.

I walked outside along the street, to pass the time, keeping an eye on my watch and turned back at twenty past, reaching the house five minutes later. Five more minutes to go.

At three minutes to the half hour, I started to walk up the broad, dark carpeted stairs, heart thumping with the persistence of a machine that would not slow down however hard I tried. I *was* frightened. I even took the stairs more slowly than I needed, still fearful that I might be making a terrible mistake. Supposing I burst in on a perfectly harmless scene between lovers who really *wanted* to be left alone for an hour a day so that Brig could show her love? And yet – how could I ignore the fear that showed in Igor's eyes at the prospect of Brig's daily visits? There *had* to be something wrong. Dammit, Igor had *told* me.

I hesitated no longer. Very, very quietly I inserted the key in the bedroom door lock. Gently, gently. I waited a few seconds more – then opened the door – I didn't burst into the room, I opened it quietly. Igor's bed at the far end was facing me so I would be able to see at a glance if anything was wrong. For a second I could not see Igor's face which had been hidden by a screen – a new one, the kind of hospital screen with four large panels which is so often put around a ward patient as he approaches death.

I had never seen that screen before. It seemed to be made of grey linen or hessian.

Turning my head slightly to one side I caught a glimpse of Brig, unchanged as far as I could see, and out of the other eye I registered the fact that the wardrobe door was open. At the same time Brig gave a scream as she saw me, as though she had been struck a blow. It was a piercing yell of fury and anger.

'Get out, you lousy sonofabitch!' she screamed at me, jumping up. Grabbing a bedside lamp she pulled it out of its socket and hurled it at me.

'This is private, you bastard! Get out before I have you thrown out,' she shouted furiously. 'Get out, get out, get out!' At the same time she lurched forward in an abortive attempt to close the screen.

Three steps took me to the bedside and there I saw how Brig had been tormenting Igor for all these weeks. From the back, the grey screen had seemed nothing more than a way of ensuring privacy round a bedside.

Then I saw the front. I let out one gasp of horror. The front of the four panels each consisted of a six foot tall blown-up photograph of a naked woman – all of her – smiling, one of her blowing a kiss to the photographer, one lying on her back legs apart on a bed, and I didn't need to ask who had taken the photographs. Another was even worse. It showed Anna and Igor actually in the process of making love, one on top of the other, and obviously taken with a camera fitted with a delayed action shutter.

Panting with fury, Brig was looking for something to throw at me but I dived past the edge of the bed and as I did so hit one of the screen photos with my elbow, tearing it right across.

'You can't do that!' she shouted.

'I can, and I did, you bitch,' and slapped her across the face. 'That's for all the torture and pain you've been giving to poor Igor. Enlarging private photographs! I'll kill you for this.'

She screamed, and then mimicked hysterically, 'Poor Igor'.

'I'll tear these bloody screens down now,' I shouted and then backed towards them trying to rip them out once and for all.

'No you don't!' she grabbed a pair of heavy tongs from the fireplace and lunged at me. All this took place near the edge of the bed, but I had no time to see Igor or his tell-tale eyes – for I was fighting a mad-woman. She missed with the tongs but went through another panel of nude photographs.

'Keep it up,' I gasped, 'then I won't have to damage the rest.'

At that moment, with the inert body of Igor only a yard or two away from me, she picked up a heavy poker – one of the fire implements that decorated the fireplace – and this time she advanced on me, twirling the poker almost like a drum major, ready to hit me. As she reached the foot of the bed I felt the blow of the poker across one shoulder with a searing pain. I shouted or yelped, I'm not sure, because she panted, 'Take that for a start you filthy interfering Russian.'

I saw the shadow of the poker as she prepared to hit me again, but I sidestepped so that she stumbled and I managed to give her a shove.

It wasn't hard, but she was off balance. With a scream she fell straight on to the thick heavy wooden frame on which she had fastened the huge photographs on their canvas, her leg twisting to an unnaturally acute angle as she fell, and I distinctly heard a crack.

She screamed again, this time not with anger but with pain.

The door burst open on a scene of chaos. The immobile man in the bed was the only one who gave no sign of life. I had been hit across the shoulder so heavily (as I later discovered when I took off my jacket) that a purple weal across my back was stuck to my shirt with blood. Brig lay sprawling and moaning, trying to get up from the tangle of broken woodwork.

First in was the sister on duty – a nun. She screamed too, but then saw several large photographed sections of a female figure – including the genitals and pubic hairs – and hardly had time to make the sign of the cross before she sat down heavily on the verge of fainting. 'What is this evil all about?' she cried.

She was followed by a shouting maid and then in strode Kornilov.

'I heard screams,' he said in Russian for a change.

'Help me, Kornilov,' moaned Brig.

Kornilov interrupted and spoke to the chauffeur who was peering through the doorway, 'Go to the telephone and tell Doctor Johnson at the American hospital to come right away. Tell him that the Countess has broken a leg.'

'Just carry me to my own bed,' she begged Kornilov.

The nun was shooing everyone out of the room and ordering the chauffeur to clear away 'this filth of depravity', as she called it and throw it away.

I forgot my pain by looking at the shining eyes of Igor. Smoothing down the bedcovers I asked him, 'We solved the problem eh? Wasn't that a good day's work?'

He blinked once – and the enthusiasm was as marked as if he had laughed out loud with his eyes. Then, as though a miracle had occurred, he tried for the first time in months to force a sound out of his mouth, through lips that hardly moved yet *did* move slightly as he croaked an unintelligible sound that seemed to be something like 'Subbon'.

'Listen,' I cried to the nun. 'He's talking.'

'Subbon!' What could that mean?

'It's a sign from God,' the nurse breathed, 'out of this evil our Lord is trying to help this poor benighted soul to escape from this wretched woman.'

'It's a good sign, but we mustn't bank on it too much, Nurse.'

Kornilov had carried his mistress to her bed and when

he returned, telling the others to help her in any way she wanted, I asked ruefully, 'What about poor Igor?'

'We shall all take care of him,' Kornilov promised.

Brig's leg had been broken in two places but, within a couple of weeks, she was hobbling about her room in a plaster cast, and asked me to come and see her.

She was keeping on the Rue St Dominique, she announced – and the staff. She told me that several of her friends, hearing of her broken leg, had been round to see her.

'What did you tell them?' I asked.

'I didn't tell them that I had broken my leg falling over pictures of my husband's favourite bit of pussy,' she replied scornfully. 'I'm not a fool. I want to be able to keep my friends.'

'Acquaintances,' I corrected her.

'Call them what you will,' and then bitterly, 'they're about the only friends I have.'

Changing the subject I asked, 'What are you going to do about Igor? Are you going to keep him at home?'

'Of course!' she looked astonished. 'You don't think I'm going to change a way of life just because some of us had a tiff.'

'It was more than a tiff – and you know it. I have never met a woman who's behaved so despicably as you have.'

In the end, and after a lot of 'eye' talk with Igor, he did agree to stay, though we made several changes. When Brig demurred I threatened to call in the police. She agreed. In place of the old bedroom door we installed a swinging door which could not be locked. It also had a small glass panel to prevent any secrecy. And I did my share by, firstly, from the ranks of Russian refugees, finding a quorum of Russian nurses. They were all respectable, some of them once rich, but most were almost destitute, reduced to selling their last pieces of jewellery. The true Russians – those who preferred death to the horrors of becoming a

Bolshevik – never flinched from the fact that all their money had gone. I might find some of them shivering in garrets in Montmartre or the cheaper *quartiers* of Menil-montant, but still poverty and dignity went hand in hand.

At least so far none of our family had been threatened. Except one. And that man was Father. Not threatened, but shattered by the German invasion of Russia. He had come to regard the Germans as our close allies and I do not think that he realised at first the extent of his guilt. He was getting old now, and was not as mentally alert as in the past, so that sometimes he would mutter to himself, and sometimes he would stare blankly at – nothing.

But as for being a traitor – I do not believe he realised anything about it until Galina casually asked during supper (dinner had been demoted to supper since the war), 'Can't we warn all the other Russians?'

'How?' I felt tired, I had no appetite, sick at what I had heard.

'Well, if you have a list of all the Russians?'

I watched carefully as Father sat up with a jerk. 'A list?' he asked. 'What do you mean?'

'There is a list,' I replied slowly.

Father's face sagged open. A trickle of spittle slid from the corner of his mouth. This was the moment when he understood the significance of what he had done.

'A lot of people on that list are now in concentration camps,' I said brutally.

'But how did they find them so quickly? That list is secret, isn't it?' asked Tasha.

'Of course. But the Germans or the Prefecture must have complete records.'

Without warning Father got up and barked, 'Don't feel very well.' He wiped his drooling away with a stiff, freshly starched napkin – Lilla's speciality – and announced, 'Think I'll go to bed.'

'What's the matter?' asked Galina.

'He'll be all right. Still shocked.'

'Something upset him,' said Tasha. 'Was it something one of us said?'

I shook my head. 'He's just sick with worry about losing so many of his friends. Did you hear that Count Shebalin, who now drives a taxi, was stopped near the Concorde and arrested on the spot and his passenger had to get out and walk?'

'Poor Shebby,' Tasha had used him several times, one of dozens of Russians who had existed by selling jewellery, bit by bit, until finally he had decided to sell the last diamond – the largest – and buy a cab.

'We'll probably never see him again,' I sighed. Poor Father. He was a traitor, but an unwitting one, and I pitied him. After all, he was my own father, a man of stature, an international figure, a close friend of the Tsar's in those glorious days, and still imposing enough – and respectable enough – to be on speaking terms with the highest in the land. And only I – and a handful of Germans, and, I suppose, Betty – knew the truth – how he had presented a list of all his friends to the enemy. It was as simple, as stark a truth as that, and I had known all along. I only hoped and prayed that he would be able to come to terms and live, harbouring such a dreadful secret while smiling and bowing to those who could have no inkling of the real truth.

After supper I went to see him. He was not ill. He sat upright in a chair regarding himself in his dressing-table looking-glass and muttering as I came in, 'Did I really do that? Am I really responsible for betraying my friends? Sending them all to their deaths – or even worse, living deaths.'

He covered his face with his hands and I could hear the sound of racking dry sobs.

'Don't worry,' I put an arm on his shoulder, trying to comfort him in the same way he had comforted me when I was in tears as a boy. 'I'm sure the list is common property – in the Russian committee for example,' I lied.

'You think so?' eagerly he grasped my arm, a solace to his guilt. 'It could be, couldn't it?'

I knew it was impossible. Each cell in the committee worked independently of any other, and though there was no secrecy, it was manifestly impossible to 'join' them up to make a complete list. 'Try not to worry,' I lied again.

'I am supposed to be the titular head of us all, of our community. What would the Tsar say if he knew what I'd done?' I felt he could see through my flimsy attempts to hide the truth from him.

From that day, as the regular reports of missing Russians came into the Red Cross, he was a changed man. He lost weight in a matter of days and only his beard hid the shrinking face filled with agony. He spent hours looking at nothing. He would never leave the house, and if he did go for a walk, it was just round and round under the globe lamps of the place de Furstemberg.

'Why don't you go for a glass of *vin rouge* at the Deux Magots?' I suggested once.

'Don't want to meet any Russians,' he shook his head. 'I'd be ashamed to. Couldn't look 'em in the eye.'

When, a week later, the telephone stuttered I had a premonition of disaster. Instinctively I answered in the French fashion, '*Allo, qui est à l'appareil?*'

'It's Father!' Galina's voice was distraught with grief.

'I'm coming!' It was all I said. I banged down the receiver, shouting to Betty as I made for the stairs, 'It's my father. Something's happened.'

I didn't wait for a reply, but almost tumbled down the steep steps. At the front door I turned right at the corner of the Institut and ran – yes, ran every step – up the Rue de Seine until I reached the Rue Jacob and finally the square. For a few seconds I stopped to draw breath in the place de Furstemberg, panting, heart pounding with the effort, even for a man of thirty-four. Then I took the stairs two at a time to the second floor. As I fumbled for my keys I dropped all of them on their key ring into the stair well. Looking over the bannister I could see them shining on the tiled floor, but I couldn't wait, so I rang the door over and over again. Galina opened it.

'He shot himself!' she cried before I even asked a question. In the background I could hear the wailing of Lilla.

'Is he –?'

'No. Not yet. But he's not got long –' the tears streaming down her face, 'Oh Nicki, why did he do it?'

I knew – I knew so well, but could not tell.

'Losing all his friends,'I managed to mutter. 'Is he in his room? Where was he?'

'In his study. He was hit in the chest, near the heart. The doctor says –' she burst into a kind of agonising cry, 'Such a good father, such a wonderful man. How could they do this to him?'

'They?' I felt bemused. I still could not grasp the enormity of what had happened.

'Killing all his friends,' she cried, wiping the tears on the sleeve of her white blouse. 'He's dying from a broken heart.'

I took Galina in my arms, stroked her beautiful hair and kissed her gently on the forehead.

'He's an old man,' I whispered. 'He can't take it – watching all the anguish around him, wondering who was going to be next. For him, death is an escape from reality. He's taken the peaceful way out. Hush, Galina darling.'

The doctor had bandaged the wound in his chest so that when I entered his study I at first saw nothing but an old white-bearded man, half comatose, waking in sudden spurts, and once smiling gently at me.

I had spoken fine words of comfort to Galina, but at the sight of him lying there, dying before my eyes, all my resolve to try and be brave began to crumble.

The doctor left with a stuttered, 'I'm afraid the Prince
. . . but I'll be back as soon as I can.'

'Where's Tasha?' I asked.

'She's gone to a concert.'

'Of course, I had forgotten. Where did he get a gun?'

'That – that toy revolver.' It was lying on the ground
near the sofa.

It was almost impossible to realise that such a tiny
revolver had the finality of death. A scene flashed across
my mind of Father and Mama entering our bedroom to
say goodnight to Rudi and me when they were on their
way to a ball at the Winter Palace: Mama in her ball
gown with her hair encircled by a glittering tiara; Father
resplendent in his white buckskin breeches with black
boots and silver spurs, his tunic emblazoned with his decorations and his beard bristly as he bent to brush our fore-
heads with his lips, the scarlet ribbon of the Order of St
Petersburg diagonally across his tunic with its golden tassel
at his left hip and the 'side-arm' (as it was properly called)
in its polished holster at his right.

It was scarcely more than a toy, that pistol, its chased
ivory handle the epitome of innocence, its silver ornamen-
tation giving it a touch of frivolity, as if its greatest mission
in life was to be put into the gentle hand of a girl to enable
her to pop peas at bobbing targets in a fairground.

But Father had not been deceived by its seeming innocence. There was a slight foam on his beard as he tried to
raise his head from the back of the sofa on which he lay.
Galina put her hand behind it and put her ear to his
lips. '"Lethal" ,' she repeated like an efficient interpreter.
'That's what he says: "Lethal".'

I nodded, still rigid with shock. He could see my amaze-
ment that that – *that* – I pointed to the weapon.

'But why, for God's sake *why*,' asked Galina again and
again.

I groped carefully for a chair and supported myself by
gripping its back while I felt the icy sweat running down

my back and sides as I held his hand. My adrenalin was not answering to the needs of the moment. I could hear the rhythmic sound of a platoon of German soldiers marching across the square, and supposed some guard was being relieved.

Father's eyes were open now. They had a glazed look about them, and I knew that it would not be long. The singed hole in his shirt front was beginning to ooze red and his hands trembled slightly in what I thought was a dismissive gesture, as if he could no longer be bothered.

I squeezed his hand, leant forward and he whispered, 'I'm sorry, Nicki – I had no idea – poor Betty, don't – blame her.'

'No-one is to blame,' I said gently. 'No-one knew anything.'

My eyes were wet, but I tried to control myself as he lay on the sofa, white beard neat and trimmed, neat as an effigy in a church, I thought, such a noble face that I forgot the last few weeks, the last few days, thinking instead of the good times we had spent together, especially at Tsarskoe Selo and Father laughingly saying to me, 'One day you'll be a Prince, my boy. You will be honest and upright and brave and you will never let your revered Tsar down – or anyone else.'

And instead of those high and wonderful hopes for a future in which we would all grow up dressed in beautiful clothes, what had become of us all? Mama murdered by fanatics, my twin brother lost except for one faded photo, and, for all we knew, dead; Igor waiting patiently for death, Olga virtually a prostitute – no, I couldn't call her that, not the mother of beautiful Tasha. Our father – a suicide.

The sound of the marching footsteps retreated, faded. I turned away and went to the window. The square was empty, the trees still. The scarlet thread had trickled diagonally toward his waist, like the ribbon of a noble order.

He spoke just once more before he died – quite clearly, as if he was determined to clarify matters.

'A matter of honour,' he said.

I bent my head. 'Of course,' I said. 'A matter of honour.'

PART FOUR

1944–1945

19

The years until the spring of 1944 seemed to pass in a miserable daze of rationing, petrol shortages, black markets, black-outs, sudden Gestapo arrests in an enslaved Europe that would never be free. Life was so long-drawn-out that Dunkirk and the fall of France were relegated to distant memories. And with the Germans constructing and strengthening a massive Atlantic wall for, in their words, 'The defence of Fortress Europe', it seemed as though the war and the Occupation would last forever.

In Russia, Leningrad had been heroically defended against siege for 900 days. British cities had apparently been bombed almost to destruction, but never into submission. Hundreds of Allied ships had been sunk but courageously replaced by new ones. Yet there was, most people agreed, no way the stalemate of slavery could ever end.

One magical day had given us a ray of hope: 7 December 1941 – the day when Pearl Harbor was bombed and America entered the war. But their main preoccupation seemed to be with fighting Japan, which also split the Allied forces, faced with the loss of Singapore and the threat to India, in a war now spread far from its original Europe, to Africa and to the Far East, changing the face of the globe beyond recognition.

The entry of the United States had one other unexpected effect for us. Brig had returned home in November 1941 in response to a summons informing her that her father had been seriously injured in a road accident. All his wealth and the finest medical attention had been unable to save him and he had died without regaining consciousness; and after his death the chaos following Pearl Harbor had extended her stay. Luckily she had made careful and sensible arrangements so that Kornilov could run the house in her absence as well as look after Igor. The hoped-for improvement in Igor's condition had not really materialised, but at least it was stable. Thus did hopes and fears alternate. Each dawn was born in uncertainty, each dusk the sun seemed to go down on a world in flames.

Against this turmoil, people still had to struggle to make something of their lives. Lovers coupled, babies were born, fathers and mothers died. In the place de Furstemberg, Father had long since gone, the sadness of his death lessened by the acts of aggression around us. And though we still thought affectionately of his memory, the secret of his treachery died with him. Not even Galina knew. Nor, of course, did Lilla, whose frailty had increased after her 'rest' in hospital. But though she had no knowledge I feel certain that her decline was hastened by her beloved master's tragic death. And the years of absence from her homeland, endured out of a sense of duty and love in a city where there was constant worry over problems of rationing, had also taken their toll. She died peacefully in her sleep one night in 1943 and a bleakness that had nothing to do with the privations of war descended on the place de Furstemberg. I saw it as a deeper sadness that her body was committed to the earth in a strange land and resolved that if ever the flames of war were extinguished her remains would be taken back to her native land for re-burial.

Olga now was not only a highly successful couturier in her own right, but she also had many German clients. She was still with Ullmann, apparently content with the arrangement – as apparently Chanel was at the Ritz – though as Galina once said, 'She has to earn everything on her back.'

Galina on the other hand received some 'perks', in a legitimate way. She was now being hailed as one of the greatest ballet dancers in the world – our restricted world, that is – and not only performed every season at the Opéra, but made regular tours to dance for French prisoner-of-war camps in Germany, for which she was rewarded with extra rations which she always shared with us; just as I received Red Cross parcels from Switzerland which I shared with the others.

Galina lived quietly at home, though every now and again, as if requiring some medicine, she would bring home some agreeable ballet dancer or official and if she liked him, he would stay the night.

Tasha and I had never married either. It seemed so unnecessary in the midst of a war, though we had announced to Galina that we *would* marry to celebrate the first day of peace, for we were now so deeply in love that every casual touch – an arm thrown over a shoulder – would send shivers of delight through both of us. It was quite extraordinary how we both desperately needed a regular release from the tensions of war by making love.

Tasha had grown into the most beautiful creature – not only firm and upward tilting, tempting breasts, but narrow loins, long shapely legs, and her golden hair had grown until it reached half way down her back. She needed to make love as much as I did and often if I arrived back and Daniela (Lilla's successor) would announce that supper would be ready in half an hour, she would smile at me – a demand, not a request – and without a word we would go into our bedroom, tear off our clothes and I would push myself deep inside her body, rubbing my strong hairs among her golden thatch, locked in each other's arms as though nothing else in the world mattered, waiting – because we knew each other so well – for the split second when one of us would cry 'Now!' and it would be over.

Galina thought it highly amusing. 'Feel better now?' she asked on one occasion, and on another, 'Hungry?'

'Ravenous!' replied Tasha.

'It's all the exercise you take just before meals,' said Galina sweetly.

Such, amidst those war-torn days, was the life we led, one of exuberant love-making, but always the repeated bouts of ecstasy clothed in a never-ending tenderness and pure love – until the day when the buzzer on the ground floor of my office warned me of a visitor. I wondered who it was. To my surprise, the voice said, 'Major Ullmann. May I have a word with you?'

I was astonished because our relations had cooled since the death of my father and the war between Germany and Russia. As a Swiss, as a Red Cross executive, I had to be polite and neutral, but it was difficult sometimes to disguise my sympathies. How I would have loved the impossible! To see a humble Germany brought to its knees by Russia!

'Good morning,' I said when he had reached the top of the stairs, thinking, this is the man whose orders have resulted in the deaths of hundreds of my fellow Russians, whose only fault was that they had fled to France instead of Brazil or America or another distant country. 'What can I do for you, Major?'

I did not offer him a seat until he more or less asked by a movement of his hands, at which I said, 'Please'. He took off his hat and gloves and then said, 'I'm not going to allow us to regard each other as enemies. I admire you, Nicki, and I've come to warn you to act quickly.'

'Warn me!'

'Yes, you. Or rather, your mistress.'

Bridling, I almost shouted, 'How dare you?'

'I'm sorry,' he replied. 'My mistake. It is the way we translate girlfriend into German.'

'Well, you keep her out of this. Just because you've' – choosing my words carefully – 'formed an association with her mother, doesn't give you the right to interfere. After all,' I couldn't help adding sarcastically, 'what's the difference between my mistress and yours?'

'That is impertinent,' said Ullmann sharply. 'Kindly pay attention to what I have to say,' and then added, with such deliberation that a chill of abject fear raced through my veins, 'If, that is, you want to save your Tasha from being sent to a labour camp.'

For a split second I thought I was going to pass out. The world swam in a dizzy circle as I tried to digest the words, and the sudden thump of my heart actually hurt – causing me a shaft of pain on the left of my chest.

'Tasha? What do you mean?' I whispered, terrified of any reply he would give me, almost afraid to wait for it.

Leaning forward, Ullmann said, 'Believe me. This has nothing to do with me. Not even Olga knows. I'm trying to stop it, and see if we can help each other.'

'But why? What's happened to place Tasha in such danger? I thought she came under your special category of Protected Persons.'

'She did. But,' he spread out his hands in a gesture of apology, 'it's that horrible man Verron.'

'But what the hell are we talking about? Verron – aren't *you* the boss? Tell him to go and get drowned in the nearest pissoir.'

'I can – perhaps – if I find out in time. The trouble is – I don't attend to the details myself – if Verron doesn't *tell* me, how *can* I act?'

'Well, you can now. But *what*? For God's sake *explain*.'

'I found out quite by accident what's happening. You remember we each made a set of rules?'

I did remember. After Barbarossa, the Germans demanded the right to intern all enemy aliens – and that meant *every* Russian. But I had persuaded Ullmann to be moderate in his demands, and to spare all those Russians doing useful work, always providing that their papers were strictly in order.

'And it seems,' said Ullmann carefully, 'quite by

accident, in a routine examination of lists and names, that Tasha's papers are *not* in order. Verron plans to call her in for questioning. It's just what he wants. The meeting will include Gestapo officers. It's going to be very difficult to do anything,' he confessed, 'in front of witnesses who know the name of – er – Olga Arensky quite well.'

I remembered there had been some vague trouble about Tasha when she first arrived in those happy days when you could take the right contact into a restaurant and order a good steak and a bottle of Beaujolais. And fix the problem.

Aunt Olga, it seems, had lost Tasha's birth certificate, as so many had done escaping in terror and at speed.

'So what?' I said. 'You can get Olga –'

'Olga doesn't know about Tasha.'

My mouth dropped open. 'Doesn't know?'

'No, not yet. As I said, I didn't want to worry her in case we can find a way to – well, to get round the difficulty.'

'Such as how?' I asked sarcastically. 'I'd have thought the girl's mother would offer *some* assistance to a top-ranking officer. Fire this bloody man Verron. Have him shot. Do *something*. Or,' still sarcastically, 'don't you *have* any real power?'

'Of course I do,' Ullmann replied angrily. 'But you must understand that I'm in the army. The *army*. And behind me there is always a shadow – the Gestapo.' He gestured with his glove as if at an unseen presence. 'If they start getting inquisitive – and Verron has friends in the Gestapo – I could be the next man to be sent to the Russian front.' Ullmann waited for a few moments while my anger subsided and then he said more mildly, 'I happen to have discovered this danger when it's only a list of names. The people won't face interrogation for a few days. I've come to you because I'm trying to help you. Don't you understand?'

'What do you suggest?' I could visualise only one agonising picture in my imagination – Tasha being pushed or shoved on to a cattle truck bound for Germany – or beyond.

'If we act we may be able to stop it,' he brushed imaginary specks from his breeches. 'Have you *any* ideas? After all, she is *your* girlfriend.'

'Ideas? Such as what?'

'Well, I could arrange for her to be sent to Vichy before Verron acts. Vichy is outside his jurisdiction.'

'No, thank you!'

'Or –' he hesitated a long time before looking at me keenly, 'if you profess to love this girl so much, why don't you marry her? It is a very simple solution to the problem. After all, you can't ask for better protection than to be the wife of a Red Cross official.'

Ah! I wondered if he would get round to that. It was the first thought that had flashed into my mind, for it was a sure shield of security. We had agreed to wait until the end of the war because Tasha still nursed a vague fear of upsetting her mother. But now?

I told Ullmann all this in a burst of frankness. I do not quite know why I did, except that I was afraid and craved help and sympathy.

'I understand,' his voice sounded gentler. 'It's a standard problem – mothers and daughters. But maybe this is the moment to change it all. Talk it over with Tasha – and tell her about the horrors, the real horrors, of the labour camps. It's a question of life or death or,' as an afterthought, 'why tell her mother? History is filled with secret marriages. Keep it secret. Nobody'll ever know – except Inspector Verron, who will then *have* to leave your wife alone.'

The possibility that we could marry quietly made it easier for a terrified Tasha to accept the idea of marriage.

'Of course I want to marry you, I've always wanted to,' she said. 'I thought we'd wait a bit – but now, I'm scared. But it's funny, I have such faith in you, darling, that it's not only fear – but fear mingled with excitement – all in one. Of course you're right! As soon as you can, please!

Oh darling! Married! The Princess Korolev. Your poor Father. He'd have wanted a grand wedding. Not for me to become a princess this way.'

'It *is* a bit of a hole-in-corner business, I'm afraid.'

It had to be done quickly. If I was to believe Ullmann, Verron was already on the warpath and he had plenty of reason to hate me anyway; but getting married in a rush was not as easy as I had anticipated. In fact, it seemed impossible. The Swiss embassy in Paris, where I naturally had many friends, could not help. They could arrange a civil ceremony given time – but we had no time. 'It might be a month before the papers and permission come through in wartime,' I was told. Nor was there any way the French could give me an instant marriage. I would have to put up their equivalent of banns for three weeks, during which our intentions would be announced publicly. The Russian church – echo of our little church at Tsarskoe Selo – was out of the question. The Germans had looted it to a shell of bare bones. I could not even find the priest.

I began to panic now. In England, I was told, a man could marry at once with a special licence. In America, the local Justice of the Peace could marry you right away. But every door in war-torn France was shut against us with a resounding bang. It seemed downright unjust. All we were asking for was a dose of happiness – man's finest medicine – yet it was forbidden by rules and regulations which in theory had been promulgated to make people happy!

Ironically, it was Major Ullmann himself who suggested the only solution. After two days of impotence and frustration, I went to see him at his office in the Crillon, and said, 'It sounds ridiculous, but there is no way we can get married in a hurry. I've tried every avenue.'

He thought for a moment and then, with a thin kind of smile, and holding his hands on his desk in a church steeple, he murmured, 'There *is* one way, Nicki. And it's very quick. This afternoon if you like.'

'Sorry, I don't understand.'

'By my battalion chaplain.' He held out his hands with an expansive gesture. 'It would give me great pleasure. As a guest of the Third Reich. And free!' he added with a laugh. 'Yes, yes, I know we are all enemies, my dear fellow – but after all, you're not always at liberty to choose your own priest when your life hangs in the balance. Either you get married, or you lose your beautiful Tasha. Think about it.'

At first I was appalled. True, Ullmann had been a great help in softening the blow for scores of Russians. But he had been one of the conspirators who had sent my father to a suicide of shame by encouraging him into the fatal card game. And to be married by an enemy priest, and a friend of Ullmann's! To take sacred vows which should have been taken in our own Russian church! Instead we were to have our troth plighted by a man whose language we could not even speak.

Almost as though Ullmann read my thoughts, he murmured, 'Our padre speaks fluent French. And, he even went to university at Oxford.' Twiddling a gold fountain pen, he said, 'And you know, he's just as good a Christian as you are. Perhaps even more, shall we say, fervent or devout. A *practising* Christian.'

As I prepared to leave with a muttered, 'I'll have a word with Tasha and phone you. Thanks for your help,' Ullmann looked up from his desk and cried with genuine anxiety, 'Don't dawdle'.

Back home, Tasha, Galina and I talked the matter through, unable – afraid? – to say yes to such an unlikely wedding. The prospect of a marriage ceremony conducted by a German was – well, horrible. Yet, what was the alternative? Banishment of a sort to Vichy? It didn't bear thinking of. Or else – the pictures haunted me of a mass grave in some distant labour camp.

Finally, it was Galina who said firmly, 'You've got to go through with it. While Germany rules France the validity of your marriage will never be in doubt. And,' drily, 'that looks like lasting for a long, long time. But if by chance the Germans ever *leave* France, the marriage certificate will be worthless, a scrap of paper you can tear up.' Laughing now she added, 'Think of it, it'll save you the cost if you ever want a divorce.'

So we married in the Hôtel Crillon, next door to the old American embassy. Ullmann had persuaded the high-ranking German officers to turn one section of a series of waiting-rooms into a sort of bridal chamber. All the people who would normally have waited there queued in the garden. One office had been decorated with flowers and Ullmann provided Laurent-Perrier champagne from the Crillon cellars. I had asked for two witnesses – both sworn to secrecy – to attend. Kornilov in a dark suit and Sergei Mensky who got time off from the Meurice and was arrayed in the levée dress of a Count attending a formal function. Its frogged high-necked coat was brilliant blue and the black silk stockings were gartered with gold braid to match the gold thread embroidery on black slippers. It was very impressive, though a little tight. Even the German padre had changed his service uniform for ecclesiastical dress and had arranged prie-dieux for us to kneel on. An ornate radiogram provided music – not the Mendelssohn 'Wedding March' of course, Mendelssohn being Jewish and forbidden, but the Bridal March from Lohengrin, and the service, in French, was as un-denominational as it could possibly be. As Tasha said afterwards, 'But for the fact that that nice pastor placed his hands on our heads, we might just as well have been married in a lawyer's chambers.'

'Not quite,' I said. I was thinking of the Easter festival in St Petersburg and the scent of incense and intoning of the choir; and it seemed that, however plain and simple a ceremony ours was, it took on something of goodness, holiness even, because at least we were pronounced man and wife by a man of God.

Afterwards, the officers who had shared our champagne all behaved very formally and correctly to Tasha, clicking their heels and bowing their congratulations.

'I could hardly stop my giggles,' Tasha said. I teased her and told her she was a disgrace to her new husband, whereupon she bubbled over with laughter and collapsed in my arms. Then suddenly she was serious, held me from her and looked directly into my eyes. 'I can't believe it, Nicki. I just can't believe it.'

'It's true,' I said. 'As true as the fact that we are now going home to make love while our German guests return to carry on with the war.'

Ullmann had even provided a car to take us back to the place de Furstemberg and had discreetly removed the usual swastika flag from its bonnet.

'I'm glad you did it,' he said to us. 'Now nothing can help Verron. Your papers are certainly in order now. And the whole secret will never come out until you want it to.'

'I wonder,' I was thanking him and the chaplain, 'secrets of this sort are hard to keep. So many witnesses! I'm a bit worried,' I confessed.

'Don't be,' he reassured me.

But he was wrong. Very wrong – and very quickly. Two days later we found ourselves involved in the most monumental row I could remember since our tragic flight from Russia twenty-five years ago.

We were just about to start lunch when I heard a key turn in the outside door lock.

'Who the hell can that be?' I jumped up to investigate. Nobody had an extra key.

It was Aunt Olga – and one look at the thunder on her face made me realise that she knew all about us.

'I didn't know you had a key?' was all I could think of saying.

'A good job I kept one, then, when I left,' she retorted. 'Now – where's Tasha?'

'In the study.' I followed her in and Tasha, suspecting nothing, smiled, 'Good morning, Mama.'

'Sit down, all of you. Yes, you too, Galina. This is a family matter.' And as everyone hesitated, Aunt Olga shouted, 'I said, *sit down*.'

'Sit down, darling,' I whispered to Tasha.

Galina, cool in a crisis as ever, said haughtily, 'I prefer to stand.'

Olga could be very domineering when she chose. She gave no quarter. She had managed to survive in a hard school – an aristocrat dumped amidst a collection of people she would normally have despised – and no doubt secretly had done.

'Now *you*,' she turned to Tasha. 'How *dared* you do what you've done – an unforgivable sin – without telling me first?'

'Wait a minute,' I said angrily. 'Since when has marriage been an unforgivable sin?'

'Shut up!' Olga almost hissed with rage, but somehow managed to keep a kind of dignity. 'I'll talk with you later. Now Tasha – answer my question – how dared you do what you've done without telling your own mother?'

Tasha looked at me. I could sense the fear in her eyes.

'Stop bullying the girl,' I interrupted.

'I said, shut up!'

'This is not your house,' I raised my voice, almost shouting, really to protect Tasha, while Galina said more calmly, 'Really, Olga, considering where *you* are living, you do make a fuss about nothing.'

'*Nothing!*' Olga almost screamed. 'You dare to say *Nothing*! You – the wife of a tapette who couldn't make love to a woman if he tried. And probably a pimp too.'

'I'm leaving,' shouted Galina.

'You'd better stay,' there was a new, almost menacing grim tone to Olga's warning voice.

I pressed Tasha's hand, as though to reassure her, for frankly, I could not really see what the hell all the fuss was about. All right, we had not told the mother of the bride. But this was not what the Americans call a shotgun wedding. We had been lovers for a long, long time, and what is more, we *had* married for a very urgent reason – to save Tasha genuinely from a fate worse than death.

'Let me explain,' I tried to calm down the shouts. 'I know we should have asked you to the wedding but –'

'The marriage will be annulled,' said Olga angrily, but more quietly, 'I shall see to it personally.'

'You'll do nothing of the sort,' shouted Tasha. 'Leave us alone and stay with your German lover.'

With an extraordinary agility for one no longer young, Olga leaned forward and like a flash slapped Tasha hard across the face. I saw the cheek turn a vivid splotch of red as she screamed.

'You devil, you bitch!' I cried.

Galina was more positive, 'And that's for you,' she cried and slapped Aunt Olga so hard that she almost fell off the study sofa.

I was aghast. I had never in my life seen women hitting each other in this fashion – women like Olga or our beloved Mama when she was alive. Like washerwomen! But I was not only thinking of that. I was feeling the first worrying signs of an unknown fear.

Olga was not the sort of woman to lose her temper in this way – certainly not because her daughter, with whom she did not even live, had married without telling her. Was there some secret she had not divulged? Was there some frightening reason why she was so angry?

She looked at us now, turning from one face to the other, and first said, 'Poor bloody fools, all of you.'

'May I ask why?'

'Let's just say,' she said angrily, but on the edge of tears, 'that you'd better get an annulment immediately.'

'Never – never!' cried Tasha. 'I love Nicki, and we're married – and going to stay married.'

Suddenly Olga started to cry, and turning to me, she

shouted, 'You promised! Your father gave his word that you would never touch this girl.'

'Don't be so bloody stupid. We're not children any more. Tasha and I've been lovers for years, even when you imprisoned her in the salon, she managed to sneak out and we'd make love. You didn't know that, did you?'

For a moment she searched for the arms of the sofa. She needed support.

'Tasha isn't pregnant, is she?' she asked in a faint voice.

I shook my head. 'We're not that stupid,' I growled. 'We take precautions.'

Now she was sobbing agonisingly as though her heart was broken. I could not understand. I was thinking of that phrase, so often used when people got married, 'You haven't lost a daughter, rather you've gained a son.' Stupid and inappropriate, but the words flashed across my mind.

'I am sorry,' I spoke carefully. 'But you really should be pleased. You're obviously angry, but you should be delighted. Don't you see, I am a Swiss, a *neutral*. And so is Tasha now we're married. Now she's the wife of a Swiss, of an official of the International Red Cross, nobody can touch her. So why the hell are you so upset?!'

'If only it was as simple as you think it is,' she wiped away her tears.

'But what *is* the trouble?' I asked. 'Don't you realise that Tasha was in mortal danger? That Inspector Verron of the French police, working with the Gestapo, was planning to have her deported?'

Her face seemed to crumple. She shook her head unbelievingly.

'Full marks to your friend Ullmann,' I said. 'He tipped me off. He didn't tell you anything, he didn't want to upset you. But he *did* arrange for us to be married.'

'It can't be true, it *can't* be.' There was a hidden terror rushing inside her, she was starting to shout and threaten again. 'Even so, I'll tell you one thing,' she said almost savagely, 'I'll have this marriage annulled.'

'Annulled! Are you crazy? Who do you think you are anyway?'

Finally, after a long pause, she said angrily, 'Yes *you* are the stupid one. Why do you think I stopped you seeing Tasha, even in her early teens? I tried to keep you apart, I didn't *want you to be alone with each other.*'

I felt a sudden angry calm – for the wrong reason. Then, face scarlet, I shouted, 'Are you suggesting that as children – that I – when she was a kid of ten or twelve –'

'No, no, I wasn't,' she shouted back. 'But now it's time I told you the truth.'

I had a sudden, awful premonition of terrible news waiting to be told, like a great stone blocking any path ahead.

'You'd better think about an annulment,' said Olga.

'Never!' I cried, but my voice carried for the first time a vague element of doubt. 'Why should I?'

'For one reason if no other. You and Tasha husband and wife? Don't make me laugh. You and Tasha are brother and sister.'

20

Tasha was sobbing as though her heart would break, despite all the tenderness of Galina trying to comfort her, while I, bewildered, was so thunderstruck I could not talk, not even think. Brother and sister! Yet also husband and wife! When Daniela, who must have heard the sound of raised voices came in timidly to say lunch was ready, I waved her away wordlessly. There was no question of any food that midday. A world war was going on; but this was something intimate, something that threatened a tiny personal relationship, and it seemed bigger than all the chaos of Armageddon.

Tasha's first reaction, after the initial shock, had been to laugh hysterically at such unbelievable nonsense – until she realised that there was no reason why Olga would invent a lie. And with that realisation, she burst into a terrible wailing sound – the scream of an animal who knows death is inevitable; an animal caught in the pain of a vicious trap from which there is no escape.

Then she fell into my arms and I just caught her as she slid on to the sofa in Father's old study.

'Get some brandy,' I urged Galina who fetched the bottle, and a small vodka glass. 'Drink this,' I helped to force some between Tasha's lips. She spluttered and coughed.

'It's not true,' she wailed again and again. 'It can't be. You're my husband.' She clung to me, crying, 'Tell me you're my husband. Tell me! Darling, darling Nicki, you're my life. I've been in love with you since I was a child. I'll always be in love with you. I can't live without you.'

'Hush, my beloved,' I held her in my arms. 'You can't love me any more than I love you.' And, knowing I was telling a lie, I added, 'Maybe it's all a ghastly mistake.'

'There must be something we can do,' Galina's eyes were also red with crying. I was thinking, she's been through a rough time, Galina, and she came through it, but this is the first really great crisis of poor Tasha's life, a baptism of fire.

'Go to your room and try to sleep,' I suggested, kissing her gently. 'It'll take your mind off things, and then we'll try to discuss what to do next.'

'You won't leave me?' she pleaded.

'Of course not,' I said, adding recklessly, 'Never!'

Almost with docility Tasha made for her room. I peeped through the doorway once and she was sleeping fitfully, though from time to time I could hear her quietly crying.

How the rest of the day passed, I shall never remember. It was purgatory. I spent most of my time silently cursing the woman who had torn our life in two, wondering, thinking, if only she had never told us, we would never have known, and everybody would have been happy!

Or would some other stroke of fate, ordained by a mysterious unknown power, have ruined our life in a different way? A child – perhaps tragically deformed? Fate has a fairly adept way of evening out scores, of telling right from wrong, even if those in trouble were not aware of it.

Jumbled, chaotic, tragic thoughts!

Late that afternoon, Tasha got up, her face blotched and swollen, and we had some bortsch and some cheese; but it was a miserable meal, for we had nothing we could say to each other.

'Let's not think any more about it today,' I advised both girls. 'Let's sleep on it. I'll go and see Olga in her salon tomorrow. Find out just what happened. Until then, I'm so exhausted, I'm going to have a precious glass of real genuine Laurent-Perrier' – Father always kept a good stock and we had used it sparingly – 'and then bed.' Though champagne, I thought bitterly, was for celebrations, not disasters.

Almost embarrassed, Galina said, turning to Tasha, 'I suppose you'd rather have your old room back. I'll sleep on the study sofa.'

Tasha looked absolutely horrified.

Rushing to the rescue, I said, 'Don't worry, Galina. I think Tasha needs all the moral support she can get. We'll sleep together tonight. After all, we've been doing this a long time now.'

Galina looked a little startled, but understood, and as for us, we undressed quickly, jumped into bed, naked as always, and curled into each other's arms, and I was just about to start making love when I recoiled – with a sudden, well, I suppose you could say 'fear'.

Tasha felt the hesitation and cried, almost fiercely, 'We may be brother and sister, but we're lovers too. Darling, I want you now, tonight more than ever.'

'I can't,' I said.

'You *must*,' she urged. '*Please*.'

Wondering whether I would even be *able* to make love, I finally stilled my doubts and worries and it was a kind of relief that surged into her warm body and then, not crying any more, but with a quiet sadness in her whisper, she said, 'Don't ever stop it, beloved. It's so beautiful and we're so tender with each other. It's the most exquisite feeling in the world. I don't care what people say, I shall not stop. I never will.'

'It *is* a sin,' I said sadly.

'It isn't. True love is *never* a sin. I shall come with you to the salon to see Mother – sorry, Olga – tomorrow,' she said just before she started to drowse into sleep.

'No, I'll go alone. Two may not be company on this occasion, but three definitely *is* a crowd, and it's bound to lead to shouting. But if I see Olga alone in her salon, she'll *have* to control herself. She can't start a scene there. And I certainly won't. I'm too shattered –' the sentence died away.

'It won't make any difference, will it?' she suddenly wakened, pleading.

'Of course not. I love you,' I muttered. What else could I say? A brother making love to a sister! I know that in many of the upper classes, brothers and sisters did experiment in love-making, but that was only curiosity, the equivalent of Hélène's lessons to me. They should not do so, of course, but thousands of brothers and sisters do, though not for love. And therein lay the difference. Ours was a passionate, almost devouring love. It had not really contained any element of curiosity, except, I suppose, for the first few times when Tasha must have been inquisitive. But for both of us, now, the concentration of love was expressed as almost 'wearing' sex, and it was the most exquisite emotion I have ever experienced. And Tasha it was who was responsible. She had this enormous gift of just touching me – and stimulating me so that I was immediately aroused. But now – and married! – was it legal? Did we have to go and tell Ullmann? We had been married by a German priest. Who would be able to annul it?

And there was that other reason why an annulment would be highly dangerous. If we were *not* married, Inspector Verron could step in and arrest Tasha. The alternative to our respectable 'married state' was unthinkable. Tasha had no papers of any sort, except those provided by the Germans. If those were taken away she would be defenceless. I could never risk that, I thought, as I lay awake, not even if we *were* brother and sister. Wild thoughts passed through my mind, even the possibility that we could remain 'married' yet live apart, so that temptation would be removed. No, that was silly.

In my sleeplessness I thought, 'If only there were no war!' Then we could bolt, start a new life in some distant country where we had no past, where the secrets of our past were shared with only a handful of relatives. And we could assume a superficial guiltlessness. But there was a war! And another thought raced through my brain: children, the dangers. Was there not an operation that could make a man sterile? But how could I dare suggest having such an operation in wartime without giving a proper reason?

Another thought puzzled me. Why had Olga not told the truth to Father when she first appeared in Paris, a woman returning from the dead? What reason could she possibly invent for having lied to him? Then *he* was Tasha's father! Had she told the truth at that very first meeting, we would never have landed in this tangle of desperate love.

It was the first question I asked when we met at Maison Olga the following morning.

She was calmer now, more composed. 'I know I did wrong,' she admitted. She was very close to tears. 'But you must see it from my point of view. I rescued this little baby, crying, newly born, still half-covered in blood, screaming, in that dirty square where she had been born. They had killed your mother and taken her body away, I took her daughter and fled, to save at least one life. And what could I do, penniless in Russia? Living in a garret – then as a seamstress, mending clothes, foraging for scraps of food for the baby and myself, no idea whether any of you were even alive. Never *thinking*, in my penniless flight, that I would *ever* see any of you again, let alone ever manage to leave Russia. I had to pass off the baby as my own.'

'But when you *did* come back,' my voice was hard, 'you came straight to my father's house.'

'It was the only address I knew,' her voice faltered.

'But even *then* you couldn't tell poor Father – *his* child.'

'I tried to. I couldn't. The words stuck in my throat. I had brought up this little baby as my own. I had only wanted to help when I saw her first. Over the years, suffering together, she became as close to me as if I had borne her. Surely you can understand that. I adored her and just couldn't bear to be parted from her.'

'And how are you sure it was Mama's baby?'

She told me in great detail the whole story of how Mama, lying on the ground, was crying to Olga that her pains had started. 'I remember an expensive carriage and pair arrived and someone was killed. Then a man saw my silk underskirt and dragged me into the warehouse to rape me. Another man started to fight for me. I hid. I was hiding for a long time before I dared to get out. When finally I plucked up sufficient courage to emerge, the square was virtually empty. Mama's body had been dragged away. The horses from the expensive carriage had been stolen. The carriage was empty. And almost alone in the square was Mama's baby. I gathered it up, tried to clean it – and the rest you know.'

'Except that you told us an entirely different tale at first.'

'I had to invent a story. I've never been married, and

you know why. Because I loved your father, only your Mama got him first. I suppose I felt entitled to his child. I'm a little calmer now, Nicki, but I am deeply – well, humiliated at what I've done to you. But I was so horrified when I learned that you had married – you could go to jail for that couldn't you? It's incest.'

'And you could go straight to a German concentration camp for living a lie the way you've done. No wonder you conveniently lost Tasha's birth certificate. She never had one. You saw to that. And you pretended to love this girl, but you've broken her heart. I don't know what to do now.'

'Don't *know*?' Her voice was astounded.

'We'll obviously have to do something,' I returned to my cold voice. 'But whatever we *do* decide, please remember one thing – the decision has absolutely nothing to do with you. You're out of it – no relation – finished.'

'But I'm her –'

'No, Olga, you're not. You're nothing to do with Tasha. I repeat, you don't come into any decisions we make. You've posed as a girl's step-mother for all these years, ruled her life – and all the time you've been living a lie, even a worse lie when poor Father was alive and he never knew. We'll decide what to do. You just keep out of it. I don't want to sound vindictive, but it would be much better if you don't come back to the house. We've already repaid your hospitality over the years and remember, it's *my* house now. I already have one step-sister, Galina. Now we've got another sister. She'll still have to live in our family house. And even if we don't think of any sexual business, we may still have to pretend to be married – for a while, anyway.'

'You can't do that,' she gasped.

'I can. And it's got nothing to do with you anyway,' I retorted. Then I reiterated why we had had to get married so hastily: She had been so appalled at the enormity of our 'crime' that she had simply not grasped the pressing reasons for it. Now, at least, she could see it in context. And if she did not approve, at least she accepted the necessity.

What I needed most of all was time. Time to be alone, to *think*, time to puzzle out the overtones of what was, in truth, a monstrous sin. I needed time to make decisions, away from the physical desire that tormented me each moment we were together, touching, exchanging glances.

As I had already thought, had this been peace time I might have escaped the great temptation against which – it seemed – I was powerless. I could have gone big game hunting in Africa, like Hemingway or sheep farming in Australia! But in war there is no escape.

Our love was constant and had been during all the years we had been lovers, during which there had never been a thought of 'sin'. Yet, with only a few words uttered, I was now beset with a great torment. For now I knew I *was* sinning.

Before, it had all seemed so simple. Sex without marriage had made no difference to our love for each other. We had been lovers for years, why should it now change? Yet in my heart I knew that this *was* a terrible secret we shared. For how long could we go on 'living a lie'? There would have to be a reckoning one day.

I did not – I could not – lie to Tasha, her melancholy giving her a strangely different appearance – a kind of ethereal beauty, so that to myself, wondering what the future held for us, I was already thinking, 'I can never give her up. I can never stop loving her.'

A little bleakly, she told me, 'There is no future for us unless we stay together.'

'I *know*, beloved. But we *are* brother and sister now. Even if we – well, do anything –'

'Not "if"!' she cried almost fiercely.

'All right,' weakly, '*when*. Is that better? But it *is* a sin, you know.'

'It isn't,' she said stroking my face and somehow slither-

310

ing so that we were sprawling over the sofa. Daniela had gone queueing for our rations, and Galina was rehearsing at the Opéra.

'Shall we?' she whispered.

'We shouldn't.'

'Just a farewell – in case –' as an excuse she always made every bout of love-making into a plea 'in case' we would never make love again because we might meet with an accident.

'You know we shouldn't. I know we shouldn't. But so long as you understand that . . . If we had a child –' it was another terror that had invaded my mind, even making me wonder again if I could have some operation to make me sterile.

When it was over, I said, gently stroking her, 'You know it *is* a sin, beloved. You can never deny it.'

'It is not,' she was suddenly angry. 'We are lovers – we were lovers before we knew who we both were. And when you feel yourself inside me, warm and ready to come, how can you talk of a sin? It's a wicked word to use for such a beautiful feeling. It would be more of a sin to love me and marry someone you don't love. Every time you did it, it would have to be a duty! With me, every time you do it, we can feel the pleasure. We were made for each other.'

'Don't you think I believe in every word you're saying?'

'Beloved man, I will never let anyone take you away.'

And so, the sense of guilt conveniently slipping away for most of the time, we slid into a world of wicked bliss – that of lovers newly married, thinking ironically of the idiocy by which marriage had given us a cloak of propriety! We could now make love legitimately! At least in theory. For it was so easy to ignore the falsehoods of my life when I was faced, as I so often was, with the apparition of a near-naked, long-legged golden-haired girl standing invitingly, waiting. I could never say no, I just stifled my guilt, which was not overpowering but occasional, like the sudden stab of pain on a bad tooth when you eat ice-cream.

311

Of course, we told no-one. Olga knew, but we rarely saw her. Galina also knew. She might not have really approved but she accepted what had happened, the decision we made, with equanimity; influenced no doubt by her own calculated and profitable marriage to a practising homosexual.

For all this I still had to watch Tasha carefully, for she remained in a state of shock. There was also a life to be lived, an important job to be performed, one in which my work was becoming more and more intense. Also, I still had to pay regular visits to Igor whose condition remained the same. He was still being cared for by French or Russian women under the supervision of Kornilov, still living in Brig's house in the Rue St Dominique, with a large supply of dollars, all in notes, left by Brig when she departed for America. Kornilov, to whom Brig had also given a power-of-attorney, guarded the fortune, changing the notes on the black market, always in small amounts, when he needed to buy food or medicines. French doctors came to see Igor regularly. So did all the family – Tasha one day, Galina (if she was not rehearsing or at the *barre*) or myself on a different day. Poor Igor. He was looking older now, and his face bore the resigned look of a man who knows that all hope has gone, even though he was able, in his limited way, to continue to talk to us.

There was something else too. The spring of 1944 was not only heralded with a spell of joyous sunshine, but everyone's spirits, after a cold and heartless winter, had been lifted by a new sense of hope which enveloped all of us. It is hard to put a finger on it and I cannot quite understand, even to this day, how everyone seemed to be affected, not just the few. Perhaps we were living on an edge of the rest of the world, where the tide *was* changing – slowly, but surely. Italy had withdrawn from the war, and the Allies were now sweeping up from the south, almost to the point of liberating Rome. The Russians were beginning to turn back the Germans. In France itself the Resistance was with increasing boldness blowing up bridges, and halting production through daring acts of sabotage, just as RAF raids were increasing too in intensity.

All this news trickled through on clandestine radio sets, by word of mouth, even illegal news sheets printed in dank cellars and distributed round the Left Bank cafés.

'*Something*'s in the air.' Galina, too, felt the same curious sense of mounting excitement, an elation as we walked along the Champs Elysées, now decked in all its finery of the glorious candles on the double file of chestnut trees.

Nostalgia swamped my memory:

> 'I come again with greetings new . . .
> To say the leaves are fresh with dew
> And dappled in the early sun . . .'

The official radio and newspapers were of course German-controlled; but the BBC in London was often able to 'jam' the controlled Paris and Hilversum broadcasts; and though people were jailed if they were discovered listening to Free France radio, we all did it surreptitiously, though with a wavelength constantly changing to avoid reprisal German jamming, so we had to do a lot of searching on the dials of our radio sets. But somehow hints leaked out – particularly through the back-street bistros where the Maquis, or Underground, were strongly represented.

'The air is electrified,' said Galina. 'It's exactly the sort of tension I've experienced so often in the theatre just before the curtain rises.'

I remember feeling the same back in 1938, on the day the English Prime Minister Chamberlain returned from Germany with his famous 'piece of paper' saying there would be no war. After the Munich crisis it was like the lifting of a cloud. Now, in Paris, people appeared to be walking with a lighter step, as if they too were going about their business in expectation, watching from the corners of their eyes for the house lights to dim and the curtain to go up.

Of course we all knew through underground sources that the Second Front was planned; and even the official German broadcasts had hinted at an immense concentration of Allied troops in England – while at the same time hinting rather more broadly at the surprises which the German High Command had tucked up its sleeve to deal with any attempt at an invasion of continental Europe. Then in the first days of June there was a persistent rumour that the BBC had broadcast the code message (it was lines from a poem by Verlaine) warning the Resistance that the invasion was about to begin. The rumour was shrugged off until suddenly, rumour became truth.

On the morning of Tuesday, 6 June, the official German radio broke into a broadcast of the *Rienzi* overture. It admitted that 'Some air and sea forces of enemies of the Reich have attempted landings on the Normandy coast of France. The fighting continues.'

Whereupon *Rienzi* resumed its martial music. Nobody listened. Nobody cared. That bare announcement was what we had been waiting for. Now we knew: the liberation of France had started.

21

'Next stop Paris!'

Behind closed doors and shuttered windows, this was the popular toast. Stocks of brandy, Armagnac and champagne, long since hidden, were brought out from secret hiding places, awaiting the moment for celebration as the Allied armies began to move forward. According to Sergei

Mensky in the Meurice, there was something approaching panic among the German High Command in Paris.

When Sergei came round for a drink and gossip ten days after the landing, he confided, 'My bet is that the Germans are getting ready to bolt. Give us another month and Paris will be French again – French with a slightly Russian flavour,' he said, adding ironically, 'I wonder what will happen to Madame Olga? The German ladies in Paris have been advised to leave for Berlin by the end of the week.'

'They have? Yes, what *will* happen to Olga? She's not the most popular of women,' I said sarcastically. 'And friends in the Resistance tell me that in Paris they've already compiled a list of girls who have been – shall we say? – too friendly with the Germans. They can expect to be hunted down and punished.'

The news of the fighting spread like lightning across a weary Europe. The Free French Radio and the BBC went into top gear. It was difficult sometimes to piece together their broadcasts, often jammed by the Germans, but one thing was clear – the long night of waiting had ended, and day was dawning.

Even on the very first day, 6 June, the BBC news reader Alvar Liddell categorically said, 'At dawn this morning an invasion force of British and American paratroops landed in Normandy.' This was followed by extended bulletins, announcing that the first American and British seaborne divisions had landed. German resistance so far was slight.

Throughout that day fragments of news piled up, sometimes with eye-witness accounts from the beaches given by official war reporters attached to the Allied armies. One of these came with miraculous clarity through the whistles and jamming sounds imposed by the Germans: 'This is Raoul Becker with the Free French Army in Normandy. The liberation of France has begun. We and our allies have secured firm footholds all along the Normandy coast and so far have had to face no German counter-attacks. Vive la France!'

A later announcement that evening said that the Germans had counter-attacked near Caen – which revealed how far the invasion forces had thrust inland during one single day. Within a week the Allies had joined up all their bridgeheads and were holding a continuous front sixty miles long and fifteen miles deep.

Even so, there were setbacks along the Normandy coast. It was clear not only that the Germans were fighting back furiously in the Caen area but that the attackers were being repulsed. The same thing seemed to be happening in the Villers Bocage – where, we heard, the Americans had suffered devastating losses.

I found it difficult to discriminate between true and false reports. Many rumours were put out by the German-controlled radio propaganda. I remembered how Maquis travellers returning to Paris insisted that the English air force had bombed Le Havre and obliterated the German naval forces anchored there, while other radio reports said that most of the English planes had been destroyed without damaging the fleet. The aim always was to mislead and confuse, create alarm, inspire despondency. One radio announcement did ring with the excitement and fervour of real truth and inspiration however. It was the Free French Radio – and none other than the voice of freedom itself, that of General de Gaulle – in a broadcast that was picked up by millions of surreptitious listeners – saying that he was now in France and going ahead with the reorganisation of the government that would take over '*as soon as Paris is free*'. Those were the magic words – the news that the invading forces were driving irresistibly toward the capital.

In restaurants and bistros waiters and bartenders could overhear high-ranking German officers talk openly of their dismay at the lack of German defence; and on 18 June Hitler and his Generals met at Soissons and the Führer (it was said) flew into a blind rage and declared 'German forces are cowards unworthy of the defence of the Reich.'

Then on 28 June the Cherbourg garrison surrendered – or, as the official German news had it, 'A tactical withdrawal was made to avoid suffering to the civilian public.' This was a crucial victory, for now the Allies had a port through which their supplies could be unloaded. But it was not until a week later that American forces crossed the Loire; and that gave the Allies the momentum to gather strength for the final push to Paris.

Rumours (which later turned out to be true) also told how the commander of Army Group 'B', Rommel, had been seriously injured in an attack by British aircraft near St Lô; and how the Vichy Minister for Propaganda, Philippe Henriot, had been assassinated. Then, a few days before we knew from the sound of heavy artillery fire that the Allies were approaching Fontainebleau, came the news that von Kluge, who had replaced Rommel, had committed suicide after his attempted defection to the Allies had been discovered. This too turned out to be true, though at the time it was just another knot in the tapestry of uncertainty. Looking back, I can relive those days as the final act of a play in which the tension increased to a powerful and dramatic finale.

By mid-August it was clear that a climax was approaching. Resistance news sheets appeared openly on the streets. Their headlines were jubilant: BRITISH ADVANCING ON ROUEN; BOSCHE RETREATING; PATTON CROSSES SEINE. It seemed that Eisenhower, the supreme commander, wishing to avoid a battle for Paris, preferred to encircle it, forcing the Germans to surrender, and avoid the horrors of street-to-street fighting.

Even so, it was prudent to stay indoors. There were German snipers everywhere. But the elation was so great that we often ignored the dangers, and made our way in turns through streets littered with abandoned German vehicles, to visit Igor with the latest news.

*

317

One day who should appear in the Red Cross office but Ullmann. I had been wondering what he was doing, but there were so many Underground fighters milling around the Crillon and the Meurice that I had decided it was safer to keep away.

Ullmann was waiting outside my office in a battered Opel, his uniform and boots dusty, his eyes dull with the hopelessness of the defeated. He climbed wearily up the stairs and I gave him a glass of Calvados, the only drink I had. As I faced him I was conscious that, through the thin veil of my Swiss neutrality, I was Russian and that I was drinking with an enemy who was on the brink of defeat.

A wry smile played around his thin lips; evidently he was thinking much the same. 'Prost!' he said, raising his glass. 'The fortunes of war. It is our turn now to go.'

'Where?' I asked him.

He shrugged. 'Who knows? For the moment we escape, while the escaping is good. General von Cholitz will surrender the garrison. He will have no choice. And the French will repossess their city.'

'The fortunes of war,' I echoed, an edge to my voice.

He drained his glass. 'Exactly. Also *mis*fortunes, my friend. Of which I come to warn you.'

'I'm familiar with those.' I was collecting them in my mind. 'But you have fuel to add to the flames?'

'Perhaps. But that is certainly not my intention. I know what tragedy is. My father was in the Kaiser's war. He died in what is now called a psychiatric ward but was then called a lunatic asylum. Shell-shock had reduced him to a mental wreck. I don't contemplate any such anguish for you; but without my – shall we say – influence? as head of the Foreign Bureau, you may find difficulties.'

'You mean Verron?'

'As a confirmed Bolshevik he will return to power with his fellow Bolsheviks – who, I can assure you, are many. We have tried to contain that now, but the worms will soon crawl out from under the stones. I think you have experienced their dislike of the Russian aristocracy.' The wintry smile; then he rose, placing his glass carefully on top of the row of filing cabinets. 'Not all Germans are of the Nazi persuasion, any more than all Russians are aristocrats. In other times, and in other circumstances?'

He offered me his hand. I hesitated. Finally I shook it.

'Thank you,' he said.

'And Olga?' I asked.

'An affair of simple animal attraction between two lonely people. No more.'

'She could have had any number of lovers among the Russians in Paris.'

'Yes. But there is no logic in these things. Any more than there is in the vagaries of war.' He withdrew his hand. 'I'm sorry about Olga. I could have got her a seat on a plane for Lisbon, where she would have been out of it all. But she refused. She intended, she said, to return to the family. And now I too must return to – no; hardly a family. The flight into Egypt comes more readily to mind.'

'Many of the bridges across the Seine have been blown up,' I told him.

'I understand that there are some pontoon bridges. We will see.'

I heard him descend the stairs and drive away in his battered Opel. There was the sound of distant shellfire. The encircling troops were getting nearer.

That same afternoon Olga came to the place de Furstemberg. The ravages of war had changed all of us; but with her the change was the saddest. Her eyes no longer had the glint of achievement in them; they were shadowed with the humility of guilt and fear of reprisal. Her hands were trembling, the long fingers with their scarlet nails plucking at her belt. 'I thought –' she began.

'I know,' I interrupted her. 'Your German lover told me.' I knew that, if I wavered now, compassion would take over and I would display weakness that Father would have condemned. He had had the courage to pay for his own treachery, and he would have expected Olga to follow his example.

'You can't come here,' I said. 'There's Tasha, apart from anyone else.'

'I shall live in the Salon.' There was a long pause before she summoned at least some shreds of dignity. With her head held high she turned and went. For the second time that day I heard the sound of descending footsteps and the distant rumble of gunfire.

All through the day of 24 August 1944, broadcasts were announcing that American troops under General Patton had decided that the French 2nd Armoured Division should be the first to enter Paris. By evening everyone knew. Multitudes thronged every main street in the city, not only to *see*, but to be a *part* of this historic day. Everyone rushed to seek vantage points. Traffic was engulfed, cars and buses were rocked by hordes of the young. Thousands of flags – Tricolours, Union Jacks, and Stars and Stripes – emerged from hidden places and soon were being waved aloft by cheering, singing, marching people.

It was impossible to keep together, the crowds were so dense, but Tasha and I had managed to reach the place de Furstemberg separately, and then set off, holding hands as the crowd almost surged over us, a sea of countless heads forming themselves into small groups and dancing up and down until we crossed the Tuileries and turned right in the general direction of the Hôtel de Ville along the end of the terraced Rue de Rivoli.

Loudspeakers were broadcasting what was happening, for English, French and American radio reporters had been stationed at all the key points. Soon after nine o'clock there was a burst of cheering which seemed to surge along towards us like a rolling carpet of sound all the way down the Rue de Rivoli. An observer announced in a voice almost trembling with emotion, 'General Leclerc's tanks have drawn up in the square in front of the Hôtel de Ville.'

The tremendous cheering and frantic singing of The Marseillaise swept over the city. I grabbed at Tasha's hand and we watched as the tears shone in both our eyes.

'After all, France is our adopted country,' I said, as if some excuse were necessary for such sentimental patriotism.

There was little sleep for anybody that night. Though the crowds thinned a bit around midnight, the sounds of music, dancing and cheering never stopped. Scarcely before we realised it, it was morning – a morning of freedom! – and the non-stop radio commentary was telling us that General Leclerc's armour was on both sides of the Seine opposite the Cité. 'We understand that the General is to establish his headquarters at the Gare Montparnasse,' the commentator was saying, 'and will there accept the surrender of the German garrison commander, von Cholitz.'

Which is exactly what happened. When the time came the German general, in the charge of a mere lieutenant of the French army, was humiliatingly hustled into the Left Luggage office of the Gare Montparnasse and there presented with the document of capitulation. Newsmen present at the signing heard Leclerc say, *Maintenant, ça y est*' as von Cholitz put his pen to the historic document.

But that was only the beginning. The real celebration took place on 26 August, by which time the army and the Resistance troops had taken over all the remaining strong-points and the enemy had vanished except for a few snipers hidden inside Notre Dame. They were quickly discovered and shot on the steps of the cathedral.

At five o'clock in the afternoon the radio commentator's voice, barely distinguishable against the background of wild cheering, announced, 'The moment of triumph has come. The leader of Free France, General Charles de Gaulle, accompanied by Generals Leclerc and Juin and the leaders of the Resistance, now begin their march on foot down the Champs Elysées to the Place de la Concorde, where they will continue their triumphant progress in automobiles to Notre Dame.' Choking with emotion over the words he added, 'Vive la France!'

Jubilation was one thing; soon the shouts of the victors were followed by cries of revenge for the blood of traitors. The Resistance had compiled their lists of names. Many were executed at drumhead court martials, others, alas, were wickedly killed in private vendettas; it was a golden chance to pay off old scores, motivated perhaps by private greed, or possibly the knowledge of where a secret fortune was hidden. There were many miscarriages of justice in the grim days that followed.

Then too, there were many who, it was felt, had to be punished, humiliated, for the way, as one newspaper put it, they had 'besmirched the fair name of France'.

The scene was repeated in many parts of liberated France. The Resistance had rounded up known collaborators 'For their public punishment by humiliation'.

So I planned to stay away from the popular boulevards where the recent scenes of joy were preparing to be replaced by the reality of revenge and reprisal. In the event, though, I found the grim reality inescapable; for the lesser streets were the very ones chosen for the ultimate degradation of collaborators. So it was with a horror like that of a rabbit petrified by a stoat that I viewed from my office window a crowd of jeering men pushing and pulling at a dozen or so women who had been assembled along the Left Bank quais near the Institut and marched in the direction of the Concorde.

They ranged from nubile girls in their teens to elderly women with sagging breasts – all painfully obvious since every one of them was stark naked and had had their heads shaven. I felt at first a shudder of nausea. Some of the women could scarcely stand, their feet left bloody prints on the road, but they were forced on by the men screaming

'Nazi whore! Nazi whore!' Some of them fell and could not move but were forced to stumble forward on their hands and knees by men who then opened their trousers and urinated on them.

I wanted to turn away from the disgusting scene. But somehow I could not, in some horrible way I stood, riveted, some of the shame washing on to me, thinking back to the not dissimilar moments when we had attempted our escape from Kronstadt. How similar the swinish mob had been then in the squares, hacking people to death with the same filthy disdain for humanity – French humanity, now – that the Russians had displayed to their fellow countrymen just because they lived different kinds of lives.

Filthy brutes, all of them! I felt no pride in the ugly mob of Frenchmen. And then a sense of shame suddenly gave way to a grim horror, so agonising that unwittingly I screamed, though my cries could not be heard from behind the windows, and with the din in the street below.

Standing almost alone, and at the end of the straggling mob stood a naked woman, not young, but bearing herself well. Her body looked firm, her breasts good, but she had been badly bruised, and her face was a soggy mess. Yet she did somehow convey the same disdain towards the crowd as those who had died in Kronstadt, and I did not need to examine her body, nude and shaven as it was.

The woman was Olga.

Then, near to her, I recognised another woman, also nude and with her head shaved. She stumbled, just behind Olga. A man pushed her. She stood upright, angry more than ashamed. She lifted her eyes as though praying to God.

It was Hélène.

I ran down the steep steps, just as they were opposite the front door of the office. I wondered what to do – to dash out and beseech someone for pity? Confess that Olga was a relative of mine? That Hélène was an old friend? As the mob changed, the decision was taken out of my hands.

All in a second, Olga stumbled, and a brute of a man kicked her and urged her on. In the same split second – so quickly I could not at first see what was happening – a man in old dungarees shouted into the crowd, then grabbed Olga's assailant and twisted him round. Then, without a second's hesitation, he pulled a Luger from his pocket and shot the man full in the face. His head seemed to split open like a ripe tomato, blood everywhere. Everyone screamed. Half the women had passed on, and most took the chance to run, naked, to the nearest side street, then hide. The small band of men stood stunned at the cool way the man had shot one of their friends. Stunned – but afraid – until violent with rage and with shouts of 'Murder', they turned on the man while I, my mouth open in astonishment, stood at the doorway. Olga slid past me – after all, she had been to that door many times in the past – I shouted 'Hélène!' She looked at me startled, started sobbing and ran to the door. I pushed her in but could not close the door for my face was transfixed by the face of the man in dungarees who had shot the other. For one split second as the crowd charged him, he looked up, and his slightly ironic face made me realise that he had seen me standing at the door. It was as though he was waving goodbye to me.

It was Ullmann, protecting his lover. He did not hesitate. Waving the gun in front of him, he backed towards the opposite side of the road on the edge of the river, just behind the path where the first portable book stores started. Still waving his gun, ready to shoot, he looked up, waved – at me? – and then put the barrel of his Luger to his temple and pulled the trigger, facing me. Quite clearly I heard him shout, in French, 'It's cleaner this way.'

As the shot rang out, the impact of the bullet made him fall backwards, straight into the Seine. I even heard the dull splash as his body hit the water.

The crowd – satiated by their fill of excitement – now began to disperse. I melted into the crowd and, when I felt it was safe, back into the Red Cross office to find blankets.

As I wrapped whatever I could find around the sobbing figures of Olga and Hélène, I realised that I was glad I had shaken hands with Major Ullmann.

The women's teeth were chattering with shock, shame, and despair. I poured out liberal doses of my dwindling stocks of liquor as Tatiana, my office assistant, put her overcoat on one woman and I lent the other my spare raincoat which I always kept at the office. To Tatiana I whispered that the older woman was my aunt, that the other was also an old friend, and that this whole beastly thing had been a terrible mistake.

Then I telephoned home. Thank the Lord, Tasha was there. I asked her to bundle up any spare clothes she had – there might be some old clothes of Olga's; I explained what had happened.

'Anything you can find,' I said, 'but I wouldn't come in, if I were you. Girls with shaven heads don't look very pretty. And one of them, darling, is Olga.'

'I won't come in,' she promised. 'Nothing would make me.'

When she arrived she thrust the suitcase into my arms and fled.

'At least I saved two of them,' I said before she ran off.

The women dressed in what they could find, after which, wordlessly, I drove them to their homes. It was the end of a wicked and revolting spectacle.

22

It was strange how, as the war drifted slowly towards final victory during its last nine months, the unsavoury incidents such as those we had witnessed began to fade in our memories. No; brutal behaviour like that could never be forgotten, especially by those who had suffered; but on the other hand they were part of the bitter, beastly realities of war.

There were many who did not think any punishment could sufficiently fit the crime for women like Olga who had openly flaunted her sexual affair with a German officer. But the tragedy was worse when innocents were wrongly punished. It may seem crazy to label Hélène as a 'good' girl but, prostitute or no, she was so proud of being French that she would never have demeaned herself by going to bed with a German.

When I drove her home to the boulevard Malesherbes, she swore to me that she had been wrongly accused, and I believed her.

'I'll come and see you again to make sure you're all right,' I promised her.

'I wish you would, and thank you for all your help.' She forced a wan smile and I drove back home.

For the most part, though, we all seemed to settle down to an almost placid existence. It was impossible to relate the distant war in the Pacific to the horrors through which France had passed. And though the fighting in eastern France and Italy was at times ferocious, it was a different kind of fighting. However desperate each battle, we were now on the winning side. Each battle might have to be fought, friends might die, but still, in the end, we won each battle. Even better, we *knew* we would win each battle before it started.

Four years ago we had accepted defeat as inevitable before each battle. Now each battle was a stepping stone to victory. It was only a question of time.

Olga apparently was doing well, the past all but forgotten. We did our best – which was not much – for Igor whose condition remained unchanged. Galina was rehearsing for *Swan Lake*, planned to be staged at the Opéra after a grand reopening, and there were vague attempts afoot to restart the ballet in Monte Carlo, though Balanchine, the Opéra's great genius of those days, had made a new home in America where he was hoping to start a new American ballet company after the war.

It was always 'after the war' at that time, and the day was growing nearer and nearer. Meanwhile, with restrictions slowly easing, the first 'visitors' soon started trickling into Paris, where the Parisians had to rebuild their spirits. Fortunately they were a robust people with a passionate pride in their country and their capital. It gave them a head start, aided by Europe's most luxurious larder, filled from a countryside with enough food (though at exorbitant black market prices) to rebuild their strength as well.

Among the first visitors to Paris was none other than Ernest Hemingway who had come a long way on the path to literary fame and glory from those happy-go-lucky days when he had spent hours over a coffee in the Deux Magots writing his short stories.

I went to pay him an early visit. He had added a little weight to his big frame, as well as to his fame, for the publication of *For Whom The Bell Tolls* had given him an international prestige we had never really envisaged in the early days. Already he was being hailed as 'America's greatest living writer', and hundreds of copies were circulating among the US troops.

He was staying at the Ritz – 'Where else?' he asked, and gave me a huge bear hug. 'How goddam long is it, Nicki?'

'Must be six years – no, longer,' I said. 'I managed to

get *For Whom The Bell Tolls* from the Red Cross and I thought it was superb. Congratulations, Ernest.'

I was still a bit overawed by his presence – precisely because I remembered my earlier meetings with him at the Deux Magots. In any case he was a big man in every sense of the word, though friendly enough as he raised himself on the bed with its pink satin coverlet and gave me a hug.

'You look as though you're doing fine,' he said.

'I'm alive,' I reflected, as I looked around room 31 in the Ritz, and its contents. On the second bed a couple of machine pistols and a crate of champagne were stacked and Ernest was drinking from a half-full bottle. He pressed a bell and within seconds a page-boy answered the summons and was rewarded with a crumpled ten-dollar bill and a request for another glass.

'You like champagne as much as your old man did?'

'I suppose so,' I hesitated. Nine o'clock in the morning seemed a bit early – though certainly Father wouldn't have thought so.

He smiled a beaming smile through his week-old growth of beard. 'Alcohol's the gift of the gods. Don't spurn it! Tell me about yourself.'

'Well actually,' I said, 'I rather wanted to hear about you.'

He gave a bull-like roar of a laugh. 'You must be kidding! I'm on assignment from *Collier's* and the *Toronto Star*, but no-one else wants to hear from me except that hick Leclerc.'

'General Leclerc? But –'

'Yeah, I know: leader of the French forces into Paris – the official liberator. And if there's one thing he hates more than a civilian it's a civilian in an army uniform.'

I looked puzzled. Hemingway's army jacket with its captain's insignia was flung over the back of a chair.

'Don't mean a thing. You've got to have a uniform if you're a war correspondent, but you're still a civilian under it. And if there's one thing Leclerc hates more than straight civilians it's newspapermen masquerading as soldiers, especially when they carry a shooter – which ain't allowed under the Geneva Convention.'

'But you –?' I looked at the guns on the bed.

'Sure. What's the point in being in a war if you can't shoot the enemy? I'm attached to the Fourth Infantry Division and I helped out with a bit of recce work. Okay, it's a bit unorthodox for a war correspondent. Some spy-eye reported it to Leclerc who is holding a Court of Enquiry, which is the equivalent of a Court Martial for the non-military. He wants to know why the American correspondent Ernest Hemingway was seen shooting at the entrance to Rambouillet and leading – *leading*, if you please! – a recce troop of Maquis! What the hell!' Ernest added, 'This troop of Maquis put themselves under my command and I got shooters for them and we went forward killing the enemy and getting information for French Intelligence. So am I scared of Leclerc? The hick! I just detached myself and my Maquis troop and we came via the Étoile and Concorde in jeeps and Kraftwagens and anything we could lay hands on.'

He drained his glass and signalled to me to hold mine out for a refill. 'One thing about the Ritz: they're still fussy about room-sharing with a woman unless you're Mister and Missus. I know: I run around with a girlfriend here, Mary Welsh, who's on *Time-Life* and a good reporter; but we also got my wife, Martha Gellhorn, booked in at the Ritz, and they let me share room 612 upstairs with her, so I've rented room 31 as an office. And I bring Mary in as a professional chum so we can talk war reporting' – he waved to the twin bed – 'move that armoury off the bed, and the Ritz is purring. French, eh? *Very* French!' He put his glass down and looked ruminative. 'Mary and Martha, eh? The two bible women – remember?'

But he was back to Rambouillet before I could answer what clearly was no more than a rhetorical question.

Changing the subject, he asked, 'And what was the name of that delicious little girl – I know it was a Russian name, but –'

'Tasha?'

'That's the one. I'll bet she turned out to be a humdinger. What happened to her?'

Half concealing a smile, I said, 'She married.'

'Ah well,' with a mock sigh, 'that's the way the best girls go.'

'To me,' I added, laughing openly this time.

'You don't say!' he cried. 'You old slyboots! Well I gotta hand it to you. You sure picked a winner.'

'I'll bring her round to meet you.'

'You do that. Give me a ring first. If I'm not at the Ritz, I could be at the Scribe. That's where the foreign correspondents are billeted, though I prefer the Ritz, but the Scribe's a distribution centre for official hand-outs, so I go there most days. And talk to the boys – and gals.'

'You don't look like the sort of newspaperman who works for hand-outs.'

'Nope, I'm not. They're strictly for the agencies – AP, Reuter, you name them. But I do *read* them. Sometimes they give me leads about future military or political movements – and if you read them with the right eyes, you can sometimes get in ahead of the opposition. Any of your old friends around?'

'Yes, there is one – or will be in a couple of days. I had a phone call last night. Your old sparring partner – François Savin – is coming in for a short conference.'

'Conference?' I could almost see Hemingway, the trained journalist, pricking up his ears. Ignoring his previous boxing bouts except for a 'Yeah – a good guy in the ring,' Hemingway asked, 'What conference?'

Shaking my head I said, 'Don't know really. He just said he wanted to fill me in with details of the repatriation of Russian prisoners of war. Just to keep me in the picture –

and for him to get a free trip to Paris. Nothing to do with me, really.'

Almost too casually, Ernest said, 'All the same, I'd like to see François when he comes. If your business isn't secret.'

'I don't see why it should be.'

'Could be interesting. Never know,' he explained. 'There's one helluva lot of Russian POWs in Europe now. What the hell's going to happen to 'em?'

'That might be what our conference is about,' I said.

'Exactly.'

'Mind you, I haven't the faintest idea,' I said. 'The Russians don't respect the Geneva Convention; so I don't suppose there's anything we can do officially. The Germans half-starved those employed on building the Atlantic Wall. The POWs are better off now under the Americans and the British. But, sure, we'll meet in a few days.'

François arrived two days later. Despite a few more years, a few more pounds, he was still the same irresponsible man who had made joining the Red Cross such good fun.

'Great days,' I sighed, though the days were even better now that I was married, despite recurring doubts about my 'sin' with Tasha which worried me regularly, though I kept them under as much control as I could. At times, though, I felt tortured, especially by chance remarks. When François, comfortably installed in the Hôtel Raspail, near the office, said in his extrovert fashion, 'And that beautiful girl of yours. God! If I were married to her, I'd want to stay in bed every night and day.'

Slightly embarrassed I muttered, 'Easiest way of getting fired.'

'Fired or tired?' François teased me, laughing. 'You obviously thrive on true and pure love, while here am I always looking for pretty girls. It must be wonderful for you to have all that beauty with an easy conscience.'

*

331

That evening we got down to what François called his 'baby conference'.

'You don't have to worry too much,' he reassured me. 'There's no way you're going to be involved because there's nothing you can do about it. But the repatriation of prisoners between all the countries may cause some questions and you'd better know the answers.'

'If I knew *what* you are taking about, it might be easier,' I retorted, studying the menu at the Boîte d'Or, just off boulevard Raspail, to which François had insisted on taking me.

'Best black market food in Paris,' he told me. 'Common knowledge. I'm on expenses. We don't get too much fun in our job, so every now and again, we're entitled to the odd perk –' he shrugged his shoulders.

The menu was impressively long, and written with flourishes in purple ink. All the prices seemed the same, so I went the whole way and ordered black market foie gras followed by a rare steak au poivre and pommes frites.

'That'll do me fine too,' said François. 'And a bottle of good Volnay – a vintage year.' This to the sommelier.

I remembered from the past – unchanged in many ways – that for all his worldliness, François was often diffident about deciding what he *really* wanted to eat, so he had the habit of taking the line of least resistance and following my choices. Reading my thoughts, he smiled tolerantly – he always smiled affectionately, kindly, that was another of his qualities.

'Always trusted your taste,' he said. 'Really, it's much easier for me to eat what *you* decide to eat.'

'Good. And now – what's my homework?'

'Wait for a coffee, and then a Calvados.'

We did.

'What I wanted to tell you is this. Unofficially the three great powers – Stalin, Churchill and FDR – have already decided on a system of total repatriation of all prisoners of war.'

I nodded. He was serious now. I had heard some rumours to that effect.

'What you don't know is that the three men are scheduled to meet soon. My spies,' with a disarming smile, 'tell me it's going to be held somewhere in Russia. And that the repatriation is going to be announced officially – with no alternatives allowed.'

'So? Doesn't everyone want to go home?'

'No they don't. There are one hell of a lot of Russian prisoners in Northern France who've been found dressed in German uniforms – and they don't want to go back. Not on your life.'

'But as they're not covered by the Geneva Convention, is there anything anyone can say or do? And even if we could help, the problem doesn't affect me or my work. My job is to look after the well-being of Russian civilians in Paris. That's so, isn't it? Civilians only.'

He nodded. 'Sure. But you do realise the implications of this plan, even if it isn't part of your job. There are over two million Russian POWs all over Europe – from the Cossacks in Austria to the men in Normandy. They've all got to go back.'

'But if someone *wants* to stay? Supposing I want a new servant and find a suitable young ex-POW and the French agree to give him a visa or whatever?'

'No go. The tragedy of what's going to happen is that Stalin insists that the repatriation must be *compulsory*. You're a POW – you've got to go home, like it or not. But millions of Russians detest Stalin and all he stands for. And the officials who are working with the Allies and the Russians on the technical details of the agreement have let a few details slip out. Stalin is terrified of having hundreds of thousands of disaffected Russians. He doesn't want them back.'

'He can't stop people thinking –'

'He can – and he will. The repatriated two million will be forced to return – by the Americans and British. And then these poor devils will face two alternatives. The lucky ones will be shot. If not, they'll take years to die of cold and starvation in Siberian labour camps. It's a horrifying prospect.'

'But you can't doom millions to death because they fought for their country which has helped to win the war?' I cried.

'Ironic, isn't it. The Cossacks, for instance, aren't even real Russians.'

François ordered another Calvados.

'Tough, but it won't save a single one of them. They'll all be sent back.'

'It's madness.'

'It is,' François twirled the stem of his glass, 'but the tragedy is that when people are busy winning wars they don't have the time to think of the peace. After all, on paper it sounds – fine. Every POW should go home. Great! Imagine the joyous welcomes for those who've spent four years in Poland when they return to London.'

'They're different. They want to go. But if you don't –'

'Stalin's as good as made it clear that if the Allies don't repatriate every prisoner to Russia, then some of the thousands of Allied prisoners from British and American camps in the east won't find it so easy to be repatriated – if ever. So what started off as a simple and normal principle is being twisted into a terrible tragedy.'

A few days later we had a celebration reunion dinner with Hemingway when François told Hemingway the details of the repatriation plans. Ernest had booked a table at the Cossack Restaurant not far from the Rond-Point. It had been recently reopened, and it was like coming home to see old friends – so long since the happy days when Igor had hosted our annual Russian lunches.

'A slap-up affair,' said Savin.

'A slap-up story you're telling me,' said Hemingway. 'You deserve it.' It was a mystery really, how the tables

seemed to be loaded with caviar, and blinis, perfect sturgeon and all the other delicacies that go to make up a
Russian meal. Hemingway had ordered vodka for those
who wanted it, but also champagne, at which the head
waiter, whom we both remembered, looked at me enquir-
ingly and whispered to me, 'Laurent-Perrier?'

'What's that?' asked Ernest.

'Nothing. It's an old tradition in this restaurant that we
always have what we used to call "Father's champagne".'

'And what's that?'

I explained how Father would only drink Laurent-
Perrier.

'What was good enough for the old Prince is good
enough for the new. And does that also suit the new
Princess, commonly called Mrs Korolev?' For Hemingway
had enlarged the guest list to include Tasha ('Who I think
is better than any champagne,') and the girl from *Time-Life*
who was married to a British war correspondent called
Noël Monks, but worked under her maiden name of Mary
Welsh. Tasha looked ravishing – so young and, if not
exactly innocent, certainly alive with the freshness of youth
and the glistening beauty of true first love, while Mary
Welsh was an equally slim, smiling girl, attractive in a
more mature way. You did not hold down a wartime job
for *Time-Life* without a comprehensive knowledge of life.

Inevitably the name of the restaurant prompted Hemingway to ask about the Cossacks, and it was when Savin
started talking about them at length that Hemingway
slapped his thighs and cried, 'That's the one! That's the
story. The Cossacks! Glamorous, superb horsemen, no
more Russian than the Lithuanians. A whole town of
them. Even included innocent women and children born
in Lienz in Austria, near the border with Italy. Yeah –
that's the story! Now we've got that sorted out let's eat,
drink and be merry.'

'You want to visit the camps?' asked Savin.

'Sure do. Lienz is in British hands. Anything to get away

335

from the French generals! I'll get my orders cut and leave as soon as I can. Won't take a long time. No sweat. I've already got on well with Eisenhower, so if I meet any difficulties I'll be able to call for help.'

'Can I come along too?' asked Mary Welsh.

Hemingway thought carefully for almost a couple of minutes then leaned across the table, took her hand and said, very gently for such a big man, mysteriously but full of hidden meaning, 'Better not, darling. One writer in the family's enough.'

I exchanged quick glances with Savin. The 'friendship' between Ernest and Mary was common gossip. It looked like becoming a family affair, though for the moment the present Mrs Hemingway – Martha Gellhorn – did look like posing a problem.

Mary gave a very sweet smile and said quite cheerfully, 'Okay. I understand.'

'I'll try to get away to Lienz later in the week,' said Hemingway. 'Go and see the officers in charge, get my five thousand words for *Collier's* and,' to me, 'I'll let you know when I'm back in Paris. Shouldn't take long to wrap this piece up.'

It was quite a night to remember, but within a few days we had all started to go our different ways. Hemingway departed to Lienz, Savin returned to Geneva, Mary just disappeared, I suppose on some assignment. I was very worried about the future plight of the POWs, but Savin's last words gave me some reassurance. 'There's nothing you can do, *mon vieux*. I just wanted to put you in the picture.'

I had been meaning to go and see one old friend in particular, Hélène. Not professionally, though! Her and Olga's appalling treatment had deeply shocked me when they had been paraded naked through the streets of Paris by the louts who were members of the Resistance. I wanted to see whether there was anything I could do, for I felt in

336

my bones that, however guilty Olga might be – and she certainly was – Hélène's protestations of innocence were true. She just was not that sort of woman and this was not the first time the Resistance groups had made hideous mistakes. They were not infallible, of course, and I would not put it past a Resistance man who had been insulted once by Hélène to pretend that she went with the Germans. Nobody could deny an accusation 'proved' by the word of a Resistance man. So I decided to pop into her house and check that she had recovered her morale, that no permanent damage had been done to her spirit, no scars left.

I drove to the boulevard Malesherbes, pressed the bell where once Father had pressed the same bell for me and I had waited so expectantly. When the young maid in a black dress opened the door I asked for Madame Hélène – her professional name. Hélène came in to see me a few moments later, took one look, and as I put an arm round her I could see the beginning of tears, barely held back. I gave her a squeeze, kissed her on the cheeks, and cried, 'You look stunning, Hélène. I'm glad your hair is growing again. I just came to see –'

'That's what I call a true friend. To come and see how I was getting on. The answer is fine.'

'I was a bit worried,' I sat down next to her on one of the old-fashioned Victorian couches with a white crocheted antimacassar. Nothing had changed, there was still an aspidistra in one corner, bringing back memories of Madame Lefarge. 'How *are* you, really?' I asked rather lamely. I did not really know what to say. I only wanted physical evidence that she was still as healthy as I had always remembered.

'Don't worry. I've forgotten the whole business, Nicki. I *had* to. For me, it's quite easy to forget something when you know the accusation isn't true. The entire affair was filthy and a lie.'

'I am sure it was.'

'And by the way,' she ordered some champagne, 'what an adorable wife you have. I glimpsed her as I was crouching behind the window in my dreadful state. I've never seen such a beautiful girl. I hope I was circumspect.'

'Perfectly. Everyone was so upset. Nobody thought – we all believed you were just another victim of stupidity and brutality. It all still makes me boil over with anger – and more than that, with shame that men can act like that, innocent or guilty.'

'I know,' she sighed. 'You've known me for years. And you'll believe that I have never entertained a German soldier in my life. They are *salauds*, but there are people who have a list of – er – addresses of places like mine, and they just pounced on me.' With another sigh, but still cheerful enough to pour out more champagne, she added, 'How sad – for me – that you are now so obviously happy! You are a real man, Nicki – a man born to be loved.'

I would never forget her. Even so, I began to prepare my exit. I did not wish to become even remotely involved.

'Well,' I stood up, 'I *am* in love,' I admitted, 'very much so.'

'I can see that,' laughed Hélène.

'So I'll be – well, on my way, saying goodbye.'

'Thank you for coming to see that I am all right. May I give you a goodbye kiss?'

'Of course.'

'And I'll always be in your debt. Any time you want any help – no,' with a laugh, 'I didn't mean *that*. But if one day there's some sort of way I can repay you I would love to have the chance to prove I am a good friend.'

'Maybe, one day.' I brushed her lips gently with my farewell kiss and made for the door. A lovely girl. I wondered if I should ever see her again.

We had received a steady trickle of Russians who had evaded capture during the heavy fighting following the Allied landings in France. Now that Paris had been liberated, large areas of the countryside were free, and one day a dirty, scruffy, unshaven man appeared at the office. I still had only the one assistant, Tatiana, who had helped me with Olga and Hélène that dreadful day.

Once the protecting power of Ullmann had gone, I became nervous of the increased power of men like Verron who were always trying to trap Russians on the flimsiest of excuses. So I had installed a 'spy hole' in the front door on the ground floor so that Tatiana could go down and peep through the tiny magnifying glass. She let the man in after asking him what he wanted.

'Escaped from a German POW camp,' I heard vague Russian words, 'Can I come in before I am questioned?' I knew this was just the sort of man whom Verron loved to catch and return to a POW camp and so I shouted to Tatiana, 'Let him in!'

'Beg pardon, sir,' the man continued to speak in Russian, head down, and I caught a glimpse of a bag of skin and bones with a haggard, grey face, and shoes with holes in the toes. His hang-dog look, his averted eyes, reminded me uncomfortably of the way in old Russia the workers on the estates refused to meet your eye until you had spoken to them.

'Come on,' I stood up and gave him a smile which he did not see. 'You look as though you could do with a sandwich and a drink. Sit down and we'll get you something.'

'Thank you, sir.' Then he muttered something, but those were almost the only words he managed to croak before he looked up, turning his face to me.

As he did so, the look of gratitude froze on his face, changing to one almost of terror or downright disbelief, astonishment. And then, mouth open as though seeing an apparition, he swayed for a moment, his eyes glazed over and without warning he crumpled to the floor fainting, barely able to speak but gurgling just audibly, 'You know Rudi Korolev?'

My mouth opened in equal astonishment. I almost keeled over too. Gripping the edge of my desk for support, I looked at the pitiful wreck of a human being and shouted, 'Tatiana – get him a brandy!' I still had the old drinks cabinet I had installed when Tasha first started coming for her lunchtime visits. Steadying myself, I got down on my knees close to him, thinking 'Poor bloody devil.' He smelt – though of what I did not at first know.

'You know my brother?' I asked holding his head in my arms, and trying to force a little brandy between his lips. He started to nod an affirmative, but could not take the liquid. The fiery brandy trickled down his filthy apology for a shirt.

'My God!' I cried. 'He knows my brother Rudi.' Cradling his head in my arms, I tried gently to bring him back to his senses until finally, warming him, wiping some brandy across his lips, he half opened his eyes. He gave me a look of abject terror, and in Russian – the language of the peasants, the serfs – I whispered, 'You're safe now.'

'Escaped prisoner,' he managed to force the words out. 'Me Rudi's good friend.'

He seemed to drift off. Terrified at the news, I tried to cajole the man into some semblance of life. It may seem brutal, but I was thinking, this man is dying. Just let me get Rudi's address. I cannot have thought that really, but all I *did* want was to know where he was.

He opened his eyes again, and this time he did not look frightened, but gave a wan smile and started to mutter some words.

'Where is Rudi?' I begged him.

As suddenly as he had opened his eyes, they closed, as though he did not have the strength to keep the lids open.

'Oh God,' I groaned to Tatiana. 'He's right out. He can't get any liquid down. Try and help me – come on – to open his mouth. Can't we get a doctor? Anything. Haven't you got any medicine?' Panicking I asked her

340

impossible questions. 'Smelling salts, or whatever, to bring
him round?' The demands tumbled out.

'I've got nothing, sir,' she was almost in tears.

'Well, let's try the brandy again.'

It was no good. I even tried to prise open his tightly
clenched mouth. Then I saw his eyes. They were open,
but his head lolled at an angle while his eyes stared at
nothing.

Only then did I realise what the smell was. It was the
smell of death.

23

I am normally so used to the vagaries and tragedies that
go with my job that I take them in my stride, but, at that
moment, with the sudden end of all hope, I broke down
completely. The thought that this poor man had known
my brother and had literally dropped dead at the moment
when he might have told me where he was, was insupport-
able.

I tottered to my feet, sat at my desk, laid my head on
crossed arms and broke into silent weeping. So near and
yet so far! How trite a phrase, yet how otherwise could I
sum up the tragedy and the agony of being thwarted on
the verge of success. My own Rudi! Here in France maybe;
no, here *surely*! The dawning recognition on the face of
the dying Russian had not been drawn from the past. It
had materialised from the present. But from where? There
were thousands of POW camps in France alone, there
must have been hundreds on the Atlantic Wall.

'Where can he be?' The question was not asked, it was
more a statement born of anguish.

'Perhaps –' started Tatiana.

'Leave me alone – please,' I pleaded, and then, feeling

341

a little calmer, I examined the dead man's pockets. The shirt bore a German maker's name on it, and I realised that the hole in his German boots had been made deliberately. They were not worn out. They had been sliced at the toe caps because they were too small.

'He must have been in the Allied invasion,' I was thinking, and as I helped myself to another tot of brandy, I called to Tatiana in the next room, 'You'd better have a little too.'

As she entered the room through the open door, she thanked me, and said almost timidly, 'I tried to speak –'

'I know. I am sorry.'

'I think I know where the man came from.'

'You *what*?' I grabbed her shoulders. The brandy spilled over the top of her glass on to her blouse and my shirt.

'You *know*! How?'

'When I spoke to him first and asked what he wanted he said that he was in a German labour battalion and added as I opened the door, "from St Lô".'

St Lô! In the thick of the second-front fighting. At the Red Cross we had heard many authentic stories of Russians being issued with German uniforms in that area. If they refused, they were shot. This must have been one of these men.

The small town of St Lô lay almost behind the centre of the sandy beaches where the invasion had taken place, a stretch of flat land a hundred kilometres long, facing due north, east of the Cherbourg peninsula all the way to Le Havre, with Bayeux ('The tapestry city' Father had always called it, showing off) in the middle.

'Get the atlas,' I shouted, and then I started to identify the places, landing beaches already immortalised by names like Omaha, Utah, Gold, Juno and Sword.

It was here where the mighty armies of Liberation had struck – just where the Germans had not really expected them – and it was here that our reports had told us of

Russians, dressed in German uniforms and armed with German rifles.

Now I was wondering if this was what had happened to my twin brother. If he had been lucky and was still alive, maybe I would be lucky too and find him.

'Perhaps he's there without the faintest idea that I'm almost round the corner,' I cried to Tatiana.

'I didn't even know you *had* a brother,' Tatiana exclaimed.

Realising that I must go to St Lô immediately, I told Tatiana to stay in the office and phone me if I were needed. She would also arrange with the police for the body to be collected. Meanwhile I dashed up the Rue de Seine to the place de Furstemberg to tell Tasha and Galina and to fetch my car.

'Isn't it wonderful? I'll have to go there as soon as I can get the necessary papers,' I explained. 'But now that most of France west of Paris is liberated, it shouldn't be difficult.'

'You'll come back? Promise?' Tasha smiled, almost shyly. She had this fear that I harboured such a sense of guilt, of sin, that one day I might escape. I never would, of course, she must have known that in her heart, but at times she was troubled that my conscience would get the better of me.

'I'll be back, never fear,' I reassured her. 'I love you too much to worry about what's right or wrong.'

Then I set about the procedure for getting movement orders – in effect military orders giving me permission to proceed to a given destination, and which would be logged as official business.

All this was arranged at the Hôtel Scribe on the Grand Boulevard near the Opera, the same which had been commandeered for the war correspondents like Hemingway and Mary Welsh. They were given rations, bedrooms, a mess and an office for arranging the trips they wanted to make. I was attached to the Scribe as part of the correspondents' team because there was not really any other branch of the armed forces into which I could naturally fit.

No problems. The Scribe gave me stamped movement orders, and then a large bunch of official petrol coupons, which I could use at the central distribution depot behind the back of the Quai d'Orsay. I filled up the tank and signed for two full jerricans of petrol which I put in the boot – just in case.

I had to discover exactly where St Lô was, then find the way to the camp – and then to Rudi, if he was still alive. And after that, if humanly possible, engineer some method of escape.

I tucked the spare petrol coupons into my pocket, and prepared to set off. The car I had been issued with was a second-hand Citroën Quinze, a powerful and reliable 23 hp front-wheel drive which had been first used by the Gestapo. When it was issued to me by the authorities, on instructions from the Red Cross, it had yellow painted rims on the wheels – the sign that it had been a Gestapo car. I had these painted black, and Red Crosses painted on the roof and on both the front doors.

As I drove to St Lô, my mind was racing not only with excitement, but also with unformed thoughts of how I could get Rudi out of the hell in which he must be living. And most of all, I was tormented by the need for *speed*. Already the British troops who had captured Russian prisoners near their beaches had started to ship hundreds over to England. Plans had already been drawn up, François Savin had told me, to send thousands of Russians to the United States and Canada. Once they left the shores of France, I would be unable to interfere. And worse still, once they were out of my jurisdiction, and the war was over, all Russian POWs would be sent automatically straight back home.

There was no time to lose. Already measures were being

formulated into what *seemed* a very reasonable arrangement – an exchange of prisoners; the British would return to Britain, the Americans to America – there, to be received with joy by loved ones; and the Russians would return to Russia – there to be received by the torture chamber or, if they were lucky, by a bullet. No exceptions. Certain death. Only as long as the Russian POWs remained on French soil did they stand even a remote chance of escaping.

It was imperative to arrange somehow for Rudi to be freed – or to plan his escape. Every Russian POW had, of course, been identified, especially the 'pro-German' ones who had carried German rifles. Special checks, I had discovered, were being kept on Russians who had actually 'fought' for Germany, desperate to help to defeat the Communists from whom they could expect no mercy. It was an incredible and ironic turnabout in the war in which 'friends' had actually fought on the same side, only to become the bitterest of enemies. And then, it seems, some of the prisoners wanted to fight again alongside those who had imprisoned them.

I reached St Lô after a miserable journey, though at least it was a journey through a part of France that was now, after five long years, once again free. There were still passes to be shown casually at check points, still villages shattered beyond recognition, detours necessary around impossible, smashed-up roads. But I finally reached the town, to find a scene of complete chaos. Though the fighting had not been as severe there as elsewhere, the troops had been there – in their thousands. And they still were.

At the first bar which I found open – called Chez Victor, and crowded despite its windows being boarded up – I was told that the prisoners were being held in a series of huts, ten kilometres from St Lô, near a small town behind the fighting, by Americans on the Utah beach called St Jean de Daye. I decided to have a quick drink at Chez Victor, and the patron was near enough to Calvados not to ask me what I wanted, but just handed me a stiff fiery drink so strong I could feel it trickling down my entire body; and when I asked if he had a sandwich – 'Anything, I'm just hungry!' I said – he was near enough to Normandy to give me a fresh baguette stuffed with slabs of square Pont l'Évêque, with the thick crust on.

St Jean de Daye, I was told, had been the scene of such heavy fighting that the Americans who had landed on Utah beach in June had not been able to dislodge the Germans before the end of July. Now, though, it had been cleared. 'But no one's had time to clean the place up yet,' said Victor as I set off.

It was starting to drizzle, almost as though to increase the miserable after-effects of war. Then, when I had almost reached what had once been a small town, and was looking around the remains of the town hall square, an American in a jeep, seeing the Red Cross signs on my Citroën, stopped and shouted 'H'ya. Lookin' for anyone?'

'The POW camp.'

'Follow me, mister, it's only a mile down the road and I'm goin' almost there.'

I followed him past the stark evidence of war all around us – smashed windows, electricity poles torn down, the skeletons of burned-out cars or trucks littering pot-holed, skiddy roads. As we approached the camp, the driver of the jeep stopped and yelled over his shoulder, 'Gotta make a slight detour round there.' He pointed to what looked like a never-ending curtain of trailing wires. They must have been some kind of trap, I never discovered what, but we struck out across the field for a hundred yards, passing what must, in the past, have been a pretty little auberge, with a car park. But outside, the whole terrace was smashed, with dozens of broken chairs, and half a dozen trees chopped down.

'It's sure one hell of a bloody mess,' yelled the GI,

'but –' pointing to some rectangular wooden huts behind the deserted bistro, 'there's your POW camp – and filled with goddam Russian traitors too. Been shootin' at us. I'd string the shits up, every one, if they'd let me.'

Ahead of me I saw the main entrance to the camp, surrounded by a double ten-foot high barbed wire fence, and acre upon acre of squat one-storey wooden buildings. And in one of these I hoped to find Rudi.

At a gap in the long straight line of barbed wire, was a larger, cleaner-looking hut above which the American flag was fluttering on a pole, and outside a couple of GIs were lolling, smoking, in front of a plain wooden bench and a large wooden table sheltered from the rain by a home-made tent-like structure. On the table stood two tins of beer. It all seemed rather casual after my experience of German HQ discipline, but perhaps that, I thought as I stopped the car, was one of the privileges of victory.

'Hi!' said one of the GIs as he drank and put the can down on the table again, 'What can I do for you?'

I leaned out of the left-hand window of the Citroën. 'Can I see the camp commandant – I'm from the Red Cross?'

'Sure. No sweat. Go right ahead,' he jerked his head in the direction of the large building twenty yards away and resumed talking and drinking.

I had not yet learned that the Americans' insatiable desire to win – to fight, to kill, but always to *win* – was marked by a startling hatred of unnecessary discipline. Their business was to *fight*. As for discipline when off duty, as one man explained on another occasion, 'That's just a load of crap for the top brass.'

I pushed open the door of the nearby hut. A voice behind a desk asked me, 'May I help you, mister?' The voice was polite, the man's clothes smart. I said, 'If you can, Corporal. I'm looking for a particular man here – a POW.'

'Russian, sir?'

I nodded and showed him my papers.

'It's the old one about the needle in the haystack, sir. I don't know as how we can help.'

'He's my brother. My twin brother.'

'You Russian? And in the Red Cross?' For the first time he looked intrigued.

'Born Russian,' I smiled. 'But I became a Swiss citizen back in 1919. My twin brother wasn't so lucky – he didn't get away when I did.'

'Tough luck,' he gave a low whistle, and turned to an officer just coming out of an inside room, ''Scuse me, cap'n. You may be able to help this Mr Korolev from the Red Cross.'

'If I can.' He was young, already with a row of ribbons on his chest and suggested, 'Come on in, sir,' and indicated a chair, 'take the weight off your legs.' He offered me a cigarette and then asked, 'What's the problem, sir?'

I explained – repeated – the situation.

'Jeez! Quite a story. We'll sure help if we can, but there's three thousand of 'em locked in those doss houses.' Thinking for a moment, he finally said, 'Tell you what. Among the prisoners we've got the Nazi major – or whatever the hell his rank is – who ran this camp before we decided on a change of management. We took all the German guards and officers who were running the camp and now *they're* locked up in separate huts. We've got a kinda waiting-room next door to this office. I'll send you this German guy. He speaks a bit of English. I'll leave you to have a talk with him.'

He beckoned me into the small adjoining room, and I heard him yell to the corporal, 'Hey Mick! Get that Kraut Schutz in here to see Mr Korolev.'

'Will do, sir,' the corporal replied and after a few minutes, the German appeared, looking baffled, and shut the door behind him.

'From the Red Cross,' I introduced myself.

348

The man looked at me, clicked his heels and announced, 'Oberstleutnant von Schutz at your service.'

Though slightly shopsoiled by now, von Schutz still bore traces of his rank and bearing. He was typically Prussian, square-headed with short cropped hair and a black monocle concealing an eye socket.

'A battle wound,' he grunted when he saw me looking at the monocle fixed as though stuck there in cement. 'Now I am what the Americans call non-combatant.'

Once again I explained my mission, and after some hesitation, he said, in broken English, 'Yes, I think I am baffled when I first see you. I think I am seeing you before, but then I think, no, it cannot be. Now you explain the puzzle. I am seeing this brother of yours in the days when I am in control of the *hundezwinger*.'

'What's that?'

'I am sorry. It is the German for – how you call it – slang. It means "kennels for the dogs".'

'And now you are a prisoner in a dog kennel,' I said, angry at the insult to Russians. 'Thank you, I shan't need you anymore.' I opened the door, and told the corporal, 'This man can go now.' The man left by himself and returned, presumably to his hut, without any armed guard.

'Is it safe to let him go alone?' I asked, surprised.

The corporal chuckled. 'That guy's going to scuttle right back to his own hut. If he goes into a Ruskie hut by mistake, he'll never come out alive.' Then, with a change of tone, he said, 'We've found out where your brother is, sir, we've got a list here. He's in Hut 23. I'll take you there.' He was brandishing papers.

'Very efficient,' I complimented him.

'Not really, sir. We had to get our lists ready because all the Ruskies will have to be shipped back to Comrade Stalin.'

'Poor devils,' I said, my heart sinking all the way down to my boots. Though I knew, of course, that the total exchange or return of prisoners to their own countries had been agreed on, I had not realised the lists had already been drawn up.

As though reading my thoughts, the young corporal sympathised, 'Maybe they'll make an exception in the case of your brother. Trouble is, though, copies of these lists have already been sent to divisional headquarters and to the French police. I guess the French'll have the job of transporting them back. Russia already has copies of most lists.' Walking alongside me, 'Don't know how it's all been worked out, none of my business. Hut 23 is over there. I'll leave you alone, but please report when you leave camp,' adding, '*Alone*.'

Heart fluttering between hope and dread I walked along the muddy slush of the path made by the constant treading over the years of countless slaves; slaves or soldiers.

The door of the hut was closed. I opened it. The place was so thick with smoke – they must have recently been issued with extra 'comforts' – that I could hardly see through it. I certainly could not make out any special features in the sea of faces.

'Korolev!' I shouted from the door into the gloomy, smoke-laden atmosphere, 'You're wanted.'

'Coming!' shouted a voice from the back of the room.

A shaggy figure in German uniform stumbled forward, a voice from the back of the room yelled in a derisive voice, 'You're for it this time, Rudi!'

He stumbled forward, reached the front door of the hut, which was lighter as the door was open, and suddenly stopped. I swear my heart stopped too – for a second, as it does when you sneeze – at the split moment when the two halves of a pair of twins looked into each other's eyes for the first time in twenty-five years. For that moment – a third of a second, a third of a lifetime – we stood stock still, riveted with astonishment, then with a double cry of 'Nicki!' and 'Rudi!' leapt forward and flung our arms round each other in a bear hug. The tears were streaming down Rudi's face.

'Sorry. Physical weakness,' he said. And then, after we had examined each other, Rudi wiped away the tears and almost laughed, 'What the hell are you doing here? And looking so bloody prosperous?'

'I might ask you the same thing. What are you doing here dressed up as a German soldier?'

His face clouded.

'Ah,' he said. 'That's a long story.'

'Come on. The story'll wait.' Putting an arm round his shoulder, I said, 'I've been given permission to use a waiting-room here for half an hour or so. We'll get a couple of mugs of good American coffee and I've got something here that might interest you.' And we trudged across the narrow path towards the guard house with its waiting-room, I produced out of my pocket a half pint flask of vodka.

'Not the best quality,' I admitted, 'but it *is* genuine.'

Rudi fingered the bottle almost with reverence. 'Two years since I had a drink of any sort. I'm going to drink this so slowly it'll last for years.'

Once in the waiting-room, with the door closed behind us, I took a good look at Rudi.

'You look terribly thin,' I said. And he did, but I could see that it was not so much from starvation but was more a kind of lean hardness that comes from physical work. His face – under a day's stubble – had a grey touch to it, and his eyes were staring.

'Hard work,' he confirmed what I thought. 'Building Hitler's famous Atlantic Wall. Ten hours a day – or you didn't eat that day. If you couldn't work – I mean incapable of work – shot on the spot. This was a real labour camp. We got lousy food, but if we worked hard we got enough – all taken from the French. But to hell with all that – tell me *everything*.'

The questions tumbled from eager lips as he sipped coffee – wonderful to him after endless years of the muck he must have drunk; and wonderful for me too. How had

I found him? How was Father? I told him he had died, but not how. And Galina? He had heard a rumour that she was dancing for the Germans.

'Not true,' I said angrily. 'She *did* go to Germany several times – but only to dance for French prisoners of war. She's French – and a top ballet dancer now.'

'She was always crazy about dancing.'

'I saw a picture of you and a friend once. It was in the papers. Did you see it?' I asked.

'Yes,' replied Rudi. 'You actually saw it?'

'Yes. In the Red Cross. I couldn't believe it. I wondered if you were being sent to Siberia!'

'No. I'd won a Stakhanovite award for the speed with which the two of us laid drains! I didn't have a bad life, until I was drafted into the forces and was caught fighting on the east front and shipped here – to dig, but not drains,' he still had the same infectious grin.

It was curious, the look of satisfaction he gave at the way in which he had won a Soviet award. And curious, too, the sudden spurt of anger when he thought Galina had been dancing for the Germans. After all, he had been captured in German uniform handling a German gun.

Still, I thought, nothing matters except that we are together after twenty-five years, sitting on two hard wooden folding chairs resting our elbows on the plain deal table between us.

'Two lookalikes!' I laughed.

'But with one difference,' there was no bitterness in his voice, 'you are in better shape than I am.'

'That's why I was able to find you,' I retorted, adding deliberately, 'before you are repatriated, wearing your German uniform, to Russia to face a rapturous welcome from Comrade Stalin.'

The cloud passed over his face again. 'I've heard rumours that we'll have to be sent back. But I imagine we'll be given some chance to stay elsewhere in Europe if we want to.'

'Don't bank on it,' I said shortly.

'How do you know so much?' Rudi asked curiously. 'Are you French?'

I shook my head, 'No. I'm Swiss. I got a Swiss passport through Father's influence almost as soon as we escaped. For years I've worked in the Red Cross.'

'Lucky you. I'd no idea.'

'I'm married, you know.'

'You *are*?'

'Yes. And you'll never guess who. Olga – remember Aunt Olga? She had a daughter, Tasha, and we're married.' Again I had to simplify my answers. Even lie.

'Well, I'll be damned. But let me tell *you* something. I'm married too.'

'Then, *I'll* be damned!' But more gently I asked, 'I'd no idea, of course. It must be hell being married – and separated. How long is it since – er – you last saw your wife?'

As though firing a bullet into outer space, Rudi grinned, then looked at me.

'This morning.' I nearly dropped the flask of vodka in my astonishment.

'*Today*! How on earth? This is no place for bloody stupid jokes!'

'It's no joke. The girl I married is young but tough. She followed me to the Atlantic coast – yes, all the way from Lienz.'

'My God,' I breathed. I could hardly believe it.

'She's now one of the camp cooks,' he added with another grin.

'How do you mean? Is she French? Is it a real marriage?'

'She's as Russian as caviar.'

'But where is she?' I asked.

'She lives in St Lô. It's all a bit complicated. The Allied advance from the beaches was so swift that all the American and British troops were too busy fighting to worry about the thousands of prisoners they took. We couldn't have proper guards or cooks, so the Americans offered the local Frenchmen and women part-time jobs to help run the camp. They get paid.'

'But your wife?'

'We married in Russia near the Polish border just after I joined the Cossacks. Some of the Cossack princes reminded me of Tsarskoe Selo, tall hats, fur coats, swords, magnificent horsemen, and beautiful girls. Some took three or four girls with them – a sort of harem. It was like living in a Cossack village. And the music! Sad and beautiful. Sometimes they sang with balalaikas till the dawn. The only thing missing was food and drink. Then I was offered a transfer with the promise of good food to help build the Atlantic Wall.'

'And you did?'

He nodded. 'I didn't realise, until it was too late, that we were to be force-marched across the whole of France. And Nataliya – that's my wife – insisted on coming along too. I don't know how we managed. In fact we nearly died, but when we finally did reach the sea, the rations were increased and Nataliya was enrolled as a camp cook. And sometimes she smuggled food in for me.'

'But when the Allies struck you moved?'

Rudi nodded. 'Lock, stock, barrel and cook! In buses, to help to defend the Nazis.'

'How old is Nataliya?'

'She's still only twenty-two. She's a great girl, my wife, and you'll adore her. Anyway, to round off the story. We're still short of American troops to supervise the camp, so again they've enrolled a bunch of local peasants who work on clearing up and generally helping out – and my wife is still a camp cook. Only there's no room for women in the camp, so arrangements were made for her to live with one of the local families. The Americans don't really *want* female POWs – and they obviously wouldn't give a damn if she just didn't turn up one morning. She could melt into the countryside and get lost. I've begged her to bolt, but she won't. Wants to stay with me.' He gave another of his grins and added, 'You know how irresistible we both are!'

What a story! But there were serious matters to discuss.

'Listen Rudi – and carefully. I don't know how, but we've got to get you out of here. And take Nataliya with you. I'm not joking when I tell you that, if you stay, the chances are that you'll both be executed when you reach Russia. Stalin has more or less said that he intends to kill every traitor. But *how* are we going to get you away?'

'There's no way without bribery,' Rudi replied brusquely. 'And that's bloody expensive.'

'If I can find some money?'

'Money's worthless,' he said. 'Forget it, Nicki. Of course I've never fought against the Allies. You know that.'

'Yes, I know. And I believe you. But will Stalin?'

'We'll just have to hope. The idea of fighting *with* Germany instead of *against* Germany is crazy. Even he must be able to realise that.'

'How did you get this uniform?' I asked.

He explained: 'We were force-marched across France to the north-west coast near Brest where Hitler was sure the Allies would attack. We had virtually no clothes, very little food. We were all lined up – those who could still stand – and the camp commandant barked out to the first man, "You've got nothing to wear. We can't provide you with civilian clothes. But you can have German uniforms. Will you wear one?" The first man said "No". Immediately – on the spot – he was shot. And the next, and the next, and the next. Finally, we all gave in. At least we all had thick warm clothes and, providing we worked hard, enough to keep us alive. The next thing, the Germans just gave each of us a gun. You took it – or you were shot. So we took it. It wasn't loaded, of course, or we'd have shot the guards.'

'I believe you. And now,' with a look at my watch, 'time's nearly up. I'm going to get you both out *somehow*, and hide you until it's safe. I don't know how – yet – but I will. I promise you.'

'That's a beautiful watch,' said Rudi inconsequentially. 'Is it gold?'

I nodded, feeling slightly embarrassed, parading even by accident this example of my good luck. 'It was given me by a girl to mark my services in bed!' That brought a laugh. Poor Brig, what an age ago!

'I've never seen gold since the old days. Never.' He said wistfully, hesitating for a long, long time before adding slowly, 'With a watch like that, I could buy my way out of this camp by tomorrow night.'

'You *what*?'

'I mean it,' said Rudi. 'We've got about thirty or forty peasants who work around here three days a week, cleaning up the grounds, bringing in food – it's a rich area and they sell their spare produce – cheese and so on – to the Americans who like fresh food and give the peasants tinned stuff in return.'

'And where do you come in?'

'The peasants come on duty tomorrow. They've got enough food – but no wealth. Nothing to trade. Money doesn't count anymore. It's a farce. *But a gold watch!* I've already sold the few things I managed to save and bought cigarettes and so on. But this watch! It's worth a fortune – in kind. I know one young chap who'd change places secretly with me, wear my uniform and give me his clothes – and then tomorrow night I'd be one of thirty-eight peasants leaving the camp at the end of the day. They only have a head count. Thirty-eight come in each morning, thirty-eight go out each evening. Unrecognisable.'

'But the man? The peasant?'

'He'd agree to stay there for a couple of days, then after I've had a chance to get clear, he'd escape to the guard house – tell how he was tied up, how he managed to untie the knots – and he can prove who he is, of course. Be no problems there. Why,' longingly, 'it's foolproof.'

I did not hesitate.

'Done,' I said. 'If you're sure. And your wife?'

'She lives round the corner. She's free to come and go in the building. She'll be there, waiting for me.' Then he changed his tone completely. 'No, I can't let you,' he said despairingly. 'If you had some money and could buy a watch for me – well, that would be different.'

'Don't be such a damned fool, Rudi. You're my twin brother, remember. And what's a watch compared to my life – and yours? Now shut up and put your hands where they can't be seen.'

Hands under the table I clipped open the leather strap of my Cartier watch and handed it across to Rudi under the table, saying to myself, 'Bye bye, Brig'. Then, 'Don't get caught,' I warned him. 'It's inscribed on the back.'

'I won't. Did you come through the centre of St Jean de Daye and see where the old town hall used to stand? One half is left, but there's an arch – about the only thing that is left standing. My wife and I will be there tomorrow evening. Between six and seven when the peasants go home.'

24

How wonderful it was to see Rudi again! Back from the dead – or nearly. Twenty-five years. Yet here he was, in the flesh. He had suffered a lot but he did not look too bad apart from the way he constantly looked around as if he was about to be struck by a guard. I only hoped he was not being naïve in believing that a Frenchman would so easily offer his place in a prison camp to a Russian! It seemed incredible – and yet it was the Frenchman who would look wronged and probably blame the Americans for having allowed it to happen.

And as for the thoughts of the Frenchman concerned, he would not only profit handsomely, but many of his countrymen secretly admired the Russians, for the blood of the millions of dead Russians who had helped to free the French. The Russian steamroller was as much a part of the liberation of France as the invasion of the Allies. The Russians had drained the Nazi forces from the west. But when the Allies attacked, they drained the German divisions from the east. Neither could have succeeded without the other. And so perhaps – especially for the price of a Cartier watch – the French did not object to helping a Russian ally, prisoner or not.

All the same, there was one worry – *me*. Even if the American guard was stupid, he must realise that I had *something* to do with the escape, though if I could prove to them a perfect alibi, if the watch were never traced, they might be suspicious but could they ever *prove* anything?

I realised, almost as soon as I had said goodbye to Rudi – promising that I would meet him in twenty-four hours – that I must return immediately to Paris. Yes. It was Tuesday evening by now, and I had to prove to the highest authority that I was in Paris on the Wednesday – *before* Rudi escaped. I had to prove it to one particular person – Verron of the Prefecture. For I had no doubt that his department would very soon be told of the strange disappearance of a twin of the Red Cross official.

I would drive back to Paris, arrive about midnight, then make an excuse to call on Inspector Verron early the following morning, then drive straight *back* to St Jean de Daye. My travel orders were undated. Any guards at any check points would probably be changed and I was a Red Cross official anyway. Even if Verron were suspicious, he would find it difficult to believe that I had been to the St Lô area *twice*.

I raced back to Paris, to be greeted by a sleepy Tasha. I told her, 'Hush darling! I'll explain everything later,' and was so tired that I slept like a dead man in her arms until in the middle of the night I woke restlessly, troubled by nightmares, unable to pinpoint why I could not sleep. My tossing and turning awoke Tasha who looked at the luminous hands on her watch and whispered, 'Sleep darling. It's only three o'clock.'

'I can't sleep. I'm going into the study for a cigarette. I'll be back in a few minutes.' She went back to sleep as I tiptoed out of the room.

As I gratefully filled my lungs with the evil smoke of a Gauloise, I suddenly realised what was worrying me, what I had been dreaming about. Here we were, making all our plans for escape with an almost military precision, yet I had ignored one vital factor. Where was I going to put Rudi and his wife? We had to find *somewhere*. I dared not hide them in the place de Furstemberg. With the knowledge that I had met Rudi officially in a POW camp just before his escape, suspicion that I was involved would be immediate. Without any question, I would be visited by someone – the police, the army, more probably Verron – but I could not tell who.

But where could they go? *Two* people! That made the problem doubly difficult. Where, oh where? I could not put them up in a hotel, even if I could afford it. Everyone had to sign a form when they checked in. The *fiches* were collected daily by the police. I tried to think of friends who might help. None. In the end I even got out my address book to check through its long list of my contacts, to see if there were any names I had forgotten.

And by God! There *was* one, departed from the scene long ago, but who had been succeeded by someone who was in my debt – and I was sure she would be only too anxious to help if she could. The sudden thought came to me when I was halfway through my address book and reached the letter L. Why on earth had I filed the name and address of Madame Lefarge? Crazy? It was plain stupid. But the old harridan had gone, replaced by the wonderful Hélène.

359

She *might* help. I could think of no-one else anyway. I would call and ask her on my way back to St Lô in the morning. I stubbed out my last cigarette of the long night, and rolled back into bed.

The next day I presented myself at the Prefecture. I invented some nonsensical questions to make sure of seeing Verron. It might not be proof that I was in Paris all day, but it would at least puzzle him. Then I drove to Hélène's flat. Past the Madeleine, I drove round the place St Augustin, and then up the boulevard Malesherbes. There I rang Hélène's bell. I did not quite know how to broach the subject, especially as I knew that mine would not be a very welcome request.

Still, Rudi and his wife would not be any trouble, I knew that, and if it really were possible – well, Hélène, as I knew, was an angel, and she did want to repay what I had done for her.

Sleepy-eyed, she opened the door, which was still on the chain and peeping through the narrow aperture asked, stifling a yawn, 'You? My dear Nicki!'

'Can I come in?'

'Of course. The girls aren't here, of course.'

'I didn't come for them,' I laughed outright.

'I didn't think you had somehow. But there must be some very important reason. Let me get you some coffee.' She undid the latch chain.

It was all arranged, typically of Hélène, very quickly. Briefly I explained our problem. 'It's only temporary,' I promised her.

'Don't worry,' she smiled. 'We've got an attic which we never use for business. It's got a *cabinet de toilette*, a bidet and so on. And if you want to go out, there's a back door that leads to the fire escape at the back of the house.'

And that was that! All fixed up in a few minutes.

Finishing my coffee, I told her, 'Now, I'm really and truly in *your* debt up to the ears. And I'll never forget.'

'Ah Nicki! I told you once that you were made for love. How easy if only I could persuade you to pay the debt in kind.'

I reached the St Lô area around two o'clock, but I did not like the idea of my car being noticed if I waited at St Jean de Daye, so I stopped three or four miles to the east at a village called Arel, where I had to wait at a level crossing while the branch-line train from Bayeux to St Lô passed through. I took a leisurely stroll through the village. There was a pub of sorts in the Rue de la Gare, newly painted with a new name: Le Croix de Lorraine; and after returning to collect my car, I went in, took a Calvados – I needed it – and had what turned out to be an excellent local dish, *blanquette de veau* with half a bottle of *vin rouge* to accompany my Pont l'Évêque cheese. Then, telling the *patron* I had to drive to Paris that night, I persuaded him to wrap up some 'rations' – for Rudi and his wife, of course.

Thus fortified, but still apprehensive, I returned to St Jean de Daye.

Once again the ruins of the village gave me the shivers. Half the back of what had been the Town Hall still stood, but empty, a skeleton, so that you could see all the inside, like the doll's house which opens in front, revealing every room in the house – rooms which should have been private.

Six o'clock. No-one there. A ruined wasteland, desecrated by man, an empty desert of broken buildings smashed as though by a massive primordial giant. I got out of the Citroën, stumbling off the roadside, and walked over the broken bricks and stones towards the arch and behind it the remains of the open 'doll's house'. It was still, the air, but I was intrigued because one of the wooden doors still standing in the skeleton was rattling, moving slightly backwards and forwards. Only there was no wind.

Then I thought I realised what was happening, and I was right. Rudi and his wife were hiding behind the door and he was signalling his presence to me. The square was deserted. How odd that door looked, just stuck to the few remaining bricks at one end of a wall, flapping in the open air.

I looked around. Not a soul. Like all peasant villages – let alone ruined villages – the doors of a few remaining houses had been locked at the end of a day's work, the windows shuttered, all except 'our' door, leading from nowhere to nowhere.

Almost impetuously I shouted, 'There's no-one around. Come out and run to the back seat of the car.'

An invisible hand must have grabbed the inside door-knob for it half opened firmly and the terrified face of Rudi peered round the door, now held still.

As a bent old woman in a shawl suddenly emerged and walked across the other side of the square, Rudi shot back behind the safety of the door. The woman never saw us, but I realised, perhaps for the first time, the long-drawn-out fear that must have soaked into every pore of Rudi's skin and every part of his mind since he had been taken prisoner by the Germans. He had *looked* in fairly good shape during the half hour we had spent together in the camp – but I had heard of a few of the hardships suffered by POWs – men beaten, tortured, used for medical experiments until death was the only hope left to a human being. And even now with Rudi (so far) free I had never seen fear so clearly etched on a man's face as when he caught sight of the old black-clad woman and darted back behind the door.

'Okay now,' I called. 'No-one here! Run for it!'

Rudi peered out, then, holding Nataliya's hand, they ran as fast as they could over the stones towards the car. I had left the back door open – though wondering at one time whether it would be possible to hide one of them in the boot. Once Rudi and Nataliya were in, I walked quickly back over the ruins and climbed into the driving seat.

'This is my wife,' Rudi introduced us.

'We'll say Hullo later,' I smiled and started up the motor.

'I'm terrified,' Rudi's teeth were chattering.

'Everything's gone fine,' Nataliya was more composed.

'Yes, fine – so far,' said Rudi. 'But you've no idea of the treatment they give you if you try to escape. I did once. They gave me the water treatment.' We were driving quietly out of the village now. 'They held my head in a bucket of water until I was almost drowned, then they brought me round – and I knew what was going to happen. I had to wait until they fetched me and then did it all over again. Ten times they did it to me. I passed out each time, then was brought back to life. I'm scared of being caught, I don't mind admitting it.'

'But the Americans!' Nataliya tried to cheer him up. 'You're a POW of the Americans. *They* don't behave like that.'

'Maybe not, but I don't trust anyone. No, you're right, for a moment I'd forgotten we're prisoners of the Americans.'

As he was in a highly nervous state, I gave them the packet of sandwiches I had brought.

'Here, share these with your wife. And when you've eaten them, tell me how you managed to escape.'

The story was soon told. By now Rudi and his friends in the huts knew most of the peasants, and the entire atmosphere of the camp, and especially the guards, was so relaxed that nobody seemed to worry. At the end of a day's work, when the peasants prepared to leave, the American guards only made a head count.

The gold watch was such a prize that there were even volunteers offering to take Rudi's place. In the end, two brothers offered to help. One stayed behind and donned Rudi's clothes, in exchange for the Frenchman's old peasant clothes. All the Russians in Hut 23, of course, had to know what was happening. The Frenchman agreed to remain there for two days – until the following day – using Rudi's bed, drawing his rations so that Rudi would have plenty of time for his getaway.

363

The brother was needed for the plot because he left normally, but taking the watch. If the other brother had been found wearing the watch, the Americans would have guessed immediately that it was a set-up.

'It's only guesswork now, of course, but when the Americans come in to make the daily inspection while the Russians are exercising, they'll look at the Frenchman – without the watch but wearing my uniform – tied up but yelling in the toilet, and the Americans will force an entry and find that one of our men has escaped. My chums will play the whole thing absolutely dumb.'

Rudi was more relaxed now that he had eaten, and we were soon speeding along the main road past St Lô and towards Paris.

'There's only one thing that worries me,' confessed Rudi. 'And that's your involvement. After all, the Americans *know* we're twins, they allowed us to talk. They *must* – *know*.'

'They may know,' I agreed, 'but if we're careful, they can never prove a damned thing. I've taken care of that. So long as they never find *you*.'

I explained how I had driven all the way back to Paris to establish a cast-iron alibi.

'Mind you,' I added, 'I don't think the Americans'll mind that much. They'll go through the motions but they're only interested in one thing – winning the war. Finally, they'll just write you off as a bad debt. I'm much more worried about the French.'

I explained the particular viciousness towards aristocratic Russians displayed by Inspector Verron. 'And he's in charge now. We lived under German rule in Paris for so long that we forget that Paris is now a French city again. He's a dangerous man.'

I had found an old tarpaulin cover which I threw on the back seats in case I had to try and hide Rudi, though I would pass Nataliya off as my wife if I had to. But we *were* at peace in this stretch of France, and I was banking on the fact that I carried Red Cross papers, that my car was clearly marked, and, as had happened before, stoppings at check posts would be nothing more than a quick casual wave past a soldier who now had no enemy to watch for.

At first, I had wondered about stopping for a meal, but had decided, No. It was imperative to keep Rudi out of sight because when his escape became known the role of a twin brother in the Red Cross would soon demand answers. And I could easily be traced in Paris and questioned. So if on the way back to Paris we had stopped for a meal and were recognised as twins, somebody would be intrigued enough to remember us and pass on the news that we had been seen together *before* Rudi was supposed to have escaped. The very eventuality for which I had constructed my alibi.

There was a long stretch of sparsely wooded straight road after St Lô and here, where any approaching car could be seen, we stopped so that I could hear at last something of what had happened to Rudi during the years before we met.

When we stopped it also gave me my first real chance to turn round and take a good look at Nataliya. She hardly looked at her best of course – neither did Rudi – but after taking in the slim figure in its ragged clothes, the youth, the brown ill-combed hair, I was immediately impressed by the – how best to describe it? – the *steadfastness* that shone out of her character. I could imagine that her determination not to die must have been an underlying factor during the long march across France. I was equally impressed with her calm grey-brown eyes, by the determined set to her jaw and the first time she shook my hand and asked, 'I've heard so much about you! Tell me, do we have a good chance?' Her grip was firm, almost like a man's, and I realised that she had asked the question not out of fear, but just because she wanted to know.

'I think so,' I reassured her.

'Now, let me tell my story,' Rudi laughed. It was wonderful to hear him laugh. 'In fact most of the time before the war – it was like living in a landscape where nothing happened. Nothing was *allowed* to happen. If you disobeyed the rules, got drunk or whatever, just wanted to have a bit of fun, you might find yourself in Siberia. Yes, it's true. You just went through life waiting patiently to be fed, to work until it was time to die. Like a horse! Of course if you were a dissident, if you protested that was different – but then I never was that sort, and my future was shaped, I suppose, by the tragedy of 1919. Most of the time I worked on farms, paid mostly in food and lodging – but at least on the farms I got better food than in the city. But it was a drab, grey existence. You couldn't call it *living*.'

'But what,' I asked, 'happened in 1919?'

'I still can't bear to think of it – not even now. Someone was *stabbing* Mama. It was utterly terrifying. Someone grabbed *me* – I don't know who or why. I kicked and screamed and I tore myself free and threw myself towards her body and sobbed and cried and kissed her. You can't imagine the scene, Nicki, but though it's all so long ago, and so much has happened, I'll never forget it.'

I could hardly bear it myself. Part of me wanted to ask him if he had seen the baby Tasha in those terrible moments. But another part could not bear to talk of yet more horror. So, screwed around to talk to him in the back seat, I encouraged Rudi to tell me more about his life.

'They dragged the bodies off. An elderly woman took hold of me, put her arms round me and led me from there. She said something, I can't remember what. She forced me to take a large swig of vodka. I do remember her saying, "That'll put some fire in your belly, my lad!" And she took me along with an elderly man and said, "I'll look after you, little boy. Pretend you're our son if anybody asks questions." Then we drove all day on an old dray. I was in the back, crying my heart out. You know how it is, once the effect of vodka wears off. You feel worse than ever. I was thinking of Mama and I just wanted to die, but the old couple – they seemed old to me – were wonderful. They did adopt me. They had a small-holding – three or four cows, chickens, pigs, vegetables – and I became a general handyman, milking, cleaning, even shooting rabbits. They made their own vodka and we didn't live too badly. Eventually they died, of course, and I left their little dacha and became a kind of freelance worker, always making for places where there were tough assignments, a kind of challenge. That's how I became a Stakhanovite and got our photos in the paper. And we built a kind of reputation. Maybe at threshing. I even won a prize of a bottle of vodka for mowing with a scythe. Life *was* grey, but there was the odd ray of sunshine in achieving things – though the war soon put a stop to that. I decided to join up in 1940. I got a medal and extra cash for that.'

'Where did you enroll?'

'With the Cossacks,' he explained. 'There were hundreds of thousands of Cossacks, their families, children, magnificent fighters, brandishing swords, wearing their tall hats. God! What magnificent horsemen – we were all captured! I thought they might make me an officer. After all, I was the son of a prince! But they said no, I wasn't a true Cossack, and so after we were taken prisoner – the entire Cossack camp – and Hitler promised extra rations to a hundred thousand Russians to build what he called the Atlantic Wall, I decided to have a go.'

'But you were married by now?' I found it hard to believe.

'Oh yes, marriage was easy in the Cossacks. No problems. The Cossacks were like a self-contained town – wives, and so on. Nataliya was the daughter of a Cossack corporal and when I proved that I was a Stakhanovite he made no objections. We were all then members of General

367

Vlasov's "Russian Liberation Army" – a sort of half-starved freelance anti-Stalin army started by the Germans. I didn't want to *fight* the Russians, I only wanted a kind of liberty, though I *was* angry that I couldn't be classed as a Cossack. "Born too far North," one of them grunted to me. It was in 1942 we were married – but we still didn't get enough to eat. And that is the main reason why I volunteered for this better job helping to build the Atlantic Wall.

'I had to go to the English Channel. When we prepared to leave, we assumed we'd be transported there. Well,' Rudi added grimly, 'we bloody well weren't. We *walked* all the way from the Italian–Austrian border area near Lienz – every inch of the way. Thousands died. But Nataliya was made of sterner stuff,' he put an arm round her, 'and she stuck it out with me, I don't really know how. And when we got to Cherbourg they made her one of the camp cooks – boiling potatoes. That was in early 1943.'

Poor Rudi gave a lopsided smile which seemed to lose itself in the hollows of his cheeks. 'When we arrived we were given good beds in "*der Hundezwinger*" and allowed to rest for days, with good meals of nourishing but digestible food that suited our starved state. And at the end of a week we were mustered and told by Schutz that the nourishing food and the comfortable beds would continue and we would be given clothes to replace our tatters.' Rudi added, 'A sort of snarl revealed his broken teeth, and I remember him telling us that there were conditions; *two* conditions in fact. One was that we would accept labour status and help build and maintain the Atlantic Wall – which was of course why they were fattening us up, to be equal to the task. The other was that the clothes they'd issued us with would be German uniforms and we'd be given German rifles too – "To fight for the Fatherland if the occasion arose", as Schutz put it. Well, I told you what happened to those who refused.'

'Yes, you did. But then?' I was absorbed in what he was telling me.

'The Allies *didn't* attack Brest or Cherbourg. They attacked much further east, and the Germans were taken completely by surprise. We were rushed to St Lô – ostensibly to fight for the Germans. Ridiculous, isn't it? Nataliya managed to come along, and now here we are, driving comfortably, eating well – and not quite sure which side we're fighting for! Oh Nicki! At least you bring a grain of sense to this crazy world. And now – where are we going?'

By this time we were driving along the main road towards Paris, but I hesitated before answering Rudi. I wasn't *afraid* to tell him, more amused, anxious to see his reaction.

So, as nonchalantly as possible, I half-turned, looking into the driving mirror in front of my right shoulder until I could make out their faces. 'Actually, I've fixed up a place to hide you in,' I said, pausing, 'in a bordello.'

'A *what*!'

'You heard,' I laughed.

'Friends of yours?' I heard Rudi's slightly ironic voice.

In a flat unemotional voice, I answered, 'As a matter of fact, yes.'

'Sounds intriguing,' said Rudi.

'Tell me all about it,' asked Nataliya softly.

'There's not much to tell. Except that it's just not easy to find a safe house. The girl responsible was a very good friend of Father's. I first met her – well, through Father, and recently – and quite by chance after many years – I was able to rescue her, help her out of a bit of trouble. And she promised me that if ever she could repay the debt, she would. I didn't know anyone else whom I could trust, so I called and asked her.'

'But what about the – well, the women?' asked Nataliya, almost shyly.

'Don't worry,' I reassured her. 'It isn't really a bordello. It's a *maison de rendezvous* – and you'll only meet the lady who runs it. None of the other – er – girls. So don't panic.'

'I'm not panicking so long as she's trustworthy.'

'Absolutely. What's more, she's not only trustworthy, but you'll like her.'

We arrived at the boulevard Malesherbes shortly before midnight and, when the maid announced me, she ushered us straight from the main entrance through a side door which I had hardly noticed before.

The maid said, 'Bonsoir, monsieur,' obviously addressing someone she knew, and I heard Rudi murmur, 'You seem to know the place well.'

On the other side of the door the girl led the way up a flight of circular stairs into a large attic which, all things considered, was quite well furnished. A large old-fashioned double bed almost filled one wall, there was an easy chair, a table the size of a bridge table, towels, soap and, on a shelf, an electric burner for making coffee.

Hélène, bless her, had left a few rudimentary provisions – bread, butter, jam, coffee, milk, some salami and a bottle of brandy, together with cutlery and glasses.

Rudi was just saying, almost with wonder, 'Do you realise that this is the very first time since we left the Cossacks that Nataliya and I have actually spent the entire night in the same bed?'

Unheard as she climbed the stairs, a soft voice said, 'I do hope it's comfortable then.' That was their first introduction to Hélène.

'I'm Rudi!' Smiling with undisguised pleasure, he came forward to greet her.

'I thought you might be,' laughed Hélène.

'And we don't know how to thank you.'

'For Nicki I would do anything,' said Hélène simply, 'and you too,' this to Nataliya, 'I hope you'll be comfortable. I'll show you tomorrow where there's a real bathroom. I imagine you must be used to getting up early. So you can have an early bath before we start preparing the house – say around nine o'clock. And of course there's the *cabinet*

370

de toilette and a bidet behind the door there. Have you got any money?'

'I gave them enough for the moment,' I interrupted.

'Good. I want to show you this.' Hélène led Nataliya to the door at the back of the house and opened it, showing the iron rungs of the fire escape, and pointed to a street lamp still shining in the midnight gloom.

'You see that lamp,' she beckoned Rudi over too. 'Directly below it there's an *épicerie* that sells everything from pâté to champagne. It's small, but a real family concern. Just tell them you're my cousin, Madame Hélène's cousin. The baker is two doors up, and next to that a greengrocer. So you won't starve.'

'I'll never be able to thank you,' said Rudi fervently. 'It's like being treated by an angel in disguise.'

To bring Rudi down to earth – and I knew I had to – I said almost cruelly, 'For the moment all's well. But remember, Rudi and Nataliya, both of you, this is only the first step. You, Rudi, will be hunted high and low. And I'm involved – deeply. The police will be watching *me* like a hawk too. I won't just be able to pop in for morning coffee. God knows when I'll be able to see you. Because though we *are* in a way free – we have to escape *properly*. How the hell we do that, I don't know. But for the moment, yes, you're right, Rudi, you're safe in the eyrie of an angel in disguise.'

'The only thing I would say is,' suggested Hélène, 'don't take any risks. I mean, don't go out to look at – well, the Champs Elysées. The police are very – how can I describe them? – not exactly trigger-happy, but they're always on the prowl, and a lot of them know you, Nicki. You've been around a long time. And we don't want some inquisitive *flic* suddenly thinking he's recognised Nicki – or is it Nicki? he'll ask.'

'She's right,' I warned Rudi. 'I'm going home now. I left some old clothes for you, Rudi, on my way in.'

'And I've got some old dresses for you, Nataliya,' added

371

Hélène. 'Can I call you Nataliya? It's such a pretty name.'

'Please do – Hélène.'

'Good. Then that's settled.'

'Sleep well,' I said. I gave a peck to Nataliya, welcoming the latest addition to our family, and a Russian-style bear hug to Rudi, and finally a kiss of thanks to Hélène, before driving home to Tasha, promising myself that after two long, tiring nights I would sleep late and long.

25

It did not take long. Five days later a police clerk at the Prefecture telephoned me.

'Monsieur Korolev?' he asked baldly.

'That's me.'

'Inspector Verron will be coming to see you at your office tomorrow morning at half past ten. Please be sure to be there then.' The phone clicked dead.

There was no 'Would it be convenient if . . .' No telephone call from Verron himself. Just a brusque announcement by a stranger of time and place, and even the words 's'il vous plaît' were a mere formality. Indeed I was flattered that Verron had elected to see me on my home territory. I would not have been surprised if I had been told to attend at the Prefecture.

I had been expecting the summons, and I knew what the line of questioning would be, but the anxiety had diminished with the passing days; the three of us – Tasha, Galina and I – had talked and talked the matter over, and we all felt that, however sure Verron and the Americans might be that I had helped Rudi, there was no way that they could ever prove it.

They could search every nook and cranny in our house,

they could tear down the bricks and mortar, and strip down the office but there was no way they could find Rudi or his wife, safe in the secrecy of a *maison de rendezvous*. All I had to do when I met Verron was to play it cool, admit nothing except that we *had* met, and feign ignorance of anything that had happened after our brief meeting.

When he arrived the following morning, Verron did not waste a moment. Ten minutes before he was due I had warned Tatiana that I wanted to spend an hour or so talking privately to the inspector, and suggested that, as we could not close the opening between the two rooms of our office, she should take the morning off, and do some Christmas shopping. She was delighted.

When she had gone and the front-door bell rang, I pressed the buzzer and a moment later heard Verron's footsteps mounting the narrow stairs from the front entrance.

Playing it carefully, I said with cheerful innocence, 'This is a pleasant surprise, Inspector! Two meetings in a week! What can I do for you?'

'For a start, you can abandon pretence,' was the reply in a softly threatening tone. 'Where's your brother?'

I raised my eyebrows in mock astonishment. 'What? Isn't he in his camp at St Lô?'

'Prince Korolev!' His courtesy was as false as my surprise. 'I said abandon pretence.' His voice was a hiss now.

'He's escaped? It's not possible! My God, from my point of view that's great news!'

His eyes seemed to diminish to pinpoints. 'I'm not here to waste time. You saw him. You arranged for him to escape. Where have you hidden him?'

'But I don't understand –'

'Liar!' Verron spat the word.

'Are you accusing me –' I hope I sounded angry.

'Huh! You flatter me by your understanding. I mean just that,' he sneered. 'You no doubt think you're very clever. Well, prince or no prince, aiding a prisoner of war to escape won't save you. And the Red Cross won't save you either. You might like to know that we've already reported the escape – and your involvement in it – to Red Cross headquarters in Geneva.'

I did not like that at all. It could spell real trouble. I decided to attack.

'You come in my office accusing me without any proof,' I cried angrily, 'then you go behind my back and tell a pack of lies to my superior officers . . .'

'Ah! You didn't like *that*, did you?' He knew he had touched a weak spot. 'Why should you worry? If, as you say, I'm accusing you of a falsehood, you've done nothing wrong. You're a pillar of virtue.' He put his ugly face close to me. 'Only I take a different view.'

I resorted to a show of righteous indignation. 'I have every right under the Geneva Convention to go and visit my brother. And I also had full permission from the officer in charge.'

'And help to plan his escape?' This time his voice had turned from threats to irony. 'You're the epitome of injured innocence; but your brother's escape was an inside job. And you organised it. You just wait!'

'How long?' It was my turn to try sarcasm.

'Don't be *too* clever.' The venom in his voice was intense. 'We've already got nearly enough evidence to arrest you.'

I laughed scornfully. 'My brother escaped – thanks for telling me; I'm delighted. When? While I was talking to you in the Prefecture? I'd have to be clever to pull that one off!'

'Never mind when. We'll find out the exact details. We'll be watching you from now on like a hawk. Your every movement will be known to us. You won't even be able to have a pee in private.'

'Thanks for warning me,' I said angrily. 'Now can I say au revoir?'

'A couple of questions first.' I could smell the garlic on his breath.

'Anything to help,' I said with assumed weariness and a hand raised to stifle a yawn.

'I'm asking you officially that, as a Red Cross officer, you swear that you did not help your brother to escape.'

'I didn't. And as far as I can see from your vague accusations I wasn't even in the vicinity. I was in Paris.'

'And you don't know his whereabouts? – Or his wife's?'

'He can be in a local bordello for all I know,' I replied. 'Come off your high horse, Verron. I'll tell you one thing – I'm delighted my brother has escaped. But he escaped *alone*. And instead of wasting your department's time questioning me here in Paris, why don't you get your bloodhounds on the scent nearer to St Lô or Beauvais?'

In the pretentious tone that policemen so often adopt, he said with a touch of solemnity, 'We have reason to believe that he is in this area.'

'Fine,' I cried. 'Maybe we'll meet over lunch one day. But don't try to blame me or you'll find yourself facing a charge of slander.'

It was his turn to laugh scornfully now. 'How clever! But it won't work. You've abused your official position. You say you didn't help? That's very funny! I don't know *what* you've done, but I know you've done *something*. Brothers don't just meet suddenly after twenty-five years, and then one of them happens to escape a couple of days later.' He snapped his fingers in a gesture of disdain. 'You're the man behind the plot. We don't know *how* or *when* – not yet. But we're patient and one day you'll make a mistake and lead us to him. And' – with an attempt at heavy sarcasm – 'we might even find you a cell with barred windows next to his.'

'See you then, eh?' I maintained the pose of airy scorn. 'In the meantime I hope I'm not rushing you – but I *do* have a lot of work to do.'

It was Verron who had the last word.

'Arranging more escapes?' he sneered.

After Verron had gone I spent a long time alone, thinking, wondering not only what *I* should do, but how much – if anything – Verron knew. His accusations had, in fact, amounted to nothing other than dark unformulated, suggestive threats, but still they were disturbing. For if he really had contacted the Red Cross in Geneva, telling them of my visit to St Lô, I could be drawn into a dangerous web of official questions – including ridiculous queries like, 'Why had I drawn "official" petrol for a private visit?' All that sort of thing. But then suddenly I wondered – had Verron in fact informed Switzerland? Perhaps he was only bluffing, trying to frighten me? Nearly a week had passed, so why had François Savin at least not tipped me off, even secretly?

What should I do? Tell Switzerland everything except details of the actual escape, or lie my way out of the whole thing? It took me a long time, pacing up and down the small room, before I reached a decision. I would say nothing. I would not make the first move. I would wait for Switzerland to approach *me*, to demand an explanation. Then I would stick to the same story I had told Verron. Because whatever anyone said or thought, there *was* no proof. That was the crux of the matter.

Even so, I must be doubly careful. Certainly any meetings with Rudi would be very difficult. It did not take long for me to observe that Verron had put a team of detectives on to watch me night and day. I soon recognised the faces of two men who seemed to take it in turns to watch me, often lounging near the front door of my office and then turning up at the Deux Magots if I went to meet a friend for a coffee.

The man would peer in through the steaming windows to make sure I was not meeting my brother, then saunter around, waiting patiently to follow me when I made my next move.

The winter was very cold as Christmas passed, then New Year and we waited patiently for the spring of 1945 – and, we hoped, victory at last as the Allies and the Russians moved closer and closer until the day when they would meet, perhaps in Berlin, and walk through the streets of a beaten and abject Germany.

I did make occasional visits to Madame Hélène and the detectives had the courtesy to leave me alone on these occasions, waiting patiently while I (so they presumed) was entertained as a client, before I emerged and then followed me home, to the arms of Tasha, no doubt smirking at what they imagined to be my repeated infidelity to the poor little girl I had married. I wished that Galina, and perhaps Tasha too, could visit Hélène's but that would have given everything away.

It seemed incredible but, for month after month, thanks to Hélène's wonderful understanding, Rudi and Nataliya languished, incarcerated in the top floor of her house. For them it must have been terrible. They had even less freedom than in a POW camp – and I knew that Nataliya was at times miserable, missing the kind of freedom she had enjoyed when living in the peasant's house each night, while Rudi desperately missed even the spurious conviviality of his fellow prisoners. The two of them were utterly alone, and there was little I could do to help them, for in the early spring leading to April, Verron still clung to me with the tenacity of a terrier. His detectives never left me alone. His threat that I could not even have a pee in private was coming damned near true.

Rudi *had* escaped – but what good was it doing him? When I saw him early in May 1945, he horrified me by blurting out, 'I can't stand this solitude any longer! I'm going to give myself up – I'd rather be in a prison camp with friends.'

'Don't be stupid,' I began.

'Don't you call me stupid.' His temper was short now and he flared up easily.

'Even if you stayed with the Americans, there's no way you could win. Now that the Yalta agreement has been ratified, thousands of Russians have already been sent back to Russia against their will. Don't *you* be a fool. It's a fate that means certain death – or Siberia.'

'I know,' he muttered. 'Sorry I blew up. But you know how it is when you can't see *any* ending.'

'I understand –' I began.

'But *do* you? You're a free man, you can walk round the city when you feel like it, talk to people. What do *you* know about how *we* feel. Sneaking out at midnight for a secret stroll! Do you realise we've lived for months in Paris and I've never seen the city? And as for poor Nataliya! I'm sorry, darling,' he put an arm round her shoulder, 'I'm a beast feeling so sorry for myself and forgetting how *you* feel –'

'I'm fine,' she smiled wanly, 'Don't worry about me.' But I had a feeling that she did, that she *did* remember those peasant evenings with the gratitude of something gone forever.

'And all we can do is spend our days in bed making love,' Rudi's voice was little more than a growl.

'Please!' Nataliya blushed.

'Sorry – but it's true. And now – I'd better get this over with and tell you outright – now she's pregnant.'

'*What*!' I almost jumped out of my wooden chair.

He nodded. 'She's missed twice,' adding with a sardonic twist to his lips, 'looks like I'll produce the heir that Father was always demanding. You don't seem –'

'We'll see.'

A child! And a prisoner. What the hell would happen *now*? As if it was not hard enough trying to think how *one* man could escape, what about two-and-a-half persons?

It was at this moment, after Nataliya had said she would

not be needing a doctor for some time, that I decided we must have at least one break.

'Tell you what, Rudi,' I made the decision suddenly. 'It's over six months since you've been here and you've never even seen Galina and Tasha. Let's take a chance and have a party. It's now early May. Let's at least go out to the local bistro not far away. The one in the Rue Bichet?' I turned to Rudi who nodded.

'Do you think we dare?'

'Why not?' I asked. 'I'll bring Galina and Tasha – you know the restaurant – Le Globe.'

'And me?' asked Nataliya with almost pathetic eagerness.

'Of course! I wouldn't go without *you*. It's not a bad little place, people tend to sing a bit and drink a lot, but the food's damned good.'

'Wonderful!' Rudi's mood was changing.

'I'll have to think how to lay it on, how to fool Verron's men – what day shall we make it?'

'I'll have to check with my diary!' laughed Rudi.

'It's Saturday today – let's say next Tuesday. I can't do it on Monday, but Tuesday's fine. Tuesday the eighth. With Hitler already dead in his bunker, there might even be peace by then.'

What intuition made me choose that date? What made me decide to go to the Globe on the Tuesday? I inveigled Hélène into booking a table for us in case one of Verron's 'tails' followed me – a table I could never have got without booking. How could I even know in my wildest dreams that a date three days hence, chosen at random, would be the day, the date, on which the war in Europe ended, the day of wild rejoicing that came to be known as VE Day?

Planning the party was not difficult, once I had proposed the visit and arranged what Galina and Tasha should do. Galina had her own car, and I showed Galina and Tasha on a street plan where the Rue Bichet was, and where they would find the restaurant, the Globe.

'Forget me,' I said, 'you make your way in Galina's car and wait in the restaurant. Ask for Mr Korolev's table and wait for me. I'll make my own way, I'll be all right.'

Planning in advance was one thing – but it was the unexpected that all but ruined our day. For though the Germans had surrendered on the Monday we did have a warning, for at midday on the Monday, 7 May – the radio, announcing the unconditional surrender, that morning, added, 'It is expected that tomorrow will be declared an official holiday.'

I had never expected a holiday like this!

With a startling suddenness as though it was a masterly co-ordinated plan, VE Day burst upon Paris. Windows were flung open and flags of all the Allied nations appeared as if from the hands of a thousand conjurors. In the place de Furstenberg the forsythias and lamp standards with their Victorian globes were draped with Tricolours. Children of whose existence we had hardly been aware danced and tumbled and turned cartwheels.

Making our way to lunch was almost impossible because of the dense crowds – even though Galina's battered old Renault did struggle successfully to get through.

'Park your car near mine in the Rue Bichet, but you can walk openly through the front door of the restaurant, then after lunch Rudi and Nataliya will leave by the restaurant's fire escape. In the meantime, I'll drive to the Ritz – the place Vendôme – followed no doubt by Verron's man – and before he has had time to make any decision other than watch my car – I'll race through the long arcade and leave by the entrance at the Rue Cambon. It's a whole block away from the place Vendôme. He won't have the faintest idea where I am and I'll grab a cab and get back to all of you. We can worry about getting the car back later.'

I reached the Ritz – but grab a cab! There was not a

single cab for hire in the whole of France. Even though the Rue Cambon – leading from the Rue de Rivoli to the Grand Boulevard – was narrow and unimportant – it was jam-packed and I realised that I was going to be late for lunch – because there was only one way I could reach the Globe. I would have to walk the whole distance!

Previously I had urged the girls in their old Renault to take the back roads, which were less crowded because everyone was making for the heart of the city. Everybody was wearing some manifestation of joy – rosettes, comic hats, toy rifles from children's playrooms. Whistles and rattles, the blare of a thousand taxi horns, the ringing of church bells split the air. It was difficult to move for in jostling crowds strangers grasped my hand and shook it; embraced me like a long-lost soul, pretty girls kissed anybody who happened to be within range – including me – and I simply edged a path through crowds that, like a tide, ebbed and flowed.

Finally, I was lucky. I managed to stand on the running board of a Hotchkiss which was also going out of Paris, the opposite way to the flood of human beings which was gathering in the Concorde and, of course, preparing to march up the Champs Elysées. So in fact I actually arrived before the girls.

Rudi and Nataliya were already there, nervously nibbling at some *radis au beurre* and drinking from a carafe of *vin rouge*. Friends – strangers – insisted on toasting them! As I entered I saw a couple of young men shake hands with Rudi then lean over and plant kisses on Nataliya.

'Vive la France!' cried the crowd and clapped.

'Have some more wine,' one other man ordered another carafe of *vin ordinaire*.

'Don't mind if I do,' cried Rudi, entering into the spirit of things just as I arrived and demanding a glass for me.

When the girls arrived too we all hugged each other,

kissed a dozen times and Rudi was in tears by the time he had introduced Nataliya and I introduced Tasha.

'So you're the beautiful Tasha,' he held her at arm's length, studying her as though wanting to paint her. 'You're downright exquisite,' he said, and I squirmed inside, as I was introducing a brother without telling him that she was also his sister.

Tasha managed to take it in her stride. 'I love the beard,' she cried. 'Just like Nicki's teddy bear!'

'Ah!' sighed Rudi. 'The teddy bear!'

But, although I had lived with the 'secret' for so long, I was embarrassed at the lie in which I was conniving in front of my brother. I *was* ashamed; and I wondered what Galina was thinking. I could not tell, of course, but *she* knew. And Tasha. And there was no way I could tell Rudi then, and ruin the happy, innocent joy of our meeting on this of all days.

'I know, I understand,' I was telling Galina something and added, 'Hélène's been an angel, keeping Rudi for all these months but soon we'll *have* to make a move. But for the life of me, I don't see how we are going to arrange it.'

One thing was unquestionably true. We could not rush. What was the *point* of rushing? We had no place to rush to and even now that the war in Europe was over, could we even begin to plan an escape?

All kinds of ideas crowded my mind. I toyed with the idea of contacting Igor's girlfriend in Avallon and seeing if Rudi could get a job farming there. He had no papers, true, but would that matter? Would it not be possible to buy the papers of a dead Frenchman? The world must be filled with 'lost' people, and at least Rudi, like all the Russian upper classes, spoke perfect if rather rusty French.

Galina had an even more inventive suggestion.

'Why don't you shave off your beard, Rudi,' she began talking quickly, 'then borrow Nicki's passport and papers – and fly to Sweden – that's the bolthole for all wanted men. Then you can post your passport back to Nicki.'

'It's a stroke of genius,' I cried. 'And most important of all, you'll never be reported as missing. With the Swedes you'll just become part of the landscape.'

Without hesitation Rudi shot out, 'But what about Nataliya?'

'She could follow later. We could look after her for the time being, give her a job in the office. Remember, no-one knows her face. And when things calm down, we could get her a Red Cross permit or a Nansen passport, and then –'

'No go, thanks all the same,' Rudi shook his head decisively. 'I'm not going to leave Nataliya. Not now, not with her expecting a baby. I'm grateful, but no, we've got to think of something else. If only we could get to Switzerland!' To me he said almost accusingly, 'Can't *you* help? You have high-up contacts there.'

'I wish I could,' I sighed. 'I might be able to get both of you freed *inside* Switzerland, but getting you *out* of France – that's the problem.'

'Well, let's have another drink,' cried Rudi, who had already had more than his share.

We spent hours that afternoon of reunion, talking, drinking far too much cheap red wine, and it was towards the evening, when dusk was beginning to fall, that Rudi sighed, 'One day we'll have to escape! But that takes money. What we desperately need is some really *big* money. A fortune! Like the emeralds Father gave to Mama. I'm a firm believer that basically money – bribery – will buy anything. Even freedom.'

'Poor Mama!' How many times in my life had I pictured her, not only her beauty when she was laughing and happy, but the awful moments of her death, murdered like a common criminal and then thrown into a mass grave with the emeralds on her corpse.

'Poor Mama?' Rudi raised inquisitive eyebrows. 'We'll never, never forget her.' He was a little drunk, and so was I, 'But I was thinking of the emeralds at this moment.'

383

Almost angrily I said, 'Dammit Rudi, I don't *believe* you can buy freedom with money. But for Christ's sake, show a little respect for the dead.'

'I can show as much respect as you,' he retorted equally angry, and then with a look that startled us, he added, 'But *Mama* didn't have the emeralds!'

The news hit me with the force of a douche of iced water, sobering me instantly.

'*What!*' I almost shouted. 'Who did have them, then?'

'I did for a time,' said Rudi. 'Then *you* had them, Nicki.'

'What are you talking about?' Galina's face had gone white.

'You had them,' repeated Rudi pointing a wobbling finger at me.

'But I *never* had them, *never*!' I cried. 'You must be crazy. And you say you had them first? You *never* had the emeralds. You're trying to lay the blame on me. Saying that I had them. It's nonsense. It's not true.'

'Quiet, both of you.' It was Galina again, but adding with a smile, 'It reminds me of how you used to flare up and fight in the old days.'

Rudi looked at me accusingly, 'You *did* have them,' he insisted.

'I didn't, you idiot. How could I have had?'

'Shut up you two,' Galina was suddenly furious with Rudi. 'Remember where you are, you fool. You're *here*, thanks to Nicki. So stop these stupid insults. We're talking about a lost fortune. Now, you, Rudi, tell me what it is you're talking about – which, so far, sounds like a lot of nonsense.'

During all this time Tasha and Nataliya had been silent, spellbound as the mystery of the missing emeralds unfolded, a story of which they were hardly aware.

'Now you, Nicki – not a word out of you, *please* darling – until Rudi has had his say.'

'All right,' I muttered. 'But I'm not going to sit here and

be insulted, if that's all the thanks I get for risking my blasted neck.'

'I'm sorry, Nicki. I was a bloody fool. I really am sorry.'

Rudi hesitated a long time, marshalling his thoughts, and finally said, 'All this is very painful – that terrible day when we lost each other.' For a moment he seemed on the verge of tears – drunk or sad or both? But he pulled himself together and continued, 'This is what happened to me. When we were rattling through the streets of Kronstadt, Mama started to feel more and more frightened. Somehow, at the last minute, I had grabbed your teddy bear. You remember that? It was a thick padded bear with a pocket in which you kept your pyjamas buttoned up inside.'

'I've never worn pyjamas!' I interrupted.

'*Please* shut up!' Galina implored me.

'Bumping along in the streets Mama was gasping, "I daren't keep the emerald necklace, Rudi. If I have to go to hospital to have the baby, somebody'll steal it. Darling," she said to me,' Rudi went on, '"You take them. There, darling," she pulled the necklace in its bag from under her blouse, but I said I was afraid.

'"No darling," said Mama. "Here, let's do this." She took Nicki's teddy bear which I had picked up at the last moment, undid the buttons and stuffed the necklace in a velvet bag into the pyjama case – the teddy bear. Then she added, "Now you guard it, Rudi. They'll never do anything to a little boy."'

After a pause, while I listened in a state of stupefaction, Rudi turned to me and said, 'Just before the end, I saw Father struggling with someone in the passage to find Mama in the Square. I wanted to give him the bear, but I couldn't reach him. I ran back to try and save Mama. I gave the teddy bear to Igor so that I could hold her. I didn't have the chance to tell him what was in it. And I haven't the faintest idea what happened after that. I always supposed that he gave it to you. It *was* yours.'

Wide-eyed, but pale and anguished, I could see before my eyes the picture of Father and Igor staggering towards the *Lysberg* – collapsing on the deck of the boat, telling me everything that had happened in one stark sentence, as Father handed me the teddy bear, 'This is all we managed to save.'

All eyes turned to me. 'Have you still got it?' asked Rudi almost accusingly.

Hesitating, almost fainting at the doubt in my mind, I managed to mutter, 'I – well, I don't know. We threw away so many things – Father insisted on it,' I conveniently blamed him, 'But maybe we didn't get rid of everything. You remember the ground floor lumber room next to the room where old Lilla used to sleep when she was married – maybe it's in there with old suitcases and so on.'

'Doesn't sound very hopeful,' said Rudi. 'A fortune in jewels and we don't even know if –' he did not have the heart to finish the sentence.

For a few moments the five of us sat in silence, the glorious day of freedom forgotten, the cups of ersatz coffee long since empty, the dirty cheese plates stacked to one side, the napkins crumpled into loose balls, the chef, still in his striped apron, sitting with a dozen friends. The untidy finale to our great celebration lunch.

Desperately I tried to throw my mind back to the days when I had first lost interest in my most treasured boyhood possession. Obviously it was when, either after my visit to Hélène or perhaps even earlier, I was beginning to feel an adult. No doubt I treated Kodi scornfully and just threw him away. Whereupon Lilla, I suppose, would have quietly taken him away. But she would never have destroyed such a relic. It was like an ikon, our last precious symbol, not only of the past, but of Father's determination that some of us would live, hoping eventually to carry on the Korolev dynasty.

I wiped the napkin round the edge of the wine glass, smeared where I had drunk after eating.

'There's only one thing for it,' I said finally. 'We'd better get home and start searching amongst all the trunks.'

'You *had* better!' emphasised Rudi. 'I wish I could come with you to help. That necklace is worth a king's ransom.'

'I saw it once,' Galina remembered, 'usually it was kept in a velvet bag, but your Mama took it out and said it was flawless.'

'Come on!' cried Tasha. 'If we find it –'

'Yes, go on,' Rudi put an arm over my shoulder, 'Go and look for it, Nicki,' he said to me, 'and we'll have another celebration if we *do* find it.'

It was long after midnight before we were able to get through the mass of people. At times the crowds simply stopped the cars, the girls kissing me, the boys showering the two pretty girls with kisses. I had long since given up any idea of returning to the Ritz to collect my Citroën.

'I'll go back in your car,' I suggested to Galina. 'Then I'll walk to the Ritz tomorrow and collect mine. Let's go by the edge of the city and come in when we think it's the right moment.'

We did that – but it took us hours, for as dusk fell on the way home, the floodlighting for the public buildings was switched on and searchlights began an erratic dance across the sky. All night the celebrations continued as people danced around monuments and landmarks. Dozens of little boys lost their parents and were sobbing piteously. We were stopped by a group of men from all three services who held a placard reading 'Pity the poor Unemployed'. Accordions squeezed out patriotic melodies at the street corners. American soldiers sang sentimental songs of their homeland like *Home on the Range* with tears smudging their cheeks; Englishmen hoisted Frenchmen on their shoulders.

What a wonderful night it was – or would have been had we not been beset with worry and apprehension, culminating at four in the morning when, bleary-eyed and weary, we reached home.

*

It was a long time since I had visited the disused ground floor rooms where, in the old days, Lilla had had her bedroom. That and the box-room next door. The stacks of luggage that confronted us as we opened the door! Discarded! Left over from the days of the Tsars, the days when Father and Mama had travelled in state with thirty or more pieces of luggage, perhaps going on to Paris from a state visit to Denmark which had required dozens of dresses, uniforms and so on. Those were the days when porterage was easy, the days of ships not planes, the days when weight was of no consequence, where, if we returned to Russia with less luggage than we had brought, we just left the suitcases behind and bought new ones for the next trip. Now I could scarcely believe my eyes – the thick leather, the safety straps that held them, the cabin-steamer Oshkosh trunks which even had drawers inside them. On top of this there was still a vast pile of 'junk' as Father always called it, despite the fact that we had given a great deal away to Russian charities.

One terrible thought superseded all the others. Had we given the teddy bear away to a charity? Or had it been retained as a toy which, however useless at our age, was still regarded as a memento precious enough to keep? Indeed, I remember quite clearly once thinking that, if ever I had a son, I would keep it for him. But had I acted on that thought?

Once inside the room, faced with the mountain of luggage, we started first to clear away old pieces of furniture – chairs, tables, even a sofa, long forgotten.

To the other two, I cried, 'Let's open every suitcase and see what's in it. It's the only chance.'

There must have been twenty of them. Trunks so large they could hardly be lifted. But even so, the job did not take long. Every case was empty except for some which contained folded tissue paper, relics of past packing. As for the rest of it – we could see at a glance that there was nothing – no clothes, no toys; all had been given away. Nothing except the suitcases and the furniture. There was a painted corner cupboard which opened. Empty too.

'I never expected to find anything!' I said in the hollow voice of a defeated man. Slowly we pushed the hat boxes, suitcases, trunks, back into the room, together with the few lighter items that we had kept – a pair of skates, where on earth had they come from? My heart was sinking, I had never expected to find them, but I still had an empty feeling as though I wanted to retch with no food inside me. I remembered my terrible seasickness on the boat to Denmark and, even worse now, I could smell the vague musty stink of old leather which brought back to me a whiff of tannin – the stench of Kronstadt where the tragedy of Mama's death had taken place.

Queasily I said, 'Everything else must have been given to Russian charities. The whole bloody lot. But how could we know?' How could I blame myself?

'Hush,' whispered Tasha, holding my hand. 'We've all managed very well so far. Be practical. You've got a good job. Galina's a *prima ballerina*. And all the necklaces in the world won't buy Rudi his freedom. We'll need another miracle for that. Come on, let's go upstairs. It's half past four. We need a stiff drink, then bed.'

As we started to walk upstairs, with Tasha locking the box-room door, she had another key in her hand, and more out of curiosity than anything else, she peeped into Lilla's old room. I had in fact started walking up the stairs with Galina, both of us exhausted.

The second Tasha opened the door, she let out a shriek – so loud, so piercing, I thought she had seen the ghost of poor Lilla herself.

'Nicki! Nicki! It's here!' Half sobbing with disbelief, she repeated over and over again, 'It's here! It's here!'

Turning on the steps I stumbled down, to behold a sight so strange that it almost *was* like a ghost. Lilla's old room was starkly empty apart from her ancient iron bedstead, bereft of all its blankets. Not a chair, not a table. All had gone. Except one thing.

Some furniture removal men with a sense of humour had propped my teddy bear against the back of the empty bedstead, it's beady button eyes looking at me with a grin.

'What's it doing here?' I gasped.

'Perhaps Lilla kept it aside as a souvenir?' suggested Galina.

'Or perhaps the people who disposed of the old things thought it was worth nothing – so stuck it there as a joke,' said Tasha.

'Open it!' Galina almost shouted, insisting, but as Tasha handed it to me, and I pressed the sturdy body, I said, 'No, I can't feel anything, it's too thick. But let's look.'

And so, on the bare wood of the staircase leading up from the bottom of the house, we played out the last scene of the drama. I ripped open the buttons of the pyjama pouch which I had never used and thrust my hand through the opening, and pulled out a brown velvet bag. Gently I undid the thin rope of gold braid that had been twisted round the neck of the bag. Then, as I opened the top, I spread out the contents.

There were the Korolev emeralds, glittering with such a potent green fire that we gasped, breathless at the beauty as we gazed at an heirloom which the Tsarina herself had presented to Mama when she married Father, and now was exhibited to an audience of three on a bare, dusty, wooden staircase!

26

The sight of those priceless relics of the past suddenly transported into the present – it was one of the most incredible moments of my life. I had only seen them once before – around the long, swan-like throat of Mama, with two matching drop earrings complementing the colour that flamed round her beautiful neck, when, escorted by Father – stiff as a ramrod, boots shining like polished black glass, white kid trousers, a scarlet sash across his chest which blazed with glittering decorations – Mama gave a ball one winter evening and Rudi and I peeped through the bannisters at the top of the sweeping, curling staircase, gazing bewildered at the galaxy of beauty below.

'Those were the days,' I sighed, but the others could hardly know what I was thinking. Galina had picked up one of the earrings and I imagined she was comparing it with the costume jewellery with which her stage friends were always decked out when performing for an audience.

For a few minutes I completely forgot the time, never noticing how dawn had crept through the staircase windows. I just sat there looking, transported into the past, never thinking of their value, only at the miracle of the emeralds' long, tortuous, and secret journey until now they had finally reached their rightful destination.

'They'll cause a sensation when they're put on show,' cried Galina. 'The whole world will stop and stare.'

'They'll rock the foundations of commercial empires,' laughed Tasha.

'You'll be famous! It's an heirloom beyond price and it's yours,' Galina said to me.

'And poor Rudi's. Though even a king's ransom won't buy him his freedom, let alone fame and glory.'

'And who said anything about letting the world see the necklace?' I asked as we trudged up the stairs to the sitting-room, with me clutching the little bag of jewels and the old teddy bear that had served us so well – left behind, discarded in the excitement, now found again.

'And don't talk about *showing* them! The less publicity we get, the less chance of robbery. And we certainly can't afford to insure them.'

'Yes, what about robbery?'

Before the question could be answered Tasha asked, 'Shouldn't we let Rudi know?'

'Of course,' I cried. 'The news is only a few minutes old, but he must be the first to know. I'll phone Hélène with a message in the morning.'

It *was* the morning, so we snatched a few hours of sleep and then, when I phoned Hélène I asked her, 'Hélène dear, this is very important otherwise I wouldn't bother you, but could you just tell Rudi that we've found my teddy bear.'

'What a message!' I sensed her ripple of laughter.

'It's stupid, I know, but it *is* important.'

'Of course. I do hope you all had a good time.'

'It was wonderful. And thanks.'

As I put the phone down I wondered, thinking of the irony of it all, what Rudi and Nataliya would think now they knew they had a share of riches beyond their wildest dreams – rich, yet they were captives. Some half-formed words from the past flashed into my mind. Something about 'a bird in a gilded cage'. What *would* Rudi do with all the money he could not touch?

It was Galina who, as usual, asked the first practical question. Treating me as the leader – which I suppose I was – she asked, 'Now the necklace has been found, what are you going to do with it?'

'I feel that rightly the necklace belongs to the three of us – yes,' despite her protests, 'to you too, Galina. I've never in my life thought of you except as my sister. Of course you get a third.'

Galina went a pretty shade of pink. 'There's no *need*,' she was almost in tears.

'Ssssh! Don't embarrass me. One third is more than enough for Tasha and me to be rich for the rest of our lives.'

Tasha asked: 'How will you – er – dispose of it?'

'I haven't given the matter any thought,' I replied cheerfully. 'This business has been something of a shock. I mean, this is beyond our wildest dreams. My first reaction is to do nothing for the moment. We can't just go out and try and sell it. I'll put it in a safe deposit box at the Crédit Suisse which has a bank just off the Grand Boulevard. We'll have to have it valued, by an expert, and *then* decide what to do.'

'Is it saleable?' asked Galina.

'I honestly don't know,' I admitted. 'It's a pretty large thing to take into a shop and ask "How much?"' I smiled. 'My own feeling is that, now the war is virtually over – except in the Pacific – peace is going to be followed by several years of terrific inflation. I know from Red Cross reports I've received that this is what the Swiss bankers believe. And they're pretty shrewd. We've got enough to live on, we ought to keep the necklace for some years and see what happens. Galina has her career, I've got my salary, we've got a free house, and we can't use the money for poor Rudi. Of course, if we could *buy* his freedom – then we'd let the whole necklace go. You agree Galina?'

She nodded. 'But we can't.'

'At least we can do something. If you, Galina, or anyone wants money, we've got enough collateral in the bank to raise thousands of dollars just by clicking our fingers. So we can't lose.'

Tasha asked an obvious question. 'But why should any bank trust us? As far as *they* know, the emeralds might be fakes. Won't you have to have them verified?'

I added, 'I've just said that. I think the best thing to do is telephone Father's lawyer – the man who got me my Swiss papers – and ask his advice. Then – with so much money at stake – I'll go to the best man, wherever he is. Probably Switzerland – or perhaps Holland – aren't they the experts in precious stones?'

'Diamonds only,' remarked Galina.

'I'll find out,' I said.

*

It had been one of the shortest night's sleep of my life, for we were all so excited that we were up breakfasting before ten o'clock. What adrenaline can do for you!

'I must go to the office first,' I told Tasha, and as we were walking to the front door Tasha spotted something, stooped and cried, 'Hullo! Here's a letter.' Picking it up, she said, 'It's for you, Galina. From *America*.'

'America!' Galina tore it open. 'I don't know a soul in America.'

But she did! Slowly, her face registering at first astonishment then a kind of exultation, she read what was obviously a long letter, and as I was preparing to go to the office, she cried, 'Wait a moment, Nicki! This is important.'

She finished reading, then without warning, the words burst out, 'Nicki! They want me to go to America!'

'America! But that's miles away.' For the moment all thoughts of the emeralds were forgotten. 'But *why*? What on earth are you talking about?'

'When?' asked Tasha.

'As soon as I can. *The ballet!* To star as *première danseuse* in Balanchine's newly formed New York City Ballet Company. Oh! Balanchine! The highest honour in the world. Listen, I'll read you the letter.' She was almost dancing with excitement.

'Come on, let's sit down again,' Tasha flopped back into a chair. 'This is too much for me. I'm not used to such late nights. What a way to celebrate victory!'

'I'm just the right age. At forty' – this was a little fib, Galina was actually forty-three – 'a ballerina is in her prime. America! *And* Balanchine!'

'Read it,' I begged her, 'before I go to the office.'

'No, darling Nicki, *you* read it,' she insisted.

She handed me a large piece of paper, and she could scarcely contain herself, twirled round in a pirouette as if she were a young girl again, then flung herself on the sofa.

I took the letter typed on paper thicker and more expensive than any I had seen since the war started. It had a dignified die-stamped heading: 'SCHOOL OF AMERICAN BALLET – from the office of the Director'.

Mademoiselle Korolev, I read, *I am directed by Maître Balanchine to issue to you an invitation.*

The Maître has for some years been directing the School of American Ballet here, and he is now considering the formation of a ballet company to be called The New York City Ballet. Such a project requires the assistance of a première danseuse with experience and reputation such as he is presently unable to command in New York. He would consider it an honor if you were willing and able to discuss the project – which has the unanimous approval of the New York Ballet Society – with him. The discussion would of course necessitate your presence here. But I am authorized to say that air transport can be easily arranged through the good offices of General George Patton and the United States Military Headquarters in Paris. All expenses and your accommodation here would of course be covered, and a fee commensurate with your standing as an international artiste would be offered.

Should you favourably consider the Maître's invitation I would be glad to hear from you by cable at your very earliest convenience. Please address your reply to me at the New York State Theatre.

I am, Mademoiselle, yours with the greatest respect . . .

'Balanchine!' she burst out as I finished reading the letter.

'Balanchine indeed,' I recalled the heart-warming man who had taken the trouble to explain to me the intricacies of theatrical costume design at Monte Carlo. 'He must be one of –'

'*The* leading choreographer of the world now, Nicki. And with such range! He works with everybody from Stravinsky to C. B. Cochran and his musical revues in London.'

'You'll accept, of course?'

'Of course!' She sprang from the sofa and hugged me. I

could see she was banking on my brotherly advice about the form her reply should take.

'Make it as simple as possible,' I said. 'Waste no words. Cable at once: "Honoured. Please advise travel details." No more is necessary.'

'I'll try to get Cable & Wireless now. I just hope the service is working, not blocked up with military calls.'

It was, of course; and I could hear her fretting at the phone as she dealt with a disobliging female operator who sensed excitement rather than urgency in her voice. But after a long delay she got her message over.

After Galina had spent half an hour trying to send her cable to New York, I left for the office. There I was able to telephone Father's old lawyer in Lausanne and explain the story of the necklace and seek his advice. Maître Dubois had long since retired – what an age had passed since I climbed those four flights of narrow stairs with Father to consult him about my passport! – but his successor M. Amyot replied quickly and helpfully. It would of course first be necessary, he said, to have the necklace valued and given a certificate of valuation. It could then be deposited in Father's Geneva bank (my bank now) as security for any loan we might one day require.

He advised me to take the necklace to a man who, he said, 'is one of the world's most distinguished gemmologists, Mr Pieter Brinkheusen, in London. I will send a letter of introduction to Mr Brinkheusen tonight,' he added 'and look forward to hearing from you at an early date.'

These lawyers! I thought. To them everything is already packeted in pink tape before a step has been taken. They see nothing of the hazards ahead, or choose not to.

I discussed the lawyer's advice with Galina and Tasha – I could not talk to anyone else – and after some serious thought, decided I would fly to London to see this Mr Brinkheusen.

'After all,' I said, 'the fare's only just £15 each way, and we *must* get the best financial advice. We must have some legal authority in case, later, somebody *does* want to show it at an exhibition. If they do, they'll have to insure it, and we must have proof of its authentic value.'

They both thought it a good idea. It would only be one night away from home, and planes were flying daily by now. I could pull rank to get some sort of priority. 'But first I must go and see Igor,' I said. 'I haven't even had time yet to tell him the good news.'

The double item of news – first the necklace, secondly Galina's plans to go to New York – had to be shared with Igor. I still visited him regularly in the Rue St Dominique where Brig – still in America, of course – had managed to siphon in large sums of dollars to help pay for added luxuries, in addition to the settlement she had made when they married. Luxury is a comparative word for a man in Igor's pitiful state. For, sadly, there seemed to be no improvement with the passing years. Sometimes he would manage to make a croaking sound, as he had done on that day when Brig had broken her leg after I saw the nude photos – but nothing more had emerged.

He received daily physiotherapy on his legs and arms but his legs particularly were more like matchsticks through lack of use and it was plain that he would never be able to walk – let alone speak – again.

I passed on the news to him, enunciating slowly and carefully to make sure he could take in every word, which he did by affirmative blinks. Kornilov stayed with us – it saved me from having to tell the story twice, and I thought that perhaps Kornilov and Igor might enjoy 'talking' about the news when they spent evenings together.

Kornilov himself, who throughout the years remained head of the household, paid for by Brig, was still hale and hearty but his hair had turned grey, and inevitably he had aged. What a selfless companion he had been for Igor – but how long it was since Igor had been a lusty young man who could never leave a pretty girl alone if there was a convenient bed handy. 'Otherwise,' as he had once told me, 'no bed, no interest.' And how long since we had met for our great lunches at the Cossacks and all had joined in the singing,

> And still the thundering cannonade;
> Our breasts were trembling, as it made
> Tremble the land.

Now poor Igor, who had always led the singing at our lunches and at the Russian Centre, would never sing again. His life had been reduced to a living hell, and once or twice I was ashamed to feel it more of a duty than a pleasure to make my weekly visit to his skeletal frame.

He could only be forty-five, but he looked twice that age and often, sensing the pleading in his eyes, the misery, I would think, 'I wonder if he would like me to help him to die?' But it was not a question I dared to broach. I was much too much of a coward.

Six days later I flew to London with the emeralds. We left Le Bourget around 10 am and landed at an airport called Croydon, which bore all the traces of having been used as a military flying base – run-down make-shift wooden huts where we had to wait in cold rooms to be 'processed'. Then we took a bus to London, about ten miles away, to be dropped at Victoria Station. From there I managed to get a taxi to the Russell Hotel – recommended by a British journalist I had met and who told me, 'Try the Russell, it's cheap and cheerful.'

London was brutalised and shabby. Vast structures were no more than twisted piles of wreckage, gaps strewn with rubble and weeds resembled some sort of apocalyptic nightmare. But the city was alive – in a different way from Paris which had lost a war, whereas London was filled with

indeed there it was, with no more than a small linen tag attached to the clasp and sealed so that no-one could remove it without detection. On the tag was written in purple indelible ink, *£40,000 stg/$190,000*. It was as brusque and simple as that. The emeralds flashed their green fire as if resentful of being ticketed like bric-a-brac at the Paris flea market.

'The Pieter Brinkheusen seal is recognised worldwide,' he continued. 'These are wonderful examples of beryl – sorry, emeralds – and this is the worth of your necklace today, Mr Korolev, in the world market. Of course, if you were to sell it to, say, Cartier or Van Cleef & Arpels, they would resell it at a handsome profit.' He reached out to caress the cat. 'But then of course selling and buying are two different things.'

I had barely returned from London when the telephone at the office rang. It was Hélène. She had never phoned there, and my first thought was that something serious must have happened to Rudi or Nataliya.

'No, no,' she said. 'It's not that.' With this assurance I had not the faintest sense of foreboding. Only when she added, 'Nicki, I've got to see you urgently. Today if possible,' – only then did I have a first feeling of worry – but of what? I had no idea.

'Don't worry,' she said, but added ominously, 'for the time being.' Then, after a pause, she suggested, 'Any chance we could meet for a talk – somewhere anonymous, though I suppose you'll be followed by that horrid inspector. But they don't know who I am. What about that restaurant near the Odeon Theatre. You remember it,' adding with a laugh, 'where you did your best to knock me over!'

'I remember,' I returned the laugh, 'come and have a bite of lunch there. One o'clock?'

We found a table at the Relais St Jacques without much difficulty. There was not a great variety to eat, so we had some *crudités* and a pork chop of sorts, a carafe of their red wine and then a cup of coffee of doubtful quality.

'Now – what's the trouble?' I smiled.

She hesitated for a long time, sipped her coffee with a slight grimace and finally, with a sigh, announced, 'I'm going to close down the house and sell it.'

'You're *what*? But why? And the house – what's going to happen to it?'

'There's a very good reason for what I'm doing,' she sipped red wine, as though to get rid of the taste of the coffee. 'I'm only getting out before I'm kicked out.'

'What do you mean?'

'Ever heard of Marthe Richard?' she gave the French pronunciation of the surname, 'Rish-ard.'

I shook my head.

'Marthe Richard is being elected a deputy, and the first meeting of the deputies is scheduled for this summer.'

'But what's that –' I must have looked bewildered, interrupted by the waiter taking away the dirty plates, and asking, 'A brandy, m'sieu?'

I nodded, 'Yes please.'

'Marthe Richard has only one desire in life,' Hélène continued, 'and she's made a vow to succeed. She's determined to close every single brothel in France and to stamp out prostitution. And she'll succeed, believe me.'

'Never!' I cried. 'It's a way of life in France. It's not even considered immoral.' I was thinking, of course, of the very simple way my own father had arranged for me to learn 'the facts of life'.

'She *will* succeed. She's determined to. As you know, lists already exist – I'm on it, partly because I was so wickedly caught up in the scandals when Paris was liberated.' She gave a slightly ironic twist to the word 'liberated'.

'But can't you – er – *quietly*?' I was so astonished at the news that so far its effect on the fate of Rudi had not sunk in.

'I hate the idea of letting *you* down,' said Hélène almost desperately. 'But for weeks now I've been offered an enormously profitable transaction for my property. I've always said no, but now – with this new law – I'm afraid that if I wait, the value of the property will be halved when it *does* become law.'

'It's yours?' I was astonished.

She nodded. 'My husband was asthmatic, which was why he had to have an outdoor job as a travelling representative for a textiles firm. His life was insured very heavily and the premiums were enormous – which was why I had to supplement our income by becoming –' She hesitated.

'A mistress of the art?'

Smiling, she said, 'You put it so charmingly, Nicki. But yes; gradually and not altogether unhappily learning the skills of the profession.' A pause. 'And when my husband died and just about the same time I heard that Madame Lefarge had decided to retire I bought the lease with the insurance money. And I can dispose of it now for enough to live on forever. But if I *wait* – but I don't know *what* to do about Rudi –'

'Don't worry about that.' I didn't mean it, but I patted her hand, she looked so concerned, feeling that she was, as she put it, 'betraying a trust where Rudi is concerned'.

'Nonsense,' I cried. 'You've been angelic. I'm always using that word about you!' I laughed. 'We'll find some way out of it, don't you worry.' After all, they had been there, lodgers, no questions asked, for months. 'He'll have to get out soon anyway,' I added. 'You've been wonderfully patient but we've – I've – we've taken it too much for granted. This news of course – perhaps it's best in one way, it's given us the jolt we need to spur us into some sort of action.'

'I'm so sorry, Nicki,' she sipped her brandy and we clinked glasses across the table. 'I hate to hurt you of all people.'

'This Richard woman – she must be a tough egg!'

'Terrible,' she shuddered. 'Probably, since we're not a bordello, more of a meeting place for friends, we could get away with it if we were very discreet, but she *is* a terror and she's sworn that within a year every single brothel in France will be closed.'

Fascinated, I blurted out, 'I don't believe it.'

'I do,' she said seriously. 'I really do.'

'But what about the – well, there must be hundreds of girls –'

She shrugged her shoulders. 'It's criminal, but they'll just go on the streets. No wretched Madame Richard is going to wipe out the world's oldest profession. She's a fool – but a very determined one. And she'll win through. One of my – er – friends is a deputy, with a great deal of power, and even *he* says gloomily that Madame Richard will win.'

'Well, I don't blame you, Hélène, for getting out, but now I've got to think – about Rudi, as well as you. How long before –?'

She hesitated, then said in a flat, dead tone, 'They're anxious to exchange contracts in two weeks.'

'My God, that soon! Rudi'll have to move. I'll think of something.'

She left soon afterwards, while I remained to pay the bill. Then I made my way home.

Rudi! I had promised to 'think of something'.

But what? And where?

27

'Right here!' It was Kornilov – ex-count, ex-butler, and general factotum of Igor's house – who suggested the obvious place to hide Rudi. 'In this house. After all, it's like a mausoleum. A dozen bedrooms, mostly empty;

there's what you might call a private wing at the far end facing the garden. It'd be ideal.'

'Will Igor mind?'

'First of all, I'm sure he wouldn't,' adding practically, 'he'd probably be delighted just to see your brother. And provided it was for a short stay, he wouldn't know, if you preferred it that way.'

'No, I think we must tell him.' As an afterthought I asked, 'What about the nurses? There are three, aren't there?'

Kornilov nodded. 'I don't think they'd bother us. In fact would they recognise him? Hasn't he got a big beard?'

'And the doctors?'

He hesitated. 'I never trust doctors. They're always asking questions. That's why I mentioned a short stay. They're always wondering if a rival's been brought in! And I know that several work with the police. But for a few days they'd hardly notice. For the most part, we know when they're coming, so Rudi will just keep out of sight when they're around.'

That was how it was arranged to switch Rudi from Hélène's hide-out to Igor's house. But how exactly were we to *make* the switch?

After talking it over at home, Galina suggested, 'Why not use Igor's car and Igor's old chauffeur, Vron. He does still work in the Rue St Dominique, doesn't he?'

'I think so. In fact I'm certain he does. But I don't quite see what you're getting at?'

'Well,' she began, 'if we explain to Vron where *we* parked our car on VE day, Igor's old car could be parked in the same place. Then Rudi and Nataliya could just walk down the fire escape and vanish *from* thin air *into* thin air.'

It *was* foolproof. Nobody knew where Rudi and his wife were hidden, so how could they possibly follow an unknown car from an unknown starting point to an unknown destination?

'You're a genius!' I cried, for, as usual, the simpler the

idea, the more likely it was to succeed. There was absolutely no reason why Vron, who, we were later told, 'exercised' Brig's beautiful Delahaye once a week by driving it down a couple of streets, should not take a spin in the direction of the boulevard Malesherbes and park conveniently in the Rue Bichet.

Rudi's stay would only be temporary though. Too many unknown people visited Igor's house. And Galina's suggestion of using the Delahaye had started me thinking how we could use that car to help Rudi escape to Switzerland. Previously I had been hamstrung by the Red Cross markings on my car. Too conspicuous by far to use for an attempt at escape. Nor could we use Galina's old Renault. It was good enough for battling through Paris traffic, but it was so old it probably would not even *reach* Switzerland. Now, though, I was beginning to work out a plan – one which I hoped could virtually guarantee getting Rudi out of France, though I was less sanguine about asking Rudi to leave his wife behind.

Much to Hélène's relief – the new purchasers were even offering a large bonus if she would vacate the premises quickly! – I went first to see Vron and Kornilov and then on to Hélène, and Rudi and Nataliya.

'We can leave right away,' I announced, rather to their astonishment. 'Tomorrow if you like. It's only a quick drive across Paris,' adding more as a joke than anything else, 'It'll even give you a brief sight-seeing tour of Paris.'

'Oh! I'd love *that*,' Nataliya spoke with such a depth of feeling that I suddenly realised what a misery of pent-up emotion, of action starvation this poor pregnant woman must have been undergoing for all these months, broken by only one lunch in a restaurant.

'Of course you will. In fact, I'll tell Vron to go the *long* way round, so you can drive down the Champs Elysées, see the Eiffel Tower, the Rue de Rivoli, then across the Tuileries, past the Louvre and home,' I promised them. 'You'll both be free – in a sense, so there's no reason why you can't make haste slowly for a change, though I won't be able to come with you.'

'It *will* help me,' admitted Hélène. 'Going like this seems such a sad rush though. And I'll be lonely without you both!'

'You've been wonderful to us, Hélène,' Nataliya thanked her on their last day, while Rudi added fervently, 'We wouldn't be here – free – if it hadn't been for you. I'll never be able to pay you – not really – I know that, but,' with a momentary hesitation, 'when we meet in the next world –' he gave his warm, affectionate smile and left the end of the sentence unsaid.

We decided to move to the Rue St Dominique in two days; and on the morning of the switch, Galina finally received an official reply to her cable to New York.

The heavy linen-textured envelope was franked OFFICIAL – US ARMY AIR MAIL and had been initialled by censors.

'Though the war is over officials still open your letters in case anyone is thinking of starting another one,' I said.

'It's been long enough getting here,' said Galina, 'but I imagine the invitation is only to advise on details.'

She read the letter then handed it to me. It was phrased in similar respectful terms to the original invitation – plus, now, overtones of pleasure:

Mademoiselle Galina,

Maître Balanchine was overjoyed at your acceptance of his invitation to join him in the completion of his project to form The New York City Ballet. He asks me to convey to you his pleasure at your agreement to discuss further details. If you will kindly advise me of the date of your arrival here in New York accommodation will be reserved for you at the St Regis Hotel and you will be met at Idlewild airport personally by the Maître. I will arrange for a Press Conference to be arranged when you arrive.

Authorization of your flight is presently being processed through United States Military Headquarters in

Paris, who will, so far as possible, meet your wishes as regards travel date.

Maître Balanchine looks forward with immense pleasure to greeting you and to what he is certain will be the happy consequence of your visit.

With the greatest respect, Mademoiselle, I am . . .

And there was the signature of Balanchine's secretary with its many flourishes.

'So now we have only to fix a date,' Galina said joyfully.

'I hope you'll wait at least a couple of weeks,' I suggested. 'I'm going to miss you.'

'I will – but you won't,' she teased. 'As an old married couple you'll at last have a house to yourselves.'

'I don't agree,' I said almost wistfully. 'Our family is still going on. Now the first priority is safety for Rudi and his wife. At least then we'll all of us have stories with happy endings.'

Rudi's switch worked perfectly. And though Igor was looking very ill, emaciated, eyes staring out of his sunken, shrivelled face, the eyes themselves lit up with a kind of hopeless joy the moment Igor saw Rudi, even with his thick blonde beard.

'My disguise,' Rudi joked, knowing that Igor could hear him, even if he could not reply. Kornilov (who told me of this meeting later) noticed the way Igor instinctively replied with an affirmative wink before Rudi and his wife were taken to a comfortable double-room at the back of the house, and told that there was always more than enough food in the house for the nurses, servants and so on, so that filling two extra plates presented no problem.

'But I must warn you,' I reiterated to Rudi when we met the following day, 'this is just a temporary refuge – for a few days. Two of the doctors are official doctors to the police and you know how they talk. Just for want of something better to do! And there's another reason. We'll need Galina's help – and she's off soon to America.'

I was preparing him for the most difficult battle I knew I would have to fight. I believed I could arrange for Rudi to escape, but not Nataliya. He would not like that.

'I don't. And I won't!' were his first uncompromising angry words, uttered harshly.

'You *will*. You will if you stop being so damned selfish, and start thinking of your wife instead.'

'Meaning what?'

'Listen Rudi!' I beseeched him. 'Nobody in the whole of France has ever heard of Nataliya. She doesn't exist, but now – if we work quickly – I think I've devised a way in which I *can* get you out of the country.'

'I don't want to leave her,' he said stubbornly.

'You *have* to. There is no way I can get both of you out. You must trust me. Damn it, haven't you trusted me before? I've got a cast-iron plan for you. Trust me not to let you down.'

Finally it was Nataliya who made the decision. Unknown to both of us, she had heard our raised voices, come to the doorway, listened to my final plea.

'Nicki's right,' she said. 'You *must* go. I insist.'

She had been – to us, having barely come to know her – such an ethereal creature, that I had hardly realised that she had a deeply passionate nature that made her now speak with such vehemence.

After a lot more argument and cajoling Rudi asked grudgingly, 'What *is* this plan? And why the rush?'

'I told you. The rush is due to one thing: we need Galina and Galina is leaving soon for America. They want her straightaway. The big shots in America are at this very moment trying to arrange VIP treatment and get her an early flight. But first I need her here to help you. So it's a question of days.'

'What's Galina got to do with it?'

'If you'd give me *time* to explain, perhaps –' I must have sounded exasperated, for as so often happened with Rudi, he smiled an apology and was suddenly contrite. 'Sorry,' he said, and what I liked most about my twin was that when he said sorry he really meant it.

'Let me take it in stages,' I said. 'At this moment, Vron, Igor's chauffeur, is taking out the back seat of the Delahaye – that beautiful car which Igor's wife bought him.'

'Will it get us there all right?'

'Like a dream. Vron runs it round a few streets once a week. It's in perfect order.'

'I don't understand about the back seat,' muttered Rudi.

'It's having all the springs taken out in order to leave a shallow hole so that if there's a crisis you'll be able to slide under the back seat and disappear.'

'So I'm being taken for a ride?' he laughed.

'You are. Second point. You shave your beard off right away.'

He nodded. 'To take your place perhaps?' He was beginning to see that I had a plan which I now outlined. It was simple but effective.

'Galina, you and I will drive from Paris in the Delahaye to Switzerland – at least almost to the border facing the Swiss town of Vallorbe, in the Jura mountains.'

I hesitated, then went on to explain the plan in some detail. Galina and I would drive. Rudi would sit on the back seat – gingerly, for the supports directly underneath the car cushions would have been removed. We would drive to Pontarlier, the last town of any size before crossing the Jura mountains, along a twisting road lined with giant trees, and then drop down to the Swiss frontier.

At Pontarlier I would get out, and remain in the local bistro, hanging around for a couple of hours or so. Rudi would climb into the front seat. I would give him all my papers – passport, Red Cross credentials – and he and Galina would cross the frontier into Switzerland without any fuss. Driven by Galina, of course, with Rudi posing as me.

Once in Switzerland, François Savin, my one-time

mentor and old and trusted friend, would be waiting in a café – there was only one – just across the frontier. With his car. All this had been arranged on the phone – all but the actual date. We estimated that the trip would take six hours at most. Galina and Rudi would join Savin for coffee and a sandwich maybe, then Galina would take back my passport and papers from Rudi, hide them, and set off back to Paris, stopping only to pick me up at Pontarlier. Meanwhile Rudi would enter Switzerland as a political refugee, backed in his application to stay by the fact that he was born in Switzerland which he could prove from the same firm of lawyers which had given me my nationality. I had given Savin a note of this.

Galina and I would probably stay the night somewhere on the road back to Paris. We would drive straight for the Rue St Dominique. My Red Cross car would never have been used, I would never have left the country, I did not see how I could be followed – and above all, Rudi would be free.

'Of course you must go!' cried Nataliya. 'You'll never get such a chance again.'

'I must say it sounds fine,' agreed Rudi slowly. 'But what happens to Natalilya?'

'Oh! She starts work for me in my office. We can do with an extra helper, we always had two girls in the past, and Tasha will take her into the house until she can get properly fixed up with a Russian family if she prefers that. Meantime I'll try to get the right papers to let her join you. It might take a little time but since she's expecting your baby I don't see why she couldn't qualify for some special treatment. After all, Rudi, didn't you tell me her father was born in Switzerland? Must count for something.'

Finally Rudi said, 'All this is very generous, Nicki, and I hate leaving her, but –'

'Of course you'll go. You must!' insisted Nataliya.

'It does seem foolproof,' Rudi agreed.

'It is,' I said. 'So you agree?'

He nodded.

'Good! You're very wise,' I said to him. 'We'll set off the day after tomorrow.'

28

By half past eight everything was ready. Galina had made her own way to the Rue St Dominique the previous night, and I left home at seven o'clock, not by car, as usual, but by a series of quick changes on the Métro which I could tell had finally baffled my 'tail'.

We had decided to start at nine o'clock, and we did; with plenty of petrol, four full jerricans in the back – jerricans being the name of a new American replacement for the old British two-gallon tins. A jerrican holds five gallons, so together with a full tank, we had enough petrol to make Switzerland, barely five hundred kilometres from Paris, hardly more than a morning's fast drive.

We were not attempting any speed records, however. Because of the discomfort for Rudi, half-hidden for much of the way, we would take it easy, arriving at Vallorbe in the afternoon.

All went well, with Galina driving so that I could lean over towards the back seat and talk more freely to Rudi.

As we approached Dijon around midday, I asked Galina, 'Do you think we dare stop at a restaurant to give Rudi a slap-up lunch?'

'Why not?' asked Galina. 'We've covered nearly three hundred kilometres, a good start. We've got plenty of time, a fast car, and I remember once driving to a small restaurant not far from here in a small valley just before Dijon.'

'Near here?' I asked.

'You're sure it's safe?' asked Rudi, still nervous at losing his new-found 'freedom'.

'I'm sure – and it has its own trout stream. It's in a small valley five kilometres further on. Shall we try it? It's certainly more secluded than the one in the main square at Dijon. It's called simply, Le Moulin – a kind of country mill turned into a restaurant.'

It was only a few kilometres along the picturesque but little known valley to the right of the N6 main highway. It seemed charming and secluded – in fact we were the only people who sat down on the tree-shaded open terrace by the side of the gurgling trout stream, slapping its way over the bottom of stones; fresh trout, of course, being the speciality of the house.

'We also make our own pâté,' suggested the patron, beaming at Galina whose easy manner and elegant well-kept ballet figure and long legs always seemed to encourage people to talk.

'Here we smoke our own ham and cut it very thin. We regard it as better than *jambon de Bayonne*.'

'I'll have that. And some melon with it?' asked Galina.

'A good mixture, Madame. Our Charentais are just ripe – in fact, superb.'

I had been sitting quietly, thinking deeply while Galina chatted on, and we all chose to have the fresh trout. For a long time – though at different times – I had been thinking that something inside me – my conscience, a guilt complex perhaps – had over the weeks been driving me into a mood of confession about my relationship with Tasha. It was something that *always* worried me secretly, but the fact that Rudi was my twin, in one sense a *part* of me, increased the need to share a secret with him above all others. This mood had quickened because if all went well and he crossed the frontier a few hours hence, it might be a long time before we met again, so when Rudi went to wash his hands, I said, almost abruptly to Galina, without specifying the subject, 'I want to tell Rudi.'

413

'I know,' she answered slowly. 'I wondered how long you would last out. I've seen this whole business brewing up – not only now, today, but for a long time. Why not? He's your twin brother, you're closer than any two people. Tell him, Nicki, my handsome half-brother, if it makes you feel happier.' Galina was always perceptive, and sympathetic.

During the meal Rudi, looking at me curiously, had asked, 'Something on your mind?'

How incredible that twins should sometimes think for each other!

'Yes, I have as a matter of fact. But did I show it?'

'No,' he replied. 'It was just a feeling I had.'

'Well, this is the first occasion we've spent such a long time together – a whole day before it's over. So far there hasn't been much time for real confidences.'

Now that I had decided to tell Rudi, I found it hard to choose the right words. After all, this was no simple truth to be told in a Catholic confessional box. It was more than the revelation of a sin, more of a crime that we had committed and kept secret for all this long time.

'Yes, it is a confession,' I admitted. 'And though it's made me very happy,' we had reached the coffee stage by now, 'It's rather – well – sordid, I'm afraid. The only trouble, Rudi, is that you of all people – I can never keep a secret from you. It's about Tasha.'

'You're not married?'

'We *are* married,' I sighed. 'That's the trouble.'

'You don't mean to tell me that you don't get on well together! I don't believe it. You were billing and cooing like a couple of love birds when we had our famous lunch.'

'No, no. I love her – I always will,' I cried fervently.

'Then what?' he still apparently thought that I was making a lot of fuss about nothing.

Taking a deep breath, I said, 'Galina knows. Tasha is – she's my sister. She's your sister too.'

'*Your what*?' he sat up abruptly, upsetting his coffee cup. 'What on earth do you mean? I've never heard such nonsense in my life. How *can* she be my sister? You're crazy! What are you trying to tell me? That Father married again in Paris? Even that only makes her a half-sister, like Galina.'

'No, no, not *that*,' I gave a wry grin. 'Father had so many girls that he didn't have time to marry *one*. No, it was Olga who told me.'

'Olga? What has she got to do with it?'

'On the quayside in 1919 – that terrible night when Mama was killed –'

'Don't – we must all try to forget that.'

'But it was Olga who saved Tasha.'

'Saved her? I thought she had married some man who died.'

'That was the story she first put about,' I explained, and then I told Rudi the entire story of how Olga had returned to the square after hiding from the men who had tried to rape her and how, after Mama had been taken away, she found Tasha on the ground, just born.

Rudi's mouth dropped wide open in stupefaction, as though his jawbone could not support his mouth, and then, without warning as the waiter looked at me, he burst into laughter – which I took for a split second to be the hysterical laughter of a madman.

'You fool!' he shouted. 'Nicki! Olga's an idiot! Where the hell did she get that idea from?'

'She told me,' it was my turn to look stupefied, but with a wild excitement racing through my blood. 'What do you mean?'

'She told you a pack of lies, though perhaps she doesn't realise it,' cried Rudi. 'Tasha isn't your *sister*. Olga might even *think* she is, but she's a fool. Mama *never* had the baby. Never! That I *do* know.'

I can't even begin to know how I managed to keep my senses. All a lie! My beautiful, beautiful Tasha, the pride of my life, truly was my *real* wife! Was this really the end of living a monstrous lie?

In my excitement, standing up, I grabbed Rudi by the shoulders. 'Are you sure?' I cried. 'Are you certain? You're not lying to spare my feelings? Promise me.'

'Hush, Nicki,' Galina too got up to separate us. 'It's obvious there's been a colossal error somewhere. Just let Rudi tell his story.'

Tears in his eyes, Rudi kissed me on both cheeks and said, 'Never fear, Nicki. What a hell this must have been for you, but don't worry. You see, I was the last person to see Mama before they took her away. And she was huge. The baby was inside her. No doubt about that. The other woman, who was obviously very rich – she had arrived in a carriage and pair with servants – was taken away at the same time. She had given birth to the baby in the carriage. And the *position* of the baby is important. It was next to the other woman and left when she was dragged away with Mama. Olga had gone by then – she had been carried off to the warehouses.'

'And I suppose Olga returned when she escaped and then –?'

'Jumped to conclusions,' explained Rudi. 'Of course. But why didn't she tell Father when she arrived in Paris?'

I explained what Olga had later told us. She had started a tale of deception and had only blurted out what she thought was the truth, long after Father had died, when she discovered that Tasha and I were lovers, and how we were finally married because Tasha had no real papers and was in danger of arrest. Then, my heart still thumping wildly at the release from sin that brimmed over my entire body, I also told Rudi how Olga had taken a German lover, and how it was Ullmann who had secretly arranged for Tasha and me to be married.

'I'm free! I'm really married!' I cried over and over again, free as though an enormous weight had been lifted from my body: that feeling of guilt which I had lived with

– even knowing that it would never be discovered – until now, when, impelled to share that guilt with Rudi, I had been made free of it.

'Tasha will scarcely believe it!' I said. For though Tasha did not feel as strongly as I did about what we had done, I know that my sense of secret wrong-doing had at times infected her, so that too often her role to me had been that of comforter and consoler in physical as well as mental love.

'I don't know what to say – I feel like singing,' cried Rudi, and as I paid the bill he threw an arm round my shoulder and, as though we were one, we sang the last three lines of our old schoolboy song,

> Delight is blowing in the air –
> I know not yet where I shall sing,
> I only know the song is there.

'I'll phone Tasha from Pontarlier tonight.'

We set off again shortly afterwards, reaching Dijon within a few minutes, then drove straight on, past the square with its imposing hotel on the left and on to the road that took us to Dôle, forty or fifty kilometres further on. Beyond that – and not far off – lay Pontarlier, and beyond *that* the frontier at Vallorbe where, with an almost incredible and instantaneous difference, the semi-derelict looking peasant farmhouses, with their untended gardens would give way, at the crossing of an invisible line, to the spick and span dwellings, the neat well-stocked shops of Vallorbe on the other side of the frontier post.

I had taken the wheel after lunch, my entire being flooded with joy and the excitement that follows when someone has snipped a piece of cord and the millstone that has for so long hung round your neck falls with a crash to the ground, out of sight, forgotten forever.

Galina sat next to me in the front seat, with Rudi lying

across the back seat – not uncomfortably, this was a big car usually chauffeur driven, so that three people could easily sit abreast. It was just that, though we had risked lunching in a public restaurant, we did not want to take any chances if we were stopped for some minor offence – turning the wrong way up a one-way street – to be suddenly discovered to be twins. It was simple for Rudi to slide off his seat and into the 'cupboard' underneath.

Otherwise we were all singing old Russian songs, memories of yesterday, and I, for myself, cannot ever remember feeling so happy.

I do not exactly know when it was that I began to have the first forebodings that maybe – only maybe – our car was being followed. It seemed the height of stupid suspicion, but a black Citroën Quinze – the big model with the tell-tale '75' at the end of the number plate indicating that it was a Paris-registered car – always seemed to be in my rear mirror. Galina, as you might expect, had not noticed anything when she was driving before lunch, but I first noticed it parked on the roadside just behind the valley where we had lunched, as though waiting for us to return to the main road.

Then I had seen it again and again. I had not noticed it before I took the driving wheel because, in point of fact, the onlooker does not always see most of the game; and for a start I had not been able to see through the rear window when sitting on the front right seat, busy talking to Rudi; but as I adjusted the rear mirror I took a careful look. Yes, the Citroën from Paris was still behind us.

'I hope to God I'm wrong,' I confessed, 'but there's certainly a Citroën on our tail – whether by accident or deliberately I don't know. No, don't look back, Galina.'

I drove on for a few miles then I decided, 'I'm going to try a small trick. Get under the seat, Rudi. I'm going to stop and see what happens. I don't imagine anything *will* happen, but let's see. Ready now, Rudi? Tucked away?'

He gave a muffled cry, 'Carry on!' and to all appearances, the back seat was empty. The Citroën was a fair distance behind us but always in view unless we turned a corner, and the roads in France were for the most part straight, wide and long.

Slowly I stopped the motor, leaving Galina sitting in the right-hand front seat, then got out and kicked the tyres as though worried by something.

It was a lonely stretch of road – the sort where any good Samaritan would try to help if I were stranded and signalled asking for help. *But I hadn't asked for help.* Nonetheless the Citroën glided to a stop abreast of Galina.

'Any trouble? Can I help?' The driver had unwound his left-hand window next to Galina.

'No thanks,' said Galina cheerfully. 'My brother is a bit fussy,' adding with a wink, 'likes to be sure there are no slow punctures. *You* understand.'

I walked round smiling and said, 'Thanks for the offer; there doesn't appear to be anything wrong.'

I took a good look at both men, smiling cheerfully, as I tried to remember their faces – I knew who they *were* – their forced smiles masked a couple of real old-fashioned Paris cops, if ever I saw any. They both looked, though only casually, at the empty back seat. I had no chance to look inside their car, and after my thanks, there was nothing they could do but start the car and drive off – ahead of us.

They stayed that way for several miles, while I deliberately took it easily and made no attempt to pass them. Then, as we approached a series of S-bends near the twisting streets of Dôle, the Citroën suddenly spurted and raced ahead. Within a few minutes, weaving past corner after corner, it had vanished. The S-bends continued for perhaps a couple of kilometres – and then with a creepy, uncanny sense of fear we reached another stretch of flat road and there, behind us again, was the Citroën. I felt the sweat break out on my forehead. It was terrifying. As

419

I slowed down, the Citroën slowed. I shot ahead. It shot ahead. Like a couple of robots, I thought to myself, but I could feel my heart pumping – not with the kind of joy with which I had started this afternoon, but now with a sinister fear.

'Christ! It gives me the shivers,' Galina cried when I told her. 'I don't like this one little bit. How the hell did this happen?'

'I'm scared too,' I said. 'Now we know. *They've come into the open.* That's why I'm scared.'

'Explain,' came the indistinct voice of Rudi, lying on the floor.

'They must know the road,' I suggested, 'and when we were on that winding bit they hid in some side road, let us pass, and then started following us again. But I believe they *know* why we stopped. To check on them. The French police aren't fools, but *why*? I can't understand why they're following us – and so blatantly! A car they've never seen, two strangers driving it – I know it sounds crazy, but I'm beginning to wonder if they know who I am – and if it's not me, that they believe you, Galina, are driving Rudi. I haven't a clue, but one thing is certain – they're on our trail and I'm scared. They must know that I set a trap – that we recognised them. But what worries me most is that they don't seem to give a damn if we *do* know them.'

'Will it make any difference?' asked Rudi.

'I hope not – but when the time comes to cross the frontier you two'll have to play the game very, very carefully. And anyway, we haven't arrived yet and maybe – though I don't think so – they might just be on a mission to see if you do go to Switzerland – and then check if I've gone. If I'm still in Paris, they will know the score. It's all muddled supposition of course – but I hope they're not going to try and stop you.'

'Will I be safe?' asked Galina anxiously. 'With my American trip in two weeks –'

'You'll be okay. Remember, you're French, Galina,

you're an international star, your picture's been in the papers together with all the details of your big trip to New York. You've given interviews and so on. No, you'll be all right. The *deuxième bureau* has a long list of persons they call *the protected*. Friends of Government ministers whose scandals are always hushed up, people who are rarely arrested for petty offences, and so on. You didn't know? Oh yes, it's true. And the police aren't allowed to interfere unless it's desperately serious – such as murder. And remember, the police know your record, what you've sacrificed for France – going to Germany time after time to dance for French POWs and keep up their spirits. You're probably on the protected list.'

'As far as I'm concerned,' Rudi had climbed on the comfortable back seat for a change, 'tell me what to do if I have to run for it.'

'If I were you, after I've left you and you approach the frontier – I'd ask Galina to stop the car about thirty yards before the frontier post. You can pretend you're going for a pee by the roadside or something like that. But on *your left-hand side*. There's a thick wood along the left-hand side, it's nearly three kilometres thick – but half the wood is in France, half is in Switzerland. The Maquis men used it. It's hard going but if you can get over the wire in the heart of the forest you'll step out near the main road in Switzerland that leads from Vallorbe to Lausanne. Not exactly a free man. I suspect there'll be a couple of men in grey uniforms prowling along the road, waiting for you to appear. But at least they won't start beating you up. Still – let's hope it doesn't come to that.'

Almost as we reached the long main street of Pontarlier, a logging town occupied with felling and transporting the vast forests, I made a sudden decision, a change of plan.

'I'm not going to wait for you in Pontarlier,' I announced. 'But on the road beyond Pontarlier to the frontier we pass through several miles of hilly country – up to the top of the Jura mountains. It's twisty and sombre, the entire countryside consists of trees for felling, and through it the road is hardly ever straight. When we reach the end of the forests – and you won't know this, Rudi – there's a long hill, quite steep in places, very long, five or six kilometres. While we're twisting and climbing up to the top, the following car will never be able to keep us in sight all the time.

'Galina will be driving after Pontarlier and that's the time, in the woods, when I'll clamber into the back seat and then you climb into the front seat, Rudi. *Then* – at the right moment, Galina will stop the car suddenly, I'll topple out of the right-hand side and hide in the woods before the Citroën catches us up. It's dead simple.'

'But why all the change?' asked Rudi. 'How are you going to exist in the forest?'

'It's only for a couple of hours,' I explained, 'then Galina will return and pick me up.'

'But you were going to meet her in a bistro at Pontarlier?'

'No more. This car that's following – there's no way it couldn't see someone getting out in Pontarlier. I told you, it's a long road, straight as a ruler. Remember, so far the two *flics* have only seen *one* man – *me*. Can't you see that if Verron ever learns that *two* men were in the car I could be held for trying to organise your escape. Then bang goes my job, our chances of success – everything! Anyway, nuff said. I've decided.'

I was thinking, planning. We changed places.

'You, Galina darling, after you return from Switzerland, the Delahaye'll have to climb the long tree-lined hill that leads away into the French forests. I expect our friends the police to return back into France first and when they've gone, I'll wait for you and flash a torch. It won't be dark, but it'll be a sign if you don't recognise the place where I'll be hiding.'

'But I don't want –' began Rudi.

'You bloody well will. Now shut up, both of you. Here!

We've just passed three sharp curves. Stop. I am going to jump.'

We had almost reached the top of the mountain. 'This'll do,' I panted. 'They'll never see us round all these corners.'

As the car, already going slowly because of the incline, stopped, I jumped, shouting, 'I've got the flashlight. See you in a couple of hours. Good luck, Rudi.' Then I dived into the nearest ditch and lay there, breathing hard in short gasps, completely hidden under a thick bank of hedge parsley, until a few minutes later I saw the police car pass me and slowly start the descent.

Only one thing worried me now. If the police believed that I, a respected member of the Red Cross, was in the car, there was no way they could stop me leaving – for my own country. Even if they tried to stop Galina, it would not be the end. She could take the car and drive back, and I (or, rather, Rudi) could walk across.

But we had to be sure that, if the police suspected the man was Rudi and asked questions, Rudi would remain calm. I thought he would. But if the questions came thick and fast, it would be a big test for him.

I looked at my watch. I reckoned it would take ten minutes down the hill, even less, a bare five kilometres, then I could picture in my mind's eye François inviting Rudi and Galina, whom he had met before, to a coffee, a cup of *real* coffee at the wayside café just on the right after you enter Switzerland. Then she would start to make her way back into France, puzzling both sets of immigration and customs men. If they asked any questions, she would just tell them that she had driven her half-brother – me – because she enjoyed the drive. And in her purse she would be carrying all my papers. She would pick me up and then make a good start, staying somewhere for the night if we still felt like it.

Time hung heavily. There was virtually no traffic. It was a warmish afternoon, though somehow the trees, blotting out the sunlight, not only hid the extra heat of the sun, but gave me the shivers. The forest had a sinister quality, like a Gustave Doré print which I remember frightened me when I read *Don Quixote*.

The silence, too, was frightening. Distance may play strange tricks with noise, but one thing it does: It *carries* noise, especially in the clear, still mountain air.

Suddenly, the stillness, the silence was broken with startling clarity; broken by that most awful of sounds, the ominous stutter of a sub-machine gun being fired at the bottom of the hill.

And I'm not sure, but I could have sworn I heard a scream, a man's scream. The shots turned my blood to ice. I started to shiver again, with a reflex action, then sweated. That was an *automatic* rifle, not the single shot of a hunter after a rabbit. That shot could never have come from a civilian. That burst, short though it might be, was the hallmark of a uniform – authority, the army, or the police.

The police on the trail of a fugitive! That was my first thought as I climbed out of the cover of the trees and started to run down the hillside to the last few yards of French territory.

I stopped, and retreated back into the woods. I must play this carefully, let time solve the mystery – if there were one. Perhaps I was imagining the whole thing. Possibly it had nothing to do with me, it could have been anything. By now, God willing, Rudi would be safe and sound in Switzerland, surrendering as a political fugitive to the authorities, taken there with guarantees of good conduct by Savin. All I could do was wait for Galina to return. Yet instinct terrified me. I felt so sick I thought I might at any moment vomit. Yet I was powerless. I could only pray and wait in hiding for Galina to return. How long? How long did I wait? Minutes? It seemed like hours.

Finally, it must have been perhaps half an hour later, perhaps longer, I heard the sound of a car approaching. The road lay straight ahead of me as the car climbed the hill. Hiding behind the canopy of big trees I saw the car turn the bend near the bottom of the hill, and I could see the smudge of its shape approaching in the distance. Finally I could make out all the details.

It was the Citroën, that I could see plainly. The hill was steep enough for the car to go into third gear which kept down its speed as its front-wheel drive laboured upwards towards me.

It was the police car, but only one man sat in front, driving. As it came towards my hiding place I could see the other man, holding a sub-machine gun, idly resting it on the back of the bench-type front seat.

And next to him, his face contorted with pain, was a face drained white with a mixture of agony and fury, a third man.

I caught one glimpse of his face, saw it clearly as it reached the crest of the hill. Yes, it was Rudi.

29

Dazed, horrified, frightened, in tears – every terrible emotion you can think of had stunned me. The agony of the tortured face at the window shattered me. I could not *chase* the police car, long since vanished over the top of the hill and by now heading towards Pontarlier – and beyond. Almost instinctively, and blinded by tears at the enormity of what had happened – all that planning, all that daring, starting with the bribery in the POW camp, all in vain for one poor luckless soul who happened to be my twin brother! – I started to run down the hill, easy on the macadam surfaced roadway.

Far away on my left a large open space beyond the heavy green trees hung like a picture postcard of beautiful Switzerland, safe and sound. On my right the dark umbrella of pencil-straight conifers blotted out the sunlight, even the height of the Jura mountains stretching for miles beyond and behind and above.

A few minutes later I heard the purr of a powerful engine. As it turned the bend and approached the long hill ahead, I saw that it was travelling fast, a sign that it was a bigger, more powerful car than the Citroën. It must be the Delahaye.

It was. It was still daylight. There was no need for hiding now. The detectives had raced ahead and I was running down the hill – running, nearly toppling over – as I tried frantically to diminish the distance between us, to discover what had happened. The car squealed to a stop beside me as I waved my arms frantically. I could see Galina crying. 'Oh Nicki! They shot him – no, only in one leg – but they've got him. They took him away. Nicki, what will you do – what can we do?'

She had stopped the car in the middle of the road. Restarting the engine, she drove it to one side, almost on to the grass verge.

'Well?' I asked.

'It all happened so quickly. Have you a handkerchief?' I gave mine to her and she blew her nose noisily, then dabbed her eyes. 'As we stopped a few yards from the frontier – near the woods as you told us – the police raced up, moved ahead of us, blocked our way. I had all the papers, ready to present them to the immigration man in the control box. Just a couple of passports and your special *carte d'identité* showing you are an accredited member of the Red Cross. The policeman got out of the car and asked to see Rudi's passport and so on, and when he had studied it carefully I said, "The man at the desk is just making notes, can I give it back to him?"'

'Without a word he handed your papers back. The other man shouted, "Bring them back after the immigration inspector has finished with them. I might need them again."'

'Meanwhile, the first man was firing ceaseless questions at poor Rudi. That was the *real* trouble. Where were you born? When did you first join the Red Cross? Who was the Swiss man who trained you? What year was that? And every now and again, as Rudi became more and more flustered, the detective would slip in a trick question, When did you leave Lienz for the Atlantic coast? Rudi pretended to look puzzled and played his part well – but he was beginning to get more rattled, especially when they fired further questions at him, What was the name of the American girl who worked for you until America entered the war? That kind of question, like a non-stop battery of demands requiring correct answers. And of course there was no way Rudi could answer all the questions. He began to fumble the replies. He became more and more jittery, unsettled, then shouted suddenly, "For God's sake stop hounding me!"

'"I may have to ask you to come back to the police station and answer more questions," said one of the policemen.

'"Never!" roared Rudi, and – stupidly, he *might* have been able to brazen it out, I don't know – he butted the first man in the stomach with his head. It was mad, suicidal! The man was bowled over flat on his back. Rudi went for the next one, sent him sprawling with a crack on the jaw. Then he made a dash for the trees.

'He had a head start. He was *almost* into the thick of the forest when one policeman shouted, "Get the gun from the back seat!"

'The man raced to the car, picked up the sub-machine gun and almost without hesitating, I watched him swivel round, aim the automatic and fire a short burst.

'Poor Rudi! He almost made it, but when the man started firing blindly I heard a scream that made my blood run cold.

'"He's over there, he's hurt," one policeman shouted, "he'll give us no more trouble."

'I knew then, Rudi had lost. The two men, one with a gun at the ready, advanced cautiously through the undergrowth into the wood, and a few moments later emerged, dragging poor Rudi, who was swearing in Russian like a trooper, more angry than hurt, it seemed. I wanted to rush in and try to help, but a sudden instinct warned me not to. If I got too close they might want your papers back, which I was holding in my pocket.'

'And Rudi – his wound –?' I asked.

'I could see some blood oozing out of one trouser leg, but I reckon it was only a flesh wound.'

She said that the two men half carried, half dragged Rudi into the back seat of the Citroën and she heard one say, 'We'd better stop at the local hospital in Pontarlier and have the wound dressed. It's not very serious.'

'My heart was pounding as though it would burst. I've never been so frightened in my life.'

'What did you do?'

'Most of all, I wanted to guard your papers so that you couldn't be drawn in. Without the papers, they had no proof. But I did try – ineffectually – to stop them putting Rudi in the car. They just pushed me away. Two customs or immigration men came from their cabins and one of them gently restrained me and said very politely, "Please, Madame, the police telephoned us ahead that there might be some trouble here. And you must not try to interfere with justice. If the man is innocent you'll see him again very soon. Come now, my dear –" He was almost like a father.

'Then once they had bundled Rudi into the car, with one of the policemen guarding him, the other jumped out of the driving seat and beckoned me.'

'"We know who you are," he said quite politely, "and I advise you, Madame, to drive your car into Switzerland – and stay there until you go to America. You are an accomplice to a crime, but not –"

'"It's not a crime to try and escape from certain death at the hands of Stalin!" I shouted.

'He replied, "I sympathise with you, Madame, and I agree. I apologise for using the word 'crime'. But a prisoner of war" – he shrugged his shoulders – "cannot be allowed to escape. It is a political matter. Maybe later – we do not know, I have no authority."

'I cried, "But it's so unfair!" I was literally sobbing. Then he looked me straight in the eyes and said quite gently, "Permit me to give you some unofficial advice, Madame. We are prepared to take a lenient view of your inexcusable behaviour in shielding this man because of what you in the past have done for the honour of France, and because I myself am a lover of ballet and have seen you many times. But please, Madame, stay in Switzerland. The newspapers have said you are going to America. Bon voyage. But go from Switzerland if you can. If you return to Paris it may be impossible for – well, others – to prevent you from being involved. Mes hommages, Madame."

'He saluted, walked back into his car, started the motor, and shot off up the hill.'

Galina looked at me, never hesitated, just said to me almost reproachfully, 'You didn't think I'd stay in Switzerland like that – right away?'

We were sitting in the car, more composed now.

'At least I saved your passport and papers,' she said with a sad smile. 'But I'll never get over the sight of Rudi being dragged, his clothes torn, dumped into that car.'

'And the man said not to return to Paris?'

She nodded abjectly. 'He was very – well, specific about it. Warned me very seriously. He wasn't a bad chap – apart from what he did. But even then, he certainly didn't look as if he liked doing it.'

'I think he was right,' I said slowly. 'You're on the edge of a new and brilliant second career in a great country virtually untouched by the war. You *can't* pass up that chance.'

'But Nicki –'

'What can you do? What can I do?' I asked. 'What the

429

hell can *anybody* do? Poor Rudi, poor devil! How it happened I don't know, the only thing I *do* know is – they've got him. I'll have to go straight back to St Lô and try to see if there's anything I can do. If I dare! I don't think I'll be too welcome there. Thank God I'm not implicated in today's events. I've never been seen. But *you* have! And that policeman's advice – yes, I don't know if it's possible, but you've got to go straight from Switzerland to America. Don't return to Paris or someone'll be after you.'

'But my clothes,' wailed Galina. 'My tickets – everything.'

'Details,' I said almost crossly. 'Don't fuss about details! Anyone can cancel a ticket – you haven't even paid for it – and arrange with the New York people to issue a different one. I wonder if there is any other way of flying the Atlantic. From Lisbon, perhaps? But now – let's plan what we're going to do.'

We sat there, filling the car with cigarette smoke, until finally I said, 'I think I've got it – what to do. How about this?'

The plan was simple. François Savin would, I hoped, still be at the wayside café on the other side of the border where the passport office and customs post was hidden by a bend in the road from the French *douane*. So there was no way – except for the sound of that shot – that Savin could know what had happened. Now, as I suggested to Galina, we would *both* drive across the frontier, ignore the baffled French immigration authorities, meet François and tell him everything that had happened.

'You can trust him?'

'With my life. Anyway, we've no option. When we've had a coffee and sandwich at the restaurant at Vallorbe, where I'm sure Savin will be waiting, I'll wait for a short time, fill up the tank and jerricans with petrol and set off back to Paris, perhaps spending the night somewhere on the way if it gets late. There I can telephone Tasha with all our good news and all our bad news.' I sighed, almost desperately. 'If only I knew *how* it happened. That's what baffles me. But it *has* happened. It's a fact. We've both seen it – you in real life, Galina, me in a kind of flash-back, as when a character in a gangster film is being held hostage.'

'What about the car?'

'I daren't take it back to Igor's place. Someone who saw us leave in it – I suppose they must have known that right from the beginning – I don't want to drive it back. Every link in the chain against me – and my job – I don't know, I'm muddled, but I'll have to think of a way of ditching the car. I imagine that the police will soon be asking questions in the Rue St Dominique about the Delahaye. Where is it? It's vanished. Kornilov can provide the perfect answer. Igor gave it to you – Galina. You've vanished either into Switzerland or even America. You'll be un-touchable.'

This plan at least worked perfectly. I spent the best part of an hour with François discussing details. It seemed that telephone and cable facilities were much easier between neutral Switzerland and America, and he would easily be able to switch the tickets. As to getting there, he promised there would be no difficulty. Helvetia Airlines, as it was called, had always kept a modest internal service going with old German planes patched up, with spare parts being sent from Germany. Now Helvetia had recently opened a service between Zürich and Lisbon, while in the summer of 1945, almost immediately after VE day, Pan American had opened their Yankee Clipper flying-boat service once a week from Lisbon to New York, the flying-boat stopping in the Azores on the way.

'There'll be no problems,' François promised me. 'Galina's international reputation, together with our Red Cross backing – we'll get her a seat.'

'It won't be dangerous?'

'It'll be fun,' laughed François, 'though as far as I'm

concerned, I would rather have your company if you were delayed.'

It was an awful wrench saying goodbye to Galina, hard to realise how close we had been, drawn together perhaps even more by our sharing knowledge of the 'illicit' relationship with Tasha. And ours had been a warm loving relationship too, built up over thirty years of a tough as well as close life. We kissed, and finally, as I climbed into the car and prepared to set off for the Swiss border post, a few yards away, she whispered, 'At least you've got your beloved Tasha. And I'm so glad that's turned out so well. It's a wonderfully happy ending for you both. And don't worry too much about Rudi. He's not dead yet.'

Driving fast, I reached Avallon that evening, only two hundred kilometres from Paris. Several miles before reaching it I remembered reading of its famous Hôtel de la Poste, and I decided that I would drive there and drown my sorrows not only in wine but with good food, in the beautiful and comfortable hotel which was renowned throughout France. And of course I was thinking as I grew closer to the small pretty city – hardly more than a town really – that the attractive Anna D'Arcy, once the secret joy and love of Igor, lived there. I was wondering how often in the past, before his stroke, Igor had driven Anna out in this same beautiful car which now I was driving.

I did not have her telephone number on me but, not surprisingly, the concierge knew of a citizen as important as Monsieur D'Arcy.

'He lives very close to our hotel,' he said, and then I asked if he would get the number, because a sudden idea had surfaced in my mind. I *had* to get rid of the Delahaye – temporarily anyway, to be on the safe side – so that *nobody* could associate me with the attempted escape of Rudi. I would park the car with Anna D'Arcy if she would let me, then take the train from Avallon to Paris.

I had always agreed that if ever chance took me to Avallon and I telephoned and her husband was there, it would be as a married friend she had met in Paris and I had promised to phone if I passed through. I had parked the Delahaye in the beautiful ivy-covered courtyard, and the concierge had been suitably impressed. He motioned me to a callbox when he had made the connection and Anna sounded delighted to hear me. Then she added, 'Come in for a drink – my husband is here' – with a significant pause – 'but I may even be able to find you a shot of vodka.' She laughed her own particularly trilling laugh that I had always found so charming. 'The concierge'll tell you where we live – five minutes away at the most. Come right round.'

The concierge pointed out to me the D'Arcy house opposite a remarkable relic of the past, hard to describe but with a particular charm of its own. I can best describe it by likening it to the ancient hippodromes of bygone days which were used for sporting events. This one consisted of a raised platform of lawn perhaps two hundred yards long and surrounded by giant trees. It was very impressive – the more so because the entire arena was lined with six or seven steps which you had to walk up if you wanted to stroll inside the rectangle of giant trees. Anna's house was at the far end. 'You can't miss it,' the concierge pointed. 'It has a blue door.'

She was genuinely delighted to meet me, and I stepped into an elegant living-room and was introduced to her husband, who seemed a decent enough chap, considerably older than Anna and not looking in very good health. Though wearing a dressing-gown he got up, shook hands, gave a smile at his clothes and said, 'Sorry about this. Just felt off colour today so decided to take the day off. But it won't stop me drinking this.'

He opened a bottle of champagne while Anna mentioned, in a happy-go-lucky way, that we had met at some reception in Paris. To make things easier, I said, 'It's a long time since we met. I think it was at a reception for my sister Galina, the ballet dancer.'

'That was it,' she lied beautifully. 'How is she?'

'Marvellous. Off to America to help start a new ballet company.'

'And why,' – a little gently – 'are you here? What brings you to Avallon?'

'I've driven Galina to Switzerland. She's got business there before she leaves for America, and I thought I would drive her down in my cousin's old Delahaye. Such fun!' Was Anna turning a little pale at the word Delahaye? 'So I drove to Switzerland, left her there, and now I'm on my way back to work. And my wife, who's waiting for me at home, tomorrow morning.'

After we had almost finished the champagne I noticed that Anna's husband seemed to be on the point of nodding off.

'Darling,' she chided him gently, 'go back to bed now. You don't look very well. I'll walk the Prince back to his hotel. I'd like a breath of fresh air.'

'Fine,' said the husband, adding to me, 'Sorry about this, but I *am* feeling pretty groggy.'

'I'm only sorry if I've tired you.'

'Not at all', meaning 'Certainly you have', as he started to climb the stairs laboriously. Anna and I made for the front door.

'Won't be long, darling,' she called as she closed the door behind her.

'Sorry about my husband,' she said. 'But he's suffering from – well it's only a question of time,' she sighed. 'There's nothing we can do. He just seems so lethargic, wasting away.'

I said suitable words of condolence and asked her, 'You haven't ever been back to see Igor?'

'No,' she shook her head. 'My husband'll be taking up all my time until –' she faltered. 'How is poor Igor?'

'The same.' I sighed too.

'I certainly seem to choose my men well!' She sounded almost viciously bitter.

Seeking to change the way the conversation was going, I asked, 'Could you do something for me – a favour?'

'If possible. If it's not illegal!' She managed a smile.

'Not quite. But I've got the Delahaye here.'

'So I gathered. That brings back happy memories! But how do I come into it?'

'I want to hide it.'

She looked a little startled.

'Don't worry,' I reassured her. 'I give you my word of honour there's nothing to be afraid of. I just want to leave it here in Avallon and return by train.'

'And what do you want me to do?'

'Leave it in a garage until I send for it, or come and fetch it.'

'It sounds very unorthodox.'

'It is. But it's essential. I'd just like the car to disappear.'

We were approaching the end of the 'hippodrome'.

'You helped me a great deal,' she said. 'So I'll help you.' She still sounded doubtful about my reasons. 'You do promise – no monkey business?'

'No monkey business,' I assured her gravely. 'I don't want anyone to know that I've ever left Paris –'

'It's not stolen?'

'Of course not. It's Igor's. Take all the papers. If you've any spare garage – if –'

'Where is it?'

'At the Poste. Here are the keys. And its *carnet* and *papier gris*. Drive it if you want until I fetch it.'

'And that will be?'

'I can't tell you. Months, perhaps years.'

'I'll pick it up in the morning,' she decided. 'I'd better tell the concierge.' We walked into the small lobby and the concierge, resplendent in uniform with crossed keys on his lapels, bowed to Madame D'Arcy, and when she said

435

she would be borrowing my car, said, 'I quite understand, Madame D'Arcy. A magnificent car.'

After a wonderful dinner I finally managed to get through on the phone to Tasha. I explained that we had been delayed and that I was spending the night at Avallon and then cried, 'Darling! I've got some wonderful news for you, something that –'

'I have to tell you –' she began.

'Hush darling! Don't interrupt. I've got absolute proof from Rudi – listen – you're *not my sister*.'

'What!'

'Yes, beloved. It's all the result of a ghastly mistake. Tasha, we are truly and genuinely married – legitimately.'

'I'm so happy for you, for us. But I've got –'

'There's something else I have to tell you,' I added in a more sombre tone of voice. 'Poor Rudi – they caught him at the frontier.'

'Oh no! And you know what's happened here –'

Hardly hearing her, I added, 'I don't know how it happened. I'm heartbroken –'

'Listen!' Her voice suddenly sounded angry. 'Will you *listen*! I've been trying to tell you something and you won't listen.'

'Sorry, Tasha. What is it?' The anger in her voice suddenly gave me that awful feeling that I was on the edge of bad news.

'Oh Nicki! How could it happen?'

'What happened?' I asked harshly.

'This morning the police came to the house while Nataliya and I were having lunch.'

'Go on!'

'They arrested her – Nataliya – as an escaped prisoner of war.'

436

PART FIVE

1946–1947

30

Almost a year of our lives vanished as though wiped off a slate; as though the atomic bomb which devastated Hiroshima and won the peace for the Allies had killed the rest of the world, leaving Tasha and me the sole survivors. All traces of Rudi and his wife had disappeared as though they had been secretly killed. Perhaps they had, I used to think bitterly, killed off or banished to Siberia by the evil machinations of Stalin, given a last-minute push to their fate by the Allies.

Men like Inspector Verron were no longer evasive because they had not the faintest idea of their fates. But he *did* tell me *how* they had been caught.

'You thought you were being clever, thinking that we were only having you followed,' he jeered. 'What do you think we are? Playing at policemen? You think we're dumber than you are. When we want something *badly* – then we leave *no* stone unturned. Automatically we put a full-time watch on the house of your cousin Count Trepov, the man with the stroke. We knew that one day, sooner or later, he would become involved.'

I swore bitterly – but under my breath. How stupid I was so obviously to underestimate a man like Verron!

'Why,' he went on in that half jeering half self-satisfied tone of voice, 'we even had a man planted in the Rue St Dominique as a gardener. And when he heard that the chauffeur was rearranging the seating – well, we just had to wait while you fell into the trap.'

I asked, sighing sadly, 'So you followed the Delahaye?'

To my surprise Verron shook his head. 'No, another Deuxième Bureau outfit took over as soon as the escape started. Nor did I –' he spoke with an almost malicious pleasure – 'have the honour of arresting the prisoner's wife. Special Branch took that pleasure for themselves. So,' he admitted after that, 'I never did know what happened to either of them. That was the end as far as I was concerned.'

He could not even resist a final jeer. 'But until then, it was too easy. The smart amateurs who thought they'd licked the professionals. Pitiful,' he shook his head. 'Let that be a lesson to you if you ever get involved again in a family squabble.'

There was another matter that doubtless Verron would have included in his sneering phrase 'family squabble', had he known of it. Olga was reluctant to accept the truth of Rudi's revelations about Tasha. She had made such capital out of her insistence on our incestuous relationship that she could not bear to lose hold of it. Had Rudi been there she would, I know, have subjected him to countless questions in an effort to overturn his story; as it was, her bad grace took the form of a rather sulky withdrawal from Tasha and me, and her rare visits to the place de Furstemberg only brought with them a strained atmosphere.

More joyful were occasional letters from Galina in New York. We caught the tempo of that city's pulsing life and her frantic itinerary among the top-drawer socialites who were backing Balanchine in his new enterprise. She also mentioned a wealthy doctor she had met at some fund-raising affair from which he had driven her back to the St Regis Hotel and invited her to dinner at his family home in Westchester.

'Reading between the lines,' Tasha said with feminine intuition inflecting every word, 'I see a budding romance between Galina and her Hugo.'

I shrugged. 'Probably just a passing fancy. She obviously lives in a social whirl.'

*

For nearly a year – until the autumn of 1946 – with the world now at peace – we had tried to find out what had happened to Rudi and Nataliya, but without even a trace of success. Even immediately after their capture, when I travelled to St Lô – half-hoping that Rudi would be there – I found the camp dismantled, and all the prisoners taken elsewhere, some to America, some to Canada, some to England. More and more, good sense warned us that by now they must be back in Russia. But I refused to think of them as dead.

Even so, slowly, with a kind of painful agony, I began to lose all hope that I would ever see them again – not with the agonisingly slow death process of poor Igor, now declining visibly; but still, the agony was there, compounded by the amateurish way I had bungled Rudi's bid for freedom, just letting the others set a trap into which I encouraged my twin brother to walk. That futile stupidity has never ceased to haunt me; not daily, perhaps, but as a recurring nightmare.

How right Verron was! What an idiotic amateur I had been.

There was only one wonderful item on the plus side. In the spring of 1946, Tasha and I had a 're-marriage' service at the Russian Orthodox Church which we had rarely attended during the last war years. It gave both of us a curious peace of mind, not only to wipe out the memory of the wrong but necessary German wedding under the auspices of Ullmann and the Nazi padre, but because of the wrong we *thought* we had done.

Then in the summer of 1946 something else happened which gave me great joy. Almost shyly, Tasha announced, 'It looks as though I'm going to have a baby.'

Excitedly resisting the comic book phrases like 'Don't you think you should sit down' I put my arms round her, squeezed her and said, 'Now, despite all our worries, I'm the happiest man in the world.'

That night we had to attend a cocktail party at the British Embassy in my official capacity as head of the Red Cross. I regret to say that even the ambassador, Duff Cooper, did not escape my buttonholing enthusiasm. Tasha was most embarrassed.

It must have been several months later when three separate letters arrived – postmarked in three different countries. One had a Dutch stamp on it, one an English postmark and the third with the red and blue airmail border and handwriting I knew immediately: Galina's. The others could wait. They were probably Red Cross business, anyway. It was Galina's latest news I wanted. And, as it turned out, what news!

Dearest Nicki:

Such excitement! You'll never believe! But of course I'm bursting to tell you! Hugo Lattimer, the neurologist I told you about in previous letters, and I were married in New York with a great deal of grandeur and finery last week. There! His parents are very wealthy, so of course it had to be at St Patrick's Cathedral with 'the full works' as the Americans call it. Just wait till you see the pictures! As you see from the address we're honeymooning (recovering!) now in Bermuda and I've only just taken breath long enough to write this scrawled note.

Of course I can see your puzzled frown about Jean-Pierre, but let me tell you nothing could have been easier than a divorce. Hugo's father is an eminent lawyer and of course he wasn't going to have his number one son marrying bigamously! But it was all right. French law allows easy divorce where one party is 'under the Republic's duress' (in jail, that means!) and both parties consent. As you know, there was never any love between Jean-Pierre and me, it was simply a professional engagement and it worked well until the poor thing got himself into a mess over that shooting. Lattimer senior had the whole

442

thing dealt with from his Paris office. All I had to do was
sign affidavits. So my conscience is clear and you can
relax the furrows on your forehead.

No time for more now. Hugo is beckoning me from
the doorway (the bedroom!). Who am I to disobey my
lord and master! . . .

Love . . .

Well! I thought: who could have foreseen such a happy
outcome of Balanchine's invitation to Galina. I felt a
glowing of happiness for her, and decided to send her a
cable right away. Tasha, of course, said, 'I told you so.'

The second letter was from London, brusque, formal,
and typed on paper headed bleakly with a name that meant
little to me. *Dear Sir*, it read, *I have been asked by your*
sister-in-law Nataliya Korolev to inform you that she gave
birth to a son some months ago. Mother and child are in
satisfactory condition but Mr Korolev has been unable to
visit her because he is detained in Fairways POW camp,
Derby, while the matter of their repatriation is being con-
sidered by higher authority.

The letter was signed with an authoritative flourish *Rose*
Castle, Q.A.I.M.N.S., Matron-in-Chief, of the Queen
Alexandra's Imperial Military Nursing Service – the equivalent rank of Brigadier, which meant that she could throw
her weight around a bit in Whitehall.

I looked at the stiff, formal letter with something bordering on – yes, almost a kind of heart-stopping panic! Alive!
Both of them! And a baby son. I felt my breath shortening
as I cried, 'Tasha!'

She rushed in. 'They're alive!' I shouted. 'Rudi and
Nataliya! They're alive!' After all these months. After all
the agonies and doubts through which we had passed, the
fruitless enquiries from every direction; even combing
through Red Cross files, nursing some vague hope that we
might stumble on a clue. And here, in a stiff and formal
letter, I had learned the truth – that, however desperate

443

their plight, however slender their hope, they were still alive – and still thousands of miles from the murderous embrace of that arch monster Stalin.

There was a third letter. I must open it, though nothing could be of importance after the news we had received. But it *was* important.

To my astonishment, the letter from Amsterdam was from the same person, Rose Castle, but it read very differently, masking the impersonal authority of the first letter. It was little more than a note, on plain paper and signed only with the initials 'R.C.' It read:

Dear Mr Korolev:

Please destroy this note immediately after reading it. Apart from my formal letter I have no right in my official position to communicate privately with you, as I understand that you aided and abetted your brother and his wife in an abortive escape bid. For that reason all mail from Russian POWs in Britain is censored and letters addressed to suspected 'friends' are not delivered. That is why you have had no news from your brother. I wanted you to know, so I have posted this in Amsterdam, where I have been staying a few days. Unofficially the baby is beautiful and well, but it is sad that Rudi has not seen him or his wife, though he has been informed of the birth. Nataliya is depressed and pining and I fear that unless someone (you?) can see her, give her some hope, and some kind of help, she may suffer a kind of nervous breakdown.

Yours sincerely . . .

What a nice letter! What a wonderful person Rose Castle must be. Her two letters were astonishing – as though the first had been written while she was in uniform, the second when relaxing. Well, in a way, that was true, I supposed. She *had* relaxed, even permitting herself to write an unauthorised letter to me. It seemed to me to show a spirit

of generosity struggling against man-made rules laid down
by Authority with a capital 'A'.

My head was reeling: Rudi free! So far. But 'awaiting
repatriation' gave me an ominous sense of foreboding.
Obviously poor Rudi had written to me but his letters were
withheld. And he was a father now.

'I must go and see Rudi,' were my first words to Tasha.

'Of course. As soon as you can. And poor Nataliya too.
She seems in a bad way.'

'I wonder if they'll let me see Rudi?' I pondered.

'I'm sure they will. Your twin brother! There's no way
they could stop you.'

'I hope not. But that second letter from Rose' – instinctively I thought of her as Rose – 'makes it quite clear that
they regard my part in the escape as proved to be guilty.
They may not relish the idea of us meeting. I don't know.'

'So you think you can just go there – just on the offchance
of meeting each other?' Tasha asked.

I shook my head. 'No. I think I'd better get hold of
François Savin and ask him if he can help.'

It *was* much simpler. After all, I had the address of
Rudi, and it was thus a fairly easy matter for the International Red Cross in Geneva (in the form of François)
with all its prestige to talk at length to the camp commandant, explain Rudi's relationship not only to me, but to
the late Tsar, the Royal connection and so on. It worked
wonders.

'The Colonel sounds very helpful,' François told me
on the phone. 'You can go and see Rudi next week on
Wednesday at one o'clock. The Colonel pointed out to
me,' explained François, 'that this will give you plenty of
time to catch the morning train from London to Derby,
and that a taxi will take you to the camp.'

'Bless you,' I thanked François. 'That's a relief. You'll
never know how grateful –'

'Forget it,' cried François. 'All in the day's work.'

'The day's *pleasure*,' I changed the old saying slightly.

'There's one thing, though, and there's nothing we can do about it,' added François. 'In view of what happened between you two before, the Colonel says there's no way you'll be allowed to see Rudi alone.'

'Oh no!'

'I know how you feel,' sighed François, 'but I must say, it *is* understandable. I think you must consider yourself lucky to be able to see him at all.'

'But it *is* bloody unfair.'

'It may be. But they won't even discuss you having a private meeting. After all, Nicki, you did that once. And they know all about the plotting that went on when you two were alone.'

'The main thing, I suppose, is to see Rudi. I wonder what he's doing in Derby of all places.'

Savin explained that a fairly large number – that was his estimate – of what he called 'the disputed list' were remaining in POW camps because there *were* some problems that remained unsolved, but Savin did add that basically all the Russians would eventually be repatriated.

'They told me there'll be no exceptions,' added François gloomily. 'It's just a question of time. I think it's only fair to warn you.'

'I know, I know; but thanks for all your help. I'll go and see Rudi and before I go from London to Derby, I'll try and contact Nataliya. I don't see why they should stop me seeing her – and the baby.'

I flew to London the following Monday, booked in at the same hotel as before – the Russell – and the following morning went to see Nataliya and Rose Castle; on Wednesday I would take the morning train to Derby, arriving there in time for my one o'clock appointment.

The interview with Rose Castle turned out to be very relaxed. She received me in her office in the Middlesex Hospital which, she told me, had been her headquarters

during the war, but now it had one annexe which was being
used to house the few women POWs who had been caught
in this beastly crossfire of peace disguised as war. At first
glance it seemed to be a cold place – endless impersonal
grey corridors, stiff, starched uniforms – I am not sure how
to describe it, except that it gave me the shivers.

On the other hand, I quickly realised that underneath
the veneer of the matron – for in a sense that was her
function – Rose Castle had a heart of gold filled with
sympathy for her charges, and in particular for the poor
mother and an innocent child caught in a web of intrigue
not of their making.

When I walked into her office, she stood up, round and
cheerful with the kind of warmth that immediately made
me feel at home, said, 'Do sit down,' and motioned me to
the chair opposite her desk, which was cluttered with
papers. She was also a woman of candour, as I found from
her first question.

'Do I call you Prince or Mister?' she asked.

'Normally Mister,' I smiled. 'But if it helps – sometimes,
well, Prince.'

'It might help you now,' she said drily. 'I feel deeply
sorry for Nataliya and we shall do everything to help her.
But rules are rules, Mr Korolev, and it is never easy to
bend rules – especially –' she added grimly, 'rules made
by Stalin. He insists that they are always obeyed.'

'It's very good of you to see me,' I began tentatively.

'I'm glad you've come, though I'm afraid you'll find her
rather depressed. We *are* very worried about her.'

I waited for her to continue, murmuring simply, 'I imagine she must be.'

'We're doing everything we can,' she sighed. 'But it's
an uphill struggle and I would not be doing you a service
if I did not tell you the truth – that I don't hold out much
hope. Let me give you a cup of tea, Mr Korolev.'

'Thank you.' I hated 'English' tea, swamped with milk,
missing the lemon and sugar, but before Rose ordered two

cups on the telephone, I managed to whisper, 'No milk, please,' and so it did not taste too bad.

'I'm just passing a little time while we get your sister-in-law presentable,' she explained. 'When Nataliya arrived in this country she only had the clothes she stood in. But now, she's got quite a trousseau,' she beamed, 'from your Red Cross – well, the British Red Cross – together with things for the baby – shoes, socks, baby clothes – everything she needs, and –'

There was a knock on the door and, after Rose had cried 'Enter!', in walked Nataliya carrying a tiny bundle in a long shawl.

'There you are, my dear,' Rose fussed. Nataliya was forcing a smile, but I nearly burst into tears myself. The girl who had been such a happy 'prisoner' in Paris had, after a year's absence, turned into a dispirited waif, a ghost of herself. Her cheeks were empty hollows, her eyes black rings as though covered in mascara, and though she had made some effort to comb her hair, it hung around her face like wisps of hopelessness, strands from an old kitchen mop.

'Oh Nicki!' she burst into sobs, forgetting Rose and nearly dropping the child. 'How wonderful to see you again – to see a friend after all this time. In all this world Miss Castle is my only friend. But now you've come –'

'Hush,' I tried to calm her, but she was sobbing bitterly. 'You're certainly with a friend now.'

She clung to me as though clutching on to a life raft at the moment of drowning. The suddenness of our meeting – even though she had been expecting it – had overwhelmed her completely. She could not stop her uncontrolled crying and I hardly managed to understand her French or her Russian.

Rose touched my shoulder. 'I'll leave you two alone for a short while,' she whispered. 'You'll be better alone. Go and take her to sit on the sofa,' she indicated the corner of the room. 'And,' this to Nataliya, 'show off this beautiful little boy to your brother-in-law. He's a wonderful little chap.'

Suddenly Nataliya stopped crying and said in French, 'Of course! I forgot.'

Carefully she withdrew a corner of the crocheted shawl which had all but covered the baby's head. It looked – to my inexperienced eye – a healthy child and the ice of Nataliya's agony was broken when both women uttered almost identical words at the same moment:

'It looks just like you,' Rose said to me.

'He looks just like Nicki,' said Nataliya.

'I should hope so. Both of us,' I said and we all laughed together.

Alone, the baby gurgling as Nataliya played with it, stroking it gently under the chin, I said to her, 'Now I'll tell you the news about Rudi. I'm seeing him tomorrow, and tomorrow evening I'll come round and tell you all about him. I hope,' I added, 'he will look better than you do, young lady!'

'I'm all right,' she said.

'You're not,' I retorted. 'You must try to lift yourself out of this depression.'

'I miss him so much! How cruel people are! Not giving the father a chance to see our baby. How *can* people behave like that?'

'I don't know,' I sighed. 'But I *do* know that while there's life there's hope. That must be your motto, your guiding star, if you want to *believe* in yourself, in the future.'

'But what future?'

'Yours!' I cried. 'You are alive, you have done nothing wrong, you have a husband, you have a beautiful baby. All right! So you're having a rough time – no, no,' I cried as she tried to interrupt me, 'I refuse to listen to any defeatist talk. You are *here*. So is your beloved Rudi. Separated, yes, but healthy and with hope.'

'I can't think like that,' she started crying again. 'If only

I could. But I know the worst is going to happen. We are no longer husband and wife –'

'Of course you are!' I cried. 'Don't talk such nonsense. For you two the war is still going on. That's the difference. And in wartime ninety-nine out of a hundred married couples are separated, sometimes for years. Some of the men die. Some of the wives are killed in air raids. Look around you at the devastation in London. But listen, Nataliya, do people separated by war go through life thinking the worst – that every day is the last? Of course they don't. They wait for the next meeting. Sure it will come. And that's what you must do. You'll meet again.'

It had been a long plea by me, and I had spoken with a passion which I think encouraged her, for she said more hopefully, 'If I really believed you – yes, I do –' she kissed the baby.

'You must. It's the only way,' I pressed the argument home. 'Otherwise you sink into a quicksand, being sucked deeper and deeper into it every second until in the end you disappear into oblivion.'

'Tell me more about him tomorrow,' she begged me eagerly, hardly hearing my warnings.

When Nataliya had gone Rose returned and in her downright manner asked, 'Doing anything tonight?'

Slightly surprised, I hesitated and said, 'Er – no. I mean, well, no, I thought I might go to a cinema or –'

'Good! You're staying at the Russell? I'll pick you up at half past seven. Like Russian food? Good. I'm inviting you and Nataliya to dinner at a small restaurant called the Suvárov just off Curzon Street, and I've asked another man to make a four. Bit more than that really,' she sounded mysterious. 'Got a plan. Might interest you.'

I was wondering if she had a beau – but the idea of taking Nataliya out for dinner made me think this was not the case. Still, it was a wonderful idea. And as for Russian food!

The Suvárov, named after the famous Russian general, was a delightful restaurant near Shepherd Market, which as she explained, was the heart of the red light district off Piccadilly, and through the windows, we could see dozens of pretty and unpretty girls strolling, waiting for clients.

It was the fourth person, though, who intrigued me. But not for long. Rose introduced him as Mr Wallis – 'Tom to you two' – and I liked him. He was about thirty – perhaps even a year or two less – quiet, and I felt he was studying us (as indeed he was) and when Rose suddenly announced after coffee, 'Tom is a journalist for the London *News Chronicle*,' I began to wonder if he was connected with the 'idea' Rose had spoken of.

He was. She had already outlined Nataliya's entire story to Tom Wallis and now he began to probe into detailed questions. They – his paper – were concerned with the plight of Nataliya, the sister-in-law of a prince, a friend of the Tsar and so on – and of course with a baby who, almost by accident, had dual nationality. By law he was as British as he was Russian, and he could, if his parents so wished, never be taken from England whatever Stalin might say. But would his parents be allowed to stay too?

'The officials are sometimes quite cross with me,' confided Rose, 'because they say I overstep the mark. Well, that's why we're keeping this little dinner quiet,' she added. 'Because I believe that Tom will be able to write a story that will set London on fire with anger that the British, who won the war, can treat a poor woman in the way Nataliya is being treated.'

'May I take a photo of you?' asked Wallis. 'I'll have a copy sent to your husband.'

Nataliya hesitated, and looked to Rose for guidance. She nodded with a smile.

'Now *you* smile,' said Rose. 'This photograph and this story could perhaps change your life.'

451

31

I had given little thought to Tom Wallis, my dinner companion, indeed had almost forgotten about the story which Rose had said was going to set an angry Britain on fire. I had, however, ordered the *News Chronicle* with my morning tea from the hall porter, and had just started to sip it when I saw the *News Chronicle* message screaming across page one:

BRITISH BABY'S MOTHER FACES DEATH FROM RUSSIANS

And underneath, on three lines was the ominous message:

MILLIONS OF SOVIETS
WHO FOUGHT THE NAZIS
KILLED BY STALIN

Underneath, on the right-hand side, was a three-column photograph of Nataliya – the one that had been taken the previous evening – looking suitably winsome, and underneath it the caption: 'This is Nataliya Korolev, mother of a British baby by birth, who wants to stay in England with her Russian husband, a Russian POW. They are both awaiting forced repatriation. Nataliya is being held in London. So far Korolev – who is in Derby, and who is twin brother of a Tsarist Prince – has never been allowed to see his own child.'

And there were no holds barred in the story either. It read:

Nataliya Korolev (pictured right) is one of millions of Russians who, as a result of a wicked travesty of justice by Britain is being forced against her will to return to Russia and a certain death or at best exile to the slave camps of Siberia.

When Churchill was PM he agreed with 'his good friend' Stalin at the Yalta conference that all prisoners of war – of whatever nationality – should be repatriated to their own countries.

It seemed a normal post-war promise. Who wouldn't want to go home at the end of a war? Answer: millions of Russians, terrified of Communist reprisals.

The result was a bungled agreement between Churchill, Roosevelt and Stalin. Churchill's decision to please Stalin at Yalta has unleashed the wrath of a wicked monster whose lust for blood knows no bounds.

Already the fate of nearly two million POWs sent from Europe has been settled. Many have killed themselves rather than go. In one shipload of 3,000 POWs leaving Liverpool five Russians committed suicide. Two men cut their arteries with the jagged edges of their camp china mugs which they had broken to form cutting edges. Three jumped to their deaths in the harbour at Liverpool.

But the case of Nataliya Korolev goes far beyond the bestiality of the treatment meted out by Stalin to other prisoners, for this involves a British boy! Conceived in France but born here, Nicki, as he has been called after his father's twin brother, is *British* by birth. So he cannot be deported. Yet his mother must go. Though his mother says she will never hand over her son to the Russians, nor will she go unless dragged on board a ship.

'I will kill myself first,' she declared to me.

Such is the wickedness of this agreement that her husband has not yet been allowed to see his son, though, as a Russian, he is a brave ally of our country whose bad luck was to be taken prisoner. He knows nothing of her present plight or whereabouts. They have never met since several thousand POWs were shipped to England.

All attempts to let them meet have been stopped. I can reveal that all Mr Korolev's letters to his brother, the

Prince, who is a highly placed official at the International Red Cross in Paris, have been stopped. The Prince has not received one single letter, and only learned by chance that his brother was even alive.

After more in this vein, the article said in small black type at the end: Page Two read 'The Guilty Men.'

I turned the page over (there were only four pages in those days), and read:

THE GUILTY MEN

It was stretched across the main feature page, and underneath it were pictures of Anthony Eden, ex-Foreign Minister and several members of the Foreign Office. Underneath that was another photograph of a man called Lord Selborne described thus: 'When he was Minister of Economic Warfare, Lord Selborne was the one man above all others who tried to save the Russians.'

Indeed, as the article told, Selborne himself had written to Eden, 'I am profoundly moved by the decision of the Cabinet to send back to Russia all Russian subjects who fall into our hands on the battlefields of Europe. I propose to address the Prime Minister on this subject, but before doing so would like you to know the grounds of my opposition, in the hope that we might find ourselves in agreement in this matter. As you know, one of my officers has during the past few weeks interviewed a number of Russian prisoners, and in every case their story is substantially the same. In the first place they were subjected to incredible hardship and ill-treatment on being taken prisoner. They were marched in many cases for several days without any food. They were placed in concentration camps under appalling sanitary conditions and were starved. They became infested with vermin, they were the victims of loathsome diseases and starvation was carried to such a point that cannibalism became prevalent. In more than one instance the Germans filmed cannibalistic meals for propaganda purposes. After several weeks of this treatment and when their morale was completely broken, they were paraded and addressed by a German officer, who invited them to join a German labour battalion in which they would receive proper clothes, rations and treatment. They were then asked individually if they would accept this offer or not. The first man when asked replied "No". He was immediately shot. The same thing happened to the second and to the third and so on until at last one man said he would, and then the others also agreed, as it was clearly the only way of saving their lives.'

The substance of the article was vitriolic. According to the author, Eden, who was preparing a memo to Churchill, had already decided, 'We surely do not wish to be permanently saddled with numbers of these men. To refuse to return them would cause serious harm with the Soviet Government. We have no right whatever to do this and they would not understand our humanitarian motives. They would know that we are treating them differently from the other Allied governments on this question and this would arouse their gravest suspicions . . . It is no concern of ours whatever measures any Allied government, including the Soviet Government, takes as regard to their own nationals.'

Churchill wavered. To Eden he sent a note, 'I think we dealt with this rather summarily at Cabinet and the point raised by Selborne should certainly be reconsidered . . . I think these men were tried beyond their strength.'

Eden retorted: 'If these men do not go back to Russia, where can they go? We don't want them here.' Churchill told Eden that 'all the apparatus of delay be used'.

Much of the blame, the article went on, for this treatment, all of which originated before Churchill was defeated and Attlee took power, was laid at Britain's door, but not all. Churchill's assistant private secretary at Yalta was John Colville, who knew that the agreement on repatriation was 'less Anglo than American' and how Churchill came back from the conference at Yalta 'downcast and disturbed'.

Colville knew that Soviet–American exchanges had taken place behind Churchill's back, with Roosevelt a firm believer that Stalin could be trusted on all matters.

'But the President,' as Churchill told Colville, 'is a dying man.'

Phew! That's strong stuff, I thought. It's going to upset a lot of people.

Sure enough it did – and swiftly too. I had barely finished my second cup of tea when the phone rang. The hotel operator said, 'Just a moment, sir. We have a long distance call for you.'

Long distance! But it wasn't as long as that. A military officer type of voice – strange how you could always tell them – asked 'Prince Korolev?'

'Who's that?' I asked.

'This is Fairways prisoner of war camp in Derby, sir.'

My heart began to thump with foreboding.

'Is my brother all right?'

'Yes, yes, sir. Please do not alarm yourself. But the colonel in charge of the camp asked me to convey to you his apologies. I'm afraid we'll have to postpone today's visit to meet your brother.'

As I started to raise my voice angrily – not quite knowing what I was saying – he interrupted, speaking rapidly, 'No, no, sir, this is not a cancellation, merely a postponement for a few days. It's the – er – Press sir. They're all demanding to see the Colonel. Apparently it's the custom in Fleet Street – where most of the newspapers are printed – that all the – er – papers get early copies of their rivals' – around eleven o'clock in the evening. And we're being besieged by journalists who drove to Derby before breakfast. And the Colonel thought – perhaps –'

'But what's it got to do with me?' I expostulated. 'I've had to pay my fare and so on to come all the way from Paris.'

'I *do* understand sir,' he apologised.

'No you don't,' I retorted angrily.

Unperturbed, the unknown spokesman said, 'The Colonel says that he's already arranged with the right people to provide you with door-to-door military transport – cars, planes and so on – when you come.'

'But this is my twin brother whom I haven't seen for a year!'

'I do appreciate that, but on the other hand, sir,' a tinge of frostiness crept into his voice, 'Your brother was captured wearing a German uniform and carrying a German gun. We are doing everything we can, sir. But Whitehall is very worried about the Press report today – and what might follow. You understand – the Labour government gets very upset about allegations of this sort –'

Somewhat mollified by the promise of free transport when I returned, I asked, 'I do understand, but tell me – when *can* I come to see my brother?'

'The Colonel says there would seem to be no reason why you shouldn't come next week when the fuss has died down. Here is the telephone number of a Major Stafford of SHAEF. He'll arrange everything.'

Suddenly suspicious, I asked, 'And there's no danger in the meantime that my brother's repatriation will conveniently be speeded up – to avert an embarrassing scandal?'

'Oh no sir!' The unseen voice sounded genuinely shocked at the thought that I could entertain such a base thought, 'You have my word, sir.'

'I'll accept that,' I said gravely.

'Thank you, Prince,' he said, 'I look forward to meeting you under happier circumstances.'

So that was that. We had obviously stirred up a hornets' nest, but such a public display of flaying the British soul and conscience could do nothing but good.

I managed to reach Rose on the telephone and tell her what had happened.

'Nataliya will be upset if you don't tell her.'

I asked if she would.

'Of course. And let me know when you come next. That was a fine article,' she spoke guardedly.

With that I drove out to Croydon airport and took the first available plane back to Paris. It was half empty. No Britons were going to Paris for the fun of it, when all they were allowed to take out of the country was £25.

32

When the phone rang I was surprised – and for a moment afraid – at hearing the voice of Matron-in-Chief Rose Castle. She was speaking from the Middlesex Hospital in London.

'No bad news,' she reassured me. 'I've been trying to find out from the camp in Derby when you are coming to see your brother.'

'On Wednesday next, if all goes well.'

'Couldn't be better,' she replied briskly. 'I've arranged for Nataliya to have an interview with an official of the Foreign Office on Thursday – the day after you see your brother. Language will be a bit of a problem but could you attend the meeting as an interpreter? After all, as well as being a member of the family, you *are* a high official of the International Red Cross, *and* a Swiss. What better credentials could you have?'

'I'll be delighted,' I cried and I meant it. Such a meeting would give me a fascinating glimpse into the ways the political machine acted – and thought. 'I'll be flying over on the Tuesday, staying at the Russell again.'

I also realised that the prospect of such a meeting, though I would have no idea of its outcome, would act as a great stimulus to Rudi's spirits when I met him.

*
458

On the Tuesday afternoon I flew in an RAF DC3, was collected at some lonely RAF airfield and taken by car to the Russell Hotel, where the RAF driver said that he would pick me up at ten o'clock the following day to take me to Derby.

When I arrived there, I found that the camp commandant, Colonel Walker, was amiable and helpful. Rudi's working party would be back at about one o'clock, he said. Meanwhile I was welcome to go wherever I wanted, ask questions, inspect accommodation, cookhouses. 'This is Sergeant Jones,' he introduced me. 'He will accompany you.'

The camp was in the woodlands and fields surrounded by outcrops of open-cast mining. The mansion, 'Fairways', set in the middle of the countryside, had been built by one of the Victorian mineowners to demonstrate his *nouveau riche* wealth, and its pillared entrance led into a huge hall with double stairways. This entrance-hall had been converted into the prisoners' dining-hall, with scrubbed wooden tables in lines beneath unseen pictures swathed in dustsheets.

The prisoners were housed in wooden huts – twenty to a hut – raised on brick piles to prevent escape tunnelling, and heated by smoky coke stoves that gave off sulphurous plumes from pipes sticking through the felted roofs. The hundred acres or so of what had once been the colliery owner's estate was surrounded by a ten-foot coiled wire fence with concrete watch towers at intervals; but these were no longer being manned.

POWs wore denim or canvas battle-dress blouses with ten-inch diameter circles of white material sewn on the backs of the blouses. Guarded by NCOs, they were taken in parties of ten to work in nearby farms and open-cast coalfields each day.

Rudi arrived just before one o'clock. I spotted him as his working party marched casually towards the front door.

Lunch was due to be served, but as the commandant

had told me a special exception would be made today, and two lunches, already served on plates, would be taken, with two glasses of milk, to a small ante-room where we could lunch together – with the stolid presence of Sergeant Jones, silent except for one sentence as the prisoner arrived, 'Don't mind my being here,' he tried to reassure me. 'I don't 'ear nuffin'. My only job is to see you don't pass over anything you shouldn't.'

'Thank you, Sergeant,' I said. 'I'll be a good brother, I promise you. I can offer him a cigarette?'

'To me sir,' he said almost apologetically. 'Then I'll 'and it on to your brother. It's the knives we 'as to watch. So many men try to do themselves in.'

Rudi did not look too bad, probably because he had been working in the fields during a reasonably warm summer and the open air had built up his face and his muscles. We hugged each other with joy – and relief that he was still alive. But the only thing Rudi really wanted to talk about was Nataliya.

After I had told him every single detail I could remember about my visit to see her, how we dined together, what the baby was like and how she looked, he sighed. 'If only I could see her. And the baby.'

'I know. Well, I'm hoping something can be done about that.' I told him about Rose Castle. 'She's the queen bee of the nursing service and high-ranking as an officer, so she can talk on equal terms with the Repatriation Committee of the War Office. In fact, tomorrow, I'm going as a Red Cross translator with Nataliya to Whitehall to make her own special plea for you both to be allowed to remain here.'

'Her own plea? But she doesn't speak a word of English! She'll only get into the same kind of trouble as I did when, once, I tried to get away with being Polish.'

'No, no,' I said. 'Rose will write it all out and *present* it to the officials in Whitehall. If she makes her plea tearfully enough it'll soften their hearts. But whether Whitehall can wriggle out of the repatriation agreement made at Yalta is another matter; and I can see international complications arising there. The Communist régime wants its pound of flesh.'

'It's all so – so incredibly unfair,' Rudi's voice was bitter. I could see his eyes misting.

'Life is unfair,' I replied. I did not want any self-pity creeping in. 'You know what Father would have said: "Fight on, m'boy; fight on".'

'Yes,' Rudi said, but there was a hollow ring to his voice. 'Fight on,' adding, ironically, 'I suppose.'

'Don't talk like that,' I said almost sharply. 'I told Nataliya never to forget one thing – that while there's life there's hope. Remember that and don't start crying for yourself. I don't see *how* the British can kick you out of the country now you're the father of a British boy.'

'I know you're right,' he muttered. 'But I get so bloody depressed about her, what she must be feeling, suffering, and the baby –'

'The baby doesn't know anything,' I said. 'And remember that Nataliya has a good and influential friend in Rose Castle. Let's wait and see what happens tomorrow.'

During all this time, smoking and talking, we had eaten our way through a dish new to me, huge portions of steak and kidney pie, with gravy and mashed potatoes and also some vegetables I could not identify.

'What's that?' I pointed to the mash suspiciously.

'Turnips.'

'*Turnips*!' I cried. 'You mean that stuff they feed to the pigs? We never ate that muck –' I almost pushed the plate away.

For the first time that morning Rudi laughed – an open, fresh roar of laughter.

'The best vegetables in the world!' he said. 'It's got a flavour all of its own. You can't tell me you don't *like* them.'

'I've never eaten them.'

461

'Now's the time to learn. We have them once a week. Go on. Try them!'

I did. The taste was something very special – as unique as, say, endives, but good, though among the Russian upper classes, no-one had ever eaten turnips.

'Well anyway!' it was my turn to smile, 'at least I've found a way to make you laugh. A magic password. Just say "Turnip!" Yes, they do taste good.'

The hour passed all too quickly and soon it was time to go. We had covered all the ground we could – from Galina's marriage to Tasha's pregnancy and Rudi's son. 'Tasha's due any day now. Cheer up – like today.' I said, promising him, 'We'll have you out of here in no time. Turnips!'

'I hope so.' He actually laughed again. My mere presence had cheered him up.

'I'll be over again soon,' I said as I prepared to leave. 'And I'm sure that if the Foreign Office can get Nataliya freed, they'll have to review your case too. After all, as I said, you *are* the father of a British boy.'

'I won't forget,' he smiled. 'God! When I think back to that day in the Delahaye, if I'd got five yards further into the thick forest, I'd have been safe.'

'Past days,' I smiled back. 'Think of tomorrow, not yesterday or today.'

On the Thursday, I made my way to the Middlesex Hospital, reaching there at 10.30 am on the dot.

'Better be punctual,' Rose had warned me in her forthright way. 'Our appointment at the FO is for 11.30, so that'll give you plenty of time to tell Nataliya all about your visit to her husband. After the interview, we'll have lunch at some small restaurant. Leave it to me.'

I did – gratefully, knowing that Miss Castle, as I had reflected before, was well named, with the solidity of structure one associates with castles. She was formidable and of no great beauty, but there was nonetheless a drawbridge to be lowered and a portcullis to be raised into the secret places of her heart. No doubt she could breathe terror into young nurses and junior doctors, and no doubt too into the spirits of shamming patients; but she would recognise the need for sympathy and understanding and bestow those qualities lavishly but without sentimentality.

I had seen her previously only in a tweed skirt with twinset and pearls; but today she was in her impressive grey uniform with its scarlet cape and gleaming badges of rank. 'It makes more of a show with the bureaucrats – like you using your title of Prince,' she said in a voice that clearly indicated that she was going to stand no nonsense.

Nataliya sat opposite Miss Castle and me in the taxi. She was thin and pale and kept twisting her hands nervously in her lap as she gazed vacantly out of the window, seeming to be wrapped in her inner thoughts. The doctor at the Middlesex had said that she needed building up after her illness, and that the mental stimulation of the visit would do her good; but she remained listless and silent until she asked in her halting French whom we were going to see.

'A Mr Massingham, a junior official of the Foreign Office.' Miss Castle paused and added disapprovingly, as if it were a fault in him: 'Who speaks no Russian. Hence your presence, Mr Korolev. No doubt he speaks French, but Nataliya's is less than adequate for the occasion. I pressed for an interpreter, and who better than yourself?' She leaned across and tapped Nataliya on the knee. 'You understand that, my dear? He will address you *vis-à-vis* in your native tongue.' Her French was almost as halting as Nataliya's. 'It is a good thing that your brother-in-law's English is so fluent. He can extract the finest nuances from your plea.' Almost as an afterthought she added, 'You are worrying about something?'

'The baby –'

'Nonsense, my dear. The baby is perfectly safe. Babies are concerned mainly with comfort and the next meal. Both are in the good hands of an experienced nurse appointed by me personally. I have seen to it.' Anything seen to by Miss

Castle would not dare to go awry. 'Buck up now; we are approaching our destination.'

The journey to Whitehall past buildings scarred by bombing, took only a little time, but waiting for Mr Massingham was another matter. A stony-faced porter took us into a dreary waiting-room in which the only decoration was a torn poster saying Careless Talk Costs Lives. As the wait lengthened Miss Castle became more and more irritated. She kept looking at the watch pinned to her uniform. Nataliya seemed to crouch rather than sit on one of the three folding chairs that were the room's only furnishings, her eyes continually moist with barely suppressed tears.

'Well now,' Miss Castle said approvingly, 'the tears are appealing, but we mustn't overdo it. Melodrama makes bureaucrats scared. You understand?'

'I, too, am scared,' Nataliya said simply.

'Mustn't be, dear; mustn't be at all. Mr Massingham is only a *junior* official, our link with higher office and political leaders; but he is merely *junior*. Polite yes; scared, no. It would betray weakness, lack of determination, the last thing we want to do. So chin up, dear, and a smile. You are justified in making a personal appeal.'

That might well be true; but I knew how much of our success in gaining an interview was due to Miss Castle, her determination, and no doubt her pulling of rank as Matron-in-Chief. She had no doubt persisted until officialdom had given in with a sigh.

At last a young ATS sergeant came to tell us that Mr Massingham apologised for the delay but would see us now. 'Will you follow me, please, Ma'am?'

'Indeed we shall,' Miss Castle said icily.

Mr Massingham's junior status was reflected in his office, which was almost as dreary as the waiting-room. His battered desk sat on a square of worn Turkish carpet and the only other items of furniture were an olive green filing cabinet, a hat-stand bearing a bowler hat, and some more folding chairs. Mr Massingham himself, though, was young, willowy, and elegantly dressed in a grey suit with a double-breasted waistcoat. The austerity of clothing rationing seemed to have passed him by. He smiled disarmingly at Miss Castle, set chairs for us, and apologised again for the delay.

'I'm afraid the Minister kept me unduly long, but with some profit, for we were discussing your case,' he stood in front of his desk leaning lightly against it, one ankle crossed over the other, 'The nub of it is that your baby, born in England of Russian parents, has English nationality and is therefore not subject to the repatriation agreement between Russia and Britain. But the Russian chargé d'affaires in the Repatriation Committee is adamant about the repatriation of you and your husband. Do you understand?'

I interpreted for Nataliya, who looked bewildered.

Miss Castle interrupted, '*I* understand only too well. You are saying in effect that the parents must go back to Russia while the child – a helpless infant only a few months old – is left to fend on its own. The English courts would have something to say about that, I can assure you. They have very strong views on the separation of mother and child.'

'Doubtless,' Mr Massingham said blandly. 'But unfortunately international law – as expressed here in an agreement between the Allied nations – prevails over a mere Court ruling.'

I could see Miss Castle's anger rising; Nataliya continued to look uncomprehending.

'The point is,' Mr Massingham continued with a gesture of his hand, 'that there is no suggestion that mother and child will be separated. The child will be given every facility of dual nationality to be repatriated with the parents.'

Miss Castle said scornfully, 'But it is precisely *that* – as I have patiently tried to explain in correspondence – which we are determined to avoid. Mr and Mrs Korolev wish to remain in England and acquire English nationality. The Communist régime is not to their taste.'

'Possibly not,' Mr Massingham said. 'But if we were all able to live according to our taste and inclination –'

'You are generalising, Mr Massingham. We are dealing with a particular case here. And it is the earnest wish of the parents that they may be allowed to state their case.'

'I was under the impression, Madam,' Mr Massingham said with some hauteur, 'that such was the purpose of this interview.'

Miss Castle regarded him with severity. 'I advise you not to exceed your remit, Mr Massingham. I am not without influence in high places.'

He had the grace to blush. 'My apologies, Madam. Now perhaps if Mrs Korolev –'

Nataliya, whose only understanding of the conversation could have been through the tone of voices, suddenly and miraculously seemed to change from a state of listlessness into one of passion. As Miss Castle said afterwards, 'Language is no barrier to the feelings of a mother.'

Words poured from her, far too quickly for me to interpret sentence by sentence. I could only summarise. She spoke of the bitter hardship that had been inflicted on them, of their devotion to each other and to the soil of their motherland, which no longer responded with freedom; of the anguish of bearing a son who would only fall victim to banishment to the Siberian wastes if he were repatriated, since he would be considered the son of traitors; of her and Rudi's indifference to what befell them if only their son could stay with them in England, which they promised to serve truly and faithfully to the end of their days. Prison, the hardest of hard work – they would tolerate anything if mercy could be shown.

At this stage Mr Massingham turned rather white. He was quite unused to such histrionics. Nataliya, revitalised

by her intensity, stood before him in an attitude of supplication, her hands clasped before her, tears wet on her
cheeks. He started to speak:

'We are not unmerciful –'

But before he could complete his sentence Nataliya was
on her knees before him, her arms clasped round his legs
in what even in a Victorian melodrama would have been
called overacting. As Miss Castle had predicted, Mr Massingham was not only scared – he was embarrassed. He
had the grace to try and lift her by her hands. But she
clung to his legs despairingly, crying 'Please, Please!' Then,
still clutching Massingham round the legs, she managed to
place her forehead on the ground in the traditional Russian
gesture, begging him again, 'Please!' 'Yes, yes,' he said
gently. 'Er – now calm yourself, Mrs Korolev. Try to get
up. There!'

Even he had seen that nothing would be gained
by harshness or ridicule. Nataliya got up, turned wearily
from him, and her dejection was so complete that only a
heart of stone could have failed to be touched. I could
see that the genuineness of her emotion had impressed
him.

'We will have to see,' he said. 'Yes, we will have to see.
I will do everything I can.'

When Nataliya had calmed a little more, and the interview had in effect ended, I saw Massingham beckon to
Rose Castle to stay behind. They only remained together
a few minutes, but in the taxi to the restaurant, Rose told
me what had happened.

'Massingham says the best thing would be for you to
meet Churchill, not a government minister. Massingham
worked for years with Churchill when he was PM, and
though the old man's out of office – more's the pity –
he still wields a lot of power behind the scenes, even
quietly with Attlee. Especially on subjects like human
rights.'

'But how do I get to see him?' I asked.

'Massingham promised me he'd fix it, and asked me if you know Duff Cooper, the ambassador to France.'

I nodded. I had been invited to his beautiful house in the faubourg de St Honoré on several occasions in the last year, such as at parties at which the presence of the local head of the Red Cross – plus the title of Prince – might have been useful.

'Good,' said Rose. 'Massingham also knows Duff Cooper – he was one of Duff's aides in Singapore before it fell to the Japanese – and Churchill is going to Paris soon on a private visit and Duff Cooper is holding a small lunch for him. He will see that you're invited. He'll warn Winston to give you a few minutes. Winston likes talking to titled princes – and hates Stalin. And I think he realises what a grave mistake the Yalta repatriation agreement was.'

Churchill! Could he produce a miracle, even though he held no official position?

Sure enough, a few days later, an invitation to lunch in a restaurant for 'an informal occasion to meet Mr Churchill' arrived from Duff Cooper, an ambassador I liked, a man of lucidity and erudition.

Fortunately it was for nearly three weeks ahead – fortunately, because the very next day darling Tasha suddenly began to have all the pains associated with imminent childbirth.

I managed to get an ambulance and took her myself to the American Hospital – much improved since VE-day, with many new top grade American doctors – and that night she gave birth to a lusty, crying seven-pound baby.

We had already decided that if it were a boy, we would call the baby Rudi, returning the compliment to Rudi who had called his son Nicki after me. He was a wonderful boy, fat and gurgling, and Tasha was smiling with happiness on a face which the strain of waiting and then delivery had made look wan and a little frightened.

I called Galina in New York, of course, and received a cable of congratulations. And something else followed the birth of our son: Aunt Olga, who had remained haughtily aloof, was among the first visitors to reach the American Hospital, and smothered Tasha with flowers, fruit, kisses and Tasha responded; after all, Tasha had for years regarded Olga as her mother, who had bestowed love and help upon her during the agonising years when Olga had half starved in Russia, and even later when they lived in Paris.

Old habits do die hard as the saying has it, and soon 'mother and daughter' dissolved into tears of happiness, forgiveness and everything else. In short, we all made it up.

Everything seemed to be crowding in upon us, all at the same time. Fortunately, in one way, the fact that Russia did not recognise the Geneva Convention saved my office a great deal of trouble, though naturally, we helped every request from Russians who needed assistance. But most of the Russian POWs had gone, and the problem of helping the few who remained lay in more calculating and unfeeling hands than mine – Stalin's blood-stained hands.

As far as I was concerned, everything now revolved around attempts to help Rudi and his family, though there was little I could do but wait, and lend moral support.

I could do nothing until I could meet Churchill, and even that meeting, I had to admit, opened up only a remote hope. For even if I could persuade Churchill to help *me*, he would have to persuade Attlee to help *him*, and it was not really Attlee's business. My gravest fear lay in the lack of activity – the lack of speed. I feared that perhaps, unknown to me, any plea for clemency might arrive too late. Rudi just might be snatched away to Russia, even though Rose Castle in the Middlesex Hospital was fighting tooth and nail for Nataliya.

At least Rose's fight 'for the decency of our country', as

she described it, was now the talk of England. The original story in the *News Chronicle* had been taken up by almost every newspaper in the land, with one scandal story following another. One was headed STALIN'S INHUMANITY; another, SHOW SOME GUTS BRITAIN; and yet another, THE SCANDAL OF THE KOROLEV FAMILY.

One story, which compared Stalin with 'The Belsen Murderers', opened, 'Stalin is as much a murderer as any of the war criminals who gassed the Jews in Belsen and Dachau.'

Our best hope that Britain might do something lay ironically in the fact that Churchill was *not* in power, for this meant that Britain was now ruled by 'friendly' Labour men who had shown admiration for Russia, and yet were horrified by the virulent stories now being printed daily in the popular press, causing much embarrassment to Attlee and the Labour government who privately abhorred Stalin's dictatorship. I was not the only person to feel – and hope – that any effort to break the Yalta agreement in the case of the Korolevs might be easier if it were made by Attlee and 'friends' of the Russian government.

Then, out of the blue, while my mind was almost wholly exercised by Rudi's problems, together with the first days in the life of *my* Rudi, the phone rang – and who should be on the line but Galina, in New York.

Though the line was poor it could not conceal the exciting vibrance in Galina's voice.

'Nicki! Is that you?'

'Yes, it's me. But you sound miles away –'

There was a gurgle of laughter. 'Of course I sound miles away: I *am* miles away –'

'– and someone seems to be frying bacon on the line.'

'Yes, I can hear it. So listen carefully, Nicki. Because soon I won't be miles away. We are coming over, Hugo and I –'

'Marvellous!' I interrupted over the hissing noise. 'To Paris?'

'Me, yes, but Hugo has to attend a medical conference of neurologists in London at a hospital – a *Middle-Sex* hospital.' Another gurgle of laughter. 'Very peculiar. But nothing to do with sex, Hugo tells me. It's because in the days of ancient history there were tribes of Saxons in the West, the East, and the South, and in the middle were the Middle Saxons –'

I said impatiently as the line crackled, 'Yes, yes, I know the Middlesex Hospital. Quite well as a matter of fact. But you? When are you coming?'

'I'm coming in two to three weeks. Hugo will stay in London. I'll fly on a connecting flight to Paris and wait there until Hugo arrives a few days later.'

'I'll be there to meet you,' I said, and added eagerly, 'We'll *both* be there.'

'Marvellous! And Nicki – we shall need somewhere to stay. Is there a room at the house? With your new family?'

'You insult me!' I laughed. 'Of course there is. For *you* – ah! darling Galina, I'm longing to see you.'

'Me too. And' – was there a moment of hesitation? – 'Hugo wants to see Igor. He promises nothing, but he's been experimenting with new drugs and – well, you never know.'

'Tell me – do you think –?'

'I've told you, darling. It's just a chance. Perhaps a helping hand to make life easier.'

'Ah! Galina, wouldn't it be a miracle – still, you mustn't waste money on long-distance phone calls. But you haven't told me the time you're arriving – I want to hang out flags.'

She gave a date in December. 'My goodness,' she said, 'it'll soon be 1947.'

'What time?' I fished in my pocket for my diary.

'Air France flight 201, arrives 1.15, lunch time.'

'Oh no!' I almost groaned. 'I can't, darling. I've got a lunch.'

'But can't you cancel?'

'I can't. I know it sounds ridiculous but –' with a laugh

471

I couldn't contain, 'I'm having lunch with Winston Churchill on that day.'

'Oh I'm so sorry,' she laughed back. 'You're joking?'

I explained the urgency of my mission, adding that of course Tasha would be at Le Bourget Airport.

'I understand. Give him my love,' said Galina. 'I'm told the old warrior rather likes ballet girls. If I can help –'

'Bless you – I can't wait to see you – but hang on a moment – it's all right – I've got my dates mixed up. I'm lunching with Churchill the week before you arrive, so I'll be able to meet you after all.'

33

Sharply at one o'clock – the card to remind me said, '1 for 1.15' – I arrived at the British Embassy in the faubourg de St Honoré, 'just up the road from the Élysée palace', as someone had once described it to me. It was not only a beautiful building; it was imposing, the double-front gates, painted a dark green, opened on to a gravelled courtyard lined with flowers and bushes, where a man took my Citroën and parked it in a corner and another man in a kind of livery led me to the front door and beckoned me inside. On the right a broad staircase led up to the bedrooms, I suppose.

Diana Duff Cooper emerged from a small reception room on the left, where I had drunk cocktails several times before the small dinner parties to which I had been invited. She was as beautiful and elegant as a living legend should be; and Duff Cooper, shorter, verging towards stoutness, a brief moustache on his upper lip, came to greet me with a casual 'Morning, Nicki, we're going to lunch at a restaurant round the corner,' and introduced me to the other guests as 'This is Prince Nicholas Korolev.' Then in strode Churchill.

I had never seen him in the flesh before, and I must say that, short though he was, in or out of office he exuded an immense sense of power. I suppose that the aura of having played such a vital part in victory for so long clung to him like a cloak of fame that he would never lose.

'Good morning, Prince,' he growled. 'Massingham has mentioned that you were coming and would like a word with me, but after the food, eh? And after the champagne. Any champagne, my dear Diana?'

He was a *lion* – or if I were English perhaps I would say bulldog – sipping his Dom Perignon in one hand and holding a large cigar between the fingers of the other. His voice was fascinating, for he spoke with a kind of slur to his words.

'Massingham tells me the Tsar was your godfather.'

I nodded assent.

'A noble man,' mumbled Churchill. 'I had the honour of meeting him many years ago. Yes, a noble man, and his end' – he screwed up his mouth into a contortion before he spat out the words – 'was at the fangs of a gang of mad dogs led and trained by Stalin.'

The lunch was extraordinary. There were eight of us and Duff Cooper placed me on Churchill's right – due to my rank, I suppose, but useful nonetheless – and Massingham on my right. Diana Cooper had only one other woman at the table of eight – Ann Rothermere, wife of an English press lord. She had an amusing, almost saucy face. 'She's very attractive,' I whispered to Massingham.

'A great many people would agree with you,' said Massingham drily. 'And she has an even more handsome husband.'

We were lunching at a small but superb restaurant, Le Drage, on the Rue St Anne, a short walk from the Embassy, where during lunch Churchill, with no sense of decorum, kept on handing me pieces of his beautiful steak.

'Too much for me! You're a healthy young man. You eat this – good for you.' I did not dare refuse.

The meal ended with a magnificent cheese tray. Churchill had ordered a Pont l'Évêque. The waiter had cut open almost half the brownish cheese and I was asking for some Brie when I sensed a thump on my plate – Churchill had again given me half his portion.

Outside the plate glass windows a large crowd had begun to gather as word of Churchill's presence spread around.

I could see the crowd and behind it, daubed on the wall on the other side of the street, the ever popular slogan 'Americans go home'.

'They don't seem to like the Americans,' Massingham whispered.

'They don't need to say "Russians go home",' I said bitterly.

'What's that?' asked Churchill.

I pointed to the 'US go home'.

'Stupid people,' growled Churchill. 'The French will never forgive themselves for having lost the war, they'll never forgive the British for *not* having lost the war, but above all they'll never forgive the Americans for having won it.'

Quite a profound thought. I repeated the words to myself in order to remember them later.

'But the Russians' – he mouthed the words – 'we fought as Allies – we had to, without them we might well have gone under – but now –' he put on his most sonorous voice '– all is changed and I view the future with great alarm.'

'I'm hoping,' I ventured, 'that I may have a few moments of your time when lunch is over to discuss the Russians – and *my* problem.'

'Very laudable, Prince.' He mouthed the word 'Prince' as though he enjoyed it.

And when, surrounded by a crowd of several hundred, a smiling Churchill smoking an enormous cigar and giving the V-sign all the time, we left the restaurant, he chuckled,

'Well, the French may not really like the British, but at least they seem to like me!'

In the hall of the Embassy, the crowds hidden by the heavy green doors, most of the guests made for the small drawing-room, but Churchill said, 'Pray excuse us, Diana. The Prince and I are going to have a little talk in my bedroom on certain aspects of the new Russia. Massingham, I think you had better come along.'

Hand on the bannister, he stumped up the broad staircase, reached his room and sat down heavily on a long chair in the room.

'Sit on the bed,' he growled to me, 'and pray proceed.'

I did. As briefly as possible I outlined the complete story with the help of Massingham, who by experience knew just how to tell Churchill the points he must make to arouse his interest. In the end, Churchill (to my mind more than ready for an afternoon nap) said, 'This is a typical Stalin scandal. I shall try everything in my power to persuade Mr Attlee to intercede on your brother's behalf.' And then, with hardly a pause, he held out his hand and said, 'Good afternoon, Prince. Delighted to make your acquaintance.' Then he climbed on to his bed as I left the room.

Massingham followed, beaming. 'Total success,' he explained. 'Well done. If Winston likes you – and he clearly does – he'll make your case his personal responsibility.'

For a few nights I could hardly sleep. Tossing and turning restlessly in Tasha's arms, I would wake and suddenly become involved in the most extraordinary dreams, sometimes erotic.

One dreaming night Rudi and Nataliya were having a picnic in the forest of Marly, but I was not with Tasha, I was actually making love to Hélène, shouting to Nataliya, 'I'll be finished soon. Can't you see I'm busy!' A kind of recycling of past life, but with Nataliya watching us!

At other times pure nightmares ruled the dark hours.

Rudi and I were in the rattling cart in Kronstadt and people were laughing as they slaughtered men and women in the street, and I must have jumped out of bed with a cry for Tasha wakened, soothed me with kisses and caresses until I fell asleep again.

Suddenly the dreams stopped.

'And I know why!' Tasha laughed as she dunked her croissant in her breakfast coffee. 'Galina's arriving tomorrow.'

Of course! That was it.

Tasha and I both drove to Le Bourget to meet the plane just before lunch. Standing beside me, Tasha looked stunning, as slim as a pencil after shedding the pounds with the birth of her baby. She looked almost like a waif, as though she needed protection, a look which she must have acquired in the early hard days in Russia and which, thank God, had never deserted her with the passing years, for it was this instinctive look of 'little-girl-lost' that made her so attractive. Everyone she met fell in love with her – and wanted to help her. Even when she needed no help.

Now, as we waited near the exit from the customs hall, half way along the long narrow grey terminal building of Le Bourget, she looked even more ravishing, for Olga, as one of Europe's top couturiers, had made her a beautiful dress in the much publicised New Look style, designed as a reaction to the skimpiness of wartime shortages in material.

Its length – almost to her ankles – seemed to add to Tasha's height and elegant figure, and the oyster satin lining of the edge-to-edge coat that she wore over it was revealed in the full-length revers. I thought she looked absurdly young to be the mother of our child; and for a moment my mind flashed back to that night in the place de Furstemberg when the lamplight had fallen on her and Olga casually announced, 'My daughter'. As we stood in the reception area with a dozen or so others awaiting the arrival of the London plane, the bleak December wind

blowing across the heathland in spite of the cloudless sky,
I felt suddenly overwhelmed with gratitude that we had
survived so much. If only Rudi . . . and Igor . . .

Astonishingly, the DC3 landed fifteen minutes early,
and a sepulchral voice over the tannoy warned those awaiting arriving passengers to remain where they were and
not impede the landing arrangements. Since the concrete
runway was at least a quarter of a mile distant we were
not likely to make a concerted rush across the stubbled
field to where we could see steps being wheeled up to the
side of the plane and the passengers alighting. And it was
impossible to make out any faces clearly at that distance.
Then suddenly Tasha rushed forward a few steps. 'I can
see her, and she's got a New Look too, and a chic little
hat – I'm *sure* it's her!' She was like a delighted child
dancing in anticipation of a party surprise.

'Well, I truly hope it is,' I said. I squeezed her hand and
smiled tolerantly. 'We *were* expecting her, you know!'

'You used to tease me like that when I wanted you to
kiss me and Olga put on that tiresome *forbidding* look of
hers.'

The little knot of passengers and the porters with their
trolleys bearing the luggage slowly approached. I could
make out Galina now, bobbing about and looking – as all
air passengers tended to do in those days – somewhat
relieved to have her precious feet again on firm ground.

She went through the customs without any trouble and
then somehow or other the three of us were tumbling into
each other's arms, half laughing, half crying, and one
saying, 'It's so good to see you again'; the other, 'How we
missed you!' I don't know who said what, though I do
remember Galina's first question, 'How's the baby boy?'

I stole a look at her. She was more poised, more worldly.
She had an aura of success about her. Of course she *was*
a huge success – and it suited her. All the same later, in
the car, the bags stacked behind, she said almost dreamily,
'*You* a proud father, Nicki! It seems only yesterday that

you were a baby, peeping through the large keyhole in that door at Tsarskoe Selo! So much in such a short space of time!' And then with a sigh, 'And such tragedy too – Father; Igor, my ex-husband; and above all poor Rudi.' The past, its weeping and its laughter, continued to rush through our minds as we drove past Les Villettes, the Paris slaughterhouses, with restaurants renowned for their steaks.

'*You* look healthy and wealthy and –' I substituted the last word with a laugh, 'and fit. Really fit.'

'Exercise. At the *barre* every day. And I also do my exercises every morning. No, not in aeroplanes!'

We were so happy, despite the tragedies around us, that the mere fact of meeting like this induced laughter and smiles that we could not stop.

'But you do look in wonderful shape,' I persisted.

'I am,' she said simply. 'Never felt better. Maybe marriage agrees with me.'

We drove along the Rue Lafayette, past the Gare de l'Est towards the heart of the city in which we had spent so much of our lives, then turned left past the Opéra towards the Tuileries and the Left Bank.

'Lunch at home. Do you mind?' I asked.

'I should hope not! Home is home!'

'And caviar is caviar – and we've got lots of it,' I exclaimed. 'I bought a large tin from Hédiard.' This shop behind the Madeleine, run by an eccentric Englishman, was the finest place in Paris to buy exotic dishes – anything from caviar and Russian vodka to sweet potatoes or Indian chutney, 'and we'll have a feast. But,' with mock sternness, 'no vodka for the baby.'

'And now,' Galina's voice was suddenly more subdued, as we drove on; switching, she said, 'Oh! It's a beautiful city, even in winter. New York is beautiful – yes, it's wonderful, *alive* – but Paris! It's so good to be back. The smell of the city! And now, do tell me more details about Igor.'

As well as I could, I outlined the latest news of his apparently hopeless case and she sighed, 'Poor Igor! He used to be such fun – and it is so cruel that he has been punished like this. And I also feel sorry for – yes, Brig.'

'*Brig!*'

By now we had reached the place de Furstemberg, and were drinking our first vodka before starting on the caviar and blinis, which our new housekeeper-cum-nanny, a middle-aged woman called Elena, was cooking. 'You mean to tell me that you like Brig! That woman who all but killed Igor. She's a bitch.'

'I've met her,' said Galina quietly.

'*Met her!* As a friend? It's not possible.'

'Yes, I did,' she said quietly. 'And I know that she *did* take a ruthless revenge. Yes, she even told me the entire story. But Igor spent so much time in bed with other women that he probably brought on the stroke himself. *You* know that. And as for Brig – she's a changed woman.'

'A likely story,' I snorted angrily. 'How on earth did you meet her?'

'She "took up" ballet, as they say. She became a patron of the New York City Ballet and is on the committee. You know the sort of thing – people buy season tickets or boxes for the entire year, they organise great balls. One day Brig came to see me – I have to make a few personal appearances, the committee seem to get a thrill if we turn up – and she's been a financial pillar of our ballet. And she knows the wrong she did Igor with all those disgusting photos.' With that naughty smile of hers, Galina added mischievously, 'Were they really hot stuff?'

I smiled back. 'They were – well, explicit.'

After that I had to retell all the latest news about Rudi – my lunch with Churchill, the hopes we all entertained of Rudi's eventual release, our fears, and the help of Rose Castle.

We talked all afternoon and then finally Galina announced that she felt she should take a nap. 'It's a long flight from New York, and I didn't sleep that well,' she admitted, 'so forty or even fifty winks won't do me any harm.'

'It's wonderful to have you back,' I squeezed her, 'and looking so stunning. Every centimetre a perfect ballerina.'

'Ah, the ballet. I nearly forgot to tell you that the maître – Balanchine, the *great* Balanchine – is coming over in a week or so. And do you know why? He's a fabulous impresario, and he's going to organise a great ball for hundreds of the richest people in Paris at the Pré-Catalan next July.'

The Pré-Catalan, in the Bois de Boulogne, was the most fashionable restaurant and ballroom, set in acres of woods, and exquisitely decorated.

'Yes,' she continued. 'Next July, and do you know, it's to be in aid of Russians in France who need financial help. You're both coming of course.'

'How much will the tickets cost?' I was half laughing.

'For you not a sou, though for the others, a fortune. But don't you worry,' she added. 'I'm going –' she paused '– no, I'll let it be a surprise, but it'll be the high spot of the evening's entertainment and I told Balanchine that my "fee" is ten free tickets. So you're both invited.'

'I'd like to meet him again, he was charming in Monte Carlo.'

'He's a wonderful man, Nicki. He's done an enormous amount for charity. Truly one of the greats. And yet, simple. He'd love to come round to your house, meet Tasha, drink your vodka and admire all Mama's old trinkets – especially her Fabergé collection.'

Two days later the news for which I had *really* been waiting came in the form of a phone call, two weeks after the lunch with Churchill. I had almost given up hope of any help from that quarter, when Massingham phoned me at the office and said simply, 'Keep your fingers crossed, Prince – I think Winston may have pulled it off.'

'*Really!*' I could feel my pulses quickening. 'Tell me – tell me everything.'

'Well,' Massingham might have been speaking next to me, the phone was so clear, 'it seems that Attlee was very upset and disturbed by all the Press reports. The newspapers are still trying to find new leads and angles and Winston asked for a private meeting with Attlee and they discussed the whole problem for nearly an hour. Of course, I don't know what was said.'

'Then how do you know? Can you be sure?'

'I think so. I met Winston that evening in the Commons. He was looking very pleased with himself and said to me, "Attlee has agreed". And in that sonorous voice, mouthing his words with their ups and downs of accents, added, "The Prime Minister himself told me that Stalin's treatment of the Korolevs is inhuman. Inhuman. That was the word he used and he will allow them to stay."'

'Mr Massingham,' I began, 'I don't know what to say. We are most indebted to you – my brother and I. I don't know how we can ever repay you.'

With a laugh Massingham replied, 'The person you should really thank is Brigadier Rose Castle. She may be a bit of a battle-axe, but my goodness, she worries like a fox terrier until things get done.'

Laughing back, I asked, 'How can I let my brother know?'

Massingham hesitated. 'I think it would be wiser to go through the proper channels,' he said finally.

'But I can't! My brother's very existence – doubts, yesses and noes – is a living torture. Why can't I tell him?'

'I do understand. But if you did tell him, and then the news is leaked to the Press before Attlee makes an official statement – there could be such a row in Moscow that Attlee might have to deny everything. Much better to keep the decision under cover.'

'It seems tough on my poor brother.'

'Better safe than sorry. It would be terrible if everything suddenly did go wrong. And things *can*, you know. Attlee is walking a tightrope in his relations with Russia. As it is, the FO is spending all its time denying officially all the Fleet Street anti-Russian articles about your brother.'

'I suppose so,' I sighed. 'But it won't be too long, I hope.'

'No, no. A week or two, and both will be free – and British.'

The next day I was still so excited that I was hardly able to take in the great news. Then Hugo Lattimer, Galina's husband, arrived. It was like a gathering of the clan!

Before anything else, I blurted out the news about Rudi.

'I'm dying to tell Igor. It's bound to cheer him up.'

Slightly bewildered, Lattimer said to Galina who should have been the first to greet him, 'That's your invalid cousin, Igor?'

'Yes. Sorry,' I smiled. 'I forgot to say hullo! I was so excited. Please forgive me.'

'Of course,' he smiled.

Hugo Lattimer looked exactly as I expected him to look. Galina had certainly described him accurately in her letters: broad-shouldered and rugged; but the surprise was the shock of thick white hair that crowned him. It gave him great distinction without ageing him – I judged him to be in his early fifties – and I suspected, from the elegant way his hair was cut and trimmed, that it was his one vanity.

After Galina and he embraced, Hugo took Tasha's hand in both of his and smiled at her with the affection of one who has built up an impression from hearsay and found it to be satisfyingly accurate. When it came to my turn to be greeted he unexpectedly used the very English phrase 'How do you do?' rather than the usual American 'Hi!'

and his accent seemed to owe far more to one of the English seats of learning than to Harvard. It transpired that he had studied medicine at Caius College, Cambridge, as well as being a graduate of Harvard.

'That *is* good news about your brother,' he said warmly as we shook hands – his grip firm and friendly in mine. And I really was delighted: Hugo seemed to me the epitome of all a doctor should be – grave blue eyes that reflected sympathy and understanding, the white hair that added to the gravity, and a contrastingly humorous mouth above a deeply cleft chin that testified to firmness of character.

Within a few minutes we were all chattering as if Hugo had been one of the family for years. By the time we reached the place de Furstemberg it had been decided that as soon as possible Hugo would arrange an initial consultation with the doctors who were attending Igor.

But before he met Dr Harvey from the American Hospital, Hugo suggested, 'I'd like to have a talk with Igor. See what kind of shape he's in.'

We went together the following morning, introducing first 'Dr Lattimer, this is Count Kornilov.' They shook hands and Kornilov held open the door to Igor's room.

Fortunately Igor took to Hugo at once. Igor's eyes mirrored his pleasure as Hugo, having easily mastered our 'blink technique', put question after question to him regarding aural, visual, and olfactory responses. He was also concerned about his taste buds and whether he could distinguish between any of the essentially liquid foods that formed his diet.

'It's like compiling a dossier of clues to the solution of a mystery,' he told Tasha and me afterwards. 'That is what we doctors really are – detectives looking for clues. And just as some detectives follow one line of reasoning and some another, so our joint efforts are sometimes successful in building up the dossier. Igor's doctors are obviously thoroughly professional, but I can't tell yet if they may not be too traditional, too hesitant to explore outside accepted knowledge. Which is one of the reasons why we have these conferences occasionally – to pool resources, as it were.'

The one Hugo had attended had not been entirely without relevance to Igor's case. 'The results of the latest laboratory experiments are collated and discussed and explained by a number of very clever but rather heavy-going organic chemists.'

'Are they different from the ones you buy aspirin from in the shops?' Tasha asked innocently.

Hugo smiled gently. 'Indeed yes. Those are pharmacists and they're specialists in the mixing of chemical substances according to what's written out on, say, a doctor's prescription; a chemist, on the other hand, deals with the properties and structure of those substances; and an organic chemist is one who deals with the carbon compounds of living beings.'

'And they've done research on cases similar to Igor's?' I asked.

'Not exactly. Research is much more general than that. It's left to us neurologists to particularise according to the risks we're prepared to take in each individual case.'

I began to grasp what he was getting at. 'And Igor's is such a one?'

He smiled. 'Possibly. Igor's is a straightforward case of what is commonly known as a stroke – the result of a clot of blood impeding the flow through the main artery to the brain. But the dispersal of the clot is by no means straightforward – not a matter for surgery. There's something relatively new, though, which we discussed at the conference. It has had beneficial effects in some cases. It's a drug called Donatol and it's a compound containing, among other things, atropine, which is extracted from Deadly Nightshade. It is sometimes called Belladonna, 'beautiful lady', because it is used as a cosmetic.'

'Never knew that,' I remarked.

'I don't want to blind you with science,' laughed Hugo,

'but atropine is a substance that inhibits the action of acetylcholine in the nervous system and aids the transmission of impulses from one nerve to another.'

'Ah!' I said triumphantly, 'thus bypassing the clot.'

Again the gentle smile and a touch of amusement in the grave blue eyes. 'I'm afraid it's not quite as simple as that. And what we're not sure of are the possible side-effects in certain cases.'

'You mean,' Tasha put in, 'it might make him worse, or even – even kill him?'

'It certainly wouldn't kill him; but – let us say it might not improve him. All the same I'm inclined to give it a trial.'

Two days later Hugo met Dr Harvey, and explained what he was proposing to do for Igor. Hugo's reputation was so well known that Dr Harvey listened with respect.

'Donatol was pioneered in the USA,' explained Hugo, 'and I've got quite a plentiful supply. Here, take this.'

He handed a large phial of tablets to Harvey.

'You'll find that its effect is to relax the muscles of the nervous system and to dilate the pupils of the eyes. I suggest a daily tablet of 0.125 milligrammes. There won't be any immediate effect – other than, maybe, the dilation of the pupils, but could I have a word with Kornilov?' When Kornilov arrived Hugo told him, 'If you give Igor the daily tablet, will you please make a very careful note of any responses such as twitching of the limbs or gurgling noises in the throat. Perhaps, Count, you could make daily – even hourly – notes of any observations. After several days a toe or finger might move, indicating that the pill is overcoming the atrophy of the nervous system. You must understand that we are not aiming at complete recovery: only of partial restoration of the muscular functions. As soon as there are any signs of this, Dr Harvey will call for a physiotherapist. The continuing doses of the Donatol plus physiotherapy might enable him to regain partial use of, say, his arms, or a croaking sort of voice.'

Turning to Dr Harvey, Hugo warned him, 'One of the side-effects of Donatol is to cause mental depression, but since Igor is depressed enough as it is, he won't notice it if he starts to achieve any benefits. Anyway, doctor, let's give it a try.'

But all this faded into the background when, returning to the office, the phone rang and a voice in London announced, 'Miss Castle would like to talk to you, Prince. Hold on for a moment.'

We were on Christian name terms by now of course, and I cried, 'Rose! So the good news has come at last.' My heart gave a great leap of joy, and I was so excited I thought I could jump through the roof. At long, long last, after months, no *years* of waiting, Rudi was on the point of freedom – already free, perhaps – and to Rose I shouted, 'All over?'

Her voice expressed none of the explosion of emotion and excitement I had expected. Instead I sensed that something was wrong.

'I don't understand,' I cried harshly. 'Massingham told me that Attlee had agreed –'

'He has, but I'm afraid' – for once her voice faltered – 'there's been a hitch. No, no, I understand the order for Rudi's freedom *has* been signed. But it takes time.'

'Bloody red tape!' I shouted. 'How long?'

The next words were like a death knell.

'We may never know,' her voice was dry, resigned, crackling with emotion.

'What do you mean?' I was frantic. 'What the hell has happened?'

'Rudi and about twenty men at Fairways have – disappeared. They received official orders to be loaded into a bus and nobody seems to know where they have been taken.'

34

What follows is such a grim recital of horror, compiled from many different sources that, for the sake of simplicity, I have thought it more convenient for the story to be assembled and related as Rudi himself experienced it. It started like this:

The first moment of drama at Fairways came when the camp commandant summoned Rudi to his office, asked him to sit down and have a cup of tea. Rudi, already aware that Churchill himself was asking Attlee to let him stay in Britain, was excited.

The hopes received something of a shock when the commandant explained, 'I'm afraid I can't go into details at the moment, Korolev, but you are being transferred.'

'And you can't say where?' pleaded Rudi.

'Well – I don't see why I can't tell you – yes, London. But the exact district – no, I'm afraid I have my orders.'

The moment of dismay passed and Rudi's heart leapt. Nicki had already told him that the pining and distraught Nataliya was in London. It looked as though they would be reunited soon! Good old Nicki! He had pulled off a miracle.

'Can you say when?' asked Rudi.

'Yes. Tomorrow. A batch of twenty of you are leaving for London.'

Twenty! It sounded odd, but of course Rudi knew he was not the only POW trying to pull strings to escape. Tomorrow! He dreamed that night (as he told me later) of lying in a luxurious bed in silken sheets like his mother's in Tsarskoe Selo, of making love to Nataliya, of cuddling his baby boy, of breakfasting in bed – of everything!

The following morning the twenty POWs boarded a bus,

and with them travelled two British NCOs armed with
tommy guns, while another armed soldier sat next to the
driver. They drove the long way from Derby until finally
they reached London.

Rudi asked one, a corporal, 'Where exactly are we
going?'

'Dunno, mate,' he replied.

The second man, a sergeant, was a little more communi-
cative. As the shattered bombed streets of the city of
London, necessitating many detours, gradually gave way
to the more impressive-looking buildings that were still
standing, the sergeant pointed out a few of the sights.
There was St Paul's, still standing, though it had been
badly damaged. There was the Tower of London. The
geography of London meant nothing, of course, to Rudi,
and yet – and yet he began to have misgivings about his
destination; nothing concrete, just doubts as the bus drove
through the shattered remains of the City and towards the
meaner, even more bedraggled streets of the East End.

'Where are we going?' asked Rudi again.

This time the taciturn sergeant uttered only four words:
'The Pool of London'.

Again the information meant nothing to Rudi. He had
read in some books about the Serpentine. That was a pool,
not a river like the Thames. Then the other man pointed
out, 'This is the district of Poplar.'

'I thought it was London.'

'It is, mate. But Poplar and Bow are areas near the Pool,
the Thames, mate, where all the docks are'.

'*The docks!*' Instinctively the twenty men in the back
shouted almost as one man. Rudi sprang up as the earlier
sense of excitement in the confined bus eroded into a sense
of terror. The sergeant pushed Rudi back into his seat with
the steel butt of his tommy gun.

'No rough stuff now!' he shouted, roaring to the others,
'Sit down – all of you, until we reach the docks'.

With a dull ache at the utter failure of a mission, Rudi,

for a moment, slumped in his seat. Victory was turning into defeat.

'But, sergeant,' he yelled, 'Mr Churchill has told me –'

'I know,' said the sergeant, almost jeering. 'And your old chum Stalin has told him to bugger off. Now behave yourselves, all of you. Anyone caught trying to escape will be shot. And we've orders from on high to shoot for the legs. So you'd 'ave to go to Russia with broken legs.'

'Keep quiet, lads,' said the corporal, more conciliatorily. 'Try to look on the bright side. You ought to be glad to be going home.'

'I've got a wife and child here,' cried Rudi. 'Where are they?' He had not the faintest idea of their fates except that he knew the child need not be deported. Perhaps Churchill had succeeded with Nataliya because she was a girl?

Behind a row of mean streets the bus stopped with a jolt that nearly knocked them from their seats. When the back door was thrown open they could smell the strange mixture of tar, dirty water, and engine oil – in short, the smell of a ship in dock.

And there it was. The bus had stopped right in front of the dockside – a conglomeration of cranes, disused railway lines, smashed up warehouses – and there loomed the shape of a big ship, moored alongside. Rudi was bundled out on to the ground, surrounded by a dozen waiting British soldiers. He caught a glimpse of a flag – a Union Jack on one corner of a red background.

'This way – and no nonsense please! Keep in line, keep moving up the gangplank. Got your mug and blanket?' Each man had been issued with one blanket and his china mug.

At first an utterly demoralised Rudi slumped forward, feet dragging up the gangplank on the other side of the railway lines. Everything was lost! Amidst the shouts and cries of the soldiers he could hear the occasional shouts – even threats – in Russian. Obviously, though it was a

British ship, it had Russians aboard to control the hundreds of Russians who were already lining the decks. Once on board they had to queue to have their identities checked. There seemed to be Russian soldiers everywhere.

Ahead of him in the queue on board the ship there was a sudden commotion. One man three bodies ahead of him suddenly bent down. As a soldier yelled at him and prodded his backside the man smashed his mug against the side of the ship and – in one movement as it seemed to a horrified Rudi – he slashed the jagged edge of the broken mug across his throat with all his force. The blood seemed to burst out of his face, gushing out as he sank to the ground.

'Free at last!' he cried, falling to the ground, blood all over his face.

'Christ!' cried a man. 'Let's get a doctor!'

The port doctor, who had been ordered to see there was no violence during the embarkation, rushed up the gangplank, took one look at the man and cried to a soldier, 'Send for an ambulance. We'll have to take him off the ship. I might be able to save him.'

But another man had followed the doctor. He was a Russian. In guttural English he shouted to the doctor, pushing him away, 'Leave the POW here.'

'But he'll die,' shouted the doctor, pushing the man off.

'I am in charge now. These men are on a vessel chartered by the Russians. We leave in ten minutes. You two' – he pointed to a couple of prisoners – 'you carry this man down the companionway and put him in the ship's hospital.'

'You'll leave this man alone,' cried the doctor angrily. 'This is a British ship. Bugger off.'

'You are not a military doctor. I am a colonel. You obey my orders on this ship.'

'I won't, damn your eyes. If he dies it'll be on your head.'

'Serve him right!' shouted the Russian as the doctor raced up to demand action from the British captain.

'There's nothing I can do,' the captain sighed wearily. 'I've seen it all. Technically a POW on board a ship is under the jurisdiction of the Russians. We just sail her because the Russians haven't got any ships, and I'm only a merchant seaman anyway.'

'It's monstrous,' cried the doctor.

'I know; but they do have a Russian doctor on board.'

'They're inhuman – beasts –' In a torrent of rage the doctor shouted down. 'You're a swine. I hope you get killed yourself.'

Rudi could hear the throb of the engines starting. His had been the last batch of men to board the ship.

As the doctor climbed back on to dry land and the noise of the engines throbbed like a funeral dirge, Rudi knew that what he had to do was to follow the lead of the poor man who had sliced his throat.

Yet that was not the way for him. No shedding his own blood like that! But still he could not live. With a roar of hate, he hit the Russian in the face with his mug, raced and pushed his way across the crowded ship and, without a second's hesitation, jumped overboard, almost at the moment the vessel was preparing to cast off.

It never entered Rudi's head to swim for it. 'I wanted to die,' he told me later. 'I would die if I returned to Russia, or at the worst lived in Siberia, never again to see my Nataliya.'

He hit the ice-cold water with a thump which he felt had cracked his skull and, almost without thinking, struck out into the oily, dirty water of 'the Pool', which was very wide, away from the dockside. In the distance he could hear bells jangling, voices shouting, 'There he is!', 'To the right!' He dived down, hoping never to come up. He swam underwater as he heard the chug-chug of a launch starting to search for him – or, as he devoutly prayed, his body. The engines belonged, as he was later to learn, to a police launch. They traced the bubbles, the ripples, and when Rudi finally unwillingly surfaced in filthy water, two pairs of strong police arms grabbed him. As they hauled him into the boat one man cried, 'There you are!'

Spluttering water, with tears of frustration and anger, Rudi cried, 'Let me go, let me go! I want to die! I must die!'

'There you are, sir,' said a policeman. 'It's just momentary stress. I know how you feel.' Adding in a feeble attempt to cheer him up, 'Feel like it myself sometimes when my old lady has a tantrum.'

'I've got to die,' Rudi sobbed desperately. '*Please* let me die.'

'Now, now,' one soothed him. 'You've caused enough bother as it is. We'll take your body –'

'No, no,' shrieked Rudi; and with one superhuman effort broke free, almost toppled the launch and slid back into the greasy comfort of the grave he wanted.

Suddenly he resurfaced. There was no way he could not have done after the first immersion. He was grabbed and hauled out in a couple of minutes, and this time one of the policemen snapped a pair of handcuffs on – one on Rudi, one on the wrist of his police colleague.

Crying desperately, Rudi lay, water bubbling from his mouth, where the police had put him. They were angry now. They half dragged the almost inert figure ashore. The gangplank which had been pulled up had been lowered again. Painfully, stumbling, still handcuffed to one policeman, Rudi stumbled on to the deck.

'Take him to the cells!' cried the Russian as the British policeman undid the handcuffs. 'And as for you,' he snarled, 'you'll have a hell of a voyage, and God help you when you arrive in Russia!'

A couple of Russians manhandled the utterly dejected Rudi, screwing his arms behind his back until he – who had wanted death – screamed at the pain of life.

'And let this be a lesson to you all!' shouted the Russian, whose name was Moligny, as the tough Russians started to take him away.

Suddenly there was another sound, an interruption, the impersonal sound of a tannoy voice, the voice unmistakably British.

'Attention everyone! Will POW Rudi Korolev make himself known. And if Comrade Moligny' – the Russian in charge – 'knows where he is, will he bring him to me.'

Stunned silence greeted the British request, relayed to every quarter of the vessel. Hardly more than a dozen in the 2000 Russian prisoners spoke English, and even had they been able to do so, they did not have the faintest idea that it was Korolev who had tried to drown himself.

Then the tannoy burst into sound again, the same message but this time in Russian.

An angry Comrade Moligny climbed up to the bridge.

'What's all this about?' he demanded angrily. 'We're late starting.'

'Thanks to your friend,' the captain said. 'Will you please find the man Korolev.'

'Why? Why should I help you?'

'Because I ask you,' the captain said. He was apparently a mild mannered man. 'If you would be so kind –'

'I don't know the name. May we leave now?'

'I'm sorry, but it's a question of the Prime Minister –'

'He doesn't count here. This is a military operation.'

The captain began to get a little angry. 'Our Prime Minister *does* matter. When he asks me for something – I *have* to obey. And I'm *going* to.'

'What does this man want, this Attlee?'

'He has asked me to identify a POW called Korolev.'

'Never heard of him,' growled Moligny.

'You are making things *very* difficult,' said the captain mildly. 'If you would just co-operate –'

'I refuse.'

During this time the original announcement, the stunned silence had given way to outbursts of shouting. Most of the crowd of POWs might never have heard of Korolev, but the twenty or so who had travelled in the last bus from

Derby *did* know him, and they shouted and screamed their support.

'I don't know him, he's not on board,' blustered Moligny. Then suddenly harsher, 'Who is *this* man?'

He jerked his head in the direction of an elegant man in a grey suit.

'This is Mr Massingham. He came up the gangplank after the police brought back your prisoner-of-war.'

'And he wants –?' Moligny left the question unfinished.

'He has come from our prime minister, Mr Attlee. To talk to Mr Korolev on Mr Attlee's orders.'

The captain was speaking vaguely, obviously trying to hide something. 'And if you don't co-operate, comrade, I shall call a roll of every prisoner on board and delay the ship for twenty-four hours.'

'You daren't!'

'I dare – and I will. Now then, Moligny, do you know him?'

'Yes I do. And he is where he belongs: in the cells. He is the man who tried to drown himself.'

The captain was so astonished that all he could say was, 'Really! I *am* surprised.' He paused. 'Well, fetch him to me. Mr Massingham wants to talk to him. Does he speak English?'

'I think so.'

'And I demand to be present during the interview,' Moligny growled aggressively.

'And you shall be,' said the unperturbed captain.

Moligny went down to the main office, barked orders to two Russian soldiers and soon the bedraggled, soaking wet figure of a half-conscious Rudi was hauled up to the bridge. He had obviously been severely treated by Moligny's thugs.

'He seems not to have any dry clothes,' protested the captain. 'And these bruises –?'

'He was violent,' snarled Moligny. 'Now, what's the trouble?'

With an enormous effort Rudi managed to open his eyes. As he remembered later, everything was a blur. One eye, black and blue, was closed. He saw a tall willowy man he had never seen before, and the only man on whom he could focus was the arch fiend Moligny.

He groaned in despair, unable to hear, listen, even see properly.

Massingham was the first to speak.

'You are Korolev?'

He nodded.

'And your wife is called . . . ? We would like to know for identification purposes.'

'Nataliya.' Something began to stir in the bemused senses of Rudi.

'And your child – boy or girl?'

'Boy,' with a gasp of pain.

All the while an angry Moligny was trying to interrupt until finally the captain warned him, 'I am the master of this vessel, sir. Be quiet or I will ask you to leave.'

A sullen Moligny clamped his mouth shut in anger.

'And his name?'

Slowly Rudi opened his eyes more widely and whispered, 'Nicki. After my brother.'

'I knew.' Massingham leaned forward and almost hugged Rudi. 'I'm a friend of your brother's. But I had to prove your identity before witnesses. Including' – with a distasteful look at Moligny – 'this man here. Mr Korolev, I have the pleasure to tell you that Mr Attlee, in consultation with Mr Churchill, has decided to waive your repatriation order and you and your wife are granted immediate British citizenship. It was a close-run thing, but I can't tell you how delighted we all are and how we love your beautiful wife.'

'No!' roared Moligny.

'Yes!' roared the captain back, raising his voice for the first time. 'Now get off the bridge of my ship.'

Only one man did not hear those last shouted words. Poor Rudi had fainted dead away.

35

By the middle of 1947 – as we approached the date of Balanchine's ball at the Pré-Catalan – our lives seemed at last to be settling in to a pattern very close to happiness.

First of all, our beloved Rudi and his family, having been saved from repatriation at the eleventh hour, had been granted their British nationality. We had raised a modest overdraft on the strength of the necklace and Rudi bought a hundred-acre general farm at a small place called Brede in Sussex; quiet, good arable land, a few miles from Battle and not far from the airfield at Lydd. Almost from the start, Rudi's venture started to show sign of an early profit. Theirs was a deliciously happy family, and there was an added bonus for us. We could go to see them for £3 return.

Yes, £3. For this reason: earlier that year a small aviation firm called Silver City Airways started to fly between Lydd and Le Touquet. In France we would drive to Le Touquet, park the car, and twenty minutes later Rudi would pick us up in his second-hand Landrover at Lydd and drive us to his farmhouse, its old beams and fireplaces redolent of the past.

And at the same time there was good news of Igor. He would never fully recover, of course. The use of his legs had gone, but he could move his arms enough to eat simple food, for the drugs had helped to release hidden tensions and strengths so that, at the same time, he slowly and painfully continued to make modest progress in the art of speaking. A normal visitor might not have been able to understand everything he said, but he was *trying*, and though he might not be able to articulate properly, in the first six months the progress was more than we had dared to hope for and only during the first weeks, when he was very tired – or very depressed by the drug? – did he have to resort again to 'blink speech'. His voice was a kind of croak, but for those of us who became accustomed to listening to it, we understood. It was a great step forward.

We even managed the occasional laugh. I had often wondered what Igor had been trying to say when I first saw the nude photos of Anna D'Arcy and I had smashed up the screen, knocking Brig around in the process. In his excitement, Igor had made some guttural sound I had never been able to decipher. It sounded like 'saybun'.

He gave a twisted, almost painful laugh as he croaked, 'It was "c'est bon!"'

Then he managed to ask, 'How Anna is?' He still got words mixed up.

I explained that her husband was very ill, and that there was little chance of meeting her.

'Better!' was the only word he said. I did add another piece of information – that after a suitable lapse of time, and with the *Englishman* Rudi Korolev safe from the clutches of Inspector Verron (who seemed to have vanished from our lives), I sent Vron to Avallon to pick up the Delahaye.

'It's in the garage, and in spick and span order,' I told him.

'Brig drive – like it –' he stumbled for words.

'You mean she liked driving it,' I said. He started nodding now instead of blinking. He *was* making a remarkable partial recovery.

'Pity – not here!'

A pity! After all that had happened between them. But then – without as much as a telephone call or a cable – who should arrive but Brig herself.

Brig! Almost wild with excitement, she was crying, 'Where's my husband?'

And as she walked into the house, where Igor sat in a wheelchair which he could propel slowly with his arms if left alone, she went straight to him, ignored his injuries, forgot the past, hardly noticed me (I just happened to be there), put her arms around his withered frame, smothered his cracked lips with kisses, and said simply, 'Dearest Igor. I have come home to look after you.'

For a moment I was thunderstruck. I had never even imagined such gall! But Brig – as we all remembered – was nothing if not determined.

To me, she finally looked up with a slight flash of amusement, as though to say, 'I thought that would shake you!' and said, 'I wanted to surprise you. We've got a lot to talk about, and we'll all be seeing a lot of each other later. No, don't go.'

Then, without warning, Brig asked Igor, 'You will forgive me?'

To her he nodded and croaked, 'You – forgive me.'

'It was my fault.' She touched his lips again and said, 'If you want a friend and companion for the rest of our life together, I'd like to come back and live here. With Count' – she stressed the word 'Count' – 'Kornilov to run the house for us.' To Kornilov, who had entered the room, she said, 'I know what you have done for your friend. No-one will ever be able to repay you, Count. But if you would like to become "Secretary" and continue to handle all staff problems and so on – will you – help us?'

She had changed. She was softer, no longer as vibrant or as exciting as the night when I first enjoyed her company in Monte Carlo. She was more mellow, but then we had all grown older, more tranquil in life. More forgiving, with the memories of war receding and – in France more than in Britain – a plentiful supply of the good things of life – food, clothes, fashion, transport, entertainment.

I must say, Brig changed the whole house around – and for the better. Of course she had the money to pay for it, but she had ideas too, and, since the death of her father, she was, as an only daughter, a really rich woman. Among

498

her innovations she had a new kind of wheelchair built, the base of which could be lowered on telescopic aluminium legs. Then she took out the front seat of the Delahaye, installed a bucket seat for the driver, leaving a large space for the new-style 'portable' wheelchair to be put inside the car, the retractable electrically operated legs telescoping to their shorter length. This meant that either Brig or Vron could drive Igor anywhere.

Then, to our astonishment – and refusing to take 'No' for an answer – she had a lift installed in *our* house in the place de Furstemberg. It would only take one passenger – because it was built for Igor's wheelchair, into which his useless legs could be folded without any difficulty. 'I know Igor will love to come often,' was all she said.

On one occasion, when I asked whether all the dirt and dust of installing a lift was worthwhile, she replied, 'Nicki, I'm going to become a hostess again. And I'm inviting no-one unless Igor comes along. Even though he'll never walk again. I know what his trouble is: he needs *company* – that's his best way of learning to talk properly. I'm going to give big parties – and he's going to attend every one. Just like in the old days!'

And I must say, he did show an astonishing improvement once he started to meet more people. She took him to Longchamps, to Maxims, to dances (though she would never dance herself), and he began to – yes, I think the word is right – to *enjoy* himself. It would always be limited, this enjoyment, but yes, he smiled more often, there was colour in his cheeks. It was wonderful to see the change.

We had never lost sight of the great summer ball at the Pré-Catalan that Balanchine was planning for July. Galina – Mrs Lattimer – had seen to that, and early in June she and Hugo and Balanchine flew over for the planning discussions.

Almost before the Lattimers were installed in our house – with Balanchine staying at the Ritz – Hugo came round to see Igor. He was astounded when I drove him to the Rue St Dominique, and said, 'It's unbelievable! That Brig!' with a twinkle in his eyes, for she was there, 'You're another Florence Nightingale! Wonderful. Keep it up, both of you.'

Hugo had nothing really to do, except talk to the other doctors and have a good time in Paris; but for Galina and Balanchine it was a different matter. They had great plans, great ideas, to put into effect.

'I'm going to make one gesture,' I insisted to Galina. 'We've got the most beautiful necklace in the world – the Tsarina's necklace which she gave to Mama, and with it two priceless earrings. I'm going to offer the earrings as a prize in a lottery on the night of the ball. Yes, I've decided. It's going to be a dance for the richest people in France – and they're the people who'll gladly pay a fortune for the chance to win not only a piece of magnificent jewellery, but a piece of history as well.'

'That'll be a perfect ending to a wonderful evening,' Galina kissed me. 'What a gift! Now, I'm going to talk about *my* gesture. We've had a wonderful idea. I want you to come round to the Ritz now and talk it over with Balanchine.'

I hesitated but Galina urged me to accompany her. 'It'll be fun, Nicki; and anyway a detached viewpoint sometimes helps discussion.'

'I can't imagine how I can possibly have any views at all on technical ballet details,' I said. 'But for you – well –'

Balanchine welcomed me with genuine enthusiasm. 'My dear Nicki! We meet again – but this time I have no stage trickery to show you. Never mind. Come and meet my other guests.'

At a small table sat two men whose faces seemed vaguely familiar but whom I could not place. One was rotund and bald with owlish spectacles and a curved pipe giving off clouds of aromatic smoke; the other was tall and gaunt with dark centre-parted hair and the look of an ascetic.

'I hardly need introduce Pablo and Alfred, I think?' Balanchine raised his eyebrows; and of course it came to me in a flash: Pablo Casals, the cellist, and Alfred Cortot, the pianist!

I bowed, quite ceremoniously. Not every day were such artists to be encountered face to face.

'What has so thrilled me,' Galina said, 'is that they are *supporting* me – two of the world's greatest artists –'

'Supporting a third,' the austere Cortot added with a gesture of his beautiful hands.

Casals put his pipe on the table and added with a childlike smile, 'Yes. A third.'

I suppose I must have looked puzzled for, after pouring some champagne, Balanchine explained that he had been puzzled how best to exploit Galina's appearance.

'Then,' he said, 'I suddenly thought, Why shouldn't she dance – and pay tribute to the famous Pavlova,' – '*Pahv*lova,' he accented the first syllable – 'and her famous interpretation of *The Dying Swan*.'

'Not an imitation, you understand,' Galina put in hastily. 'Nobody could do that. But to re-interpret it in my own way. Pavlova was at the Imperial School as a pupil before me and I had to do an essay on her technique before the passing-out exam.'

'*But*,' Balanchine broke in, 'she was an inspired artist in movement, and an individualist, and people went to see her rather than the ballet as a whole. And the technique of the ballet had been perfected. But it had become, with its *pointes* and *entrechat*, an end in itself; and against the artificiality that ballet seemed to be drifting into, Pavlova brought it back to nature. And what more proper in this beautiful forest of Fontainebleau than to set our *Cygne*?' He giggled slightly at his pun.

Cortot peered morosely into his champagne flute glass. 'The music worried me for a moment,' he murmured. 'As you know, *Le Cygne* is a musical representation of a swan from Saint-Saëns' *Carnival of Animals* suite, and it lasts

501

for barely three or four minutes. The cello gives an impression of the grace of the swan and the piano the rippling effect of the water on which it glides. Our problem was to link it to something that could give the same sort of effect but would be an extension of it and offer the opportunity to return to it at the end when our artist' – he raised the forefinger of the hand that held the glass – 'is ready to sink to the ground in the agonising sadness of the bird's death. It was Pablo who found the solution. He telephoned me from Prades. "Rusalka," he said. "There is our music." And I knew at once that he had the answer.'

I didn't know what they were talking about! Casals took up his pipe. 'An opera by Dvořák,' he said jovially, 'about a water-sprite who falls in love with a human. The music is' – he paused – 'yes, it is *undulating*, with harps, and our orchestra could express themselves with great joy before Alfred and I return to *Le Cygne* for the close as the lights dim and silence falls.'

Lofty and interpretive artists they might be, but their feet were planted well on the ground, as Casals proved, for, chuckling, he tapped on the table with the stem of his pipe and told me that he had once read the diaries of the English writer Arnold Bennett after Bennett had seen Pavlova dance. It amused Casals so much that he could quote it exactly: '"London Palace Theatre. Pavlova dancing the dying swan. Feather falls off her dress. Two silent Englishmen. One says 'Moulting'. That is all they say."' He chuckled again. 'For an Englishman to reveal any emotion would be a calamity.'

The great night of the ball finally arrived.

Rudi and Nataliya flew over – with young Nicki, of course – and slept in the old room once used by Lilla, where we had found my old teddy bear. Rudi looked in wonderful shape, and almost the first thing he did was to go and see Igor. 'And then we're going to dance the night away,' he said. 'I've even hired a dinner jacket.'

'Makes my dress look dowdy,' sighed Nataliya. Olga solved that one. It was a regular business to lend model dresses to famous people on major occasions and Olga had no trouble finding beautiful clothes – just for the night – for Nataliya.

We had prayed for good weather – what *would* we have done had it rained? But it did not. The evening was warm and there was a full moon as the jewelled guests, the scores of millionaires, all made their way in chauffeur-driven cars through the Bois de Boulogne, to the centre of it all – the Pré-Catalan, one of the most sought-after places in Paris in which to stage an evening of splendour and beauty. Every restaurant guide – flourishing now the war was well and truly over – praised everything from its famous fresh salmon to its extensive wine list, together with ecstatic descriptions of the surrounding woods of the Bois in which the restaurant was set, and in which the long tables, in fine weather, were hidden from the rest of the world, the tables arranged in such a way that they stretched out from the central restaurant and stage like the spokes of a wheel, or to put it another way, the huge stage – a restaurant in rainy weather – was the point from where the tables fanned out in a semi-circle – not unlike the 'ribs' of an open fan, so that every single person – up to five hundred – had an excellent view of the stage from the straight lines of tables.

Overhead, the branches of giant trees spread like a canopy under the starlit sky – not blotting it all out, but letting one catch a glimpse of two or three twinkling stars, vying for supremacy with the artificial fairylights hanging from virtually every branch of every tree.

At the back of the stage soft music played from the orchestra while the guests drank cocktails and sorted out the place cards for their seats. Galina would dance later to the orchestra of the Paris Opéra, which had donated its services, and of course to the even more famous Cortot and Casals.

Balanchine – great showman that he was – had left

nothing to chance; nothing but the weather. He had had to gamble on this, but on the night, late in July, there was even a sprinkling of white sharkskin dinner jackets dotted among the more conventional black. Balanchine, with the head chef's advice, had chosen the menu himself: bortsch with peroushki, followed by koulibayaka (to take advantage of the Pré-Catalan's well-known fresh salmon), strawberries with fresh cream, while already ice-filled buckets of Laurent-Perrier champagne were dotted at regular intervals along every table.

'I love Laurent-Perrier,' Balanchine told me, 'and this is my way of toasting your father, the Prince. He never drank anything else, did he?'

'Nothing else but that,' I smiled. 'And a lot of it!'

'Poor Galina,' Balanchine sighed. 'All that beautiful champagne and all that wonderful food – and she can't eat or drink until after the show.'

It was half past nine.

'I must start *my* performance now,' Balanchine made his way to the tiny part of the stage in front of the closed curtains and signalled for a roll of drums to the band in front and below him on the ground. When the band struck up a sonorous chord for silence, Balanchine cried, 'Chebvinograda mir Bog,' which freely translated means 'In this wine and bread lie the peace of God.'

It was our Russian way of saying grace. He then announced, 'Dinner will be served in ten minutes, but first let us charge our glasses to our incomparable stars, Galina, Cortot and Casals.' Two small stages had been erected, one on the right, one on the left of the proper stage. 'On this one,' Balanchine indicated a baby grand piano, 'will be Monsieur Cortot. On the other,' where a music stand stood before a chair, 'will be Señor Casals. They will be playing while Galina dances, and after that the dance band will replace the ballet orchestra, and there will be dancing, and of course the draw for the late Tsarina's famous earrings which match the emerald necklace, given to the mother of the present Prince Korolev. We shall meet him later. Meanwhile, I hope you will enjoy your food.'

The slight bow was a signal for scores of waiters who seemed to spread out like a swarm of busy ants. The service – for which the Pré-Catalan was justly famous – was astounding. All five hundred guests seemed to be served at the same moment – and the wine waiters – each with his silver tasting dish draped round his neck – made sure that no champagne glass ever remained empty.

Finally we reached the coffee stage. The waiters brushed away crumbs, covered stained tablecloths with fresh napkins, put out bottles of brandy and fat round glasses, together with *petits fours*, including *fisalisse* – tiny Cape gooseberries which had been dipped in melted icing sugar to take away the tartness.

And then, the preliminaries ended, all the waiters vanished and, in a mysterious hush of expectancy, the great gardens seemed to be wrapped in a shroud of silence as the chattering stopped, the sudden spurts of laughter ceased, and then as the lights dimmed – in a tension almost tangible – the curtain rose to reveal a stage in total darkness. Against a whispering of violins from the hidden orchestra, a blue radiance invested the stage. By some mastery of lighting we seemed to be part of some aqueous ambience that enveloped us in its undulating ripples. Then by another trick of stagecraft an impression of white wraith-like shadows mingled with the softly flowing blue. This enchantment lasted for several minutes, until the whispering music faded almost into silence, the undulating shadows mingled as it were into themselves and, very faintly, could be heard the sound – *pianissimo* – of Casals' cello playing the limpid melody against the flowing accompaniment that Cortot's fingers shaped so exquisitely.

Galina seemed to make no entrance, as such. She was just, suddenly, *there*, as a presence, her movements for a while almost indistinguishable from those of the delicately rippling lighting – as indeed was her costume. Her designer (a pupil of Diaghilev's master of décor, Léon Bakst), had avoided the obvious and designed her dress in tulle rather than feathers. It was so diaphanous that as Galina moved unhurriedly through her graceful improvisations her body seemed to glow from within, imparting an ethereal quality to the swathes of the dress that was far more subtly swan-like than any attempt at realism.

As the rich notes of the cello faded, a change of mood seemed to overcome Galina. The harp in the orchestra picked up the music from the piano, the lighting changed to a silvery radiance in which Galina, arms upraised and body suddenly tensed, expressed her impassioned plea. I could hear a sharp, audible intake of breath in the audience, as if we too had joined in her supplication; and as the climax of the orchestral accompaniment diminished, the reprise of the Saint-Saëns melody changed the mood and the lighting once again. Casals' cello, in full throat now, could never have sounded more rich, nor the filigree of Cortot's accompaniment more delicate.

Galina seemed to retreat within herself as her arms fell from the shape of ecstasy, and as the music quietened she sank like a wraith to the floor, her dress embracing her like closing petals, head and neck curved forward to her bosom. Beside me, Tasha's face glistened with tears, and my own trembled on the brink of my eyes. The lights faded. For a moment there was a complete, stunned silence, then there was a roar of cheers, a thunder of clapping, showers of flowers picked from the table vases and thrown towards the stage.

Time after time the curtains swirled back to give Galina yet another appearance before the audience, hand-in-hand with Cortot and Casals, who bowed as she made the traditional curtsey and then from one of the large bouquets that were presented to her, she plucked out two roses and handed one to each man. And finally, when calls of, 'We want Balanchine!' forced him to appear, he too received rapturous applause, and he too received a rose from Galina.

At last the clapping and cheers subsided, nothing left but the chatter of voices, the clatter of plates, the occasional clink of glasses as people toasted each other. The musicians from the Opéra had quietly gone, to be replaced by the dance band. And then from the stage, in front of the curtains, the figure of Balanchine emerged again.

The crowded guests, fingers twirling the stems of elegant champagne glasses, halted in mid-conversation and looked up expectantly.

'Ladies and gentlemen,' Balanchine began. 'I am not here to make a speech –'

'No, no! Speech, speech!' several guests interrupted, especially the rowdier ones, tapping spoons on glasses to attract attention.

'No, no, ladies and gentlemen,' insisted Balanchine. 'I am only here to ask you to toast our incomparable Galina for travelling from the United States and giving her services for this beautiful dance, and for our masters of music, Monsieur Cortot and Señor Casals for the honour they have done us.'

At that, with everyone in a state of great euphoria, the audience again rose and stood up to drink their health, as the three joined Balanchine, after which Balanchine held out a hand and asked, 'Now I want to introduce to you – although I am sure you know him – the son of our last doyen of the Russian fraternity in Paris – the late Prince Korolev who died during the war. I have the honour to present his son, Prince Nicki Korolev, named after the last Tsar, who was his godfather.'

I had been expecting the call, of course, and did not have much to say, as Balanchine gave me a hug and withdrew, while I stepped to the microphone and said briefly, 'My task is very simple, ladies and gentlemen. As you know, you have all subscribed most generously to the tombola for the Korolev emerald earrings.'

None had seen them – or recognised them – because the earrings, set in diamonds to match the Korolev necklace, were at that moment adorning Tasha.

There was a pause. A couple of waiters brought a kind of barrel on to the stage, and started to turn it round in full view of the audience so that they could understand the way in which the tickets were being jumbled up.

Holding up a hand for silence, I added, 'Those of you sitting next to my wife Tasha might have noticed that she is wearing the Korolev emeralds this evening. For those too far away I am going to ask her to step on the stage, make the draw and this will give you all the chance – the last chance – to see the beautiful matching earrings, once the property of our beloved Tsar, with whose children I was brought up. When the name of the winner has been declared my wife will take off the earrings and hand them personally to the winner.'

There was a burst of applause, mingled – and I could see this from the platform – with a touch of almost greedy anticipation, excitement, hope. For these were royal earrings. Someone, somewhere in this room, was going to win the most spectacular pair of earrings in the world.

As the curtains were drawn back, Tasha walked from the wings out on to the centre of the stage, not exactly shy, but with that special waiflike beauty, enhanced by her low-cut gown, showing her beautiful white neck set off now by the necklace around her long, slender neck. She had been warned to stand on a certain spot, marked in chalk on the floor with a white cross. When she reached it, powerful floodlights were suddenly switched on, almost blinding her as they had been beamed straight at her face.

A spontaneous cheer broke from the guests. Not only was the necklace beautiful, but she touched her earrings to draw attention to them. There was a kind of communal gasp of astonishment at the sight of such beauty – the necklace and the model – and then, as one, they brought down the starry 'roof' with their cheers. Out of the corner of my eye I could see Igor, in his wheelchair, giving a little wave.

Then, as I signalled for silence, the audience sat down and at the same time, and when they were all seated, breathless with excitement and anticipation, I whispered to Tasha, 'Dip your hand in the tub, ruffle the papers and pull one out.'

She did just that, and holding up the winning ticket announced, 'The winner of the Korolev emerald earrings is . . . number 387, and it has just one single name on it – Giselle. Will Giselle please make herself known and join me, so that I can present to her these beautiful emeralds' – she gestured to her ears.

There was no need to look around. From one of the long tables there came a shriek of unadulterated joy and a girl, who looked no more than twenty, jumped up, waving her ticket and cried, 'It's me! It's me!'

She jumped on the table and ran quickly along it – far quicker than along the narrow alley made by the backs of the diners adjoining her table! 'I've won!' she cried, half-laughing, half-crying.

I had not the faintest idea who she was, but she finally reached the stage breathless, and without any warning, cried, 'It's wonderful!' and kissed me. Then she turned and curtsied to Tasha who was busy taking off the earrings, which she then handed to the girl who, with the experience of an older woman, quickly and deftly put them on. Her name, she said, was Giselle de Contades, and she was a student at the Sorbonne, so I announced the name of the winner, congratulated her and she then left the stage.

At that moment, as I was trying to make a quick exit – I wanted to restart the dancing – someone handed me two crumpled notes. One was from Olga.

I asked for another roll of drums and then, having re-read the note announced, 'Ladies and gentlemen, the famous couturier Olga has offered us a second prize – she is prepared to make for the lady who draws the winning ticket any item of clothing from her current collection.'

There was another gasp of pleasure – and the second prize was drawn by Tasha and won by a French lady whose name meant nothing to me, but who was almost as excited as the girl who had won the earrings.

Everyone presumed that this marked the end of the excitement, but no – there was something else.

I was almost getting tired of asking for music to demand silence, but the drummers obliged, and then I said my final piece.

'No, ladies and gentlemen, this is not to announce another tombola prize,' laughter from them, but suppressed excitement for me. 'This is to tell all our Russian friends who are here – and those who could not afford to be here – that the Count and Countess Trepov – the gentleman in the wheelchair, and his American wife of many years – have presented us with a truly remarkable gift for the Russian community in Paris.'

I paused to let the words sink in.

'They have bought an entire building in the Rue des Sts Pères almost opposite the site of the new Medical College. The offer is for a freehold building, and the Count and Countess have donated a large capital sum, whose interest should provide enough money for running expenses. I need hardly say that this is one of the most generous and wonderful gifts we have ever received. It will provide a new Russian Centre, and mean great happiness to the poorer members of our fraternity who will now have a place where they can meet, play cards, gossip – and where there will always be a samovar ready for tea. May we all drink a toast in gratitude to the Count and the Countess.'

Brig stood up behind Igor's wheelchair and then, as he managed a wave, she leaned forward and kissed him. It was a very touching moment.

Finally the dancing started, and as we were already on stage, Tasha and I led off. It seemed the natural and proper thing to do.

'Beautiful creature,' I kissed her neck gently as we danced a slow foxtrot cheek to cheek.

'And a wonderful husband,' she smiled back. 'I can't kiss you back. It wouldn't look proper. But later tonight – well – you know what I'm hoping for!'

'It won't be long.'

'I love you my husband and father, my Prince. And I always will.'

And so the glittering occasion ended – a memory for all our years. For us Korolevs and all the émigré Russians in Paris there was renewed faith in the future. Our lives had tangled with the dramas of war and death and love, but old Russia had never been far from our hearts. Now the years ahead lay like hopeful paths to be explored with courage. Courage indeed! – but the paths were there.

Night and the stars faded. Dawn tinged the sky and birds sang in the trees as we made our way home.

MORE TITLES AVAILABLE FROM
HODDER AND STOUGHTON PAPERBACKS

NOEL BARBER

All these books are available at your local bookshop or newsagent, or can be ordered direct from the publisher. Just tick the titles you want and fill in the form below.

Prices and availability subject to change without notice.

Hodder and Stoughton Paperbacks, P.O. Box 11, Falmouth, Cornwall.

Please send cheque or postal order, and allow the following for postage and packing:

U.K. – 55p for one book, plus 22p for the second book, and 14p for each additional book ordered up to a £1.75 maximum.

B.F.P.O. and EIRE – 55p for the first book, plus 22p for the second book, and 14p per copy for the next 7 books, 8p per book thereafter.

OTHER OVERSEAS CUSTOMERS – £1.00 for the first book, plus 25p per copy for each additional book.

Name ....

Address ....

....